The Barefoot Child

To Victoria + Chris

Hope you enjoy.

lots of love

Michelle

x x x

The Barefoot Child

Michelle Dixon

The
Book
Guild

First published in Great Britain in 2025 by
The Book Guild Ltd
Unit E2 Airfield Business Park,
Harrison Road, Market Harborough,
Leicestershire. LE16 7UL
Tel: 0116 2792299
www.bookguild.co.uk
Email: info@bookguild.co.uk
X: @bookguild

Typeset in 11pt Minion Pro

Printed and bound by CPI Group (UK) Ltd, Croydon, CR0 4YY

ISBN 978 1835741 078

British Library Cataloguing in Publication Data.
A catalogue record for this book is available from the British Library.

To Andy, with all my love.
For always understanding and never giving up.

Part One

1   Jess

Dad had to lunge for the door without making it look like he was lunging. He had to balance me on one arm, carry our suitcase in the other, double-checking for his van keys, all whilst reassuring me in a low voice that he'd definitely not forgotten to pack Pinky the elephant.

'Absolutely sure?'

'Course I'm bloody sure! Believe me, not important right now.'

'Can we go back for my doll's house?'

'No!'

'But I need my doll's house.'

'No time! No room! I'll buy you another!'

He'd sneakily filled the van the night before, packed several spare pairs of knickers, three skirts, two T-shirts and my favourite summer dress, enough to see us through the next few days (he'd forgotten a spare pair of shoes and didn't even consider socks). He'd also forgotten my Thomas the Tank Engine wellies, my pink padded coat with the fur-lined hood and thousands of other things I'd never see again. He did it all while you were upstairs in your room, too pissed to realise.

We'd been trying to escape for months. Made several half-hearted attempts, got as far as the end of the drive, on the verge of celebration every time, only to find you always sobered up at the critical point. Not that you particularly cared about keeping us, you just couldn't bear to see us happy.

This particular night, Dad tiptoed across the kitchen, holding me against his heaving chest, heading for the back door. Black-and-white checkered lino beneath my dangling feet, noisy to walk on, sticky with grime. The sink piled high in unwashed plates and cups; the cooker coated in immoveable grease; not that you ever did much cooking to put it there in the first place. I'd been living off takeaways and cheese sandwiches for months, wearing grubby clothes, attracting piteous glances from passers-by. You'd let yourself go, a cause of concern for everyone who knew you. People had tried to help but you wouldn't have it. Screaming in their faces. The whole world against you, even your own daughter. Eyeing me suspiciously, as if I'd been plotting in between school and CBeebies, which, as it turned out, wasn't far off the truth.

'Come on, not hanging about.' A new edge creeping into Dad's voice. He'd been promising me a new life for months. He'd painted the picture swirling round my head. A garden big enough for a swing, perhaps even a trampoline, a large bedroom decorated any way I liked, even a rabbit or guinea pig once we got settled. Just the two of us, free to laugh as long as we liked, without interruption.

'And stay there forever?'

'Forever. Well... till you get sick of me,' he said, laughing, which was never likely to happen.

'And never come back here?' I'd double-check, because I didn't want to be fooled by anyone, especially him.

'Never.'

We were only two or three steps from the door when you silently appeared, like a wild woman framed in the dining-room doorway. Long wavy dark hair tumbling either side of your face, large hazel eyes flashing hatred, long slender nails gripping the doorframe, ready to catapult towards us. Even a slow trickle of blood running from the corner of your mouth, glistening deepest red, though I might've made that bit up. Pushing my face into Dad's huge chest, praying the next time I looked up I'd find myself in the safe place he was always promising.

'What the hell do you think you're doing? Not having her! Jess! My daughter! Bastard!' You'd given up using coherent sentences long ago, but it didn't matter, we always knew what you meant. The tone unmistakable.

Hurling something at Dad. I could feel him flinch, the suitcase dropping to the floor, his large hand cradling my head. His shirt smelling a mixture of sweat and grass, the odd dried blob of ancient cement scratching my cheek. He'd just got in from work and not had time to get changed.

'We're going now,' he insisted, trying to stay calm.

'Bloody not! Let her go!' Launching at him as if your life depended on it, desperately trying to knock him over. You didn't care what happened to me, just as long as we didn't escape.

Eventually, he set me down on the sticky lino and nudged me behind his leg as he tried to fend you off with both hands. Double your size, he could easily haul a wardrobe up two flights of stairs without breaking into a sweat; the last person you'd ever imagine being beaten by a woman. If he'd told anyone, run to someone for help, which wasn't his style anyway, they'd have laughed in his face.

You took a step back, gasping for breath, readying yourself for a second attack. Amazing how you never did anything half-hearted once it came to your attention. Pushing everything to its natural conclusion, forcing a result either way. Only winners and losers in your world.

Whilst you drew breath, you took the opportunity to scream at Dad. God knows what exactly. My mind already in that place he'd promised, leaping towards a cloudless sky on the trampoline he hadn't even bought yet. Afterwards – many years afterwards – people filling the gaps for me. According to Dad, you were wild and unstoppable, incoherent and rambling. Clawing at your own arms according to Aunt Carol, Dad's older sister, who was miles away at the time but still knew more about it than anyone. And according to Ellie, my half-sister, not even born back then, nothing less than a psycho; an absolute nutter.

While I cowered behind Dad's leg, trembling but still standing firm. He realised if he gave way that you'd win, and I'd lose. My only ally in this world, the only ally I'd ever known.

God knows what happened next. So fast there was little time to stop it. Something hazy in the background refusing to show its face. Something dark and unpleasant inching towards me, reaching out, almost grabbing hold… what was it exactly?

I tried to peek round the side. Dad nudging me back, covering my face with his shovel hands. 'Keep back, Jess. Do as you're told for once! Stop being a nuisance!'

Then it happened, the moment life changed forever. A serrated knife glinting through Dad's legs. The big knife we used on Sundays to slice meat. God knows where you'd pulled it from. Perhaps you'd been planning it all along, just as we'd been planning our escape. Dad begging you to put it down, pleading with you.

'Be reasonable!'

'Can't do this! Legally you can't! My daughter!'

'Not bothered about her. Let her go, for God's sake.'

'No!'

'Jess! Keep away from the knife!'

He desperately tried to nudge me back. Far too interesting, despite the knife. A piercing scream, I think it was from you, couldn't have been anyone else. A mad scramble for the door, my head sandwiched between somebody's leg and solid glass, no room to breathe. Hot tears sliding down the rippled glass.

And something else, something dark and fuzzy, drawing near once again. Worse than a knife? Even worse than a crazy drunken mother? Pushing it off with both hands, an almighty shove, a piercing scream, refusing to let it near… determined to escape at last…

I glanced down at my white cotton dress, an unfortunate colour as it showed every mark. I'd been in the garden earlier, waiting for Dad to get in from work. Covered in black smudges and fresh grass stains. A new colour suddenly blooming, a dark runny red trailing through the embroidered flowers, dripping onto the black-and-white floor. I reached up to my throat. Red on my hand. Covered in the stuff. My screams suddenly ringing loud and clear, competing with your own.

'What the hell have you done?' Dad yelled. 'Trying to kill her?'

'Oh my God!'

'Maniac! Look what you've done!'

You were staring at me, bending down to my level, running urgent hands all over me. For the first time, noticing my skinny frame. While I noticed your funny eyes, dark pits beneath, the look of desperation that will haunt me for years. Sobbing uncontrollably, losing faith in Dad. Not so wonderful after all. Then suddenly he scooped me up in his arms, somehow managing the suitcase as well, threw open the door and finally we burst into the sunshine and fresh air, free at last. A light breeze on our faces, birds in the trees, a child's laughter floating down the street. We'd done it at last! Unbelievable. How on earth would we cope on our own?

The white van parked on the road, coated in a layer of summer dust. I'd been in it loads of times. Dad often sat me on his knee and let me steer and change gears. Somehow he threw open the passenger door and lay me gently on the seat, pressing a handkerchief to my throat.

'Hold it steady and no peeking. Lay still, we're leaving.'

'Are we coming back?' I sobbed.

'No! God, no!'

The seat dusty and torn. On cold days he often struggled to get the van started but couldn't afford a new one. Couldn't even afford new boots, his socks always protruding from some part.

'Where we going?'

'Christ knows. Away from here. Who cares?'

Speeding through town, swearing impatiently at every red light and pedestrian crossing, as if it were better to knock somebody down or get pulled for speeding than stay another second in that miserable house. Every so often glancing down and telling me off for not holding the handkerchief tight enough. While I sneaked a peek at the mottled pattern, trying to turn it all red until not a patch of white remained. Fascinating, despite stinging pain.

'You looking?'

'No!' I sobbed.

'Jess! Do as you're told for once, this is serious!'

As we left town behind he seemed to make up his mind where he was going; the only option open to us. Aunt Carol's small two-bed mid-terrace over fifty miles away. She was used to phone calls from Dad in the middle of the night, used to offering support, and just as importantly, she lived alone and could handle people trailing blood and tears across her living room carpet at a moment's notice.

Your cries still echoing in my ears by the time he pulled up, we hadn't travelled far enough to leave them behind. Dad carrying me into the dingy back room and laying me on the cream sofa while Carol freaked out at the sight of me, freaked out at the state her new sofa might get into, then finally came to her senses and fetched plenty of towels and blankets.

'Should be in hospital, daft sod. Why you bringing her here? I'm a hairdresser, not a bloody surgeon.'

Dad shaking, panting heavily. 'You know why. You know the story.'

'So ring the police then!'

'No police... Carol... no police...'

'Yes! Gone too far this time, Ray.'

'Carol, please. Just let us stay a few days, then we'll get

ourselves sorted, I promise. I know somebody who's got a cheap flat we can have; owes me a favour, did him an extension last year.'

'Damn idiot, for once in your useless life, put your brain into gear.' I think she even whacked him at that point to reinforce her words, which I later discovered was perfectly normal, while Dad tried to weave out the way, as if he knew what was coming.

'Carol!'

'Give you bloody Carol. Think what you're doing before it's too late. Never get away with it, even you can't.'

'Can't take her to hospital, too many questions.'

She paced up and down in front of the gas fire and lit a fag, rubbing her chin. What was she thinking? How best to hide a six-year-old from the police? Or how best to keep a six-year-old off her cream shag pile carpet?

'You know what a useless bugger you are. Never two pennies to rub together, how the hell you going to pay to bring up a kid? Like a big kid yourself.'

'I'll manage somehow. Always put her first.'

'And you think that'll be enough? Won't be a kid forever, will she? Not be throwing her over your shoulder much longer. What then? Look at her, she's filthy for a start.'

All the while lunging at me with blankets, yanking them into place so they covered every part of me except my head poking over the top. Peering close, taking in every inch, as if I was some strange creature she barely recognised. She discovered I'd had no tea and hadn't been particularly well fed for a while. With minimum fuss – but plenty of moaning – she prepared a dish of pasta and set it on a small table at my side with a glass of juice. A proper meal, one that said a grown-up was thinking of me. Tasted strange but not unpleasant.

'She's stopped bleeding,' she muttered, peeking behind the handkerchief. 'Might leave a scar though. Shaking like a leaf. Looks like she's hurt her hands as well. You'll have to tell people she slipped and cut herself.' Blowing a thick plume of smoke towards the ceiling. 'That's what we'll do, Ray.'

He sighed heavily. 'Thanks. What the hell would I do without you?'

'Bloody fool, never think things through, do you? What would Mum say if she were here? Eh? Down to me to point out the obvious every time?'

My heart still hammering in my ears, threatening never to slow. I'd finally stopped crying, somehow calmed by Carol's presence. Later on, I drifted in and out of sleep whilst they argued on the other side of the room. Carol still unhappy, struggling to get Dad to see her point. Dad's only argument to gesture towards me and point out the state I was in. Still Carol argued, telling him it wouldn't be that easy, how could he look after a small kid on his own? How would he manage work at the same time? Pay bills and put food on the table? What did he know about the needs of a six-year-old girl?

In the end she could tell he wouldn't budge. No argument good enough to make him take me back. The hands on the mantelpiece clock ticking round. We waited for the knock on the door, but it never came. Waited for the phone to ring but it never did. Somehow, miraculously, there seemed to be no objection. Carol realised she had to stop judging, patch me up and help Dad get away with it.

While I tossed and turned into the night, the two of them quietly planned the future.

2 Lisa

The bastard was shouting from above. Yanking me up by my hair to screech in my ear, a familiar pain that didn't hurt as much as it used to.

'Listening, bitch?'

'Yeah.'

'Listening?'

'Yeah, I'm listening. Alex, please, for God's sake…'

'Your bloody fault, your damn fault! Stupid bitch!'

He let go so I could slump to the cold hard floor. Gratefully digging my nails into the lino, creeping to the farthest corner, curled in a shivering ball. Even holding my breath in case it pissed him off. Bastard.

Seconds ticking by. Minutes, maybe hours. Mesmerised by the blood on the black-and-white lino, my daughter's fresh blood marbling the tiles. She was okay, thank God, a brief text from Ray half an hour after they'd gone. I closed my eyes, trying to recall exactly what happened. He'd lifted her up in his massive arms, sweat trickling across his forehead. Racing down the drive to his knackered old van, touch-and-go whether it would start. Jess crying out in shock as much as pain. Tear-stained face searching for mine, still trusting me somehow. God knows how. What would he do with her? Where would he take her? Somewhere safe, away from Alex? Was there such a place?

I shuffled round and peered through my fringe. The bastard was slumped against the sink, panting hard, still clutching the bloodied knife. He'd never done anything like it before, never quite like that; only towards me, which didn't count. Yesterday he took Jess to McDonalds, jigging her home on his shoulders like any father. Rolling across the floor if he was in the right mood. Nobody believed me.

Finally he let the knife clatter to the floor, suddenly clutching his side. Did he know what he'd done? That he'd just tried to stab her? Had stabbed her. Our daughter. Watched another man carry her out as if they were never coming back.

'Alex?'

'Shut it!'

'Alex?'

'For Christ's sake!'

'Jess's blood. Look!' Stabbing my finger, swirling a pattern. A turning point, surely. This was different to all the rest.

He pushed me roughly back against the unit, cracking my head. Eventually he shuffled into the back room and threw himself on the sofa. A bottle of vodka from somewhere. I held out my hand, pleading with him. The last one.

More seconds ticking by; my left cheek squashed against cold gritty tiles. Eventually dropping off, not wanting to wake, sobbing when I did, realising nothing had changed. I propped myself against a unit, my head spinning, tasting vomit. Alex in the back room, still clutching his left side and swearing repeatedly. He shouted at me to clean it up, sick of looking at it, even though he wasn't looking at it. I grabbed a cloth from under the sink and rubbed at the stain. All over my hands and T-shirt, seeping under my nails. The more I scrubbed the more it spread, smearing the whole room.

I picked up the knife and stared at the blade, mesmerised by the line of deep red crusting the edge. Realising through a thick haze that it had become my knife all of a sudden, with my prints on it, in my hand. People not pausing to listen. Louise had been right all along. I'd turned into that kind of person. I had been for a while.

I dropped it into the pedal bin with a clatter. Barely three hours since collecting Jess from school, joking with the other mums as we strolled home, laughing as if my life depended on it. What the hell would I tell them next time I showed my face? Sarah with her designer shoes. Amy with the property portfolio. Clinging to a cliff-face while they smirked.

My heart suddenly bursting to life, hammering my chest, the whole room swaying in a shimmering wave. I gripped the cooker for support. He'd attacked our daughter while I scrubbed the evidence. Any second now, a knock on the door, strangers entering our lives. Firing questions, turning the place over, prying into our business and seeing how we lived. Somebody asking Louise her opinion. She'd give it as well; she wouldn't hold back even for my sake.

'I've done it. I've finished. Alex?' Still desperate for his approval. Stupid bitch.

'Shut up, can't you see I'm in pain!' Gasping for air.

I threw the cloth at the bin and slumped against the wall, sinking slowly to the floor. Staring at the bottle in his hands as he quickly drained it, screaming at me in between. Vodka. Jess. Vodka. And Jess. The knife in the bin. First a drink, then save Jess. Somehow do both. Still time.

*

I used the dim light from the window to guide me. The sickly orange glow of the streetlight, the thin curtains, even the headlights of the occasional passing car. It was raining too, slopping over the guttering at the front. I used the noise to lower my feet to the floor, levering myself over the edge, the bed springs groaning under trembling hands. Holding my breath, close to tears. Tonight was the beginning of the rest of my life, a turning point at last. Or yet another terrible mistake, back to square one.

He was downstairs, still sprawled on the sofa, gasping for a drink. Desperately calling my name half the night, almost pleading. Bastard.

My mouth parched, aching for a long cold drink. My head throbbing and limbs tingling; perfectly normal at this hour. What happened last night wasn't, however. Jess and the knife. Alex crossing a line. Thank God for Ray, keeping her safe.

A dog howling in the distance. I dropped to the floor and crawled out the door, scurrying across the dim landing to the safety of Jess's room, allowing myself a few silent flowing tears.

Her bed still bore the shape of her body, the duvet flung back. Her pink toy elephant half tucked under the pillow. She'd be devastated. Once I found her we'd go somewhere safe. I couldn't imagine it clearly but knew it was out there, special places for people like us. That's what we were: a recognised group. Louise had told me till she was sick of saying it. My know-it-all sister. Shoving leaflets under my nose, the name of a website I could never recall. Losing her temper if I turned away. Basic, perhaps, freezing in winter, with few luxuries, but above all else, safe. Louise's sarcastic tone ringing in my ears.

For Christ's sake, Lisa, what you waiting for next? For him to fling you and Jess out the window? Not happy till he breaks your necks, is that it?

I dragged the case from under the bed and ran through the contents. How much time had I wasted the last few hours? The last few years? My thighs covered in bruises. A throbbing pain in my wrist where he'd slammed me against the oven.

Jess's birth certificate, my passport, paperwork that wasn't easy to replace. Her first pair of shoes, the tiny cardigan my sister knitted her with the pearly buttons before she left hospital. School pictures, including the painting of just the two of us standing in front of the house, huge smiles plastered across our faces as if she'd somehow managed to wipe out Alex altogether. Jewellery belonging to my mother, a photo of my father on his allotment one scorching summer years ago. I grabbed the elephant and rammed it down a side pocket.

I'd had another brief text from Ray earlier. Jess still in shock, still reeling. He'd taken her to his sister's, miles away. I'd never even heard of the place (or the sister). What the hell would I have done without him? The way he talked to her, on a level, almost as if she were his own, distracting her from Alex. Flinging her about the garden and racing round the front room. The way she responded, trusting him from the start, saving all her laughter for when he showed his face. Why couldn't I have ended up with him instead? Why couldn't life be that simple?

Last summer when Alex was in prison for six months, it was Ray who stepped in. I'd have gone to pieces without him. Within a matter of weeks, Jess had stopped calling him Uncle Ray and started calling him Dad, no matter what anyone said to her. She'd chosen him over Alex and who could blame her? Whenever Alex disappeared, Ray was always poised to step in.

Finally, I dragged my clothes from under the bed. A jumper and a pair of jeans. I dressed hurriedly, checking my pocket for the twenty-pound note and small change. The change wrapped in tissue. The twenty nicked from his wallet while he drifted to sleep, surprised by my own boldness. Alex had crossed the line.

About time. Silly bitch. Should've done it years ago. Everybody else saw through him, why couldn't you? If you weren't so pissed half the time...

I picked up the case and crept onto the landing, shivering at the top of the stairs. If he suddenly appeared I'd end up slammed against the wall, his hand gripping my throat. I could picture it more clearly than anything, even Jess's tiny face waiting for me to do something. Lying in a twisted heap, neighbours banging the wall, the dog in the distance starting again. Making excuses next day, just like the time he held my hand over the gas ring and Louise spotted it straight away. She knew it was there without even looking.

I inched down on tiptoe, holding the case clear of the steps. When I reached the bottom I slapped my hand over my mouth to stifle my own joy, as if I'd never been out the house before. Stupid bitch.

I crept through the dining room. He was still flat out on the sofa, face down, his hand inches from the empty vodka bottle. Just pretending or gone for the night? Tousled hair, bare feet sticking over the edge. Almost like the old Alex, when we first met, idling the weekend at his poky flat above the *White Lion*, planning the future. Struggling to get my head round the idea of never seeing him again, letting go of that future. Always telling Louise I'd rather die than leave him, even throwing her out the house for suggesting it.

I shuffled towards the darkened kitchen, holding my breath, an overwhelming stench of vomit in the air. The floor still sticky with the residue of Jess's blood. My throat on fire. I pulled open the top cupboard, knowing it was empty but still hoping. Crumbs and a lone tin of beans.

What the hell was I waiting for? I should've been gone hours ago, miles away before he realised. Lou was right. The leaflets had always been there. The website I forgot.

Can't do it, can you? Never wanted to stand on your own feet. Never wanted to be a decent mother. Always using that twat as an excuse.

I tried to answer back, not so easy with such a gob on her. What did she know about parenting? Always easy from where she stood. Ought to try it sometime.

Bullshit. Jess is the easiest kid in the world. Want to start appreciating her before it's too late.

What if I went back upstairs and slid the case back under the bed, pretending the idea never entered my head? At least

I knew where I was with Alex. I'd barely known anything else since Mum and Dad died. Not even a bank account to my name. He'd managed to wipe me out bit by bit, day by day; in the middle of it before I could tell.

I once did thirty hours a week at Morrisons after leaving school. 10% discount, make-up, shoes, the latest fashions, two or three nights out a week. Plenty of friends to share it with. Even a pension like everyone else. Until Alex felt threatened by it, resenting the smile it put on my face. One day he sneaked my mobile out of my bag and wiped the address book, leaving me with less than half a dozen contacts, the ones he could bear.

In one swift movement I unlocked the door and fell onto the driveway, relishing the rush of chilly air, looking up into the rain, like fine mist quickly covering my shoulders.

Years ago, not long after Jess was born, Louise gave me a scrap of paper with a number on it. She pressed it into my hand on the doorstep. The people at the other end waiting to talk. I told her to piss off and slammed the door. Protecting Alex from her interference. Protecting the three of us.

I pulled out my mobile and sent Ray a brief text. Quick change of plan. I needed to see Jess urgently before it was too late. Tiny face, confused and hurt, struggling to understand. Thank God for his sister; a friendly female face, somebody she could cling to until I reached her.

But first a drink, just a small one, with Alex's money. One of those twenty-four-hour mini-Tescos a couple of streets away. Help me concentrate. Help me sleep if I had to curl up on a bench for the night.

In the distance a few seconds later – or maybe several hours later – a siren of some sort, whirring closer. Police? Ambulance? On my heels. Screaming my name through the light-polluted streets. Silently sobbing and stumbling my way towards freedom.

3   Jess

The rest of those early days a blur. Snippets of conversation coming back now and again, the odd image when I least expect. Weird things barely making sense.

Dad scrubbing at the black mould round the window frame, cheerfully insisting he'd found us a palace. Give him a few minutes, he'd soon have it sorted. Carol's cramped spare bedroom at the back, overlooking next door's gloomy yard. Waking each morning to find the window steamed up, condensation dripping to the carpet. Scrawling my name and watching it slide to the floor.

Dad consigned to the two-seater sofa in the back room, his knees up to his chest, his head scraping the woodchip wall, a giant trapped in a doll's house. Laughing as if we couldn't believe our luck.

'Don't blame me,' Carol snapped, missing the point. 'Can't expect Jess to sleep on the sofa after what she's been through. I'm not used to catering for kids. If I'd known the two of you were turning up. Give us some damn warning next time.'

Long hot days merging into one. Scouring the house for toys and games, among the dusty glass ornaments and photos of strangers. Flinging open cupboards and rifling contents, boredom driving me on. Pouncing greedily upon a couple of pens and a pad of paper, stashing them under my pillow at night, scribbling furiously throughout the long stifling day.

Kicking my way round the scrappy yard, hunting for a skipping rope or ball. Behind the shed, under the shed, peering on tiptoe through the grimy window. Where had they all gone? Who'd taken them? After a while, finally understanding, amazed by the answer. They were never there in the first place.

Carol shaking her head, puffing away. 'No idea what to do with herself, has she? Can't sit still two minutes. She always been like it?'

'Confused, that's all,' Dad would reply. 'After everything she's been through, who can blame her?'

One day, sat in my room scribbling on the pad, a strange noise filtering through from outside. I jumped on the bed, hurriedly prising open the window at the top. A child's laughter in the distance. A girl the same age as me. Scanning the horizon, trying to see over the tops of trees, garages and fencing. A glimpse of something bright three doors down, perhaps a swing or slide. My heart beating out of control, suddenly moved to tears. Dizzy with excitement, almost tumbling through the gap.

I fell back onto the bed and grabbed the pen, scribbling a picture. She looked a lot like me. Same colour hair and eyes, almost identical. We played in her garden till it turned dark, perfectly safe, making a den down the bottom, no adults to disturb us. A red slide, blue swing and loads of other things she was happy to share.

Hazy summer days. Scribbling furiously on the diminishing pad, drawing my own happy future while they argued over it downstairs.

*

'Not too late, Ray.'

'Bloody is.'

'It's not! Still time to come clean. Stop being so damn

19

stubborn. What happens when summer's over? Eh? When other kids are going back to school and she's stuck here? Not for me to look after her. Not my responsibility, is she?'

He pulled me towards him protectively, his answer for everything, to keep me close. 'Alright, aren't you? Just a bit bored, that's all. Got an active mind, she's that clever she can't help it.'

I nodded eagerly. I'd searched every cupboard while Carol nipped into town and hadn't found anything remotely interesting. Only shelves full of fluffy white towels and rows upon rows of bottles and lotions that smelled nice when I sprayed them in the air, till my eyes started stinging and I had to shove them to the back before her quick tread on the stairs.

'Course she's bored, there's nothing here for her,' Carol snapped. 'That's why she's rifling through my cupboards all day, making more work.'

'I'll buy her a few jigsaws then, a few cheap toys. Left in a hurry, didn't we? Can't see her complaining, can you?'

'And if I have to bring someone back? A client? What then? Like being a prisoner in my own home, jumping every time the doorbell goes. If someone walks past the damn house. How the hell do I know who to look out for?' Blowing smoke rings at the yellow ceiling, trying to convince us she was terrified, though it was hard to imagine, even if you battered down the door and held a bread knife to her throat.

He leant forward and muttered something I couldn't catch. Something about me. She had a quick answer for him but then Dad had an answer in return equally quick. He seemed to have the final say and it shocked them both.

'Have it your way. Just have to hide upstairs, won't I? Wait for her to grow up. Only another fifteen bloody years to go.'

She stormed out the room, making a racket in the kitchen. Biding her time until bedtime, till she got him alone and told him what she really thought.

Laughing after she'd gone, rolling on the floor till my head ached. So funny the way she behaved, always forcing us closer together.

'Don't worry,' he whispered, gently stroking my hair. 'She's just sulking as usual. Gets like it sometimes. It'll sort itself, I promise.'

*

It was strange without your voice echoing in my ears. I'd got used to your screams and the sobbing in the night. That funny noise you made in your room when you thought I was asleep, like a small animal in constant pain. I should've been happy about it but sometimes, for no reason, found myself crying when nobody was about. Staring out the window at next door's rotary washing line, disappointed in Dad for the first time. Nothing like the picture he'd painted in my head. The guinea pig. The rabbit. The trampoline where we planned to jump for the sky.

That dark fuzzy thing never far away. Returning without warning in the night, as soon as the house had fallen quiet except for the odd creak and the occasional sound of Dad tinkling in the little toilet under the stairs.

I'd creep down after Carol had gone to bed, into the darkened back room where he slept on the two-seater. His chest rising and falling, casting a mountain shadow on the far wall. Lunging towards his belly, reaching my arms around him as far as they'd go.

'Jesus! Where's the fire?' Every time, even though he knew it was me.

'I want to sleep down here; I don't like it upstairs.'

'Don't like it, eh?'

Quickly drifting off in his arms while he turned on his mobile and sent text after text, muttering from time to time to check I was okay.

'Just a bit confused, that's all. Eh?' Patting my leg. 'Trust me, getting it all sorted. Not be long now, I promise.'

*

More random images jumping out. My bedtime routine, a mystery to Dad as much as Carol. Easy to fool them both. Gawping at me from the doorway, uncertain whether to butt in.

'Has she brushed her teeth? Does she know how to do it?'

'I don't know, do I?' He turned towards me. 'Brushed your teeth, sweetheart?'

'Don't ask her! Make sure she does it. Don't take her word for it.'

Marching me into the bathroom and miming cleaning his teeth. Like being three all over again. The two of us side by side. Shouting to Carol that I'd cracked it, nothing to worry about there.

Carol hovering in the background, butting in with advice. How to iron my clothes, what to give me for breakfast, how to do my hair in a morning. Yanking me out of his grasp and doing it herself. Dad winking over her shoulder.

'Like this, you do it like this… you watching, Ray?'

'Course I'm watching.' Winking.

'All a big joke as usual. Eh? If you don't watch, how are you expected to learn?'

Arguments over how much to feed me. Dad believing I was on a par with himself, ready to stand alone. Carol convinced I was straight out of nappies, not to be trusted.

'Far too much! Heaven's sake!'

'She'll leave it if she's not hungry. She can make up her own mind, can't she?'

'She's six!'

'Exactly.'

'Don't put salt on it! Getting her into bad habits. Plain simple food. Start how you mean to go on.'

Dad believing it was sorted even before we'd begun, desperately trying to get a smile out of her. Working hard to make her happy. What was she moaning about all the time? Another box ticked.

'Jess has been independent for years. Way ahead of other kids because she's had to be. It's sad but that's how it's always been. No idea how smart she is, honestly. How do you think she's survived till now?'

Carol's stony silence, eyeing the two of us in turn. Not quite sure who was the biggest fool.

'No time for being cavalier, is it? Time the two of you woke up before it's too late.'

Dad still winking over her shoulder. So funny at times.

*

Another stifling summer's day. Sobbing quietly in my room while Dad slipped off to work in his dusty van. Carol downstairs with a client. The two of us circling each other warily. Every so often popping her head round the door. Did I want a drink? Did I need anything? Breathing a sigh of relief when I turned her away, scribbling silently on the pad.

She'd bought me some new knickers printed with different days of the week. Dad hadn't packed enough. He hadn't thought of anything useful or practical. Always making work for others.

I yearned to go home, to see you again, even with the knife in your hand, wild hair tumbling about your face. I tried to picture you standing in the kitchen, light from the window catching long greasy hair. Hanging washing in the yard, slumping against the wall for a fag. Collecting me from school, head down when somebody called your name across the street. The funny smell of your breath as you held me close, insisting you loved me, over and over, trying to convince us both.

Getting much harder. You were doing things without me, beyond the endless rows of terraces, garages and fencing. I was doing things without you, like reading a book Carol had finally shoved under my nose. *Ice-cream. Attempt. Obvious.* New words that nobody realised I'd figured out for myself. Launching them into an empty room till they sounded right.

I stood on the bed, staring out the window into the distance. Were you out there, hanging out washing in the yard? If only I could escape the house without Carol realising.

After a while flopping back on the bed, struggling to concentrate on the book. The same words spinning round and round, nobody to ask if I was getting it right. Dad and Carol insisting it was confusion. Summer of confusion. Not even sure what it meant. Asking them to explain. Over and over.

*

Dad's funny reaction whenever a book passed under his nose. Even one of mine, with the big writing and pictures taking half the page. Perched on his knee before bedtime, launching with enthusiasm.

'What's that say?'

'Ask me an easy one, why not. What's Carol playing at, giving you such crap? I've got a better idea.' He lobbed it over his shoulder and tipped me to the floor. Grabbing my hand and pulling me outside.

It was more fun doing it under Carol's nose. Dragging a sheet off the line, the pink one you could almost see through, creeping back inside and throwing it over the back of the sofa, pinning it to the windowsill with glass paperweights. Creating a gap between sofa and wall that I could creep into easily and Dad could squeeze into with much swearing, his feet poking out the end.

Strawberry laces he'd bought from the garage on his

way home. A large bag of coconut mushrooms for himself. Provisions from the outer world.

'Not be here forever,' he confided, lowering his voice just in case. 'Once I've finished this big job. Just a few more weeks, then I'll get paid and use it as a deposit.'

'Deposit?'

'It's what you need to buy a house. Once I've got it, we'll be laughing. Don't worry, got something really special lined up.' Tapping the side of his nose.

I stretched a lace as far as it would go, smacking him in the eye. Draping them over his head like pink dreadlocks, struggling to hold it in as Carol approached swiftly from outside, thunder rumbling across the carpet. Determined to spoil our little game.

*

Reading on the settee in the front room with a large bag of jellies and a carton of juice. Dad glued to his phone. Carol flicking through a magazine. We'd been doing it years. Years and years.

A sharp rap on the front door. Frozen in an instant, exchanging glances. Eventually a second rap, breaking the spell.

'Who the hell's that at this hour?'

'Back room, quick!'

'Upstairs?'

'Either. Just get moving! And take her toys with you. Go on! Didn't I tell you?'

Dad bundling me into the back, slamming the door behind. I perched on the sofa and watched his reddened face as he pressed his ear to the door.

'Who is it?'

'Shhh!' Pressing a finger to his lips.

'Mummy?' Trying hard not to cry. Nobody had heard from you in weeks and now suddenly you might be lurking the other side of the door, seconds off dragging me back to my old life.

25

A strong draught rolling across the carpet as Carol opened the front door. High-pitched voices as she tried to sound surprised. Should I keep quiet or make a noise? Terrified you wouldn't try that hard. Caught between two worlds. My old grubby life and this strange new one.

Dad lunging forward, pressing a finger to my lips. 'Don't want to be discovered, do we? Eh? After all this time?' Beads of sweat on his forehead. 'Do you love me?'

I nodded shakily. It meant so much to him. Safety this side of the door. The guinea pig and the rabbit. The trampoline still to come.

He pressed his ear to the door again, breathing a huge sigh when he finally worked out who it was.

'Bloody Cathy! Frizzy perm next door but one. Wanting a trim at this hour. Hen party tomorrow night. Would you believe it?'

He mouthed something as he leaned back against the wall. Sit tight and be a good girl. Soon be over. Half an hour and she'd be gone.

*

There wasn't much to pack the day we finally piled into the dusty van. An armful of clothes, some books Carol had bought me and a drawing pad to keep me quiet on the way. Carol standing on the front step with folded arms, glancing nervously up and down the street.

'God knows what I'll do without you rifling through my cupboards all day.'

'Don't rifle through your cupboards all day. Not anymore.' There was no point. Even the lotions all the same.

'No, that's true.' She reached out to ruffle my hair, not quite sure how to do it. 'Not so bad, are you? When all's said and done.'

She looked worried, despite Dad's constant whistling and the fact we were only going ten miles. She yanked my cardy into place, doing up the top button. Turning chilly all of sudden. Summer almost gone.

'Carol?'

'Call me Auntie.'

'Auntie Carol? Thank you for the books. I can keep them, can't I?' I knew I could, she obviously had no use for them. Just wanted to hear her say it.

Instead, she lunged towards me and pulled me into a hug that neither of us found comfortable, my nose squashed against her flat, hard stomach.

I might've imagined it, but her eyes looked misty when I glanced up. Even Dad seemed amazed. Then she insisted on redoing my hair, which took a couple of minutes, into a tight ponytail, before Dad grabbed hold and swung me into the passenger seat, clipping me in for what felt like the final time.

'Thank you for letting us stay with you.'

She smiled and nodded, folding her arms.

'It's been a very long time,' I added.

'Long time! Two months to be precise.'

Exactly. A long time.

I waved as he pulled off. She raised her hand and held it there, a funny look on her face as we rounded the corner, as if she couldn't imagine spinning round and going back into the house again, her old life, after we'd messed it all up for her, even though she'd spent half the time shouting and moaning.

'Can you believe her? All that bloody grumbling.' Dad shaking his head.

Rows and rows of houses, country roads and twisty corners, as if he was deliberately trying to get us lost so you'd never find us again. Tapping my leg every so often to reassure me.

He finally pulled up outside a new-looking house on a quiet street. Explaining that it was a semi, three years old. Taken from somebody who couldn't afford it, so we'd got a bargain. It needed a bit doing but that was no sweat. Rubbing his hands together. The first house he'd ever bought. It meant a lot to him.

'Carol's just jealous, don't listen to her.' And from the corner of his mouth, in case she might hear, 'This is the kind of place she'd love to afford herself, so expect a few snotty little remarks when she sees it.'

I nodded. Understanding fully.

We went inside and it was immediately obvious it was nothing like the old house. No dark corners, tiny rooms or spidery cupboards under the stairs. Nothing dark or fuzzy awaiting me when I dropped my guard. Impossible to imagine you sat in the modern kitchen-diner or leaning against the back wall with a fag.

'School's only round the corner. I've put your name down; it's supposed to be decent. And I'll get you some lovely pink bedding and pink curtains once I can afford it. Just give us a month or two.'

I nodded again, a bit more enthusiastically. We'd discussed bedding and curtains many times. I jumped up to peer through the kitchen window at the garden. Nothing like Carol's. The grass looked green, room for both a swing and a slide. The other houses further away, not on top, pinching all the light.

He was telling me about how he'd come to buy the place. It was hard to keep up, though he seemed to think I should and rambled on. The last owners were stupid, but we wouldn't make the same mistakes. They'd only lost the house because they'd been daft.

'Dad?'

Checking the tiles above the sink, rubbing the grout with his fat thumb. Telling me what improvements we were going to make once he had time.

'Are we staying here?'

He spun round. 'Eh?'

'Staying here?'

'Staying here? Bloody living here, aren't we?'

I looked down at his mucky footprints on the grey tiled floor. He'd already emptied his pockets onto the worktop. Bits of tissue, chewing gum, betting slips, spare change spinning off the edge. The first time in weeks. Stuff he'd never dare leave all over Carol's.

'Jess! Stop being silly! You'll break that cupboard in a minute.' Disappointment in his tone. 'I thought you were smarter than that. I've explained enough times. It's been decided, okay? This is home now.'

I nodded silently, letting go of the door. Confusion over.

4   Lisa

The whirring siren was for me, nobody else would do. Stumbling and sobbing my way down the street that dark night, my case rumbling against the tarmac. Mere inches ahead. Permanently within Alex's grasp.

Fag burns trailing my chest. Stinging cuts and bruises littering my thighs. My left wrist broken in two different places. Why hadn't I realised the full extent? Most people would've worked it out years ago. Almost as if I was making it up and had something to hide. They wanted to understand, they'd seen my type before.

I woke hours or maybe days later in a clean bed, surrounded by whitewashed walls with a needle strapped to my arm. A long winding corridor somewhere on my right where people in uniforms wheeled trolleys and shouted instructions into the distance. A small window to my left, a glimpse of summery sky between horizontal bars. I could stand if I wanted and shuffle round the small room as if about to leave, only for a brief second before somebody noticed.

'Take it steady now, one step at a time.'

'I need a drink. Where the hell am I?'

'Sit down, will you? You've had a terrible shock.'

'I need a drink…'

'I'll get you a drink, just sit down.'

They took it in turns to gently prod. First a softly spoken

man in a flowing white gown, checking the monitors over my shoulder and scribbling against a clipboard. Followed by a young blonde woman with a spiral notebook, noting every word as if I might have something vital to say. Her pen poised, taking her time to get it exactly right. Nobody had ever listened so closely.

My daughter, Jessica. Did I know where she was? Could I remember?

'She's safe, She's with a friend. He's looking after her.'

They'd taken my phone and wouldn't return it. I gradually noticed they'd taken everything. No, I couldn't leave just yet. I wasn't well, surely I could tell? They needed to ensure I was alright first. They needed to know everything, however long it took.

'What friend, Lisa? We need to find her, this is so important, we need to know.'

Ray had taken her, my ex-boyfriend of three years who'd never really got over me or moved on with his life. He was always desperate to help, and this was his chance. He'd watched me fade into a shadow of the woman he'd known. My dark wavy hair turn dull brown, every curve he'd once loved turn skin and bone. I could trust him more than anyone.

'Can you remember anything about that night, Lisa? Remember how we found you? Remember where?'

Century Park. The top of the bridge, high above the swirling black river. Somebody wrestling me to the ground, thinking I was about to jump, even though I hadn't quite decided. I bit his wrist and kneed his groin, surprised by my own strength when it came to it, convinced it was Alex trying to drag me back to the house and throttle me. Actually, a ginger man with an overgrown beard and a Morrison's carrier bag on his way home, desperate to interfere.

'Can you remember how you felt?'

Nobody had asked how I felt in years. I'd even stopped

asking myself. Suddenly the most important question floating round the room, my entire future hanging on the result.

'Jess…'

'Where is she, Lisa?'

'Nobody can hurt her.'

'One of the neighbours reported a man in a white van. This is so important, Lisa. We need to make sure she's not been hurt. We need to know where she is.'

I turned over to face the wall. The tantalising glimpse of blue between the bars. I drifted slowly to sleep. The only way to shut her up.

*

I sobbed for days as it sank in. Louise had been right all along. I'd been abused by Alex. Me and Jess. They needed all the details; they had a right to know. How long had it been going on? As if they thought it started one particular day.

The blonde woman with the notebook again. It turned out she was a police officer. Smiling kindly, implying she was on my side and stopping all the nastier questions from reaching my ears.

What happened in the kitchen that night? Yes, of course they would understand. They'd seen Alex's type before and he'd clearly been drinking heavily. But what actually happened?

'I can't remember; it just got out of hand and went too far.'

'We understand but we do need to know the sequence of events. It's important you get it right.'

What if I got it completely wrong? They'd searched the house and seen how we lived. The blood on the floor and the bottles of vodka in the back room. They'd talked to the neighbours either side. Alex's family. Alex's friends. If I told the truth I had nothing to fear.

'I know there was a scuffle but that was all. Please believe me, please…'

She coughed politely into the back of her hand.

'We found a knife in the pedal bin, Lisa. A kitchen knife. Can you remember?'

'No.'

'I must point out we've had it tested; we know exactly what's on the knife.'

'I've told you, why do you keep on asking? I want to go home now; I'm well enough to go home. Where's my bag? What've you done with it?' Levering myself off the bed and lunging towards her, shouting in her face. I wanted to go home, even to Alex and the blood on the floor. It might not be too late.

'It had your prints on it. Can you remember touching it? Think carefully before you answer.'

And before I could do anything, before I could prepare an answer or even change my mind, she stood up and let somebody else in. As if she couldn't stop them, however much she'd tried. Much harsher questions crowding the room, a different tone. They'd seen my type before.

5   Jess

He was far jumpier than me. Butting in as I skipped along the pavement to school, dodging cracks and counting the number of red cars that whizzed past before reaching the corner of Thomas Street (red vans didn't count). The record was four. If I stepped on a crack I had to stop dead and think of something else, like bikes going in the opposite direction or sparrows hopping in the gutter.

'Stop running ahead, will you? How many more times?'

Freezing in an instant, gazing at the terraced houses, cars jammed into scrappy front yards, people scurrying towards town. Were you among them? Watching from the shadows, waiting to pounce.

'What you hanging about for now? Come on, Jess, be bloody late at this rate!'

My new school was so amazing I'd almost forgotten my old one. A huge reptile tank and a floppy-eared rabbit, a colourful garden where we were all allowed a patch each (lessons outside on sunny days). A massive cupboard overflowing with tissue paper and material scraps. Nobody complained if you used too much or spilled it all over the floor. Mrs Shipley wanted us to use our imaginations. Racing home with glitter in my hair, floating like fairy dust in the bath, clinging to Dad's work clothes and dusty eyebrows.

Not to mention Sophie Clayton with the blonde pigtails, from the big house on the corner. Giant tree house at the bottom of the garden, two older sisters and a growing mountain of the latest toys. If we couldn't sit together at lunch time I'd fold my arms and refuse to speak. Sophie got upset too but not quite as much.

'Can she come for tea tomorrow?'

'Eh?'

'Sophie!'

'Who?'

'Dad!'

'Let's get settled first. Just give it a bit longer, a few more months.'

Dragging my feet against the pavement. Changing pitch to a whine. 'Settled? But why?'

'Because I've said.' He glanced over his shoulder again, scrutinising the innocent-looking cars and vans whizzing by.

God knows how she'd take it. I'd already told her she could come and we'd make a den in my room afterwards. What if she ended up at Olivia's instead? Olivia Harris with the twelve-foot trampoline, two red swings and double slide.

'Can I go to Sophie's instead?'

'Haven't I just said?'

'No.'

'When we're settled.'

'But why? Is Mum coming after us? Have you seen her?'

He dragged me close and gripped my hand, forgetting his own strength. Pushing and pulling through crowds, all of a sudden lifting me clean off my feet and dodging down a side street, missing Thomas Street altogether.

'Dad!'

'Just hold on!'

'Put me down!'

Hearts thumping as one. His breath coming in great gasps, sweat trickling down his forehead, drenching his shirt. Maintaining a rigid smile throughout.

'Try not to worry, try not to cry, no need to panic.' Setting me down once the coast was clear. 'Alright, sweetie?'

I hugged his leg so hard he had to uncoil me to stop from tripping over. 'We'll be alright, Daddy. I won't let her hurt you, I promise.' Not an easy thing to say. That dark fuzzy thing still hovering, especially if I closed my eyes and had nothing better to do.

Not that I was worried about myself for a sec. You'd clearly forgotten me long ago. For some reason, only out to get Dad these days.

*

He could do anything, which was just as well because we had no choice. In it up to our necks. He spent most of his time showered in dust, fine powder on all he touched, mucky footprints on the new tiled floor. Ready at a moment's notice.

They phoned at all hours, desperate to get hold of him. Often jumping out of our skins, thinking it might be you. I couldn't hear what they said, I could only guess from his replies.

'No problem, mate, done it no end of times. Planning permission? For that little bit?' Or: 'Take a couple of hours max, probably overestimating at that.' Or: 'Wiring the whole house? I don't see why not, can soon give you a quote. Want me to pop round?' Or my favourite, because it made him sound like he really knew his stuff: 'They say you're supposed to get certificates and whatnot, qualified this and that... to be honest, never had an issue. Health and safety gone bonkers as usual.'

They came round at night with small brown envelopes stuffed with money. Straight into his back pocket so we could go for a drive-thru at McDonald's for tea; the picture he'd painted finally coming alive, the colours vibrant and real. Or if he didn't get paid he'd drag me round to Carol's, barefoot and starving, the two of them shouting in the kitchen while I slumped on the settee in front of *Toy Story*. A week's worth of pick-and-mix meals to follow. Beans on toast or half a sausage roll. Two jam sandwiches or five slices of toast. No milk for two weeks but a cupboard full of chocolate digestives. The picture flickering, turning dark and ugly, threatening never to return.

Not that I minded about the job. One day he brought home a pile of old wood that used to be somebody's shed and on a sunny Sunday afternoon transformed it into a swing and painted it red while I did cartwheels round the patio. A few weeks later he dragged home an old tyre and made another swing, which I told Sophie to stop her going to Olivia's. And it seemed to work because nobody else at school had quite the same. They could recognise something different when they saw it.

*

On cold winter mornings the old van coughed and spluttered on the drive before bursting to life. He breathed a sigh of relief when it did or stamped his feet and swore repeatedly if it didn't.

'Thank Christ. In serious shit if it decides to pack up now.'

'Why? Because we might need it to make a quick getaway?'

'Getaway? I need it for work, silly.'

Every Saturday morning I climbed onto the dusty passenger seat with as many toys as I could carry, a carton of juice and a bag of jellies. If I needed the loo it was my own fault; should've gone before we left.

He parked the van on somebody's drive miles from home. A wall needed rebuilding, a patio laying or a roof mending. He'd be finished by one, so we could go to the park for the afternoon.

'Alright?' he checked before climbing out, as if we had much choice.

I nodded, glancing quickly left and right. The coast clear.

'Only over yonder doing that wall. Shout if you need me.'

He worked quick, only pausing for a cuppa when somebody

brought it out to him. Carrying three bricks in one go, resting on his right palm like LEGO as he coated them in cement the same way he buttered my toast in a morning: a bit on top and plenty round the sides. I wanted him to go for more, try for a world record. Sophie sat beside me. Mrs Shipley and the whole class.

The wall appearing from nowhere. It swallowed his ankles and reached the knees of his ripped jeans while I opened my book and started to read. Glancing up between chapters, the pile of bricks at the side slowly shrinking.

What if he disappeared altogether? If I never found him again? Left to survive on my own. But then he'd glance up and mouth something, never in doubt. *Alright, nuisance? How you doing over there?*

I finished my juice and started on the sweets. It was a good book, about posh kids always discovering secret tunnels, getting kidnapped and finding treasure maps. I could always tell how it was going to end – the same as last time – and that was the best part about it. Devouring chapter after chapter, hungry for the next page, halted only by the odd strange word or phrase. No point asking Dad; he'd just laugh and walk away, shaking his head.

I finished a chapter and glanced up, swiping my chin on the back of my hand. The garden empty. A strong breeze stirring plants on the patio and bending the branches of the trees down the bottom. He'd disappeared. The wall still standing, Dad's trowel resting on top, but Dad himself gone.

I jumped up and squashed my right cheek against the window so I could see to the left. Squashed my left cheek against the other window so I could see to the right. Glancing in the mirror in case he was hiding behind, gripping the dusty seat with both hands.

Counting to ten, twisting the book to pieces, teetering on a watery precipice. I shouldn't have nagged him about the park over breakfast, sulking on the front step. Didn't really mind if we didn't go. Didn't mind if we never went again.

What if you managed to find me? Dragged me back to the old house, the dark rooms, the spidery cupboard under the stairs. That dark fuzzy thing finally catching up.

Tears falling steadily to the gritty floor, staining the book. Juice all down my dress. I'd starve without him. Couldn't do anything without him. School uniform hanging off the back of the door, hot milky drink before bedtime. Couldn't even swim without him. One of his shovel hands under my tummy at all times, even though I didn't need it, always there.

I glanced in the mirror at the silent houses across the street. I'd have to knock on one of those doors and explain, find somebody to take me in, starting all over again. New school, new friends, new routine. New Dad. More tears, much heavier, dirty stripes scouring my face.

I turned quickly to my right. A sudden tap on the glass. Big grubby face pressed to the window, squashed strawberry nose, rolling his eyes as if I was four all over again, eyeing up the jellies on the dashboard.

'Mine!'

'Dad!'

He'd only nipped inside for a quick pee, two minutes if that. For heaven's sake. I threw open the door and launched into his arms. Behind my back swiping half a dozen jellies before I could stop him. Carrying me over to the wall, dabbing my tears on his gritty sleeve.

'Thanks, Daddy.' As if he'd never been away. But no, he didn't understand the funny words in chapter ten. Why did I read such daft books? *Indignation* and *scornful*. Never even heard of them. I'd have to pester Carol if I really wanted to know.

*

Old Mrs Patterson across the street was a million times better than stuffy Mr and Mrs Williamson on the corner. She had a greater selection of chocolate biscuits and didn't mind how many I took. Even if I smuggled a couple home in my pocket and helped myself to strawberry yoghurts out the fridge.

'Not hungry again, my love? Let's see what we've got.'

She nipped into town especially for me, visiting the right shops just to get my things. A large round face that was always red and smiling no matter what she was up to. It lit up in my presence as her eyes followed me about the room. I could scratch my bottom and it was fascinating. Cartwheels across the garden worthy of a gold medal. My scribbled drawings plastering every surface, prized like the works of a grand master. Untidiness and chaos bringing tears to her eyes.

'Can I borrow your duvet to make a den, Mrs Patterson? Down the bottom of the garden near the hedge? Won't get it dirty, I promise.'

'Duvet?' Her eyes lighting up as the idea sank in. 'Well I don't suppose it'll do any harm, just make sure you stay where I can see you. Don't like you going out of sight.'

Her only son Clive had died in a motorbike accident. Wasn't even his fault but he'd still died. On the corner near the chippy, where people had complained loads of times. Dad reminded her of him because they both scraped the ceiling and were good with their hands. Maybe if Clive had lived he'd have had a daughter exactly like me. Watching me was almost like watching her own granddaughter. Confiding in me one day while I coated her tiny kitchen in flour and emptied the contents of her cupboards to make fairy cakes. Always the right ingredients.

'Here's some socks, my love. Pack of six. If you need any more, just let me know. And some new knickers with ladybirds and butterflies.'

She remembered the names of all my school friends; she cared about Sophie as much as I cared. If anybody was mean, if

I got a certificate worthy of putting on the fridge. Maths due in a week next Thursday.

While knitting me cardigans in bright colours using remnants of wool whilst I investigated her massive back garden. Frank Sinatra or Matt Monro in the background. Tapping her foot while I knocked over a pot or chipped one of her ceramic birds. Chaos far better than the alternative. Her neighbours' manicured lawns and child-free homes.

'What relative are you?' I asked. Knitting balls spread halfway across the floor, red on the right, blues and purples to the left.

'Relative?'

I nodded. Probably to do with you. She'd never even heard of Carol.

'We're not related, my love.' She laughed, as if I'd cracked a joke.

'So…'

'What?'

'So why is it you're always looking after me and buying me things? If we're not related?' And let me stay in her spare room while Dad worked away. Tucking me in like a grandmother (like I imagined a grandmother). Turning back twice to double check. Gently shaking her awake in the middle of the night, sobbing by her side. She'd even bought me a butterfly nightlight. Who else was going to use it?

'Well…' She squinted at the pattern on her knee. 'Your dad fixed that guttering, didn't he? Had that broken bit at the back he did for free. Then cut down that conifer taking all the light, did a smashing job, taking all that rubbish away. Then the grass at the front, I can't manage with my knees anymore.'

'So that's why you do it?'

'Of course, my love.' As if I should've known.

I went quiet for a long time. Swapping the colours about, red on the left, blue on the right.

Mrs Patterson looking concerned. Not like me at all. Finally bursting out, 'And my apple crumble, of course, can't forget that. Lovely to have someone to make it for again. Never turns it down, does he, Jess? Jess?'

I grabbed one of the large red balls, determined to keep it for myself. And another yoghurt out the fridge. She wouldn't mind.

6   Lisa

It wasn't nearly as bad as some people made out, just as long as you didn't focus on the name. Some of us felt almost normal. Some of us could walk out the door and start all over again.

'You don't have to tell me why you're here, not in any detail. I won't tell anyone, sod all to do with anyone else. Just keep it to yourself, who cares?'

Rachel Unwin – shocking pink bob with studs creeping up both ears, a toothy grin no matter the occasion – constantly chipping away. Huddled together over meals and swapping secrets in corners; it made us feel different to the rest. Daniel, her ex, hadn't chain-smoked like Alex, he'd slashed her with a razor instead.

'I'm not gonna say anything, you know what I'm like. Lisa? You know what I'm like.'

'Same reason as you, pretty much. What else?'

She pulled me close and whispered nonsense in my ear. I wondered who she'd used before I came along. Who would she turn to when I'd gone?

Other than Rachel, the awkward questions had ground to a halt. Everything appeared to fit; they'd seen my type before. Plenty of boxes to tick, explaining it all. My prints on the knife in the bin, running crazily through the night. The neighbours had taken in so much more than I thought, especially the nosey bitch at number five. She'd heard us squabbling in the yard and seen Alex shove me roughly to the ground several times. Susan next door spying from her bedroom window for weeks. She'd filmed our drunken rows just in case. When it came to it they were all desperate to tell. I'd repeatedly lied but only because I'd panicked. Anyone would do the same.

'Wow,' Rachel burst out when I finally made a confession (not completely of course, that would be impossible). Just confirming what she half suspected, something she could easily recognise. 'No wonder you're in here, I'm not surprised.'

'I've got a little girl called Jess, she's absolutely gorgeous.' Bouncy dark hair like mine used to be, frizzy at the front. Skinny sunburnt arms. Tiny mole between flexed toes. Strawberry birthmark below left ear.

'So where is she?' Rachel whispered.

'With friends. She's perfectly safe.' What kind of mother did she take me for? Other people might be clueless where they left their families. Husbands lurking in the shadows, children behind closed doors. Jess was different; I knew exactly where I'd left her.

Snippets of information slowly filtering through. Ray had managed to buy his own house and sign her up for a new school. He'd visited twice and asked me everything he could think of. I'd held nothing back for Jess's sake. The name of her doctor and dentist, her complete medical history. All the stuff he'd never done before – buying her clothes and cooking her meals – he'd somehow figured out. She barely mentioned Alex, as if he'd never existed. Barely mentioned me but that was different, I'd be able to explain everything once I escaped. She'd cry but that was all. We'd move on and accept whatever help we could.

'But they might not let you anywhere near if they think you pose a risk. Lisa? If they think you pose a risk.'

Just because other people posed a risk and couldn't be trusted. The toothy grin again. I felt an overwhelming urge to slash her face. Who could blame Daniel?

'They won't, not with my own daughter, they can't. Are you listening? Whatever's happened, they actually can't.'

Park Field Psychiatric Unit, Ward 2b. My case clearly different to all the rest, whatever they liked to think. None of them had seen my type before.

7   Jess

One Year Later

'He's severely dyslexic. Won't admit it so there's no point telling him, might as well save your breath. He'll only ever work for himself so he can be as daft as he likes. Imagine the carnage if he had to answer to someone else all the time.'

'So it can't be cured?' A stubborn lump lodging in my throat, refusing to budge. Carol remaining stony-faced.

Dad had the same thing as Thomas Phelps, who had to sit on his own in the library with special paperwork and a different teacher twice a week. Except Dad didn't bother with paperwork or the special teacher, just laughing his way through, praying nobody would notice.

'Won't be long before he's asking you to sort through all his paperwork and take charge.'

I tried turning a cartwheel under her nose. It always worked on Mrs Patterson.

'I can see it coming, young lady, so you beware.'

'Carol? I've got to do a project on ancient Egypt next week. I need to do a map of the Nile. Can you help me please?'

'Has he started already?'

'What?'

'You know what, don't play the fool with me. I'm asking because I'm concerned, that's all.' Blowing a thick plume of smoke, wafting over the rotary washing line and next door's shed.

All I'd done was read some paperwork for him over breakfast, the difficult bits he struggled with. Handing me the white envelopes, telling me to go ahead. No secrets between us.

'That's the only drawback to being smart. Sooner or later you'll be so far ahead he'll be relying on you for everything. Running his business, telling him where to go and what to do before you've even left school. I've warned him. Might like to think you know it all.'

I tried another cartwheel, falling just short of her grasp. Trying to grab a sheet off the line.

'You get that mucky and you're for it, young lady.'

'Mrs Patterson doesn't mind.'

'Far too big for that sort of thing; you're not kidding me.'

She stubbed her fag on the ground, grinding it into the dirt. Slowly coming after me as I raced down the yard, the sheet billowing behind.

*

Another driveway, another season. Skeleton leaves battering the dusty van's windscreen before tumbling down the street. An umbrella torn inside out in the wing mirror, cartwheeling across the road, snatched from somebody's desperate outstretched hand.

Another book, this time set in a boarding school, where posh kids were sent years ago. I'd discovered the meaning of *indignation*. Carol felt it when Dad turned up on her doorstep and explained we'd run out of milk again. But now there was *queer*, *jersey* and *pluck*. Not to mention ginger beer.

Dad pacing up and down, double-checking his phone and mumbling under his breath. He had to dig a pond and make a fountain. He'd never done it before, although he'd sounded confident on the phone. If he needed the loo he was going to tell me because of last time. I needed to stop panicking; I was being daft. Like the time he abandoned me at the tills in ASDA and rushed down aisle three for loo rolls and toothpaste. Where on earth did I think he was going?

I watched him dig a large hole in between chapters. He'd be done by one so we could go to the park early. Stepping back to wipe his forehead, crushing a large pink flower. Over his shoulder into the bushes. Spreading black material in the hole, stamping on it to make it flat. Yanking out the hosepipe and filling it with water. Not so tricky after all.

I grabbed a pencil and underlined interesting words. *House mistress. School tunic. Scarlet fever.* Even Carol wouldn't know them all. Starting to get annoyed. Why did I have to know everything?

When I next looked up there was a large bald man stood beside Dad, jabbing a finger at the hole and pointing to the other side of the garden. Gesticulating wildly with a mortified expression. I opened the door a crack, letting in a draught of cold autumn air.

'Told you I bloody wanted it over there. We agreed for Christ's sake. Can't you read the plan?'

'Well…' Dad shrugged and laughed awkwardly. Perfectly normal, although it annoyed some people. 'It's done now.'

'Done now?'

'Can't be changed, can it?'

'That all you've got to say? And what about this?' Pointing to a statue of a naked girl hiding in one of the flower beds. 'Eh? For Christ's sake.'

Dad tried to convince him he was just as well to leave the pond where he'd put it than move it down the bottom. Nearer the house far better. He could enjoy the full benefits of the wildlife all year round.

'I knew I should've listened to Derek Smith. Warned me

you were a tosser. I want my money back now. No excuses, no bullshit. Not even level, for God's sake. And you'll pay for that statue, it was a birthday present for the wife, or I'll report you for that bloody van.' Turning to the house. 'Beryl? Come and look at this heap of shit.'

Dad looked red-faced and confused, nudging the liner with his toe. 'Slight problem, mate. Haven't got the money, have I? Spent it on this little lot. Look, I'll come back next week and put it right, it's not nearly as bad as it looks. I've got some glue for that statue.'

Another voice chipping in from the patio doors. A woman hurrying forward and picking something off the grass, examining it closely. Full of indignation, with a perturbed expression. 'Tom? That off my statue? How's that happened?'

'How? He's a bloody fool, that's how. Crushed your climbing rose as well.'

'You're joking.'

And within seconds I found myself standing in the middle of it all – no choice, our only hope – book in hand. Small and vulnerable, yet strikingly mature at the same time.

'Can't you see he's doing his best and he's offered to put it right,' I explained. 'He's tried to negotiate sensibly but you won't listen. Just get it in perspective. Some things matter a lot more than a crappy old pond and broken statue, things like that can easily be replaced.'

Beryl's face softening slightly as she took me in. Grubby cotton dress, Mrs Patterson's hand-knit cardy, ladybird socks. The climbing rose and chipped statue briefly forgotten.

'If Dad says he's got some glue then I don't see what the big fuss is about, not as if he's made it any worse. Just trying to improve it.'

I glanced down. Dad's hand locked onto my wrist. He started dragging me towards the van, struggling to hold it in.

'What the hell are you playing at?'

49

'Nothing.'

'So rude at times.'

'Dad?'

'Told you before, haven't I?'

He hadn't.

'I think you need to apologise, young lady.' He mouthed something above my head. Beryl smiling weakly, Tom shaking his head. 'I'll be in touch once I've found this glue.'

He opened the door and threw me onto the seat, shaking his head. Starting the engine and shooting to the end of the drive, gripping the wheel, arms straight. Nodding briefly at Beryl and Tom, united in understanding.

Tears falling steadily onto the gritty seat. The posh books clearly putting him off. Only pushing him further away.

'I didn't mean to upset anyone. Dad? I'm sorry, I didn't mean it, just trying to help you out.'

Once we pulled onto the main road, the house out of sight, his face collapsed in an instant, back to its familiar shape. 'Bloody hell, Jess!'

'What?'

'Where did all that come from? Good job Carol taught you all them big words.'

Swiping hot tears on the sleeve of my cardy.

'Don't be silly. I said I'd take you to the park, didn't I?'

I nodded silently.

'Didn't even put you up to it. Must be a natural, eh? Nothing but a natural.' Laughing quietly to himself.

8   Lisa

They left the house at quarter-past eight every morning. Jess
out first like a pink rocket, skipping along the pavement till he
ordered her back, having to be told at least twice. Her hair much
darker than before, tied into a scruffy ponytail. Different coat
and shoes, different uniform beneath, inches taller every time.

'Dad! Hurry up!' Words slicing me in two. The smug smile as
he grabbed her hand, taking ownership, growing in confidence
by the day just from having her by his side.

They turned left at the end of their road and onto Portland
Terrace, over at the crossing – chance for him to look the full
length of the street – then down Thomas Street, usually jammed
with parked cars and the odd van, so I could linger at one end
easily with my hood pulled across my face. Glancing at my
watch as if waiting for a lift.

Jess's left sleeve within touching distance. Chance for me
to reach out and grab hold, bundling her into the back of a car,
even though I didn't have one, explaining rapidly it wasn't me
who'd slashed her with the knife, it was her dad; surely she could
remember. Give me another chance and I'd soon make up. Yes,
I knew I looked like shit because I'd not been well but getting
better all the time. Still Mummy.

But then she'd do something really strange and unexpected,
like jump on somebody's front wall or trespass on somebody's
garden if something caught her eye, all over the place in seconds.

Spinning cartwheels and hiding round corners, throwing leaves in the air. Unstoppable. Ray perfectly used to it, even joining in at times, turning it into a massive game just to keep her happy. How the hell would I keep up? Had she always been like it?

Then all of a sudden he might get wind of something. For no reason whatsoever yanking Jess out of her daydream and dragging her down Richard Street, picking her up if she wasn't quick enough. Running with her on his shoulder, which always seemed crazy. Not as if I didn't know exactly where they were going.

Ten minutes later standing at the school gates, trying to blend in. Too many kids and parents knocking about to notice. Standing beside someone who looked as if they wouldn't mind, an outsider like me. They'd ask if my kid was in the play or signed up for the trip, moaning over ridiculous amounts of homework. Nobody noticing there was no kid by my side, that I often stumbled and seemed lost for words.

Ray always sticking out a mile. Wherever I stood I could hear every word. Attracting funny looks, the odd whisper behind his back. So big and clumsy beside Jess, who seemed torn between not wanting to leave his side and an irresistible urge to run with the other kids.

I'd watch him bend low and whisper in her ear, convincing her of something, even though we'd lied enough. What else was she being told without my permission?

He relished the attention, quickly working out how to turn it to his advantage. Exchanging comments with teachers and parents, winning over the women whilst keeping his distance from the men, who seemed to trust him far less. Dishing out business cards and noting addresses.

'Fit it in this week, no sweat. Half a day max. Give us your address, I'll pop round later.'

He made it look so easy, squeezing into a new life, whatever the shape, convincing everyone of a blatant lie while I struggled to convince people of the truth. Watching Jess out the corner of my eye, wondering when to butt in. How was it possible to abduct my own daughter? From a man who wasn't even her father? He'd promised he was only looking after her temporarily but now couldn't let go. Surely if everybody knew the truth, they'd understand and help.

Then something strange would happen, something inexplicable. January melting into June. August merging into December. Whole days lost in a fog while I struggled to crawl out of bed. Convinced I'd spotted Alex in Pizza Palace opposite, hiding behind an oversized menu and biding his time. Creeping behind me up the stairs in the dark. Far too bitter to let go without a fight.

Then when I emerged, thinking I could finally crack on, Jess's seventh birthday had come and gone. A new school year, new coat, new shoes, new everything. More assured and settled. Her laughter ringing clear across the playground, her step more confident. A different child without me. If I took her back and couldn't cope, what then?

*

My flat was a one-bed, second-floor rabbit hutch sandwiched between a Thai restaurant and a twenty-four-hour off-licence. I was upset about the one bed and couldn't get over it, imagining where Jess would sleep when I eventually got her back. I insisted to the council I needed more space, struggling to explain why. Didn't I realise I was lucky to have that much? People crying out for places like mine. Surely I understood how it worked?

Black mould creeping across the chimney breast, the silhouette of somebody watching me walk into the room. An icy chill that never escaped the building even in summer. I'd have to wrap Jess in a blanket and layers of clothes. Take her to the library to keep warm.

Steamed chicken seeping through the walls. The ever-present stench of grease, despite empty cupboards for half the month. Not that it mattered for my sake, but what about Jess? I'd have to give up at least half my meals to ensure she ate enough, as long as she thrived and there was a smile on her face. Baked beans, reduced bread, stuff on its sell-by date. Visit food banks if necessary, shout a bit louder. With Jess by my side I'd be able to.

On cold winter evenings, endless screaming and shouting from the street below. I almost craved Alex's presence, the comforting warmth of his back against mine. Poised to forgive, despite his footprint against my cheek, the thumbprints shadowing my windpipe.

Sometimes I'd perch silently with a cup of tea and take in my possessions. A battered old leather sofa from a charity after emerging from hospital, a small table and couple of chairs somebody had understandably left behind. Curtains and cushions from Age Concern. The only thing of value, stuck to the fridge and pinned to the bedroom wall, Jess's old pictures, scribbled nonsense she'd done at school. The only bright spots in the whole shitty place.

The mantelpiece cluttered with bills and appointment cards (usually a postcard or two from my sister, a new one each month). Bite-size pieces of info. Having a wonderful time in Australia, unlikely to return for another year at least. Her only method of communication, no longer interested in what I might have to say. She'd heard enough.

*

I only joined the self-help group to keep Dr Shipley sweet. The most important thing in the world, to shut him up.

'What's there to lose?' he posed, holding up both hands to show he wasn't hiding anything. 'Couple of hours at most. Wednesday evenings. Free tea and coffee, free bickies, can't go wrong. Won't force you to do anything you don't want. Had a couple of patients get on really well there. Shall I put you down?' He already had.

Not long after I left hospital. All those little looks, threatening to send me back. I'd escape the first opportunity. Who could tell?

'I'll give them a ring. It's called Helping Hands.'

Which I liked the sound of. It could've been anything. Three rooms above a Christian bookshop in the centre of town. Separate access down a mouldy side passage but you still felt you had to behave. A cheery logo on the glass door, a stick couple holding hands beneath a vibrant crayon rainbow. A large airy room where we all gathered to sit and talk, a small bathroom and dated kitchen with mismatched mugs and peeling 1970s cupboards. Not too overwhelming or sparkly. I could hide in such a place for years.

During the day it was home to a knitting group. Intricate patterns pinned to the walls, trays of tightly wound balls of wool stacked on shelves, a washing-up rota sellotaped to a kitchen unit. Knitted figures stacked in a corner. Jack and Jill going up the hill, Humpty Dumpty falling down. Organisation and productivity in technicolour.

While we left nothing behind, not a trace of our existence. Creeping home in darkness, no promises made of a return.

You didn't have to give your name if you didn't want. You didn't have to give your real name, I should say. Just turn up once, then disappear, never to be heard of again, which I liked the idea of, not being pursued. I felt virtuous by turning up almost every week. Free tea and coffee, as Shipley promised. Chocolate digestives if we were lucky, sometimes the only thing I'd eaten all day.

'My name's Lisa, I'm twenty-seven. I've got a drink problem. Just out of hospital. Come here to get better; I need all the help I can get. That's about it.'

It was run by Steve, an ex-alcoholic in his late forties. Crumpled blue-stripe shirt, heavy bags under pale blue eyes. Forcing himself to stay awake just so he could talk some sense into us. Dumped by his wife and two kids; disgusted at what he'd turned into. He'd slept rough for six months before turning his life around, an example to us all.

He nodded patiently while I explained about Alex, stretching his legs into the circle and crossing his arms. Young girl meets older man who seems wonderful at first. Before she knows it she's doing all kinds of stuff she was never brought up to do. Her family disapprove and cut her off, they seem to think she can stop it easily if she wants and that she's being awkward for the sake of it. They get offended when she won't take advice, as if it's all about them.

Steve making me question everything. Whether Mum and Dad had loved me the same way they'd loved Louise. Whether they'd actually pushed me towards Alex and ensured we'd stayed together. I couldn't manage an escape because I didn't see it as one. I was grateful for everything he gave me. Mum and Dad's sudden death within months of each other left the overriding question floating in the air. Had they loved me as much as my perfect sister? And if not, why not?

'My sister had a leaflet for everything. She said I'd let everyone down. The more she interfered the more determined I was to do the opposite, just to spite her.'

Had I been a heavy drinker before I met Alex? Had he encouraged me? Had I felt obliged to keep up? The first time I'd ever been asked. The first time I had to search for an answer.

'I think so.' A long pause, unwilling to bring Jess into it. God knows what they'd say if they realised I'd given up my only child to strangers. Even worse, if they realised I hadn't the guts to get her back.

At the end of each session I gathered everyone's mugs and plates, staying later than most, tidying round and washing up.

'Seriously, it's not necessary,' Steve insisted. 'You're the first person who's ever bothered.'

'Really?'

Laughing at the look on my face. I genuinely enjoyed it, sweeping crumbs and wiping coffee rings, making it tidy for the knitting group the following morning. I didn't want them thinking the worst.

'Don't worry, you're doing a great job, Lisa...' Patting my shoulder as he wandered past. Pausing briefly over my name, never quite sure if it was real or not. Perhaps it was the only time it mattered, when everyone had gone.

I kept my head down, running scalding water over the mugs. Perhaps it was true, everyone taking the piss and rushing home early, but wasn't it obvious I needed a bit more than them? I craved the routine just as much as the advice. I needed to feel I could be useful again.

*

He always made a point of not answering the first call. Or the second or third. Eventually, I'd glance at my watch, realising I'd rung six times in an hour. Carol rolling her eyes, accusing me of pestering him and being hysterical, frightening Jess for no reason.

'Ray?'

'Lisa?'

'Why don't you answer? I've left three messages. We need to talk.'

Something crashing to the floor. 'In the middle of doing a kitchen, I've not got time for checking the ruddy phone every five secs.'

'How is she?'

'Eh?'

'Jess! I've told you, I'm free Saturday, you said you'd think about it, you promised.' Sinking to the floor. Rapidly running out of credit, knowing full well he'd never ring back.

'Alright, stop flapping for Christ's sake. She's fine. You can come Saturday, only problem is, Carol's going to be there, that's all.' Breaking off to shout at someone to turn on the tap. 'Go for it, Danny!'

Vying for my daughter's attention with some bitch who had no right to be there. Who the hell was she? No interest in kids till Jess came along. Now a massive expert all of a sudden. Someone vulnerable she could sink her teeth into. A female version of Alex. Would I ever be free?

'We've got to start somewhere. If I can just have a bit of time alone with her, you know I'll not do anything daft. I know Carol means well and she's been a godsend but there's no need, honestly.'

'Hang on a sec.' Turning away. 'Switch it off, for Christ's sake!'

'I'm running out of credit!'

He came back in his own time. Always on his terms. 'Sorry, sweetheart. So how you getting on then?'

'What?'

'Feeling a bit better?'

'That's not why I'm ringing.'

'Still going to them session things?' He'd told Carol, the two of them lapping it up, refusing to trust me. Desperately keeping me at arm's length in case I did something daft. Like what? Take my own daughter and tell her the truth?

I took a deep breath. Something I'd carefully prepared. 'I feel ten times better than last month and I'm sure next month I'll feel better still. It's a slow process but I'm getting there and that's all that matters. I've been onto the council again. Looks like I'm not allowed a second bedroom. Doesn't matter what I say, they won't budge.'

'Oh bloody hell. Told you, didn't I? Carol said the same, didn't she?'

'But it doesn't matter because she can sleep in my room, and I'll have the sofa. Plenty do far worse.'

'Bloody hell! Getting a bit ahead, aren't you?'

'We have to start somewhere. Just let me see her. We can start with a weekend, then build from there.'

'Can't do that, can you? Need at least one more bedroom. Can't go from here to staying in some crummy one-bed.' A hint of pride in his voice, at what he'd given her. The same person who once thought nothing of kipping on a stranger's settee. 'You can't just waltz out of hospital and expect everything to fall at your feet, doesn't work like that.'

'Will you stop going on about it, for God's sake? So I've been in hospital. I'm out now, okay? At some point we'll have to tell her the truth; it's better if it comes from me. A miracle it's gone on this long. She's getting near that age where it has to come out whether we like it or not.'

A lengthy pause.

'I don't know. How she's going to take it? Who can say? She never even mentions Alex. Barely mentions you. And another thing: stop following us around, will you? Bloody school run, for Christ's sake, I'm not daft!'

'Then stop avoiding me! And stop hiding behind Carol! Let me see her. There's no need for Carol to be there, she can do whatever she likes, we don't need to bother her.' Still talking, long after realising I'd been cut off. No idea how much he'd heard. I'd bought her some new shoes. Socks and knickers. Next month perhaps a winter coat, followed by a pretty dress. Carol didn't need to tell me the size or point me in the right direction. I could work it out for myself.

I rushed round the flat, desperately trying to scrub the kitchen floor. Grabbing a cloth and wiping mould from the kitchen window, determined to make it mine.

I couldn't afford more credit till the end of the month. Couldn't afford all the stuff he was telling me I needed. Perhaps

I'd never be able to, but I was Jess's mother and even a terrible mother was better than what she was living with. God knows what they were telling her. No better than Alex. Ray fooling me into thinking he had my best interests at heart.

Time to take control. Even if I fell flat on my face. Even if people thought I was hysterical, and they put it down to the meds. Time to take back my daughter.

9   Jess

You hadn't budged an inch in over two years. Still hanging out the washing, slumped against the back wall, lighting a fag while I played at your feet. Wait a sec. Doing something new for once. Gently pressing a finger to your lips, glancing over your shoulder at the house. Not that I was frightened, of you at least. United over something.

'Try to play a bit quieter, Jessie. Try not to shout.' Hands twitching, arms jerking, the usual. Something to do with the house, a place of fear and loathing. Somewhere to stay clear at all costs, for us both.

While I scrabbled in the sandpit with the red bucket and blue spade. Yellow plastic rake and mini green watering can. Stretching it out till bedtime, waiting for Dad to get home from work. Forever six, in the grubby white dress and dirt-streaked face. Crying out your name, working for your attention, never losing hope…

'Jess! What the hell's this? Get your arse down here!'

I snapped open my eyes and rolled off the bed, standing at the top of the stairs, dragged reluctantly into the present. Dad below, hovering near the front door, amazed at something arrived in the post.

'How am I supposed to make head or tail of this? Credit card crap.' Holding it limply in the air.

I stomped down and snatched it. Pages and pages. His name at the top. A long list of numbers and descriptions. Stuff he needed for work from the Builder Centre. Sand and cement, a wheelbarrow, a ton of gravel. Other stuff that always appeared. eBay and Amazon mostly. His entire movements for the last few months.

'They're asking you to pay. That's what they do, don't they? You need to pay.' I read a couple of sentences. 'They're charging you for late payment again.'

Not entirely sure. I didn't want to be forced into understanding. I wanted to hide in my room and message Katie instead; find out if she'd got her new trampoline yet. Make up something about myself.

'Why are you always surprised, like it's never happened before?' Tempted to snap at him, like Carol, force him to sit down and sort it once and for all. Then run into his arms so he could kiss the top of my head and tell me everything was okay; he'd never bother me again.

He bent down to snatch another two envelopes off the mat. 'Just leave 'em in there, I'll have a look later. No rush.'

I watched from the kitchen window as he wrapped up and went into the garden, wind whipping his hair about his face. Lugging paving slabs, bags of cement, piles of bricks, making phone calls in between.

If he caught sight of me he'd flash a smile and a big thumbs up, tripping over his size twelve feet. Shaking his head if I didn't laugh straight away.

I sat at the table and tore open the letters, spreading them in front of me. Better than stuffing them down the side of the sofa unopened. Circling important words. At least, words I thought were important, in capitals or red ink.

After a while the numbers and words merging into one. Nothing like school. Nobody to ask for advice, nobody to tell me I was doing it right. I fought the urge to run back upstairs and plug in my earphones, shutting out the world. So much easier to be six and a half up there.

Half-three, the breath of winter stinging my hands and face. Launching into the front room after discarding both jacket and rucksack on the way. Skidding to a halt on the blue-stripe rug. A small blonde woman perched awkwardly on the settee, holding a pink teddy towards me, my name stitched across its chest.

'Hi, Jessica. Nice to meet you. I'm Karen. Good day at school?'

Backing off to the safety of the doorway. Dad perched on the small footstool in the corner, as if he'd suddenly shot there in the last few seconds. Explaining with a red face, explaining too much, his tongue tripping over the words. An old friend he'd recently bumped into. Known her years. Something to do with a bakery in town. He smiled nervously, trying to make it sound fun, too much hanging on my response. Repeating himself in case I misheard or thought something far worse. Like what?

'Hi.' Throwing myself on the settee, burying my head in my phone. 'What's for tea?'

A quick burst of nervous laughter, making me jump. A new voice in the house, light and sharp like my own. A wave of flowery perfume invading my nostrils. A pair of heels and a leather bag hurled into a corner, a pink jacket draped over the back of a chair. No memories of you doing the same. What would Carol say?

'She's really funny,' the woman burst out, as if I wasn't sat right under her nose.

'Oh she's funny alright. Wait till you get to know her.'

'Bet she looks after her old dad. I mean, I bet you're really close, just the two of you.'

'We look after each other. Had to, haven't we, Jess?'

I took the teddy and rammed it down the side of the settee. Somebody else trying to take your place. Glancing from under my fringe. What was so funny? How was I supposed to react?

Dad suddenly sitting upright, much taller than usual, even picking up his mug differently. Taking polite little sips instead of great big gulps. What was wrong with the normal way of doing things? He looked both uncomfortable and incredibly happy at the same time.

'So what have you been up to today?' she asked, leaning towards me. I didn't like the way she did it, as if she might be around a long time.

I mumbled something about my rainforest project. Yes, I was really enjoying it. I'd researched it online with my Auntie Carol's help. Did she know her? No, not yet but she looked forward to meeting her at some point.

'Maybe I could have a look when you next bring it home?'

I shrugged. Dad sitting up even straighter, tea slopping over the side of his mug.

'You can bring it home tomorrow, can't you? Maybe Karen can help. She'll be ten times better at that sort of thing than me. Ever so smart.'

'Okay.' Tapping away on my phone. My voice coming out strange, vision starting to blur. Six and a half all over again.

10   Lisa

I got there early, so as not to give them an easy excuse. I knew
they were looking for one. I could hear Carol's voice already,
warming up. *How can we trust her when she's never on time?
When she can't even drag her arse out of bed?*

Carol's tiny terrace I'd once spent half a day staring at from
the opposite side of the road after leaving hospital, on the off-
chance Jess might be inside. Finally admitted on their terms,
according to their rules.

'Remember what we agreed before they get here. No scaring
her, no jumping the gun, no little remarks.'

'Carol, she's my daughter. Why the hell would I scare her?'

'I've told you; she's confused. Can't just blurt it out without
thinking.'

'I'll let her take the lead, you know that.'

She lit a fag and paced in front of the mantel while I perched
on the sofa, trying not to twitch.

'Well make sure you do. Don't want to make the situation
any worse, do we?'

In reality I didn't know what the hell I might do. Rush at her
and squeeze the life out of her perhaps, give her no choice but to
accept me. Surely some instinct would kick in for us both that
Carol could never understand. To hell with their rules, insisting
I sit in a corner and politely watch.

Half an hour and two cups of tea later, Ray's knackered old

van announced their arrival just as I thought he'd chickened out. I gripped my mug and locked onto Carol's face. Her mouth set in a grim line. God knows what she'd do if I pounced too soon. What would they tell Jess after I'd gone? My stomach lurching at the thought of them being right after all, the sudden realisation I might've got everything wrong. An unstable mother, incapable of raising her own child. Not to be trusted anywhere near.

Too late. She launched through the back door and into the room on a wave of cold air. My daughter. Within feet of where I perched. My mouth set in what I hoped was a warm smile, even though I looked rough as hell, perhaps even scary to a small child. Except my own child, of course.

'Carol! Look at this!'

'What is it?'

'A unicorn, can't you tell?'

She handed Carol something she should've handed me. Something she'd done at school. Ray watching from the doorway, blocking the light from the kitchen. We exchanged glances, just a brief nod. He twisted the cap in his hands, his attention focused on Jess.

'Is that what it is? I'll put it up here out the way. Do you want a drink?'

She hadn't turned to look at me. She sat cross-legged on the rug in front of the fire, as if it were her usual place, dragging something from a toy box in the corner. She could see me out the corner of her eye. She hadn't flinched and didn't seem upset. Surely now was the time.

'Alright?' Ray asked, as Carol nipped into the kitchen. He sounded out of breath.

Didn't they realise this was the biggest day of my life? The biggest day of Jess's life. Shortly we were going to hug and cry and perhaps argue to start with. Mother and daughter again.

'Jess!' I whispered tentatively.

She spun towards me, dark hair whipping across her face. A plastic toy horse in one hand. I smiled and leaned forward. A brief flicker between us before turning back to the box.

'Bloody cold out there,' Ray broke in, rubbing his hands.

'Here.' Carol shoving a steaming mug at him. 'Where you working?'

'Jackson Street. Bit of pointing. We're not staying long; I'll just have this.'

'I've got you some socks for Jess. And a pair of pyjamas. They should do her for winter.'

Any minute Jess was going to jump onto my lap and show the two of them how close we used to be, while they discussed pyjamas and socks. She pulled out a jigsaw from the box, scattering the contents across the rug. Carol carelessly ruffling the top of her head as she wandered back towards the mantle.

'Do you want any help?' I offered, ready to lunge towards her. Face to face there wouldn't be any doubt. My hair was shorter, that was all, perhaps a little greyer. Puffy under the eyes, down to the meds.

'No thank you, I can do it on my own.'

Thomas the Tank Engine, far too young for her. As she slotted in the final piece I slopped tea down my jeans.

'That was good,' I whispered. Any second she was going to throw in my name. Mummy. And their whole world would crumble.

'I've done it before,' she answered, refusing eye contact. Breaking up the jigsaw and throwing it back in the box. In her own little world.

Who on earth did she think I was? A friend of Carol's? Another client popping by for a trim? Somebody unworthy of attention because she'd never set eyes on me again? I glanced towards Ray. He gulped his tea, resting against the doorframe. Carol puffing away as if she'd seen it all before. A slow shake of her head as I began to open my mouth.

'We'll get off then,' Ray announced, nodding towards Jess.

'Already?' They hadn't given her a chance, hadn't given me a chance. Of course I looked different, everything was different, it proved nothing.

'She's tired, aren't you?' Carol butted in, grabbing hold of the collar of her school dress and yanking it straight. All for my benefit, to show how things worked. My daughter needed sorting, the two of them could handle it.

Before I could stand and move towards her, she'd skipped into the kitchen and started playing with magnets on the fridge. Arranging her own name out of the plastic, coloured letters. Ray placing his hand on the back of her head and steering her towards the door.

'See you soon,' he muttered, avoiding eye contact because he knew he was about to lose her. Just one little comment. It was going to happen whether they liked it or not.

I spun towards Carol, ready to scream in her face but she was too busy pulling out a plastic bag from behind the sofa, stuffed with socks and pyjamas. Also for my benefit. Whatever my daughter needed they could provide.

I opened my mouth, ready to come out with it. Cold tea slopping across the rug. Stopping myself just in time. Carol's grim face within inches, lowered eyebrows, a clear warning. My breath coming in tiny gasps. Alright. On this occasion I'd bide my time.

*

'Underselling yourself as usual. How do you expect to get a job by being straight?' He took out a red pen and started crossing out everything except my name, address and date of birth. Even that he didn't seem too sure about.

Whilst I leant against the kitchen units, nursing a cuppa, convinced I'd made a huge mistake. Showing Steve my CV after everyone had crept home. Half a page of nothingness that could've been about anyone.

Always first to arrive and last to leave above the Christian bookshop. Newcomers could be forgiven for thinking I had a vested interest in the place. Why else would I always ensure the place was immaculate for the knitting group, even scrub the grotty toilet if necessary?

'Qualifications?'

'I've told you, nobody's going to employ me. Bunked off school too much. You won't believe me, will you?'

Staring steadily. Tired blue eyes, barely blinking. For the past few months looking exactly the same. Used to dealing with stubbornness; plodding on regardless.

'Work experience?'

'No.'

'Not even at school?'

'Nothing.'

'Volunteering?'

'Who'd have me? Seriously.'

'Still not giving up. You do realise?' A warning look, still not quite sure what he was dealing with. 'I know you don't want anybody knowing anything about you, which is fine, I can fully understand where you're coming from, but when it comes to finding a job you've got to put something. Got to be someone. When you've got a big gaping hole in your life like we all have here.'

I pulled up a chair and perched, the CV between us, feeling a pang of guilt for wasting his time.

'I know what you're afraid of,' he said.

I couldn't help laughing. He hadn't a clue. Lowering his voice so I could barely hear. The shop downstairs closed hours ago, the whole draughty building to ourselves. No need to be so gentle.

'This Alex character. You're terrified of putting down too much on paper. Got into the habit of being secretive, right?'

69

All the times I'd imagined him skulking outside my window and loitering in the street, always imagining the worst. The doctors right all along, I simply couldn't see how ill I must've been.

'These past few months I've realised how pathetic he really was. All that time, afraid for nothing. All that time wasted.'

'It doesn't matter now, just move on.'

He was right, of course. What else was I used to doing except hiding? What else was I good at? Being straight with people? Grabbing life with both hands and going for it?

He sighed heavily and glanced at his watch. He'd recently made up with his eldest daughter, though still fragile. These sessions getting too much for him. He'd even hinted somebody might take over, that it could be for the best as far as the group was concerned.

'You know what you've got to do, otherwise you wouldn't have brought me this.' He jabbed the paper. 'And that once you've found that job you won't need this place anymore. You'll have a proper life, proper friends, money, everything everyone else has. No need to hide anymore. Free to move on.'

He'd known all along. Coming here was my way of having a life, except it wasn't really a life, giving me an excuse to keep my head down. An excuse to avoid doing all the things I desperately needed to be getting on with. Somehow he'd recognised me, he'd seen my type before.

'There must be something you've been dreaming about all this time. Not just giving up the booze. Some goal at the end, something you can close your eyes and picture. Something that gets you up in a morning, whatever, whoever it is.' Leaning back so he could look at me properly. His tough pose. He'd finally had enough. 'Because I'd hate to think that by coming here every week you've forgotten it. That's not why I set up this place originally. If you're well enough, healthy enough, strong enough to go, that's what you've got to do. When did you last have a drink?'

'You know when. Months ago.'

'Then you're as fit and healthy now as you'll ever be. Nobody's worried about you, nobody's looking for you. The slate wiped clean. Something's given you the strength these last few months. A purpose. Whatever, whoever it is, don't forget it now. You're nearly there. Closer than you think.'

'I just need to get my head round it. There's somebody in the way, somebody I need to overcome.'

Narrowing his eyes.

'Don't ask. Just somebody who gets under my skin. I've let them take advantage. That was my biggest mistake, not taking control.'

I glanced at the paper. Hardworking and punctual. A quick learner, both good in a team and working as an individual. He'd created a new person, professional and self-confident.

'You've done this before. You put the same for everyone.'

'Course I put the bloody same for everyone! How else do you think I get rid of 'em?'

I pulled it towards me, taking ownership. This person was going to get my daughter back. She was going to stand up to Ray, look Carol in the eye, all the things I'd never been able to do. Better get used to her.

'What do I have to do?'

*

'You barely gave me chance,' I accused Carol. 'Ten minutes, for God's sake! You're not being fair on either of us.'

'So being fair means caving in. Giving you exactly what you want, is that it?'

'It means giving her chance to work things out.'

'She didn't recognise you. She didn't want to recognise you. She was more interested in a jigsaw. Don't blame us for that!'

She'd invited me round in between customers. My voice

71

quivering out of control. The cold hard stare while I twitched and shuffled on her sofa.

'And what's this about a girlfriend? Karen? Here I am, trying to get back on my feet while he's playing happy families. God knows what effect it's having on her, somebody's got to tell him.' Panting for breath, perhaps the longest speech I'd ever given her. 'Who the hell is she?' Blonde, brunette, tall, short, fat, thin. I couldn't imagine anything that wouldn't cut me in two. Close to Jess, whoever she was.

Carol puffing away, gazing out the window at her shabby yard. My words making no more impression than if I were talking to the window itself. When she spoke, almost to herself. 'As daft as he is no doubt. Why else would she be interested? By the sound of it she's got her feet firmly under the table.'

'Already?'

'Talking about foreign holidays, weekends away. Obviously got a bit of cash. I know what he's like; money's always been his weakness. She'll have him worked out by now.'

My hands trembling as I gripped my mug. Dust mites dancing in the shaft of weak winter sunlight. Silence hanging between us for what felt like hours, Carol perfectly happy, puffing away. Always the advantage. She'd known for a while, only telling me when she was ready. Plenty of time to plot and plan. She didn't need as long as me.

She'd already decided there was no way I could turn my life around, taking it for granted. Could anyone meet her high standards? Part-time hairdresser, forever interfering in her brother's life. Hanging around awaiting mistakes, picking up the pieces other people left behind, including my daughter.

I'd known Ray years. It felt natural talking to him and arguing with him, but God knows how I'd ended up here, visiting Carol's dark poky terrace as if we were intimately related. How had I let it get this far?

Because we were desperate. She'd kept our secret if nothing

else. Ray would never have managed without her. She'd told him what to do when he hadn't a clue, when I was in no fit state, guiding him through those early months. Problem was, she knew full well.

'I know he's had money troubles; he's always been a bit...'

'Inept. Any idea how much he owes me? Even I've lost count so there's no hope of him remembering. Started writing it down but then made it so damn complicated, dragging Jess into it, playing for sympathy. Not above using her as an excuse. You could say she's been highly convenient for him at times.'

I stared at the carpet, avoiding her harsh stare. Sorely tempted to tell her about my CV and the jobs I'd applied for, the future I had in mind. A round of applause from Steve and the group just for trying.

'You're saying he's in trouble?'

'Trouble?' she snapped. 'Never out of it. Jess might've changed him initially but not anymore, once the cuteness wore off. Just going back to the way he always was. Didn't expect him to cope forever, did you? Didn't expect him to be interested forever. Must've been desperate if he was your best bet.'

'Of course I was desperate, surely you could tell?'

I insisted that Jess could come to me if Ray was obviously struggling. Now was the time. He was moving on with his life, just as I was moving on.

'In a one bed flat?' She sounded disgusted.

'I'll get a sofa bed. It's not the end of the world.'

'For a child?'

'For me. She can have the bed. She's still young. Once it's all explained. They can accept things like that when they're younger.'

'The truth? After all this time?'

Flicking ash into a small glass bowl on the mantelpiece. Swiping dust with a bony fingertip. One of Jess's pictures propped behind a clock. Brightly coloured people standing in a flower garden. Who the hell were they? Toys and books stacked in a corner, awaiting her return.

'Living with Ray she's bound to be more grown up than most kids. You do realise she opens half his post? Has to manage his business when he can't? I reckon it's happened while you weren't looking.'

I tried to summon some of the resolve Steve had told me to muster, remembering my goal. Without sounding hysterical, without it being put down to the meds. 'She's mature for her age, she's been through more than most. But grown up or not, she's still my daughter. Whatever I've done, however stupid, however many mistakes, nobody can change that, even you.'

She paused for a split second, not expecting a personal comment. 'Problem is, Lisa… and I realise it's not entirely your fault with everything that's happened, but who do you think paid for her uniform? School trips? All the stuff that matters?'

'Okay, okay.'

'Holidays? When they've been away, who's made it possible? Who's paid for half her meals when they've been starving? Who's given her as normal childhood as possible? Who's made it financially possible and never taken credit? You think it's been easy for me?'

'I'm sorry, Carol. You've been fantastic but you're still not her mother. Even Jess knows and look how confused she is. The truth is the truth.' I sat up straight, talking confidently in Carol's back room. Perfectly sober, making sense. The first step towards normality. Who gave a damn what she really thought?

'Not so simple, is it? Ray likes to pretend he's bringing her up but half the time he isn't. You like to claim you're her mother but have never acted like it. Neither of you wanted responsibility. Neither of you capable. How do you undo all the lies without a fuss? What are you going to tell her about her father? Surely it's better if she believes Ray's her dad? Surely anything's better than the truth after all this time?'

'We'll think of something, once she realises who I am. Just let me have a few more meetings. Let her get used to me. If we start telling the truth now, at least that's in our favour. We can be honest, can't we?'

'We? Lisa. I've never been anything else.' A long pause. 'Think it through, for God's sake. Once you start blurting out the truth, who knows what might follow. Surely you don't want her knowing every single detail?'

'Of course I don't want her knowing every single detail!' My heart thumping in my ears. That terrifying thought again. What if they were both right? Carol might be a bitch but could still be right. An unstable mother not to be trusted. 'So who the hell am I supposed to be if I can't be her mother yet?'

I could hear the cogs whirring away. She'd thought of something already. She'd thought of it long ago.

'I might have an idea. Leave it with me.'

Her words reverberating round the poky room, following me home afterwards long after I'd escaped. Jeering at me from the corner of my bedroom as I failed to fall asleep. I couldn't pick and choose, she'd make sure of that. I couldn't reveal so much and stop. All or nothing, as far as Carol was concerned.

*

'So you've been doing voluntary work for the last few months? In a bookshop?'

'Yes. Been very rewarding.' I sounded out of breath, as if I'd been running up a steep hill. 'Two or three days a week.'

'Excellent.'

I gripped my knees to stop my hands doing anything stupid. Making eye contact was the worst, though Steve had insisted it was crucial. Steely grey eyes that barely blinked. Mine feeling watery in comparison. Instantly annoyed by her confidence and her assumption that having a job, a wage and a pension was the norm. Knowing no different. Not to mention the dark blue suit, a million miles from my dark blue suit: the fabric, the cut, even the buttons. Was there nothing that didn't give me away?

It was ridiculous to get so wound up over such a menial job. Forecourt assistant. Twenty hours a week, a shade above minimum wage.

'And what exactly were you doing?'

'Sorry?'

'Duties?' Raising her eyebrows.

'Dealing with customers, stock-taking, using the till.' I tried to recall Steve's list. Like revising for an exam. All about looking and sounding good, not actually being good. I could practise that later.

She nodded slowly, flicking paperwork. A name badge pinned to her chest. *Sue Watkins.* Thoroughly bored, not necessarily at me but the whole process, asking a hundred questions to fill a crappy position anyone could do.

'So you're used to handling customers and taking the flak. Two references, I see.'

Thank God for Steve's friendship with Liam, the kindly bookshop manager. We'd barely exchanged two words over the last few months, yet he was prepared to lie to see the back of me.

'Okay. What about family?'

It just came out. I could've told her about Jess without going into detail. I could've admitted I had a daughter from the start, but like Carol said, far too complicated to go into now.

'I'm single. No kids.'

'Hobbies?'

'Cycling. I like walking as well, to keep fit. Two or three times a week, as often as I can.' I answered without hesitation. The life I wanted to lead, the person I wanted to be. After finding a job I'd be able to do it easily. Outdoors in all weathers, the satisfaction of regular exercise. Taking Jess along. Having money for the first time.

She scribbled it down, making it official. 'Great. Just one other person I need to interview before we decide. Thank you very much for your time, we'll be in touch.'

I shook hands and escaped. Steve had always said it was about putting on a show and pretending to be the right person. As long as I was better at it than most, I'd have no problem fitting in.

11

Jess

A Few Months Later

Of course, Karen didn't try to change us straight away. Wasn't like she marched into the house and told us we were living like pigs. She waited till I was at school and Dad at work. She waited till the coast was clear.

'Like a walking Argos catalogue.' Dad beamed. The highest praise he could think of, like she'd done something really smart.

'What? Don't you want me to do it? You've only got to say.' Resting her blonde head against his shoulder. Curled up on the sofa, tiny feet tucked in. Not much bigger than mine. 'I feel so comfortable with you, especially the way you've brought up Jess on your own. How many men could do that? I just want to help whatever way I can, make life a bit easier with a few treats. What's so terrible about that?'

'Nothing. Nothing at all.' Big grin stretched across his shining face. 'Nobody's having a go. You're doing all these wonderful things we've just never got round to. Both ever so grateful, aren't we, Jess? Can't believe we've found someone like you, can we?'

Hour after hour. Karen making him happy the way I used to make him happy, arms wrapped round each other, fleeing to Carol's. That night we ran away, drawing on his strength, which he seemed to crave more than anything. Confident he could put a smile on my face, chase away all my doubts.

It wasn't long before she'd swapped the living room curtains so they matched the cushions for the first time. A new blind in the bathroom, a full-length mirror in the hallway that showed every bit of you before you rushed out the house. Pink instead of beige, purple instead of brown. Everything shiny and new, with a funny smell as if it had just been unwrapped. And a growing mountain of rubbish in the backyard, our old life ready for collection on bin day.

'I'll only carry on if it makes you both happy,' she announced.

'You've given us a new lease in life. Jess? Made us realise how shitty it's been for us all these years, struggling on our own. I don't know how we've coped now I come to think of it. Jess?'

I turned to my book instead. Dad's happy face, exactly like it used to be, scrabbling in the backyard, glancing over our shoulders. So desperate to let go of the past. While Karen, dabbing at tears and managing a small smile, couldn't even remember it.

*

'You can have whatever you want,' Dad insisted.

'Anything?'

'Yep.'

'Absolutely anything?'

'Get a move on! Stop overthinking!'

'Not overthinking.'

As if I were being awkward, failing to grasp the new rules.

'She always like this?' Karen whispered, nudging him in the ribs.

'I'd like egg-fried rice and some spring rolls but Dad always says it's too expensive.'

'Too expensive! What a load of crap!' He turned a dark mottled red, insisting I was a picky eater, that was the problem.

'But it's over five quid. Egg fried rice is £2.80 and two spring rolls £2.40.'

'Over five quid!'

'How old are you, Jess? I can't believe you're only nine. Shouldn't be worrying about stuff like that at your age. Should she, Ray?'

'Bloody shouldn't. Sick of telling her.'

'Shouldn't even be thinking about it.'

Dad nudging me with his big toe. Always the little things. Glancing at me as if he didn't know me anymore. Worse than that, slightly disappointed. Surely I could tell everything had changed?

*

'So come on then, what's the latest? Still flashing her money about?' Carol's gloomy back room. Carol already shaking her head as if she knew the answer.

While I perched on the cream sofa and tried to explain. Nudging closer to Auntie Maggie, who looked pale and worried at the latest developments. I could hear her breathing just above my right ear.

Karen had stayed the night several times. It only took a few weeks. We'd sat opposite each other over breakfast, and she'd swiped nearly all the milk before realising we didn't have an endless supply of everything. She'd apologised, then said she'd soon nick some more from work.

'Roberts Bakery,' Carol muttered.

'Doing what?' Maggie asked.

I shrugged. 'She puts the jam in doughnuts, I think.' No idea. Maybe the jam was already there.

'Part-time?'

I nodded.

'So she's on peanuts then?'

'She's allowed to bring home flapjacks if they're a few days old. We had doughnuts for tea yesterday, with pink sprinkles.' Karen could lay her hands on more fresh cream cakes than even I could handle. I'd spent most of my time stuffing my face since she'd entered the house. Only a matter of time before somebody stopped her.

A quick exchange of glances above my head. Hard to tell who was most upset. Carol's face set into grim lines; Maggie looking distant, her mind elsewhere. Another funny turn perhaps. She had lots, according to Dad. One eye on Carol, awaiting her decision. They were sisters but Carol always firmly in charge.

'So she's got her feet under the table and he's lapping it up, helping her spend all that money.'

I nodded. Could hardly remember the old Dad. He'd disappeared and been replaced by somebody really cheerful, yet deadly serious and picky at the same time. Scrubbing the oven after work. New pink towels in the bathroom. He'd even screwed a handle on the downstairs toilet door.

'It had to happen at some point, I suppose,' Maggie burst out. 'He can't be alone forever. But should he be having her round with Jess there, especially at night? Does he know he can trust her?'

I chipped in with what I thought might comfort them both. Karen had helped with my rainforest project. She'd bought me a book on South America with a fold-out map.

'So she's trying to buy you then? That should make him happy. All his dreams come true.'

'Rainforest project?' Maggie butted in, face falling to the floor. 'What do you need? If I'd known you wanted something…'

'School books are expensive, Maggie, shouldn't bother if I were you. Best leave it to this woman if she's that way inclined.'

I insisted I hadn't asked her. Dad had practically shoved it under her nose because she'd got a GCSE in Geography.

'And he tidies the house whenever she's coming.'

'Properly?'

'Properly.'

'Not just playing at it? You help him, you mean?'

Carol struggled to picture it. What about the bathroom? What about his tools lying all over the place? And half the stuff he'd broken, like the shower and cooker, the garage full of crap, all the stuff he'd never got round to finishing properly, what about them? Didn't any of it put her off?

I told them how he didn't live in his work clothes anymore. He'd started taking them off as soon as he got in. And combed his hair and brushed his teeth more often although he hated me pointing it out, claiming he'd been doing it years.

'I keep embarrassing him. He just wants me to shut up in case I say something.'

Carol staring out the window, deep in thought. I took the opportunity to lunge towards Maggie, who kissed the top of my head and stroked my hair, gently rocking back and forth. Almost enough to disguise her constant shaking. I breathed in against her shoulder, relishing the smell and shape of her. A woman who cared, who might be able to give advice if she stuck around long enough. She might even know the answers to some of my endless questions.

'And she's got a brand-new convertible BMW,' Carol suddenly announced.

'Convertible BMW?' Maggie sounding even more alarmed, ten minutes behind as usual. 'How's she afforded that?'

'Keep up. Her grandmother died and left her a bungalow or something. Don't get that on minimum wage.'

I hesitated before telling them the next bit. They'd only find out anyway. Perhaps it would hurt less coming from me. It wasn't just the fact she'd bought him loads of presents and taken him by surprise. Or the fact that whenever we ordered a Chinese she insisted on paying. Or that she had a nice car Dad could never afford.

'What? Spit it out.'

The wispy blonde hair and soft blue eyes. The fact she couldn't have been more different to you. A fragile-looking creature, still squeezing into kid's clothing, hardly bigger than me. Exactly what he'd been waiting for.

'He likes her even without the money,' I burst out, causing them both to freeze. Carol insisting I'd got it wrong. Maggie pulling away, too much to take in. 'I think he just likes her anyway.'

*

'Does she have to? My room, not hers. If Karen loves pink butterflies so much she can do them all over her own room.'

Fresh bedding to match. Fluffy pink lights strung across the headboard. A new desk to help with my growing mountain of homework. Some of the stuff she even ran by me first, the rest she confidently picked herself.

'She's just trying to give you the room you deserve, that's all. The one I always wanted to give you but couldn't.' Dad pulling me close as we curled up on the sofa, precious time while Karen was at work. Naturally slipping back into the old ways. 'We've waited long enough so let's make the most of it. Karen as well, she's gone through the mill with her ex, so she appreciates all this. We've all struggled and now we're reaping the rewards. If you have to put up with a few daft butterflies here and there, who cares? Look at my room. Suede purple blind and sheepskin rug! Don't think that's my choice, do you?'

'But it won't last forever, will it?'

'Eh?'

'The money. Acting like it's never ending. If we're all

83

spending it on stuff then eventually we'll run out, won't we?' On the verge of tears. The thought of him being miserable afterwards, the way it always worked.

He squeezed me so hard I had to tell him to stop. They were teaching me crap at school. Worrying over the price of a Chinese, fretting over a loaf of bread. There was a time in everyone's life for purple suede blinds and this was ours.

'This is what we've been waiting for. Struggled enough, haven't we?'

I leaned against him and listened. Maybe he was right. At least Karen could open the post in a morning and tell him what it meant. At least she could take control.

'But what about all the rubbish dumped outside? Our old stuff. Just getting rid of it without even asking.' My old bedroom rug wrapped round a bathroom cabinet. The spare bedroom blind poking from the old kitchen bin.

'Oh, come off it, she's doing us a favour.' Rubbing my shoulder till it hurt. 'What use is it these days? Not like we're going back. Called progress. Moving on.'

'Dad?' I spun round to look at him. 'You know next weekend when you're away? Can I stay at Auntie Maggie's for a change, instead of Carol's? She can help me do my homework on the Nile.' She wouldn't, of course. She never had a clue.

'We've been through this before. Maggie has funny turns; she can't be doing with kids running all over the place.'

'I could sleep on her sofa. It's not like she hasn't got the room.'

He chewed it over for a while, like he often did before letting me down.

'Terrible nerves, sweetheart. That's why she lives alone in a crappy old flat. Not exactly child-friendly, is it? Don't go mentioning it, only make it worse. Don't want to make it worse for her, do we?' Whistling cheerfully. His own sister. His face slightly flushed but that was all. Turning suddenly to his phone.

I lunged towards his middle, gripping hard. Slightly thicker than it used to be, especially since the takeaways started. Burying my head against his shoulder, breathing in his dusty smell, relishing it like never before. Didn't feel like mine anymore.

*

'You do realise it's not Christmas every day? Are you listening? You can leave some till tomorrow, you know. Grandma worked hard for that money. Think about that every time you open your purse.'

Karen's mum. White-haired, even smaller than me, usually to be found in pastel cardigans and a beige skirt, on her way into town or on her way back, a large shopping bag in the crook of her arm, just popping in for five minutes that usually turned into a whole afternoon. Her mission in life to persuade Karen to leave some money in the bank for future.

'Give it a rest, Mam.'

'Somebody's got to think of these things. Pretty obvious nobody else is round here.'

Blue eyes sweeping over me, refusing to melt, settling for a few seconds, as if she couldn't quite work out where I'd sprung from. How we'd found ourselves in the same place, connected to the same people.

'Jessica. How's school? Finished all your homework?'

'It's Jess. That's what everyone calls me. Haven't got any homework today.'

'I thought they gave you homework every day. That right, Karen?' She wandered to the sink and grabbed a cloth, flicking in all directions. 'I'll soak it ten minutes. Covered in germs. Look, Karen. When did they last clean this?' Picking up our mess between finger and thumb. Not satisfied till she found it, which made Dad really happy.

I got upset when I imagined the two of you bumping into each other. I laid awake at night thinking about it. How she'd shake her head over your long greasy hair and allergic reaction to housework. How you were everything she was fighting against on a daily basis, everything she couldn't understand. How she'd grab hold and feel the need to give you a good scrub. Dumping you in the garden with all the other rubbish. Your only answer, to grab hold in return and throw her violently against the nearest wall, sorting her in no time.

'What do I have to call her?' I asked Dad. 'I can't ignore her every time she walks in.'

'Well… I suppose she's your grandma in a way, though we don't want to upset her at this stage.' Talking out the corner of his mouth. 'Let's introduce it slowly. Win her round gradually.'

'She's not my grandma. I haven't got a grandma.' I'd never had one, except Mrs Patterson, sadly not around anymore. Dad always trying to make people fit. How could I have a grandma like that and still be your daughter? 'If Mum were here she'd soon sort her.'

A muscle tensing in the side of his jaw.

'She wouldn't like Karen's mum. She'd hate her, wouldn't she?' I didn't tell him I was pretty confident you'd hate Karen too. Not to mention the endless butterflies and purple suede blind. 'What about Carol?'

'What about her?'

'Always questioning me every time I go round.'

'Give it a rest, will you? No need for Carol to know our business every five secs. Or Maggie, come to that. Time they both butted out. Now we've got Karen we don't need to be running to other people all the time. This is what we've been waiting for, remember. This is our time to enjoy, let's make the most of it, let's not spoil it over crap.'

*

86

A cold windy night not long after Karen entered our lives. Gone ten when I finally felt tired enough to drift off. Dad and Karen downstairs in front of *Newsnight*, cheerfully planning a conservatory. Dad shocked at the scale of her plans. Karen insisting it was what she wanted, sod her Mam. My name occasionally floating up. Things they planned to buy me. Places they planned to take me.

Next door's two cats scrapping beneath the window. In the distance a burglar alarm activated by the strong wind, howling through the overgrown pine. A plastic bag scratching its way down the street.

Imagining you, bursting into the house and catching them on the settee, ripping them apart, forcing your way back into our lives. Laughing in her mother's face, undoing all her careful cleaning. In one swift movement, hair tumbling about your face, binning the peach and mango air freshener, tearing dusters to shreds, trashing the blind and butterflies, creating a huge pile in the garden for the binmen next Tuesday.

I smiled into the darkness till my cheeks ached. Karen could fill my room with half the rubbish out of Argos; you were still my mum, I hadn't forgot.

Eyelids drooping, ready to go. Suddenly a whisper along the landing, something rubbing against the wall. Dad. For a large man he could be surprisingly quiet when he needed to be. I closed my eyes and lay still. He nudged the door, struggling to hold his breath. The noisiest part about him. Once he got it under control he'd be unstoppable. He inched towards the window, his bulk outlined against the curtains, only spoiling it last second by stubbing his toe against my new desk and clutching his foot in agony.

'Shitting hell! Where's it gone?'

The wooden toy chest beneath the window, a birthday present from Carol. He prised open the heavy lid and dropped something inside. A whisper of paperwork. Spinning round, sparing me one quick glance, then quickly gone. Back downstairs in seconds. Laughter slowly drifting up. The conservatory back on course. Had he ever been away?

I rolled onto my side and faced the wall. After a few minutes I sat up straight, staring into semi-darkness. The wooden chest. He'd made for it straight away, without shaking me awake. Or shouting from the bottom of the stairs, asking me to explain, even though half the time I couldn't. And what about Karen? Ignoring her too.

Within twenty-four hours, whatever he put in the chest had gone.

12   Lisa

'I'm not cut out for this,' I admitted to Jenny. 'The till, the special offers. Everything.'

Customers gawping, thrusting greedy hands, desperate to get on. My fingers fumbling across the till, terrified of the consequences. One after another, firing impossible questions, walking off before I'd even begun.

'You serious?' Jenny filing lime-green nails. She'd been told to tone them down but didn't give a stuff. 'I'm only staying till I've saved enough to finish this course. Living wage? More like bloody slave wage. Don't reckon I'll even put it on my CV. Part-time garage assistant. Who gives a shit?'

She hadn't a clue. I had every intention of milking the place for all I could. What else did I have?

'It's just working out the change. Remembering all the prices of the stuff outside. I don't know how you do it.'

There was a pile of logs, barbecue coals and bunches of flowers stacked outside the door. Three for two offers that changed every week, stuff without barcodes, a multitude of pitfalls every time I went on duty.

Thank God for Will's uncanny knack of never being on time – he always looked like he'd just tumbled out of bed or was ready to tumble back in – along with Jenny's natural instinct to do the exact opposite of what she was asked. Making me look almost acceptable. Jenny's tongue stud, distracting whenever she opened her mouth. Metallic red hair deepening with every shift. Will swiping his nose on his blue fleece top rather than bother to bring a tissue. Upsetting customers and driving Sue up the wall. Least I didn't do that.

Towards the end of my second week Sue called me into her office. I'd scanned a car magazine twice and taken ages to put it right. Then allowed somebody to take three sacks of logs, only charging for two, not realising the deal had ended. The final straw, surely.

She lowered her glasses so she could peer over the top. Piercing grey eyes. If she sacked me now at least she'd never discover the truth.

'Don't look so terrified all the time, I'm not going to eat you. I just wanted to say I think you're settling in extremely well and I'm really pleased. I know I've not had much chance to show you the ropes, but you seem to be picking it up okay. Was really hoping Jenny might offer a bit of help but you can see how it is. Probably for the best.'

'Right.'

'So is there anything you feel unhappy about or want to ask? Now's the time. Anything you need?'

Looking as if braced for an onslaught. I offered some kind of squeaky-voiced reply.

'God, I wish we had more like you. There is something else, actually. Would you be prepared to do a few extra hours? I know the contract states twenty but in the run up to Christmas I think we could easily offer you another five to ten per week.'

I left the office in a daze. Went straight back on the till as if I owned it. Who cared if I pressed the wrong buttons occasionally? While it was quiet I scribbled out a note about the logs and the latest three-for-two offer on flowers, propping it behind the till. Who cared if Jenny sneered? She always did, not just at me.

An extra ten hours a week. Another sixty quid at least, the

kind of money that at one time had to last a fortnight. Alex would've whacked me across the kitchen for far less.

I wandered home a few hours later, noting different streets and different faces, different cars whizzing by, even different shop windows glaring back in the dark. The world didn't have to seem like a forbidding place. I could join in if I wanted. It felt like this. When I got in I whacked up the heating, ignoring the meter whizzing round. Staring out the window at the wind tugging people's coats, feeling insulated for the first time in years. In the distance, on a street corner, a young man settling down for the night on a sheet of cardboard.

Hours later I lay in bed, bathed in the sickly orange glow of the streetlight with roast chicken wafting through from next door. Sue's words floating round the room. She wanted more like me. I couldn't imagine her saying it to either Jenny or Will.

Alex retreating by the day. How had I allowed him to get so close for so long? Plotting behind my back, lurking round every corner.

I rolled over to face the wall, the dim light catching a curled corner of one of Jess's paintings. Holding hands with Ray in a flower garden. Catching me off guard. I hadn't spoken to her all day.

*

'The till's a pain but I'm not as bad as I was. I'm not the only one who makes mistakes. Will's always half asleep. Jenny's not bothered if she puts the wrong code in. At least I admit I've done something wrong, which Sue reckons is the best thing you can do, it makes her job much easier.'

Steve biting his lip, struggling to hold it in.

'What?' I snapped.

'Nothing. Just enjoying the new Lisa. That a new pair of boots?'

'So?'

'New jacket?'

'I needed a new one. Didn't expect me to walk around in a ten-year-old jacket the rest of my life, did you?'

Every Wednesday evening when I was free. Glancing round desperately for something to do.

'You managed to find the dishcloth then?'

'Exactly where you left it. Nobody's irreplaceable, Lisa, even me.' He scrutinised my face, searching for clues. 'Don't get me wrong, it's lovely to see you and everything but if you've found new friends we won't be offended, honestly.' Gently teasing, our relationship constantly shifting around us. On an equal footing for the first time, simply by finding work and having money in my pocket. 'We're more than capable of wiping down a worktop and rinsing a couple of mugs.'

'I never doubted it.'

'New starter. Derek. Bit OCD, between you and me. Quite handy if I'm honest.'

I insisted I still wanted to come, that work changed nothing. Blushing furiously. He'd heard it all before.

'Another month and you'll not be thinking about us anymore. Slightly embarrassed when you wander past the door. Who knows where you'll be this time next year. Not long before you've met somebody and settled down. The number of people who've brought their families back here just to rub my nose in it.'

What was he on about? I had a family already, the reason I was here in the first place, because I'd screwed up.

'How else do you think it happens? You've started the ball rolling, too late to stop it now.'

I turned away and tried to wipe the spotless worktop. A sudden hatred towards Derek. Damn his OCD. A new washing-up rota sellotaped to a cupboard door; names I didn't recognise. Even the knitting group had moved on.

He lowered his voice, gentler this time. 'Don't panic. You are ready. Just last to realise, as usual. This Sue person, whoever she is, she's obviously got no idea about your past. When she looks at you she sees someone enthusiastic, willing to learn, everything she wants in an employee.'

'She says she could do with more like me.'

'There you are then. This is what you've dreamed of, don't forget. Remember your goal? When you first came here you said it was impossible. If you had a job, if you had money, if you had a social life. All these things holding you back. Can't say that anymore, can you?'

How could I be honest now and explain what I wanted? To reunite with a daughter I'd given away and be a proper mum for the first time. Just as importantly, take a stance and not be pushed around ever again. I'd allowed Ray and Carol to do it just as much as Alex. I'd allowed everyone to do it rather than take responsibility.

I straightened up and threw the cloth at the sink. On duty at five in the morning.

'I've never been straight with you. I know you keeping saying you've heard it all before, but this is different. It's got so big now, I'm terrified of telling anyone, even you.'

He leaned forward and kept his voice low, even though we had the whole draughty building to ourselves. 'Known each other a while now, right? Guess what? If I bumped into you in the street tomorrow, not in this environment, I'd never guess there was anything wrong. No need to advertise it. Every day that goes by, everything new in your life, every new person, is one more thing between you and that past.'

I nodded.

'Whoever this person is holding you back, you're every bit as good as them. Stop pretending they're better because it gives you an excuse. Do what you need to do. If you don't do it now, you never will.'

I turned away and grabbed the cloth one final time. My last chance to get nearer Jess, before it was too late. Auntie Maggie. A temporary measure, bringing me one step closer. I turned back and caught him smiling. He'd known all along.

*

'You after promotion?' Jenny snapped. 'Not like there's anywhere for you to go, is there?'

'Just doing my job.'

'Yeah. But there's doing your job, then there's doing your job. Who you trying to impress anyway?'

She was puzzled by my enthusiasm. Angered at times. Screwing up my little notes behind the till and lobbing them at the bin as soon as I went through the back. Sue's sarcastic comparisons only making it worse, something she never had to endure before.

I'd never paid much attention in school. Left with no qualifications, only a desire to spend the rest of my life with Alex. The absolute certainty I'd never need anything again. Yet here I was, feeling an overwhelming urge to know it all, an overwhelming need to fit in, however late. I explained that I'd been unemployed for a while. It was just a relief to have a job and have my own money. What would a normal person say? What would she relate to? I'd had years of people looking down their nose at me, now all of a sudden I was being pulled up for being too good.

I tried to concentrate on Jess whenever she had a go. Her voice dragging me out of bed in a morning. Whenever customers were sharp. The Jess I used to know, scrabbling in the backyard while Alex slept it off inside. The current Jess, laid flat out on her bed, listening to her iPod, rolling her eyes at Ray's goings on. Slightly harder to picture, slightly grainy, but still there, clinging on till I reached her.

94

I'd bought her three dresses and a pricey pair of trainers. A maths book for school. All the stuff she'd had to turn to Carol to provide. Next I'd sort the extra bedroom. She was sick of Ray making a mess of their lives. Karen turning everything upside down and her mother constantly interfering. Surely everything was playing into my hands?

Little things bringing me closer to my daughter. Things I'd never had chance to do before. Soon I'd be able to hold a conversation with a stranger and they'd never know. My curves slowly returning, all the things that once made me attractive.

So it was hardly surprising while I kept my head down, picturing Jess, there were other things going off behind my back, just as Steve predicted. While I obsessed over the till and awkward customers, all the mundane stuff. Things I never expected would involve me.

13   Jess

Six Months Later

He'd been chewing it over for days. A misty-eyed look over his cornflakes. While sipping his tea in front of the six o'clock news. Finally ready to commit.

'I reckon a holiday. That way we can all enjoy it and there's no complaints. Disney World, Florida. Jess would love it. Been nagging me for years.' Trying to catch my eye. 'That right, nuisance?'

'Or maybe,' Karen chipped in, 'a new patio, some garden furniture and one of those patio heaters? And if there's any left, a chiminea? We can have massive barbecues in summer. Surely Jess would love that far more than a holiday?'

She mouthed something at Dad while my head was down. Dad mouthed something back. Only since they'd got married. When I looked up they both flashed beaming smiles.

'Alright, Jess?'

I nodded. 'Especially when you're whispering behind my back. Here's an idea. Why not save the money, then spend it on something later? You might need it for a sudden bill or if the boiler packs up.' One of Carol's favourite scenarios. Obviously I was the only one paying attention.

Karen refusing eye contact. Dad clapping his hands to

regain control. 'So how much is it exactly?' His pen poised over a scrap of paper, calculator to hand. 'Fire away.'

She checked online and gave him an exact figure. Just over a grand. After a few calculations, he wasn't sure it would be enough for ten days in Florida for the three of us. Even ten days in Skegness. Karen might have to rethink the chiminea.

'That's that then. Bloody great.' He slammed the pen to the floor. Tapping the calculator, trying different ways. Shaking his head, then starting again.

Karen gazing out the window, chewing her nails.

'Where's it all gone? If we started off with sixty, where have we spent over fifty-eight? Can't see it anywhere, can you?'

She gestured round, looking towards me for support, always assuming we should be on the same side. I buried my head in algebra, following Carol's advice.

'Conservatory, the wedding, Jess's lovely bedroom, new carpets…' Starting to lose steam, then picking up as she ran through each room in her head. 'Bathroom suite, fridge, clothes, set of ladders.'

'Don't start making out it's all been spent on me!' The calculator slipping to the floor. Growing increasingly red. 'Last thing we bought was your laptop.'

'Why shouldn't I have a laptop? You encouraged me. Look how much Jess uses it for school. Biggest thing we've bought is a conservatory. Can't say we've not all benefited from that, can you? And what about your fancy watch?'

'What about your mobile?'

'What about it?'

'If you'd kept within budget on the wedding. You said ten grand max, came out nearer twenty. Couple of bunches of flowers and a fruit cake!'

'Flowers and fruit cake? That how you sum it up? All that effort for nothing?' She jumped to her feet, drawing herself to full height. At least half a centimetre taller than Dad while he remained seated. 'This is what I get for trying to make our lives a bit easier? With my bloody money? And what's your contribution? Thinking up ways to spend it all?'

On the verge of tears. Dad not rushing towards her straight away. Too busy staring at his calculator, waiting for the right figure to pop up.

'Wish I'd never had it in the first place. Supposed to make us feel happy and secure, all it's done is prove what a total knobhead you are.'

I left them to it and escaped to the kitchen. Another pointer from Carol. Flinging open cupboards and drawers. Mouldy crumbs and an empty wrapper wedged in a corner of the breadbin. No milk either and nothing for pack-up tomorrow. Not so easy for Karen to nick stuff from work since they gave her a written warning.

I glanced round while their voices drifted through. Double glazing, laminate flooring sweeping through into the hallway, conservatory blinds, solar fountain on the patio. They'd forgotten it all. One of the blinds already snapped. The solar fountain always hit and miss.

Some of it supposedly for me. To keep me on side. To shut me up. I perched at the breakfast bar and closed my eyes, trying to block out their voices. Gripping the worktop, concentrating hard. All I could picture was the grubby black-and-white lino. Poky backyard, plastic toys littering the path, dirty sandpit two steps deep. Your voice cutting through. Was it still harsh? Had it softened slightly over the years? Hair still tumbling about your face, blood trickling from your mouth?

Craving detail. Had I started making it up? Doing it for a while, everybody letting me get on with it. Dad laughing uncomfortably when I claimed you had soft hands. Carol shaking her head and turning away. Even Karen joining in, doubting it could be true.

We used to bake fairy cakes together. You'd show me how

to gently fold the mixture to let in the air, as if it were something your mother showed you. Then you'd let me lick the bowl clean to keep me happy. We'd both smile as they came out the oven because we'd done something together for once.

I managed to dig two custard creams from the back of a cupboard, slightly soft but okay. I nibbled off the biscuit to reveal the sticky yellow centre. Becky Harris got five quid every day to buy lunch. Alicia Brown thirty quid a week, more if she asked.

Suddenly a commotion. Raised voices next door. Dad rifling through his wallet for receipts, Karen trying to remember where she'd put the one for the fridge.

'Hardly used 'em anyway.'

'Eh?'

'Ladders.'

'What do I need a laptop for? Told you, barely used it. Here's the receipt, take it back tomorrow, then start again.'

A brief pause. Hushed voices. Something to do with an Xbox game.

'Never played it, has she? Got the receipt?'

I pulled a creased fiver from my pocket, left over from Karen's last spurt of generosity. Enough to buy a sandwich in the morning at least. Perhaps two sandwiches, two days in a row. Becky sniggering behind my back. Alicia raising her eyebrows, struggling to understand.

*

'New shoes?'

'No thanks.'

'New coat?'

'Karen, I'm fine.'

'Must be something. Some trainers like Becky's?'

'Why would I want trainers like Becky's?'

A nervous burst of laughter. 'We don't want everyone laughing at you, do we? Honestly, Jess, when I was your age,' she pulled me close, lowering her voice, 'and before you start, don't keep on about money all the time, this is a fun day out. You sound just like my bloody mother at times.'

Girly days out with Karen were nothing like girly days out with you. You wouldn't try as hard. You wouldn't be seen dead trying as hard. Threading your arm through mine in the middle of Waterside, asking my advice on clothes and shoes, calling me 'hon' and 'sweetie' as if we'd secretly agreed it between ourselves.

Saturday morning, the whole day stretching ahead. Every weekend threatening the same. Reaching for my hand, a massive smile stretched across her face. A ready-made daughter all to herself. Still some money left but not much. Swearing under her breath every time she went near a cash machine.

'Let's do lunch,' she announced cheerfully, like it was perfectly normal. Nobody had ever asked before. Twenty minutes later squashed into a corner of Sam's Diner, another warning not to worry over prices. 'I can cover it, sweetie. This is so nice, just the two of us, don't you think? Over the last year I feel I've not only gained a husband but a daughter as well. Does that make sense?'

More like I'd gained a tiny sister. I was two centimetres taller already. It stopped us being able to swap clothes.

'Every girl, especially your age, needs a role model. I don't know how on earth you've coped to be honest. No wonder you're fretting over money all the time.'

I sipped on a Pepsi whilst patting my jacket for my purse. Ten quid in case we couldn't get home, or she couldn't afford to pay. Phone fully charged so I could ring Carol at least.

'I know Carol's been brilliant to you and your dad, but she only knows so much. You've got to remember she's no kids of her own. Not as if she's had any life experience. Dad's just too scared to tell her to bugger off.'

'She's been okay. We stayed with her after we ran away.'

'And all these neighbours he used to dump you on.' Lowering her voice. 'You know he'd have got into serious shit for some of those things? No idea who half of them were. What if they'd done stuff to you?'

Mrs Patterson? A flash of happy memory. Knitting needles clicking back and forth, Matt Monro on the player, cartwheels across a sun-drenched stripy lawn. Had I missed something?

'Anyway, it's all over now. When Dad's at work we can disappear for the day and have a giggle. And if I need to nip out for a bit or fancy a day to myself, Mum can always baby sit for a few hours; she'd love that. Get on okay, don't you?'

Burgers, fries, onion rings, coleslaw. The table quickly overflowing. Karen ordering extra garlic mushrooms and another portion of fries.

Yesterday I shared a bag of cheese and onion crisps with Alicia. The day before, half a jam sandwich and two chocolate digestives, my stomach rumbling through geography. Even Mrs Skelton thought it was a joke.

'Carol's not my real mum, only my auntie. Never thought of her as my mum.' Chewing steadily, trying to make it last. 'Just don't like to hurt her feelings.'

'Course not. I'm just saying it's not your fault she's been your only female role model. Not your fault she's a bit rough and ready.'

I took a deep breath. Time to let her know my intentions, as she couldn't seem to work them out herself. 'One day I'll find my mum again. Can't be that hard. There's a girl called Ruby in my class, lives with her dad at the moment, her mum's in Newcastle, but when she gets older she's going back there. When she's got a job and can afford it. So thanks for the offer but really I'm just biding my time. I know I've had loads of babysitters because Dad's had to work, and some have been really nice, but that's all they are. They're not my mum.'

We picked over the food. Karen because she had the appetite of a three-year-old. In my case it felt weird scoffing everything in one go.

'Jess?' A mouthful of coleslaw. 'Don't get your hopes up too much. It's really sad but there are people who can't be good parents for whatever reason, they just don't have it in them. I'm sure there's a good reason for it and maybe we'll never know.'

'She was drunk all the time, that's why. I don't need Dad telling me. Sometimes couldn't even pick me up. Kept dropping me downstairs. She was always heartbroken, couldn't stop fussing over me. Sometimes she'd fall asleep when I had to go to school; I had to wake her up. She'd leave the gas ring on and wander off. I had to keep an eye on her in case she hurt herself.' I paused, not too sure about the next bit. 'Some of the stuff Dad and Carol have told me doesn't make sense. She wasn't always that bad. I don't care if she was anyway, not anymore.'

She reached across and squeezed my hand, feeling sorry for me again. Something else though. A hint of panic, having to deal with it on her own, without Dad to back her up.

'You were far too young to remember. Only six, weren't you? Getting a bit muddled, that's all.'

I'd not told anyone the next bit. I'd kept it all to myself. No idea where it came from. 'One day she pulled me into the bathroom and locked the door. There was someone on the other side we were hiding from. She was drunk but still trying to look after me. I sat on her knee, and she hugged me really tight and started talking in a loud voice to distract me. Some kind of nursery rhyme, except she kept getting the words mixed up. Pretty rubbish like that. Really weird.'

'Jess?' Trying to distract me with onion rings. Waving them under my nose. 'Don't let it go cold.'

'So I don't need anyone telling me it didn't happen. It did. I wasn't the only one who was terrified. Mum was more terrified than me half the time. So explain that.'

'Well I can't, can I? My guess is that she's moved on after all this time. Just a shame you're tormented by all this crap.'

Something in her tone making me sit up. 'You know where she is?'

'Don't be silly. How on earth would I know?' Trying to laugh it off. When that didn't work, shovelling in fries. 'So what are you spending your money on? What about a lovely dress? Get you out of those jeans and show off your legs. Can't get away with being a tomboy forever.'

I finished my burger slowly. Of course she knew something. All those nods and winks behind my back. A lump suddenly forming in my throat, making it hard to swallow. Why did nobody care how much I missed you? Your skinny arms gripping me close, your nervous laughter ruffling the top of my head. They'd spent so long trying to find somebody else. Going shopping with somebody else. Arguing with somebody else. Somebody else providing answers to my questions. Why couldn't they realise somebody else was never enough?

'Can we take some food home with us? We could have some tomorrow and spread it out throughout the week.'

'You know how ridiculous that sounds?' She paused. I'd been asking far too many questions. She might pass me onto her mother next time. 'Why don't we finish up, go home and have a girly night in? Get on our onesies and watch a DVD. Yeah?' Which nobody else had ever said before either.

14   Lisa

He was almost impossible to spot at first, for someone like me.
Just one more customer rushing in before work for a paper and
a scratch card. Two or three days a week, halfway through my
shift. Perhaps one of our meal deals for lunch. Chicken wrap,
packet of crisps, choice of fizzy drink.

He spoke once or twice. Not everybody did. Usually to do
with the weather or to ask if we still sold matches. Gradually
forcing me to look up.

He was attractive. Not in an Alex kind of way, thank
God. Smoother and cleaner, more wholesome-looking, which
wasn't hard. Chestnut hair, spiky at the front, concealing the
fact it was beginning to recede. Slim hands and fingers as he
slid the paper across the counter, something sensual in the
movement. A deep voice but not unpleasant, enough to make
me fumble.

'Shit. Sorry.'

'No problem, it happens.'

Scanning his crisps twice by mistake, interfering with the
meal deal offer. Several seconds to put it right, which always felt
like half an hour with a queue out the door.

He smiled for no reason, which maybe he did all the time.
How could I tell? Some connection to Alex perhaps, dropping
by just to torture me. How could I kid myself that travelling a
mere fifty miles meant escape?

What if somebody walked in – anybody from my past – and recognised me instantly, blurting something out? My new life shattering in seconds. Sue's shocked response. Having to confess in the back. Not the person she thought I was. I didn't deserve a job, didn't deserve a chance, didn't deserve anything. Her slow withdrawal, her pretence of support but never looking at me the same again.

Just as things were turning round, my three-month trial coming to an end. I'd opened a current account for the first time since Morrisons. My real name, complete with national insurance number, staring back at me in black and white. They even knew my real address and phone number. It felt good telling the truth. Not just a novelty but as if I deserved extra brownie points for being brave. I'd got this far, what else was possible?

I sent Jess a text and found she'd been waiting three days, slightly annoyed but okay, so I had to explain it was to do with my shifts, the first opportunity I'd found. She came back straight away.

No problem, another time. I'm round Alicia's this weekend anyway. Speak soon. xxx

Alicia who? Picturing wherever it might be. I didn't need to know all the details every time.

I scribbled a short note to my sister, the first time I'd had anything decent to report since Jess was born. Imagining the look on her face. I'd waited years and would never see it. Initial disbelief followed by jealous annoyance. She'd settled outside Sydney with no intention of coming back. I told her about the job and left it at that. It didn't matter if she didn't reply or even if the letter got lost. Surprisingly easy to let go in the end.

*

'Why don't you go for a break? You've done over two hours.'
'In a minute, just want to get this sorted.' There were two

types of chocolate muffin at the end of the first aisle, not all reduced, yet somebody had mixed them up.

'Seriously, Lisa. I can cope for twenty minutes on my own without a childminder. Somehow managed before you arrived.'

'I know, I just need to...'

'Go! Just go! Doing my head in!'

I dropped the muffins and walked through the back, red-faced and trembling. Being efficient and making friends didn't go well together, Jenny forcing me to choose.

I expected to find the staffroom empty. To sit in peace and quiet for twenty minutes and stare out the window, chatting to Jess over Alicia. I wouldn't be able to see her this Saturday because I was working, but I'd bought her an Xbox game she'd mentioned in her last text, on the ball for once.

Today was different. A quick adjustment required, hard to make in a split second. Sue stood over the kettle, hand on hip, having a laugh with somebody sat in my usual chair. A man vaguely familiar. Chestnut hair, spiky at the front, slim fingers wrapped round one of the few decent mugs. Where had he sprung from? So busy organising cakes I hadn't spotted him slipping through the back.

Sue cracking open the best biscuits, chocolate-chip cookies, usually reserved for weekends. She glanced up and paused.

'Oh no, what's up now? Getting Jenny sorted?'

'Getting on her nerves more like.'

'Sounds about right. That girl needs somebody getting on her nerves.'

He was scrutinising me. Steady, confident gaze. He'd been in the shop several times, asking pointless questions that forced me to look up. I grabbed a mug off the side and popped in a teabag, scattering sugar across the worktop. Who the hell was he, confidently wandering into someone else's workplace? Intruding on my time with Jess.

'This is Jim. Jim, this is Lisa I've been telling you about.' Lowering her voice. 'The only one who's not a pain in the arse. Actually comes to work to work.'

'Bloody hell, must be a first round here.'

'I told her to tidy some shelves the other day and she did it.'

'Now you're having me on. Didn't tell you to do it instead?'

A peal of laughter from Sue. 'Guess what? She doesn't think I owe her a living, doesn't get pissed off or bring her troubles to work.'

'Wow. You've hit the jackpot there.'

I went even redder. Staring at me as if I were a freak. They'd been talking about me in detail, as if they had nothing better to do. No corners to hide in – he'd pinched mine – Sue casually propped in front of the door, so it wasn't easy to escape. How could she?

Perhaps she'd told him what I could be like. Different to everybody else she'd ever worked with, painfully weird. Inviting him in just to make fun. So damn good-looking. Surely he had something better to be doing.

His deep voice washing over me, gentle and soothing at the same time. Hard to concentrate on the words. Smart grey suit and electric-blue shirt. He had money and presumably a decent job. What the hell was he doing here? Sue's boyfriend? Sue's husband? I'd forgotten how people like that behaved and what was normal and what wasn't.

'Jim's my cousin. He's just popped in on his way home.' She turned towards me. 'Anyway, what's wrong with Jenny? Moaning about her shifts next week? I've told her, she can't always have her own way, selfish madam.'

'No, not that. Chocolate muffins.'

'Come again?'

'Not supposed to show any interest in stock. Not allowed to care if prices are wrong, customers nick stuff, coffee machine's knackered or the roof caves in. Just supposed to stand at the till reading a magazine, blanking customers. Then I'll finally fit in.'

They were both gawping at me. Sue with one hand on her hip, coffee cup in the other. Jim leaning back in my chair with his hands behind his head.

'Exactly like our place,' he said. 'Show any initiative and people hate you for it. You've got to ignore people like that.'

I sat down and sipped my tea, in the middle of the room. Nowhere else to go. Slowly taking a biscuit. They were cousins, that's why they seemed comfortable with each other.

'What do you do?' I asked.

'Sales rep for a plastics company.' Pulling a sour face. 'I know, sometimes I could die of excitement.'

Out the corner of my eye Sue pulled out a folder from a shelf and settled down at the far end of the room. Any minute he was going to make an excuse and scarper.

'So what did you do before you came here?'

I opened my mouth and lied far more convincingly than I ever could have imagined. Volunteering in a bookshop whilst struggling to find work. He nodded in sympathy. No shame in that, everyone in the same boat.

Immaculate white teeth and unblemished skin, although perhaps he was no younger than me, just an easier life. What was he doing here? Humouring himself on his way home.

I touched my fringe which was sticking up at the front as usual. Why hadn't I glanced in the fridge door before barging in?

'What kind of bookshop?'

'Er… Christian mostly. Educational.'

'Oh right. Specialist stuff then.'

He flashed a warm smile. Impossible to tell if he was the same with everyone. In the far distance, a screech from Jenny. Something clattering to the floor. Nothing to worry about, just her usual way of attracting attention. Sue shaking her head.

'There she goes, stubbing her toe on a fruit flapjack.'

We carried on drinking in comfortable silence. Smiling occasionally as Jenny's voice drifted through. For the first time in years it felt good to be different.

15   Jess

Karen's mum's bungalow was nothing like your place; fag ends floating round the sink, blood-splattered walls and broken glass carpets. Or like ours, bursting cupboards at the start of the week, panic and despair by the end.

Dark ancient furniture passed through the family, so well-scrubbed it could pass for new. Green-and-pink carpets, flowery curtains, wallpaper so old Dad would mutter it had come back into fashion five times since. Silent faded world even while I was part of it. Hunched over homework, fascinated by elementary algebra, the difference between metaphor and simile. Any white van whooshing past the window, hopefully Dad come to rescue me like he'd promised. The distant laughter of a child in somebody's yard.

No place to go hungry. No place to fling open cupboards and wonder where all the food had gone. At the same time, no place to pig out. Just enough of everything, always at the right time, in the right place. Karen's mum forever writing long lists and sticking to them. Dad couldn't have found anybody more sensible to wipe you from my mind.

The kitchen boasted mustard-coloured units and a green-tiled floor. Clean and shiny enough for me to slide across in my socks, smacking into the cooker at the end if she wasn't looking. Dad said he'd have it ripped out in half an hour, shove in a breakfast bar, bi-fold doors onto the patio and a utility/wet room in the corner.

'What's the point in changing it if it's not broken?' she'd snap.

'Doesn't have to be broken to change it.'

'So why change it at all?'

He shrugged. 'To get something new? Something up to date? What people do.'

'That's what people like you do. Never satisfied with what you've got. We bought that kitchen in the summer of '75, just after we married. Karen's dad put it in himself to save money and it's still like new. Can you imagine how much it's saved us over the years?'

They stared at each other in stubborn silence, wondering how they'd come to be in the same family. How did we all come to be? Who made all these decisions?

'I'm genuinely sorry, sweetheart,' he'd say, sighing, whenever he dropped me off.

'I'm old enough to look after myself now. Don't have to keep doing it to me. Please, Dad.'

'Pains me to leave you with her, the old bat.'

On the verge of tears. Anger spreading through my entire body. Twenty quid in my bottom drawer, enough to look after myself for a few days, no need to involve anyone else.

'Just ignore her. She's only getting at me. Do your work, can't you? Books and what have you. Makes no difference where you do it.'

'You mean homework? What people my age do.'

'I know, I'm not bloody daft!'

'So why aren't you interested?'

'Course I'm interested!'

'Then what am I doing in history at the moment?'

'Oh come off it.'

'The name of my favourite teacher?'

'I didn't know you had one.'

'Sometimes wish…'

'What?'

I left it hanging in the air. Hanging for months. Not six anymore. Plonking me in front of a stranger's telly, hoping it was enough. Trying to convince me that stranger was part of my life when he'd only bumped into her five minutes before. Trying to tell me they had more right to be there than you.

'I'm sick of spending half my time with strangers. Shoving me onto all these people, making out it's normal. Alicia lives with her dad but still sees her mum at weekends. Doesn't have to spend half her time with other people.'

'Strangers? Talking about Karen's mum, for Christ's sake. Part of the family, silly old bag that she is. You know I've got to work. You've always been used to staying with other people. Absolutely loved Mrs Patterson, couldn't wish for a better grandma.'

'So you got lucky from time to time. She lived at the end of the road. You once fixed her guttering.'

'What else could I do? Karen's mum might be a pain but at least she's sensible, least you're safe with her.'

He wanted me to figure out his paperwork but with everything else he'd rather I was a fool. We weren't related to Mrs Patterson. He hardly knew Mr and Mrs Williamson. The first time I ever clapped eyes on Carol was the day we ran away. I'd never been to her house before in my life. No wonder I was scared to death.

'Jess!'

I slammed the door as I jumped out the van. He didn't understand and never would. It didn't matter who he left me with, however sensible, however stupid, they still weren't you.

*

'I always brought Karen up to sit at the table. I don't believe in slumping in front of the telly for meals. Can't be good for the digestion, I don't care what anyone says. I expect your dad's never told you that.'

He hadn't told me loads of things. Karen's mum made cottage pie, steak and kidney pud, steamed veg, fish without batter I'd never tried before, beef stew, ham salads. All from scratch. The plate wiped clean or endless questions. The odd bit of joy, like a sponge pudding with a splodge of jam in the middle, soaked in custard, not too much in case I got carried away. No cream doughnuts or huge bowls of ice cream, the kind Dad would grab from the garage on his way home. No crisps or sweets, Pepsi or Coke.

She was missing the point anyway. I'd got used to sitting at the table to eat. Used to sitting on the floor. Used to just about anything. Mrs Patterson always dined off a padded tray on her knee, decorated with Siamese cats. Mr and Mrs Williamson said grace before we were allowed to touch a crumb. Mumbling the words till I got them by heart. Carol standing over me, fag dangling from her mouth, questioning me on what I'd eaten throughout the week and where it came from. Auntie Maggie, on both occasions I'd eaten in her poky flat, chattered nervously to hide the fact she wasn't eating herself, just as long as I was okay.

Kindly Mr Shaw from the newsagent's, dark eyebrows merging into one, allowed me to pick a Fruit Shoot out the fridge and a lolly from the freezer. The chatty Chinese couple, whose bathroom had fallen through into their front room, encouraged me to squash in next to their own daughter so I could share noodles while Dad rushed to the builders' merchants before it shut. Simon and Debbie above Perfect Pizza offered me a bed for the night while Dad moaned about juggling work and childcare.

'Don't worry, I'm used to it,' I mumbled, picking over my jam roly-poly. 'This is the norm, with Dad's job and everything. He's always left me with other people.'

'Now why doesn't that surprise me?'

The worst thing was not knowing what to call Karen's mum. Mumbling awkwardly under my breath if I pushed past. I dreaded the day the house caught fire, or somebody came to the door while she was hanging out the washing.

No more cartwheels across the lawn. No more applause for silly things anyone could do. Far too many prized ornaments. No music in the background, even stuff I didn't like. No music at all. If I dropped a glass or plate she could always tell, even from another room.

'I still can't believe it sometimes,' she'd mumble whilst sewing in front of Coronation Street.

I nodded, still fuming. Dad already half an hour late, pushing it every time. What if he didn't turn up one day? If he decided I wasn't part of his new life? What if I suddenly ended up connected to somebody completely different, without any warning?

'Even the wedding didn't feel real. Until now.' She glanced towards a dark corner of the room. Karen's corner, except Karen wasn't there anymore, only her clutter. Magazines piled on a bookcase, a line of multicoloured nail polish, pink furry slippers awaiting her return, out of place among the dark furniture.

I picked out a nail polish and held it to the light. Deep purple mingling with silver stars. Reminded me of you. Karen's mum shot me a look, so I put it down.

Then it occurred to me she was just like Mrs Patterson, struggling to let Clive go. Holding onto his stuff in the hope he might return. And it made me feel sorry for her for a sec, which I didn't like.

'She'll know exactly what's missing if you pinch one.'

'I wasn't. I don't pinch things.'

She shot me another look over the top of her round glasses. I was missing the point.

I didn't want to understand her. Not my fault something was missing from her life. After a long pause she started firing questions. What did I think of the matter? Hadn't I got used to being on my own with Dad? Didn't it feel strange having to share him with someone else? How would I adjust?

'What choice have I got? Nobody asked me, did they? We're both in the same boat.'

'I suppose it's been a way of life for you, passed from pillar to post. Since you left your mother, at least. I suppose...' A long pause, catching herself just in time. About to say something she shouldn't.

'Dad says we're all one big family now. Got to muck in together whether we like it or not. Says we'll have to get used to it because there's no alternative.'

I knew it would annoy her. The idea of being stuck together. Going nowhere. For some reason, even more than it annoyed me.

*

Rain bouncing off the pavements, flowing steadily down the middle of the street. Headlights obscured by mist and spray. Dark stormy November night. Returning home from Carol's, sent there all day to escape. Something different this time. Letting me play games on her laptop without a word. Rubbing the back of my neck as she wandered past.

I creaked open the front door, on the lookout for change. It was waiting for me. Something sweet and unfamiliar hanging in the air. Plastic bags littering the hallway, colourful wrapped presents on the table, unopened boxes on the floor. Clambering over to reach the stairs.

I climbed quietly, gripping the banister. A new life waiting at the top, threatening for weeks. Be quiet, they'd told me. Careful and calm. Dad no longer laughing in front of the telly. Karen shouting at him for something he'd forgot.

The tiny third bedroom at the back. Dad's old eBay dumping ground. He'd had his moan but caved in towards the end. Painted a fresh B&Q tropical lemon, Karen and her mum discussing the shade for months. Baby giraffes, baby elephants, baby zebras, baby everything running round the walls. You'd never have done that for me. Picked out bedding and a matching lampshade, agonising over the right scheme.

I crept towards the cot beneath the window. Inside, the squirming bundle I'd been told to expect by people who couldn't contain themselves. Strangers in the street. Nosy neighbours. Mrs Walters at school. Tiny, bunched hands waving silently for attention. Squashed vulnerable pink face. I held my breath, my arms hanging limply by my sides.

I reached out slowly and grazed her cheek, suddenly yanking back. I'd get used to her, people said. Help look after her and enjoy it eventually. Familiar, yet unfamiliar. Part of the family I knew, part of something else.

I glanced towards the window, a sudden urge to throw it open and do something drastic. Not hurt her, just get her out the house before she did any harm, before it was too late.

Impossible to turn back. More than anything that had happened since. The future wrapped in a fleecy pink blanket. New names for us all.

A sharp creak on the stairs, excited footsteps, hushed tones. Everybody rushing up, the whole lot. Karen's mum determined to get there first. Finally she had a name that would put a smile on her face and bring much needed noise into her silent world. Grandma.

16 Lisa

'Er, really hard this one, let me think, really tricky. Could it be that he fancies you?'

'For Christ's sake, keep it down!'

'If you weren't so obsessed with organising pot noodles you'd have noticed weeks ago. You know when he asked if you'd been to see the new Bond film? What he really meant was, "do you want to go see the new Bond film?".' Jenny at the top of her voice, starting before he was even out the door.

'Just making conversation, he can't just stand there.'

'And when he asked if you liked dogs and said he'd got a German shepherd, what he really meant was, "would you like to see the German Shepherd?". At his house, just the two of you. Alone. Probably hasn't even got a German shepherd.'

'Not everybody thinks like you.'

'Oh for Christ's sake, where the hell have you been hiding?'

He smiled for no reason, when there was no one else about. He asked questions that didn't need answering, just for something to say. He found an excuse to be in the staffroom while I was on break and lingered in the shop while I was on the till.

He travelled the country selling plastic mouldings (whatever they were), briefcase to hand. The sharp business suit and the sparkling Audi. What could we possibly have in common?

'He only comes in to see Sue. They're cousins.'

'Yeah right. Would you come in to see Sue? Never bothered before. Accept it, he fancies you, and you're blind. If I were you I'd put him straight before it goes too far. Just being cruel, dragging it out.'

'He comes in to buy his lunch and the odd magazine. Only when he's passing. He's got a customer up the road, so it makes sense.' It made no sense. Even weirder than Jenny realised. People like him didn't spend half their time hanging round somebody else's workplace for people like me. I couldn't get to know him properly because I'd have to speak to him and exchange information, impossible without wiping the slate clean.

I still cut my own hair, except when I allowed Carol to have a go. I bought most of my clothes from Age UK or Cancer Research, as long as it was shapeless, even though I wasn't overweight and had nothing to hide. Hospital ingrained in my face. Deep lines either side of my nose, jittery body language that made people stare. How would Louise react if she could see?

When Alex fancied me years ago it was obvious. I could recognise it and join in. I could tell when it was coming and where it was coming from. The smiles and the flattery, the initial compliments. Had I stopped looking over the years, thinking it would never come my way again? Being a mother driving such thoughts from my mind. Except I wasn't really a mother, hadn't been for years, however many snatched conversations, however many pretty summer dresses, however many books and games I scraped to buy on the side. Not really anything anymore.

*

I'd wiped down every single unit. The special-offer shelves fast becoming my pet project. Jenny forever nudging older stuff to the back. Even customers not that awkward.

'Always absorbed in something, every time I come in here.'

I spun round. He had a way of creeping up on me. Did he remind me of Alex? Give me a great excuse to tell him to back off.

'Sorry.'

'Don't apologise. Sue in?'

I shook my head, feeling rising panic. She'd nipped to the bank. Jenny in the back on an extended break.

'Mind if I get a coffee? Had a totally shite day thanks to an awkward customer.'

'Help yourself.' I wasn't used to being in charge.

'Want one?' he threw over his shoulder.

'Er...'

'Not a trick question.'

'Tea. Two sugars. Thanks.'

Would he expect to sit with me? God knows how I'd keep him happy. I'd done nothing all morning except serve customers and wipe shelves. A minor problem with one of the pumps.

Five minutes later he came back with two steaming mugs, plonking one in front of me on the counter. Tumbleweed blowing across the forecourt. I leant against the lotto machine, trying not to stare. Electric-blue shirt again, fourth time at least, contrasting against his slight tan.

'Good day?'

'Yes, thanks. Bit quiet.' Painfully polite. Enough to put him off, if only I could stop gawping.

He wandered up and down both aisles, pausing to stare at car magazines on the bottom shelf, one hand in his pocket, sipping coffee. Jenny was right. Definitely after me for some weird reason, probably because I couldn't stand up for myself. What if he followed me after work? If he got funny because I brushed him off? The fact he was Sue's cousin. How did that complicate things? I couldn't afford to lose my job over some silly misunderstanding.

I opened my mouth, ready to burst out with it. Back off. Sick and tired of control freaks thinking I was easy game. Finally getting my life back on track – nothing he'd understand and none of his business anyway – Jess my only concern.

'Have I ever told you about my dog, Sky?'

'Sorry?'

'I did steak for tea yesterday, turned my back for literally ten seconds and she'd wolfed it down in complete silence. Last year my sister made me a chocolate birthday cake, scoffed that as well, honestly thought she was going to keel over. Looked so sorry for herself, I couldn't bring myself to tell her off.'

I must've smiled because he went on to tell me what else she'd done. I found myself imagining his house, his furniture, what he wore at home, what street he lived on, if his neighbours were okay.

He reached for his phone like a teenager, showing me picture after picture. Large sorrowful brown eyes staring at the camera. A row of oak kitchen units in the background with a spacious dining table beyond.

'She's gorgeous.' Nothing else to add. Not used to discussing dogs, everyday things, for the sake of it.

'You okay? Look a bit pale. Sue not overworking you? She's not used to anyone working, that's the problem.'

'Jim?' The first time I'd used his name. Washing inside my mouth. 'Look, I'm really flattered by your attention.' Blushing like mad, no turning back. I gripped the counter for support. 'Jenny's been winding me up actually, she reckons... it's just, I'm not looking for anyone at the moment and I'm not really your type anyway. Been through a bad patch these last few years and this is my chance to get back on my feet.'

He looked surprised at first, quickly followed by amusement. Just having a laugh while he was passing. The same with everyone. The dog pictures, the story about the cake. Jenny setting me up to look a fool.

'Sorry.' I sipped my tea. Alex was always furious when I apologised too much, any reason to beat the shit out of me.

'Shame. I only popped in to ask you to marry me.'

I smiled shakily.

'Might as well get to the point. Cut out all the crap in between.'

When did Alex last do that? Rolling on the bed laughing before Jess came along. Wasting whole evenings. One of those pointless activities that achieved nothing yet meant everything.

'I take it that's a no then? Oh well. How about a meal instead? What about a film, then a meal, or is that pushing it? Can I drag you away from the pick-and-mix for a whole evening?'

I wouldn't stand a chance if he was really determined. Impossible to allow him close.

'Don't overthink it, you'll only make it worse. That's your problem, isn't it?'

I'd not eaten in front of someone for years, more than a cuppa and a digestive, even Jess. Would he pick over my appearance, even if it was just a joke? The space closing between us. Chance for him to see all in microscopic detail.

'I worry over everything. That's what I'm like I'm afraid, I'd drive you up the wall.'

He set his mug on the counter. A customer marching across the forecourt, searching his pocket for change. Our little world over in a matter of seconds. Before they entered he gave me his full attention, determined but kind.

'One evening. That's all I'm asking. If it's a total disaster, we'll never mention it again and I'll clear off for good. Okay?'

*

Of course I fretted over it all. What to wear, what to eat and drink, what it would mean if I allowed him to pay. How I'd manage the rest of the month if he didn't.

He picked the place himself. He knew these things because of his job. *The White Horse*, just round the corner from my flat. I wouldn't tell him in case I needed to make a quick escape. A reserved table at the back, overlooking a courtyard. Nobody anywhere near, the place half empty.

'So where you from originally?' he asked.

The nitty-gritty. Giving me his whole attention, unhindered by Sue, car magazines or customers nipping in and out. Piercing blue eyes. He could tell my accent wasn't local. I threw him a few crumbs, not too much just in case.

'So you've no family round here? Shame. Must be pretty tough.'

'I've got an older sister in Australia. She's been out there a while, looks like she's staying.' So grateful to tell him. I could share a million things about Louise.

We both ordered French onion soup for starters. Over six quid apiece. God knows how I'd manage the rest. While he had a mouthful I took the opportunity to fire questions about his family and his job.

'Just my parents and younger sister. She's at uni studying some crap. Media studies? Quite a big age gap so we've never been that close. There's Sue obviously and a couple of other cousins I've always been close to. So how you finding her? Seem really grateful for the work. Things been that tough?'

Chicken breast covered in some kind of creamy sauce. A bottle of red between us, my glass miraculously refilling itself. Too terrified to explain I didn't touch the stuff. Life a shitty mess. What if I burst into tears and blurted it all out? Misjudged how much he could take?

'I should never have come. I don't even know why you asked. What a joke!' Wedged between laughter and tears. At least I didn't have far to run, while he was in the gents' or at the bar. 'Jenny's been taking the mickey all week; she thinks it's hilarious.'

'That idiot you work with?'

'That idiot.'

'Who cares? You want to know why I asked? Because you're honest. Clearly. I know you're hiding something, I'm not bloody stupid, but at least you're honest about it. You're a crap actress and I like that. Wouldn't be interested if you were a good liar.'

'Cheers! My main attraction.' How much had I drunk?

'Long as you've not killed anyone.'

'Sorry?'

'You've just had a shitty time, probably at your own hands, like everyone. Any idea how long I was out of work before I got this job? I thought I'd be living at home forever.'

'So I look haggard?' I didn't want him to think that anymore. I wanted him to see something wonderful in me. My ghostly reflection in the dark glass over his shoulder.

'You need to learn to take a compliment. Don't let a nobody like Jenny pull you down. Half the time it's insecurity or jealousy that sets them off.'

I decided to do a deal. Tell him the lesser evil and perhaps he'd overlook the rest. Put him off the scent, so we could move onto the next stage. What next stage?

'I've had a drink problem for years, ever since I can recall. Twelve, thirteen. Skiving off school, nicking from Tesco. I can't remember my childhood. Louise was the perfect one, she cornered the market and made it impossible for me to be myself. That's my excuse, anyway. For the last year I've been going to this self-help group. Not just drink but confidence and self-esteem. It's all linked.'

He grabbed the bottle and pulled a face. 'You mean I didn't have to share?'

Ironic that I had to have a drink for it to come out. He'd put all my behaviour down to that. Every look, every twitch, every comment. Not that the relationship was going anywhere. What relationship?

'Nothing to be embarrassed about; nobody's going to judge you for it. Nobody that matters anyway.' He grabbed my hand, looking even happier than before. I'd become interesting all of a sudden. 'I thought you were going to say something really terrible for a sec. Half the people I work with have a drink problem. Not that I'm saying it's not serious, just nothing to be ashamed of, especially if you're dealing with it.'

I wondered what might shock him, what he'd consider a step too far. Drip feeding information. One small step at a time. This was my chance to finally make Jess proud of me. This was my chance to be something other than an ex-alcoholic. By the end of it she might actually want me as a mother.

'I'm dealing with it. Just have to be patient I'm afraid.'

A slow smile. 'Anything else?'

I reached out for his hand. A long pause. 'Not for now.'

Part Two

17   Jess

Eight Years Later

Late September. Stuck at the back of an endless queue in Walkers Newsagent's after school, feeling the weight of lose change in my pocket dragging me down on one side. Three pound coins, two quid in twenties, the rest in tens, fives, twos and pennies, scraped together over the last twenty-four hours, a contribution from all four corners of the house. From Karen's copper jar to the darkest depths of Dad's pockets. From the back of every drawer and cupboard to Ellie's piggy bank as a last resort, after much screaming and shouting on her behalf.

'Not spending my bloody money on stupid electric again! How many more times?' she screamed, aiming a last-minute kick at somebody's shins. Dad wearing his most determined expression, the one he always saved for those tricky occasions where he had to prise money from an eight-year-old.

'Now calm down, young lady. Stop being so selfish, it's for everybody's benefit. Use electric like everyone else, don't you?' Slamming her bedroom door and leaning against it with a heavy sigh, as if he'd managed to contain a wild animal. 'Promise it's the last time.'

'Sod off, you liar!'

And I could only hope they'd counted it right for once, that

I wouldn't reach the front and find myself twenty-three pence short like last time.

'Look sharp,' he'd told me before I left. 'On the emergency reserve so it'll not last till tomorrow.' Like it was my fault for not keeping an eye on it. Slumped on the settee, head in his hands, broken and beaten. 'Bloody crap, aren't we? No bread, no milk, can't even have a sodding cuppa. Where's it all gone?'

I glanced at the cushions he'd thrown on the floor, the TV remote he'd slammed against the coffee table. Ellie sulking in her room above, Karen sulking in hers, the house unusually silent for once, as if we couldn't even afford to make a noise till payday.

'Last time ever. Are you listening? I won't always be here to sort your shitty mess. Gotta start doing it yourself.' And I rushed out the house as fast as I could, all the way to Walkers before closing time at half-six.

When I reached the front of the queue I handed over the electric card and the embarrassingly large amount of change, trying not to glance at the assistant – Susie Smith's stroppy older sister – who'd served me so many times I kept expecting her to refuse.

'How much you giving me here?' she snapped.

'Should be ten quid exactly.' Glancing out the window, trying not to care. I could cope without electric in my life.

'Should be? Haven't you got anything bigger? Like two fives? Or a tenner? No?'

Pretty obvious I hadn't. Pretty obvious I was starving, Ellie skipping breakfast again, nothing in for tea, both desperate for new shoes for winter and not sure I could take much more without following Ellie's example and smashing my head into the nearest door.

'Sorry.' A polite smile plastered across my face, everybody gawping at my back, clearly recognising a freak.

'Not supposed to accept this much change.' Counting slowly, deliberately going wrong just to make her point.

My stomach rumbling painfully throughout, eyeing the Maltesers and Wine Gums inches from my hand, even the stuff I didn't normally like. What if I nicked a couple of bags? Was that the answer? The only answer these days. Making fists in my pockets, staring at the floor. My mobile going off, a text coming through. Dad, short and sharp.

What's taking so long? Nearly run out, getting desperate, hurry up! Any chance u can pick up some food while you're at it? Love lots.

I switched it off and rammed it deep in my pocket. He knew he'd only given me ten quid. Where the hell did he think I was going to get money for food?

Eventually, Susie Smith's sister agreed it was ten quid exactly, credited the card and handed it back without a word, clearly pissed off, as if I'd no right to be buying electricity with coppers. Made it inferior somehow, wouldn't work the same as if I'd used notes.

I burst out the shop in relief, forgetting my stomach for a sec. Five seconds later I spotted Chloe and her younger sister Lauren crossing the road in front of me. Chloe knew all about you. The only person at school who did, except teachers, of course, who had a right to know in case something kicked off. Nutter of a mother who might turn up any sec. Chloe forever bitching about her dad and his endless succession of girlfriends. If I told her about you she didn't raise an eyebrow. That was the deal. She had a crap father and I had you.

'Chloe! Where you going?'

She spun round. 'Hi. Just to my dad's for the night. His girlfriend's gonna be there though. Thought he'd have dumped her by now, don't know what he's messing about at. Two months already, crazy bitch.'

I'd already switched off. She was scoffing a large tray of chips drenched in salt and vinegar, waving them under my nose, casually slotting them into her mouth between words.

Salivating like mad, I couldn't help it. Do anything for a chip. Even the scrapings at the bottom of the tray, swimming in vinegar, dusted in salt. Even the crumbs dropping unnoticed to the ground. One single sodding chip.

'These taste like shit.' She tossed them into a bin, half falling to the ground in a greasy pile. 'Not hungry anyway. Get a burger later. You coming?'

'You're okay, I've got to get home.' I swallowed hard and glanced away. Chloe was a genius at school, could spot an iambic pentameter at fifty paces, yet totally useless at understanding the stuff that really mattered, like when her best friend was starving and too proud to admit it. I sat next to her hour after hour, month after month, year after year. Just her pale skinny friend with the frizzy hair, a bit quiet occasionally, slightly picky over food.

I tried to concentrate on what she was saying. Her dad was a tosser and she'd had enough. Chloe's parents never really together. Before she turned two her mum had moved onto someone else, and her dad had filed for divorce and moved into his own flat. Chloe lived somewhere in between, mostly with her dad and his latest girlfriend.

'You're so lucky. Least your mum can't be found, Jess. Wish my dad would piss off to the same place.'

We had a brief chat, then parted at the end of the road, the two of them arguing loudly over whether to go for pizza or a burger, voices floating down the street. My mouth watering. At first I started walking home but then quickly changed my mind. My last meal a small ham sandwich at school, using the last two slices of bread, over six hours ago. No idea what they gave Ellie or what they ate themselves. I managed to scrounge a few salt and vinegar crisps from Hannah at break, followed by a bruised apple from Lucy at dinner, which she was about to throw away. Later on, a tampon from Katie, making out I'd run out. She could always tell.

I delved into my pocket and pulled out a shiny two-pound coin. Usually stashed in my bottom drawer inside a rolled-up sock. Sometimes as little as a quid, sometimes as much as twenty if I was lucky. I hid it from Karen and Dad when they questioned me over the electric. Not that difficult. Last thing they suspected was initiative.

I crossed the road and headed quickly for Tesco. I'd look for the cheapest stuff possible. A small loaf of bread, tin of beans, pint of milk. Enough to ensure Ellie had something before she went to bed. Perhaps Dad and Karen as well. Enough for all four of us until tomorrow when Dad hopefully got paid. Karen's payday still six days away, equivalent to half a lifetime in our house.

At the supermarket I optimistically picked up a basket. Wandering aimlessly, distracted by other people's baskets and trolleys, always more exciting than mine. Imagining going home with them, living their comfortable lives, scoffing their food, ignoring starving people like me because I could afford to, not even aware they existed. Oblivion.

I managed to find a dirt-cheap brand of beans hiding on a bottom shelf. From the reduced shelf at the end of one of the aisles, Karen's favourite haunt this time of month, I picked out a small squashed brown loaf. Picked it up like someone who'd got plenty of choice, who actually preferred squashed bread to the fresh variety, a far superior taste. Then I remembered Dad's comment about wanting a cuppa. I'd have to get some milk. How? Sneak it through the self-scan tills and make out I didn't understand if they caught me? Edging closer every day, on a slippery slope, shoplifters always starting out like me. Resisting for a while, swearing they'd never do it, only caving in because they had no choice. Perfectly okay with a good excuse.

Panic over. At the front of one of the fridges a half-price pint of semi-skimmed on its sell-by date. I added it all up twice to make sure, felt confident it came to no more than £1.90 and headed for the tills. Sidetracked a couple of times, imagining what it might be like to buy a new pair of jeans or a magazine. A small bar of chocolate, packet of mints. Teasing myself by picking them up in turn.

I glanced round for you when I reached the end of an aisle. Totally insane, as if you were likely to be stalking me in Tesco or anywhere these days, when you couldn't even remember my birthday. The 12th of September, in case you were interested.

I wandered past the end of one of the clothing aisles, lightly grazing the jumpers and jeans, suddenly interrupted by a familiar voice at the counter, questioning the assistant. I froze. Dad. His back towards me, still in his work clothes and dusty boots, holding up a white blouse in his callused hands. Laughing and joking with the assistant, one elbow propped on the counter like he'd been there all day. Only thirty minutes since I left him on the sofa, head in his hands, too ashamed to look me in the eye.

'No idea what size she is these days to be honest. Best not to ask. What's the standard?'

'No standard as such. This is a twelve.'

'Go on then, I'll take it, can always bring it back if it's wrong.'

'We do full refunds within twenty-eight days if you keep the receipt. Would you like the hanger?'

I watched him hand over the money – two crisp tenners – while the assistant folded the blouse and popped it in a bag. She handed him a penny change, which he told her to keep, closing his wallet with a big grin and spinning round, the happiest I'd seen him in weeks. Since last payday, in fact.

'Sweetheart! What you doing here?'

Dad hadn't got a twin brother living a parallel life. Hadn't got a brother at all. This was Dad, the same person on the sofa earlier. For some stupid reason I hid the basket behind me, ashamed of its contents.

'Just bought Karen a little pressie to apologise.' Squeezing my arm. 'Don't worry, got something for you and Ellie as well.'

'Please tell me you're having a laugh.'

He removed a black box from his pocket. A delicate silver heart pendant nestling in his hand. 'Like it?'

'Great. She's got six exactly the same.'

'I've got you that Xbox game you wanted. Thirty quid, right rip off.' He sensed my hesitation and took it the wrong way. 'Can't leave you out, can I?'

'I thought you were skint. Where's all this suddenly come from? Why can't we be normal for once? Dad!' Trying to keep my voice down even though it was impossible. Posh people with full trolleys, normal people gawping as they wandered past, looking down their noses. I felt like launching into him, crashing him into the large display of Pepsi Max just like Carol if she were here, grabbing a two-litre bottle and smashing it repeatedly over his skull.

He grabbed my hand and dragged me down the aisle. 'You know Dave? Harris? Little dark fella with the squint? Popped round after you left, owed me two hundred for doing his patio last month. Told you to remind me. He's alright, Dave, keeps his word eventually.' He noticed my basket and suddenly stopped, pulling it out from behind me. 'What's this? Thought you were fed up of beans?' Holding up the loaf, pulling a face. 'Squashed bread? Not starving, are we? I'm going for a Chinese in a minute. Karen wants chicken curry; Ellie wants special fried rice. What about you? Beef in black bean?' He dumped the basket on an empty shelf and continued towards the exit, pushing me in front, unwilling to let me out of his sight. I might act like an adult and really show him up.

On the way home he gripped my hand tight, like he used to before Karen and Ellie came along, smiling broadly, anticipating the joy he was about to unleash the second he opened the door. My stomach rumbling like mad, smelling the chicken curry and black bean sweating in a plastic bag in his other hand.

'We can't carry on like this. We can't.'

'Eh?'

'Where's it going to lead? Why don't we learn anything? It's like we're going round in circles all the time.'

'Don't be silly. No harm, is there? This is normal. Perfectly normal. Come on, don't spoil it.'

The worst bit was not knowing what we were. Rich or poor, lucky or unlucky, feast or famine. How could I do something about it when I didn't even know what I was supposed to be doing?

When we got home both Karen and Ellie were downstairs, as if they'd forgotten the reason they stormed up in the first place. Arguing about Ellie wanting her friend over at the weekend, the one who trashed her room last time she stayed.

'I'm having all the rice!' Ellie shouted, pulling the tray towards her. 'And where's my pocket money? I want it back with interest, you're not getting away with it this time.' Jabbing Dad in the ribs.

'You don't need all the rice,' Karen interrupted, grabbing the tray. 'Plenty for everyone. You eating, Jess?'

I nearly snapped her head off. Almost two days since I'd had a proper meal. Wasn't anyone paying attention?

In the end I scoffed more than anyone, finishing off the black bean and nicking some of Karen's curry. I might be pissed off but could still play along if I had to. Feeling just as full as I felt starving earlier. No in between.

After we'd finished we all sat back in rare silence. Dad reached into his wallet and gave Ellie her pocket money, with interest on top. She grabbed hold and did the sensible thing, running upstairs before he could change his mind, locking the door with a resounding click. He handed me a fiver and told me to treat myself, winking as he let go. I folded it into my back pocket with a scowl.

'You want to spoil yourself for once.' Turning up the volume on the telly, settling back with a contented sigh, his huge feet blocking the view.

I opened my mouth, ready to snap back, stopping just in time. He thought he'd done enough to distract me. Confused me enough to keep me quiet. Didn't matter. He was running out of answers to awkward questions. Running out of places to hide.

Jigging me on his shoulder that day we ran away. What the hell were we escaping? My worst nightmare or his? Just because he couldn't face you. Just because he couldn't turn back.

Always telling me what to be afraid of, trying to convince me I was better off without you. The best yet to come. After all this time, how could he possibly know?

Forget sadness, forget the tears (they dried up long ago), I simply wanted to know why you left me with two idiots, ducking all responsibility, telling yourself this ending was the right one. Never thinking of me again, leaving me to work out everything for myself. Or even worse, perhaps you didn't give a damn if I didn't work out anything at all.

18   Lisa

It was important enough to have a name. *The Brambles.*
Seventeenth-century local stone, Grade II listed. A utility room
bigger than my old kitchen. Two cavernous sitting rooms but
no lounge. Outhouses stretching down the two-acre grounds
towards an ancient apple orchard, herb garden and crystal-clear
stream. Five bedrooms, including four doubles, overlooking
either the village at the front or grounds at the back. All the years
I'd tortured myself over the one-bedroom, stingy space and lack
of options, forever holding me back.

'Think of yourselves as custodians for future generations,'
the solicitor had urged before we signed. 'Historically important
for the village, not merely your home.'

'Sod him,' Jim had snapped behind his back. 'Our house,
not his, we'll do what the hell we like.'

'You saw the state of my flat. I can't even hang wallpaper the
right way and you're expecting me to handle a grade-two listed
building?'

'Er, yes.' Checking his phone, clicking his briefcase and
shovelling breakfast down his throat. 'I've told you, just get
somebody in. And don't go ringing me at work over pence. We
can afford it, so let's splash out.'

Easy for him, he'd done it all his life. Spending twice as
much on a kitchen light fitting as I once spent in a fortnight. My

electric bill for six months equivalent to the heritage wallpaper I chose for the landing.

'Why are you obsessed with showing me the receipts?' He'd sigh. 'Happy with it? Then that's all that matters. Admit you enjoy spending just as much as the next person. We live up to our means like everyone else. Stop pretending you have to punish yourself forevermore.'

So I had to source somebody to sort the crumbly floorboards. I hired a gardener from the village to clear the largest trees. The whole process helping us fit in. Poring over colours for the bathrooms and kitchen, the stuff where I couldn't go wrong. Spending far more than was necessary without another word.

Every time he walked through the door I'd drag him round the house. 'What about the pattern? Not too dark, is it? What about the curtains?'

'Perfect. Couldn't have picked better myself.'

'Great. Now open your eyes.'

'I'm knackered, will you give us a break? You've cracked it! Panic over!' A quick peck on the cheek. 'You're good at these things, just like everyone else. What have I been telling you all these years?'

*

Six years ago he whisked me to Paris for my birthday. I was still working at the garage at the time and able to contribute in a small way. Kidding myself I could keep my old life whilst dipping in and out of his.

I'd never been abroad before so had to apply for a passport. Seventy quid, a huge chunk of money. I'd also never been on a plane, queued at an airport, exchanged pounds for euros. Endeavoured to speak French, booked into a hotel or tucked into a continental breakfast.

'You're seriously telling me you never wanted to go abroad in your whole life?' He laughed. 'Even France?'

'Not a matter of not wanting to, just never been able to. Can't you tell the difference?' I'd snap. That familiar tone to his voice. The way he took so much for granted, assuming his experience to be the norm.

I'd told him something of Alex. Not the full horror, of course, just a hint of what it was like. If I drip-fed him info perhaps he'd be less likely to run away. Perhaps I'd be less likely too.

We strolled round Montmartre in the sunshine while he explained why it was so famous. I'd never even heard of the place. Paid for somebody to sketch my profile, which everybody seemed to be doing, only it was hilarious in our case. No such thing as a cliché.

Sprawled on the grass in a crowded park, eating crepes as the sun went down. Another cliché. Running through them all. He loved being with somebody who knew nothing, his confidence swelling, feeling like an expert even though he admitted he wasn't. Telling me stories and getting it slightly wrong. Impossible to correct him. Trying out his broken French while I kept quiet and trusted him implicitly.

He would've appeared normal to anyone else. I made him feel special by being stupid and slow.

'We'll do a cruise tonight. Can't come here without going on the Seine. And Notre Dame. And the Louvre. You've got to say you've seen the Mona Lisa at least, even though we'll get nowhere near.' A warning look.

'Don't panic, it's one of the things I really want to see.' In case he thought I'd dropped from another planet. I pulled him close and let his head fall onto my lap. Other couples doing the same. I relished that more than anything. This simple life had been going on while I lived with Alex and Jess, all those years. Couples lounging in Parisian parks, eating crepes, laughing over nothing. While Alex shoved me down the stairs and held my wrist over the gas ring, people were paying ten euros for a quick sketch. Laughing and joking. Buying tacky key rings and T-shirts from cheap stalls along the banks of the river.

'I still can't believe I'm here.' The heat roasting my eyelids. Jess somewhere in the background, skipping beside us as we strolled through the park. Did she still skip? Turning back with an impatient glare. Somewhere in the future she'd join us on trips abroad. Not entirely sure how it would come about, details always hardest to picture. 'I'm gonna wake up any sec.'

'Stop thinking then.' Even with his eyes closed, he could sense I was doing it. 'Enjoy the moment, don't keep spoiling it, please.'

He gripped my hand, stopping me from being in that other place where I could so easily have been. Impossible to be in two places at once.

*

It all started coming out halfway through that trip. Being far from home forcing it out of me. Parisian glamour replacing cold hard reality. Surely nothing in my past could dampen all that light and beauty?

'So this Alex was a bastard? You struggled to get away but did, to your credit. Stop giving yourself a hard time. You didn't ask for it, you did nothing wrong. Bastards like that trash people's confidence, that's how they succeed. If he shows his face we'll just call the police.'

Montparnasse Tower. We stood at the top in darkness and gazed over the twinkling city, a million miles from home. He pulled me against his chest, promising never to let go. Another person had made those mistakes, entrusted Ray, failed to do the right thing. I felt ready to tell him about her.

We tucked ourselves into a quiet corner of a small restaurant across the street. Just before the first course arrived the truth spilled out of me without any warning. The state I'd been in and the issues I'd had. Most importantly, my time in the psychiatric unit.

'What?' He smacked his glass on the table and turned his left ear slightly towards me. A large group pushing in behind. All that time we'd been laughing over crepes in the park. 'Psychiatric unit?'

'Yes.'

A brief pause. 'Over a year? And you hadn't thought to mention it before?'

My voice trembling. Not exactly the response I'd been expecting. 'He was abusive, I told you. I had to get away but had nowhere to go. Easy to say I should've left him but where was I supposed to go? Have you any idea how terrified I was? I thought he'd followed me, convinced he'd tracked me down.'

'That's not the point; I'm not blaming you for being a bit down.'

'Bit down?'

'Not blaming you either way. I'm blaming you for hiding it from me in the first place. You really think I'm as bad as Alex? You don't trust me any more than you trusted him?'

The first course arrived, breaking us apart. He struggled to stomach his salad and look me in the eye. I reached for the wine and took a large gulp without him noticing. How the hell would I get home on my own if he buggered off? Come to think of it, how would I even find the hotel? Some unpronounceable name down an unpronounceable street.

If he felt jealous over Alex, who I detested, how would he feel about Jess? Ten times worse still to come.

How could he be so surprised? Surely he'd seen I belonged somewhere else? He couldn't kid himself I'd moved entirely into his world. Couldn't punish me for being afraid.

The meal wore on and he questioned some more, clarified a few things. Paris turning ugly through the grimy window. The twinkling lights no more special than those back home. What kind of treatment did I receive? Was I still having it? Was I cured? Did I ever feel like going back? Question upon question, snapping them out.

'You don't have to tell me, of course, if you don't want. If it's that private.'

'Course I want to tell you, I came here wanting to tell you, just not that simple.'

He took a large gulp of wine and stared over my shoulder. He might've travelled the world, but he'd led a straightforward life. I'd been to places he could barely imagine, seen things that would scare him to death. Could he really be so innocent?

'You said you'd forgive. I wouldn't have told you...' I sensed him drifting away, his mind elsewhere. How had he got so close in the first place?

'I know, I know, just never expected this. Bloody hell.' He swallowed half a glass full and stared out the window to give himself time. 'Let me think. Need time to think, that's all.'

I reached for his hand. Used to finding it. He grazed my knuckles, then quickly withdrew.

'Let me process it first, get my head round it. You've just caught me off guard, that's all.'

*

Jim was the first person I'd ever wanted to tell but he still felt hurt I hadn't trusted him enough. He'd always boasted he could handle anything but when it came down to it, unless it fit into his cosy little world, unless he could recognise it, he went to pieces like everyone else.

I wandered off on my own down deserted alleys, pausing on benches and browsing shop windows. Yearning to go home. Back to my old life, bickering over flapjacks. I ended up near the river, breaking through ranks of excited schoolkids, feeling I'd blown it. When I told him about Jess he'd be ten times worse, let alone the rest.

The night before we returned home I walked into our hotel room and found him staring out the window, hands deep in his pockets, his shoulders sunk. He spun round, looking both shattered and pissed off at the same time. The first time he'd not got his own way.

I perched on the bed and searched for his hand.

'Sorry.'

'For what?'

'Being an arsehole. Of course you were afraid to tell me. I shouldn't take it so personal all the time.'

'I thought I'd never be able to get a job, never hold down a normal life. What bit of confidence I've got is down to you.'

He came towards me slowly. A bit of praise all it took. He grabbed my hands between his. No idea what he was about to say or which way it would go. Was this the end I'd always seen coming?

'You know this was just supposed to be the start? Coming here? I only want the best for us both.'

'We can still do all that, I'm not going back to that place, even without you.'

'You do realise this promotion's not the end? If Tony leaves like he's threatening, I'm in line for his job. That means more money and more responsibility. Whatever I've got is yours. We're a team, right?'

'I don't give a shit about money.' Burying my head in his chest. 'I've survived on three quid a day, there's nothing you can threaten me with.'

'I'm not threatening you, for Christ's sake.'

Next time I looked up, face wet with tears, he'd silently pulled out a small velvet black box. His sister teasing for months.

'Jim?'

142

He lowered himself to the floor, groaning under the strain. An old squash injury he'd never shaken off.

'The lengths I go to.'

'Don't be ridiculous.'

'Will you do me the honour...' Removing the ring. A stunning square-cut diamond. Presumably. I'd never seen one before. 'Before anything else goes wrong.'

Like an old black-and-white film. The family next door banging in the corridor, kids complaining of another museum trip. Rain splashing the glass. Jess hovering in the background, waiting impatiently for the answer.

'Well?'

'I'm thinking. Nobody's ever proposed before.'

'Think about my knees.'

'I want to enjoy the moment.'

'For Christ's sake!'

'Yes! Course I'm going to say yes!'

I helped him up and we hugged and kissed. He picked me up and threw me onto the bed, his knees suddenly recovered, and his face flushed. So strange. I'd pictured proposals dozens of times, heard the words and relished the scene, yet never imagined the other person even happier than me.

'Sure?'

'Yes!'

'Happy?'

'Always happy with you.'

So overwhelmed to have him back. I didn't give a shit about money or conditions. Forty, fifty grand a year, all a fortune to me. My only chance of normality, the only chance I'd ever had. Jess hovering over his shoulder with folded arms. Pleased I was happy yet slightly sulky at the same time. Getting to that age.

Ray and Carol also hovering. What would I tell him? That they were old friends? That Jess was Ray's daughter, as so many believed?

His heart pumping in my ear. He'd been genuinely nervous, genuinely scared, as if I might say no. I twisted the ring on my finger. Perfect fit. How did he know these things? His knack of sorting everything with minimum fuss.

*

Since we married the house had taken up masses of time. Grade II listed gave me a great excuse to fuss. Rules and regulations to uncover first, stretching every minor job into major upheaval. Besides, I wanted to do it right, to prove that I could.

I stared out the window at the front garden and the street beyond, one eye on the clock beside the fridge. Elaine from the post office usually wandered past about now. Sometimes Jeff from round the corner with his two bull terriers. Next door's ginger tom stalking sparrows in the hedge. We'd been here long enough to set the clock by such things.

Jim away in Belgium till Saturday. He'd kept his word about the promotion. Tony conveniently moving on, leaving his export sales manager position open. An extra ten grand a year, better company car, more time from home.

I found myself drifting off as I watched the cat tirelessly stalking the birds. Jim always ticking me off. Retreating to a place where he couldn't join in. Not that he was anything like Alex, thank God, we were just close.

I spun round and clocked the time. Nearly half-three. Shit. I rushed into the hallway and grabbed my coat and bag.

Thankfully only the other end of the village. I jogged down the high street, waving to Jeff as he rounded the corner in the distance. See him down the pub at the weekend with a bit of luck.

Two minutes late as I entered the yard. He was swinging on the climbing frame, trying to kick his best friend in the face. I grabbed his shoulder and yanked him away.

'Stop that, we're going.'

'Five minutes more!'

'No! Now!'

He was the only person I'd ever been able to correct. The only person I'd ever been able to talk to like I was in charge. Damn good job. The day he was born I seemed to find a new voice just in time.

'Pack it in, Harrison!'

I couldn't imagine him ever coping without me, the way Jess had coped without me. He desperately needed me for everything, from picking out his underpants in a morning to running his bath the same time every night. Jess had somehow worked these things out herself. Wasn't that what Carol had told me for years? That my daughter didn't really need me, she'd even taken charge of Ray's life years ago.

When Harrison didn't get his own way he'd scream in my face, not just because he was spoilt as Jim loved to insist, but because he couldn't bear his routine upset, he couldn't handle it. My life with Jess had been one long disruption from beginning to end, forcing her to work things out for herself.

I thanked Mrs Spence, his poor teacher, grabbed his sleeve and pulled him screaming through the gate. Sometimes the only way. Halfway down the high street I fell into step with Alison, from one of the ex-council houses the other end of the village. Her daughter, Nina, tried to distract Harrison with a game on her mobile, giving me five minutes precious peace.

'Love the bag. That new?'

I nodded. I knew she'd want it. I found myself picking things up that I didn't really need but knew certain people wouldn't fail to notice, then feeling guilty if they tried to keep up. Alan had been made redundant in April.

'Present from Jim. He went to Milan the other week. I told him not to, we're supposed to be saving for a holiday home.' I lunged forward and grabbed Harrison just before he tried to jump somebody's front wall. My arms six inches longer since he was born, not to mention the energy. Where had it been before?

'Where's that?'

'South of France hopefully.'

Alison's face – a mixture of envy, yet distant at the same time – the way mine used to be.

'Inside, please. Now!' I guided Harrison to the front door, pulling him away from the shrub he seemed determined to kick to shreds. Enormous patience, as well as a commanding tone. Sometimes he was the best kid in the world when he lunged towards me and squeezed the life out of me with one of his big hugs, making it all worthwhile. I smiled at Alison, feeling guilty for a sec. Stuck in a rut, struggling to survive. Next time definitely invite her in, it wouldn't do any harm. 'We'll have to meet for a coffee sometime, once I get sorted, promise. Sorry, got to rush, see you tomorrow.'

Gently but firmly closing the door in her face. So cruel at times, especially in a village, but what was the point in giving people the wrong impression about the way we were going to be?

19   Jess

Lisa Sharpe on Google images. Pretty ones, ugly ones, fat ones, thin ones. Blonde ones, ginger ones, dead ones, living ones. Tracing every line and wrinkle, every scrap of evidence. Discounting most straight away. Laughing ones, friendly ones, less aggressive-looking ones. As far as page seven, till it started getting silly. Racehorses, somebody's prised yacht, a lawyer the other side of the world.

'Honestly, this is a complete waste of time.' Chloe grabbing hold of the keyboard. 'Give it here.'

'Hang on a sec!'

She typed quick, straight onto Facebook, giving specific details I'd never have dared. You were a psychotic mother, last seen roughly twelve years ago. You liked a drink, too much half the time, totally unreliable and frequently late for school run. Approach with caution.

'Chloe!'

'What?'

'Delete that last bit.'

'Why? You want to find her, don't you? I'm only telling the truth.'

'Okay but keep your voice down.' I glanced towards the bedroom door.

She was using Carol's description far more than mine.

Perhaps I should add my own. *Okay, really. Not as bad as first thought. Please get in touch for second chance.*

'Look,' Chloe pointed out, like it was a logical maths problem. 'There's only a certain number of Lisa Sharpe's in the whole country, right? We'll tick off every single one we hear about through Facebook till we've got her cornered. She's got to be out there somewhere unless she's dead.'

I paced up and down in front of the window. Once I found you I'd have to force you into acknowledging you were my mother, so we could have it out in a safe place with loads of people walking by. I'd wave my GCSE grades under your nose. Two A stars, four A's, the rest solid B's. Not quite as impressive as Chloe's but pretty good, nevertheless.

And you wouldn't shower me with useless gifts. Jewellery, clothes, tacky crap I'd never asked for in the first place. Amazed how I'd got on in life without a fuss. If you were braced in the doorway, eyes flashing, hair tumbling, the odd trickle of blood, you'd pause for a sec. Frozen mid-air. The knife clattering to the floor. Paying attention for the first time in your life. More than that, you'd be mildly impressed.

*

'If I find you've been at it again after everything I've said. Am I the only one in this damn house who worries about putting food on the table and electric on the meter?' Karen slamming the fridge door and turning on Dad over breakfast, threatening the end of his nose with a wooden spoon.

'No,' I piped up, seriously annoyed. 'The meter's on less than two quid and it'll probably run out tonight. Not my fault nobody listens.'

Her face softening. 'Okay. Are me and Jess the only ones who worry?'

'No!' Ellie sticking her hand up, striving to reach the ceiling.

'I worry all the time. Sick of going to school with a slice of bread and manky old apple. Everybody thinking I'm a joke.'

Karen bit her lip, trying to hold it in. 'Ray, what I'm trying to say in simple terms is whether *you* give a shit about putting food on the table and electric on the meter or is it just me and the kids these days?'

He remained calm throughout, quietly confident he could turn it round with a bit of manoeuvring. Chewing steadily, fixed on the kitchen window, blocking out all else.

'Look. You get paid Wednesday, don't you? Got Derek paying me for that bit of plumbing any time this week, I'll ring him later to make sure. You can nick some bread for sandwiches from work. Maybe a few cream cakes or whatever they've got left over. We've almost two pints of milk left so we're alright for tea and coffee. As for the meter, just have to take it steady. This is how everybody lives, not just us. Perfectly normal.' A short pause, pleased he'd sorted it. 'Just don't have a bath or use any appliances when you get in from work and we'll be fine.'

'Great! So I can't wash my hair tonight because I can't use a dryer, toast for tea again and I've got to send my daughter to school with a bloody cream doughnut. What sort of mother do you think I am? You know what bugs me most? Years ago we used to pay for electric like everyone else. We were normal. Now we've got a meter and nothing to put on it half the time. All that money from Gran, wasted on crap.' Glaring at him, still clutching the spoon. 'I don't know what the hell you're up to but when I find out…'

'Not up to anything. God, so damn suspicious.' He poured a second cuppa just to prove we'd got plenty of something in the house. 'Hang on a sec. What happened to all that I gave you last week? Eighty odd?'

Karen turning red.

'I asked you to sort the electric.'

'Told you, I went to the hairdresser's. Not my fault you forgot.'

'For Christ's sake! Can't you ask Carol instead? Hell of a lot cheaper!'

'No, I bloody can't! About time she butted out of this damn family.' A lengthy pause. 'Any idea how many times this last month I've had to miss a meal to make sure Ellie gets something? How many times it's a straight choice between us?'

'Don't be so dramatic.'

'How the hell would you know? Since when did you make it your business to find out we're alright? When things go wrong, you're nowhere to be found. Only interested in the good times.'

I tried to concentrate on Ellie's face as she chewed her toast, on the basis that if I looked at something innocent I wouldn't look too guilty myself. Three slices between four, which even Dad could tell didn't work out. Me and Ellie allowed one each, Karen and Dad sharing the third. Ellie's had the thickest coating of spread, mine slightly thinner with the odd mould spot, Karen's and Dad's only slightly moist in the middle, desert-like round the edges.

Dad nibbling delicately, savouring every mouthful, trying to prove we were being spoilt and fussy. Half a slice of toast enough for anybody to survive on till dinner time.

'Everyone's the same. No different,' he muttered.

The wooden spoon at the side of Karen's plate, inches from her hand. God knows what she was planning on doing with it. At least when you lashed out you did a proper job, no half measures, to hell with the consequences.

'Can you pass the sugar, please?' she asked, keeping a steady eye on Dad.

I leant over, careful not to break contact with my chair. Dad glancing across to ensure I was alright. Ellie also glancing, not quite sure what she was looking for but aware there was something. Would she keep quiet? Not long ago she'd have shouted at the top of her voice, pointing the finger, treating it like a game. Was she beginning to realise there might be consequences that affected us all? The wooden spoon giving it away.

'Now then!' Dad suddenly scraping back his chair and clapping his hands, making us all jump. Nobody could fault him for cheerfulness in a morning, whatever the atmosphere when he walked out the door. 'So I'll give Derek a ring, tell him I need that money this week. Crack on with this landscaping job. Not much to it really, even Pete can manage a bit. If it turns out alright I'll put some pictures on the website. Alright, love?' He pecked Karen on the cheek, winking at me above her head. Ellie taking it all in.

'Dad? What about pack-up?'

'What about it?'

'Tired of nicking somebody else's.'

Ruffling the top of her head. 'Don't be daft. Your mother'll sort it, don't panic.' Ignoring Karen's frosty stare.

After he'd gone we sat in silence for a few minutes. I'd made my toast last as long as possible, poured a third glass of juice I could barely finish. Crossing my legs, leaning forward.

'So what you up to today?' Karen asked. 'Apart from revising? Don't mind cleaning the loo, do you?'

'No problem.' As long as it got her out the door quicker. Why was she taking so long?

Ellie ran into the front room to watch telly. Karen loaded the sink, staring through the conservatory, lost in thought. Searching for Craig next door probably. He had a habit of poking his head over the hedge whenever she stood at the window.

Suddenly she spun round and leaned back against the sink, arms folded. A hard, searching stare. I shuffled awkwardly, itching to escape to my room. Those days long gone.

'Wouldn't do anything stupid, would you? Understand each other, right?'

'Sorry?'

'Don't play the innocent, I expect more from you, Jess. Acting like your father.'

'You know I'm always worried about the meter. Probably look at it more than anyone. I wish I could forget it for two minutes, give my brain a rest. You know how I feel about the food, it's demeaning. Either feast or famine, I've always said that. Why do you think I want to find a job so bad?' All the while my arse burning. A miracle I managed to stay seated.

'Good. Because the way your dad behaves affects us all. I'd hate to think you were on his side just to please him. If he's doing something stupid he's shitting on us all, not just me.'

After she'd finished the washing-up she grabbed her bag and raced past the front room.

'Be good!' she shouted to Ellie. 'Jess can take you to school.'

'Mum?' A whine from the sofa. 'Starving. What's there to eat?'

'I'm late for work. Have to ask Jess, won't you? Try to get something for tea, promise.'

She slammed the door. Finally just the two of us. I stood up and unpeeled the white envelope off my chair, addressed to Dad. I was first down at half-seven, standing in the kitchen wondering what to do when Karen burst in. No choice but to either hand it over or sit on it.

I tore it open, leaning back against the sink. It was from the bank, to do with the mortgage. Seven months behind with payments, over five grand in all. They were concerned he hadn't kept an appointment two weeks ago and wanted him to make another. At the bottom, in italics, a sentence jumped out. *Your home may be repossessed if you do not keep up repayments on your mortgage.* And all I could hear were Carol's words, over and over. Eight years old. A warning to be careful, telling me not to laugh. Turning cartwheels under her nose.

'That Dad's?'

Ellie in the doorway, holding Cinderella upside down by her ankles. Maybe it was the guilty look on my face or the way I was holding the letter, but she could tell straight away it wasn't mine.

'It's about a job I've applied for.'

'I saw him winking at you. Don't worry, I won't say anything.'

'Yeah, okay. I'm looking after it till he gets home, that's all.' No point hiding stuff. She probably knew more than anyone.

'No big deal, is it? None of my business.'

And with that she lobbed Cinderella over her shoulder and ran upstairs, slamming her bedroom door. Which was perfectly normal half the time. She'd always been sharp but really that sharp? How come she'd suddenly aged five years? She'd normally make a huge fuss, threaten to run to Karen or at least text Gran.

I took the stairs two at a time and burst into her room. She was perched on the bed colouring in a picture, doing her best to look innocent, tongue lolling out on one side.

'Okay, what's going on?'

'Nothing.' Scribbling over Sleeping Beauty with green crayon, scrubbing at the paper till she almost tore a hole in it. 'Just trying to make Dad happy, aren't you?'

'Not really. Just helping him out while he gets sorted. He's promised he will, and I believe him, okay?'

She scribbled over the prince as well, obliterating his face with brown crayon. Not normally so angry with her own stuff.

'Don't care what you get up to. Don't care about Dad. Nothing to do with me.'

'You got something to tell me?'

'No.'

'I'm not daft. Where've you been hiding it? If you don't tell me I'll turn this whole room upside down.'

'Sod off!'

'How long's it been going on? Might as well tell me. If I have to start throwing stuff about, things might get broken.'

She glanced quickly towards the window, shuffling back, out of reach. Not entirely sure what she'd done wrong, just enough to hide it. I dived towards the window and her red plastic toy box. Just lately she'd become the tidiest kid in the world for no reason whatsoever. Karen never had to get involved.

I tipped the box on its side and watched the contents slide across the floor. Jigsaws and battered board games, soft toys and dolls. She cried out as a make-up case tipped open, contents rolling under the bed. She grabbed Buzz Lightyear and launched him at my head. At the bottom of the box was what I was looking for. Far more than what I was looking for. A thick wad of brown and white envelopes, loose paper, leaflets, even a credit card with Dad's name on. I stood in the middle as it slid across my feet. Far more than he'd ever hidden in my room. I leaned against the wall, struggling to take it in.

She shrugged and went back to her colouring. 'You know what he's like.'

'Oh I know what he's like. A complete tosser.' I picked up a loose sheet, searching for a date. Almost two years ago. Was that how long he'd been using her?

'You're not the only one, Jess.'

'Sorry?'

'He knows he can trust me; I wouldn't tell anyone.'

'It's not a competition, Ellie. Whatever he says, it's not, okay? We're not competing, do you understand?'

'He said he wanted somewhere to hide stuff and I told him he could use my box. I don't hide it for him, he just puts it there.'

I gathered everything and threw it all back, feeling ancient. Ellie had the perfect excuse for not understanding. What was mine?

'He's being a prat at the moment. He's got into trouble and needs to sort it before it goes any further. You've done nothing wrong. I'll have a word with him when he gets home.'

'Is it something to do with your crazy mum?'

'What?'

'They're always talking about her.'

'Don't be daft.'

She nodded. 'Always whispering. Anybody would think she lives with us.'

I perched on the bed. 'They like to go over old ground. Karen's probably jealous.'

'Why would she be jealous? Doesn't make sense.'

'For obvious reasons. My mum was Dad's first partner and Karen doesn't want to think of him with someone else. She wants him to move on.'

'He has moved on. So why keep talking about her when she's not here? Not important, is she?'

'I don't know. Forget it. I don't know everything just because I'm eighteen.'

Throwing herself flat on the bed. 'Jess! Starving! Please help me!'

'Just let me deal with it. If Karen happens to find out about the paperwork, make out you're stupid, shouldn't be difficult. Just act like her little girl.'

A few minutes later we went downstairs so I could put together one of my specials. She used to hate them at first. Hurling them at the conservatory wall, jam and tuna sliding to the floor. Till she realised it wasn't likely to get any better.

'Let me see.'

Two stale Jammie Dodgers. A slice of wafer-thin ham but no bread. Half a tub of marg. Five tins of beans.

'Can I have a chicken sandwich and some cheese and onion crisps?'

'Yeah, sure. I'll just pull them out my back pocket, hang on a sec.'

I stood on a chair and searched the top of the cupboards. A slim chance there might be something long forgotten. Pulling out every dusty pot and pan, digging to the back.

In the end I found a small tub of Pringles, two carrots, which I cut into sticks, and two out-of-date strawberry yoghurts.

'That it?'

'Yes. And you need to pay attention to what I'm doing so you can do it yourself one day.'

She broke off from slapping Cinderella against the wall. 'I'm not doing it. You can do it.'

'And if I'm not here?'

'What?' Her face falling for the first time. 'Jess?'

'I'm just saying. I've got things I want to do in life. Before I go, I'll go through it all properly. Easy once you get the hang of it. Just need to save some of the money they give you and hide it, then in an emergency you can look after yourself.'

As I took in her tiny face, a mix of anger and confusion, I felt a sense of desperation. How come I'd turned into a crappy version of Mrs Patterson? Desperately trying to inject normality into her life, as if I knew what it was myself.

Dishing out the kind of advice I'd never received from you, the kind routinely passed from mother to daughter. I wouldn't even have minded if you'd got it completely wrong. Of course, we'd have argued, I'd have ignored you at first and made out I'd not taken it in. Of course, I'd have listened to every single word.

'You've got to learn to be sensible,' I added, trying to sound as if I knew from experience.

'Sensible?'

'No choice I'm afraid.'

'Not yet, Jess. Please?' A long whine.

'Okay. Not yet. Now get your shoes on, we'll be late.'

20   Lisa

'Again!'

'Let's choose a different one for tonight.'

'Again!'

'Just for a change, Harrison. Please listen for once.'

'Again!' Right in my ear. Squirming to the bottom of his bed.

Cranky Crocodile. Seven nights in a row, the pages falling to bits, shouting and giggling in all the same places. Jim waiting impatiently downstairs, a Liam Neeson film lined up on Netflix. Bottle of red in the fridge, box of mints, our usual Saturday-night routine. If I was lucky he might even switch off his phone.

A fleeting glimpse of Jess as I flicked the tattered pages. Tucking her into bed and reading her a story, reminding her to clean her teeth. Slurring my words and losing my place, having to be told. Sometimes getting it just right against the odds. Creeping downstairs to join Alex. Then what? Did she ever crawl out of bed and stand at the top of the stairs? Did she always fall asleep before he started? How much did she take in?

I kissed Harrison goodnight and gently closed his door. Surely my biggest achievement was the fact he couldn't tell. One mother, one child. When he told me I was the best mum in the world he actually believed it.

I slipped into our bedroom just in time to catch my mobile

vibrating on the chest of drawers. I pressed the button, nudging the door shut at the same time.

'What now?'

'Lisa?'

Ray. Sounding desperate, as if he'd been trying to reach me for months. I pretended not to know.

'Okay?'

'No I'm bloody not! Don't you check your phone these days or is it just me?'

Some stupid idea that I was too good for him, fuelled by Carol's bitterness. Sticking his nose in the air when my back was turned.

'Don't tell me, it's about the money. I put it through the door when you said, you must've got it.'

A brief pause. 'Yeah, I got it.'

Five hundred, probably squandered already. How much did he expect? In so much trouble he'd lost all sense of proportion.

'Not being funny, Lisa. I know we didn't exactly set a figure as such.'

'No, we bloody didn't. How much do you think I can get my hands on at such short notice? I've had to lie as it is. Can't just walk in and ask for thousands without Jim knowing.'

I ran my finger along the blue-and-cream wallpaper. Cavendish Stripe. They did silk cushions and throws to match. I once made the mistake of telling Carol the price.

He sniggered down the line as if he could sense what I was doing. Last time we met he'd commented on my white gold earrings, a present from Jim after his last bonus, as if it were unusual the way we lived. Convinced I was doing it just to spite him. One day he might drive past, climb out his van and come down the drive, curiosity getting the better of him. Squashing his rough reddened face against the front window, making an offhand comment, thinking it was funny.

'Must have your own bank account. Can't believe he leaves

you short. For Jess, not me. How much do you think it costs to feed a growing lass?'

'I can't give you any more without making him suspicious, you'll have to wait. It's not my fault business is struggling. Perhaps you need to retrain or try something different. Have you considered at least? Looked into it? No?'

Two years ago he slipped off a conservatory roof and tore a ligament in his knee. Of course, they had nothing to fall back on while he was out of work for six months and now it seemed to be everyone else's fault they were in a mess.

'Shelled out a small fortune over the years, not as if I've asked for anything before now. Only fair, especially now you've had a bit of luck.'

'Bit of luck?'

'Well you have!'

'You know your problem? Everyone who does well is lucky, everyone who works hard, saves hard, tries to make something of their life.'

'Just asking for a bit of flaming help!'

I bit my lip, tasting blood, trying to focus on the stripes. All the years he begrudged me crumbs. Waiting all day for a three-word text. Now suddenly desperate to share, just because I had something finally to share. Something to lose.

'How many times did I offer to take her for the afternoon, drop her off at school or take her to the park? How many? And how many of those times did you even answer the phone? Be honest! What choice did you give me?'

'And how many times were you in a fit state? Could barely stand up half the time. What choice did I have? Had to keep her safe, had to think of her.'

'I was ill! I didn't go into hospital for a holiday, did I? Didn't choose to be sick.'

'Alright, keep your hair on.' Somebody listening in the background. Panicking again. Why the rush all of a sudden?

He'd managed the last twelve years. Couldn't he just carry on?

'I might've made some terrible decisions but at least I had an excuse. You honestly didn't notice the state I was in?'

'Wish I'd never bloody asked.'

I struggled to keep it down. Park Field Psychiatric Unit, Ward 2b. Overlooking the shabby courtyard with the cracked paving and half-dead climber shadowing the opposite wall. Ray and Carol exchanging glances behind my back, wondering if I was safe. The inconvenience to their lives. They even had me apologising for it, begging for another chance.

'I always knew Alex had taken advantage, I knew it even while he was doing it, but you did exactly the same. You used me and used Jess to get what you wanted. Carol as well. Like a great big kid. While you're interested, everything's fine, soon as you lose interest you're looking for a scapegoat.'

'Jesus.'

'So don't go accusing me of letting her down. Don't throw it in my face. You've treated her like a toy. You wanted her back then but now can't be bothered to give her the attention she needs. Too smart for you, that's the problem, she sees straight through you.'

'Talking crap.'

'And now you've run out of money, all of a sudden I'd make a perfect mother. All of a sudden you can't wait to tell me what's going on.'

'I thought you'd be interested!'

'Life's moved on for us both, not a matter of being interested. Surely even you can see that.'

I paused. A sudden creak on the stairs. Loose board, fourth one down. Jim about to barge in and see the truth in my face. Perhaps he knew already and was just waiting to pounce. Wasn't I always last to know?

'Over five quid apiece. Thought she was having me on!'

'What?'

'Moroccan bloody tiles!'

Eventually a few more creaks and a light cough, followed by the clicking of the bathroom door.

'That all you and Carol have to talk about?' Bitch. I'd only shown her the brochure because we had nothing else to discuss. Couldn't he grasp the truth? It was nothing to do with money. Jess was smart, I could hide my sudden interest ten years ago. A dodgy haircut wasn't likely to fool her today if I got too close.

'Christ, Lisa. You want to listen to yourself sometimes. How you've changed.'

'And how you haven't.'

God knows how I'd ever thought him smart or looked up to him. Completely out of control. I should've seen it coming and done something sooner. Moved further away. He could wander past any time he liked, knock on the door and throw everything in my face.

'Of course I want to help, it's just not that easy. Tell me exactly what you want, and I'll tell you what I'm prepared to give.'

'Not so simple, is it? She's asking questions. Carol, me, anyone she can get hold of. It's like her whole life has been leading up to this point. One of her friends has been egging her on. There's no telling her, she's that determined. You know what lasses are like once they get together.'

Blue-and-white stripes merging into one. Impossible to visualise Jess fitting in, even if Jim managed to accept her. The house, the village, my circle of friends. Not really friends, just people who held a certain view of me. She belonged on Taylor Avenue, somewhere I could visit whenever I felt like, not here. She'd only set eyes on Harrison twice, round at Carol's when he was little. I felt sick at the prospect of it going further. Trying to have both and losing it all. I'd made my choice and learnt to be happy.

Harrison's mummy. People shouting it across the playground, the doctor calling me it as if I'd never been anything else. The slate wiped clean the second he was born. I didn't care if I never went back to being Lisa. Whatever Ray might say, it wasn't just the money. For the first time I'd become someone I didn't want to destroy.

'And how is extra money going to stop her asking questions exactly?'

'She's asking because she's not happy. They've cut Karen's hours so she's not bringing in as much. Not everyone can have big flash cars and fancy clothes. If I can make things a bit easier maybe she'll not be so concerned about someone she's barely set eyes on in years.'

We talked some more, the toilet flushing and the tap running. Eventually settling on a figure that was more than I would've liked and far less than he was hoping for.

'That's it. You hear? Give me a few days to sort it, then I don't want to hear any more.'

I ended the call and switched off the phone. Done with gratitude. Those days long gone.

21   Jess

'Can't live in the past forever. Got to look forward like everyone else. About time you started applying for a few more jobs. No point daydreaming all the time, where's that end?'

How could I move on when I wasn't ready? What happened to the past? Did it remain where it was, awaiting my return, or did it become impossible to return to? What if there was something important lurking in the black and white kitchen, something I'd not finished with yet, that I needed to tackle first before moving on for good?

'You can't keep using what happened as an excuse,' Karen droned on. 'Shouldn't think you can even remember it that well.'

'Jess remembers everything,' Ellie chipped in. 'Her mum's eyes were like this on stalks. Blood dripping from her mouth like a vampire. Used to throw her from the top of the stairs like this...' Launching off her chair with a loud cry.

'Ellie!'

'She used to lock her up in a cupboard for days on end with no food or water. Two packets of crisps and a KitKat to last a whole month. Jess had to lick it off the floor like a dog, like this...'

'Enough!' Karen snapped. 'About time you both forgot. Time we all moved on.' She slapped Ellie's hand from the last slice of toast, looking unreasonably pissed off. 'Not discussing this the rest of our lives. That clear? Sick of hearing about her, damn woman. Had enough of an impact round here.'

She grabbed the toast and lobbed it at the bin, collecting plates and mugs at lightning speed. A bustle of activity that seemed to come from nowhere. Me and Ellie exchanging glances, struggling to keep up. No idea she hated you so much.

*

I paused in the doorway, instantly feeling I'd got the wrong place. A small freezing room opposite the headmaster's office, normally reserved for meetings or other things that didn't involve pupils. My uniform permanently abandoned. Faded skinny jeans, T-shirt, tatty trainers instead. The future an unknown place, exciting yet terrifying.

'Hi, Jessica, have a seat.'

I perched on the edge, keeping my jacket on. He'd thrown his on top of his briefcase, loosened his tie, ruffled his mop of dark hair. Wrong-footed for a brief sec. He should be middle aged, perhaps a flowing grey beard. He looked as if he left school three days ago.

'Call me Nick.'

'Right.' Almost laughing in his face. What if somebody marched in and told me off for being cheeky?

A mass of paperwork in front of him, different coloured forms neatly sorted into piles, including a list of all my GCSE results and the A levels I was about to sit.

'So tell me about yourself.'

Silence.

'What you enjoy at school, what kind of things you're into. Just so I can help.' Determination behind the polite smile. He was used to sorting people out, even the ones who didn't want to be.

'Nothing to tell really. I'm not like Chloe.' I glanced sneakily at his list. He would've seen her this morning. She'd have marched in, told him what she wanted and left shortly after with an application form. Several application forms. Her whole life mapped out for the next twenty years. 'She wants to go into child psychology. Always wanted to. Never changed her mind. And I'm not interested in college either, so there's no point suggesting it. There's nothing jumping out at me so what's the point?'

He leaned back and looked me straight in the eye. 'I assume you mean Chloe Roberts? I saw her this morning. I'm asking about you, Jessica; this is your interview. There must be something. What have you been thinking about the last couple of years while you've been doing your A levels? Have you considered office work perhaps? Retail? Higher education?' Trying to rephrase it. 'What appeals to you?'

Obviously I'd been thinking over the last few years, pretty much non-stop. I couldn't switch off like everyone else.

'There is something, but you'll think I'm an idiot.'

'Go on.'

'It's not even relevant. Nothing to do with having a career.'

'You're my last appointment. Plenty of time.'

'It's stupid.' Wishing I'd kept my gob shut.

'I'm used to stupid, that's my job. So far today I've had one student faint on me, another spent most of her time texting her mate, one said he wanted my job and could do it better, another wanted to sign on because it represented his best option in life. I've never met a student with an unsolvable problem. I'm sure you're not the first.'

I touched the scar on my throat. So small I had to search round for it. 'I haven't seen my mum since I was six. We had to run away because she was a violent alcoholic. There, I've said it. That's what I've been thinking about the last couple of years. And probably why I'll get shit grades and end up stacking shelves the rest of my life.'

A lengthy pause. 'You've barely started your exams yet.'

'So? I've hardly revised. I didn't even think about what subjects to take. I've been bored stiff in psychology for two years just because Chloe needs it for this stupid course. It's like somebody's living my life for me. This thing has got inside my head and until I get it out I can't move on. I need to find her, even if she just tells me to bugger off.'

He frowned at his mass of paperwork. I'd knocked him completely off course. 'Is there somebody you can talk to? Relative perhaps?'

'They just think I'm being awkward, which makes me even more awkward. If somebody told you your mother wasn't important, what would you think? If they told you to forget, what would you do?'

'Not really for me to say, is it? Whatever happens in your private life, no reason you still can't think about a career. Can't put everything on hold. My parents separated when I hit sixteen. They'd been waiting for that particular moment, I think. Last thing I felt like doing was applying to college. Felt like sitting in my room for the rest of my life, waiting for everyone to clear off. They didn't. I went to college anyway, got the qualifications I needed. Decided my parents weren't going to screw up my future the way they'd screwed up their own.'

'I get what you're saying but sometimes...' Why the hell was I telling him? A complete stranger. 'I don't even know who I am. Everybody else knows so it's easy for them to decide the future. I don't even know the basics that everyone else takes for granted. Why I've got frizzy hair that won't do as it's told. The reason I've got different-sized feet and find it hard to find shoes that fit. Why I'm so useless at maths but brilliant at crosswords. Was my mum the same? And that's just the trivial stuff. What about the important things?' I took a deep breath. 'Everybody in my family lies, especially about the past. They've been feeding me bullshit from the start.'

166

He started pulling together his paperwork, glancing at his watch. 'You walked into this room like somebody was holding a gun to your head. Guess what? You're eighteen now. You can claim benefits, work full-time, play the lottery, get married, have kids. You're in charge now.'

My heart pumping. He was talking to me like I was an adult. Looking at me like I was an adult. Even if Dad and Karen thought otherwise.

'I don't normally say this to students because it's not usually appropriate, but you can do what the hell you like now you're an adult. Be outrageous. Be daring. Be brave.' Dragging his briefcase from under the table. 'From what I can gather, most of your classmates have been doing it years.'

'Thank you.'

'Here. In case you change your mind.'

I rushed out the room, clutching a couple of leaflets. He might've been gutted he hadn't ticked a box for me or filled out a form. He had no idea he'd given me exactly what I'd been waiting for.

*

'Don't worry, I'll pay you a proper hourly rate,' Dad insisted. 'All above board.'

'Really?' I laughed. 'And what about Pete?'

Dad's workmate for the last eight years. Probably his closest friend. Owed over two months' wages, not to mention all the unpaid overtime nobody had been counting.

At first Pete had been understanding and even laughed it off, which he tended to do about most things in life. 'Only beer money, Ray. By the time you've finished you'll owe me five hundred pints. Don't think I'm not bloody counting.' Until it stopped being funny and became quite serious. Pete's parents – who he still lived with at thirty-five – started complaining about his lack of contribution towards the mortgage and council tax. Even getting half his wages would be a start. Anything better than nothing. Pete passed this nugget of information onto Dad, who acted like it was a revelation. Didn't Pete realise he was doing his best to keep the business going? Wasn't it in both their interests to make a temporary sacrifice? Course he'd pay him as soon as he could. Had he ever run away from his obligations?

'Sorry, mate,' Pete ended up apologising, feeling rotten for asking so much. 'I can see you're working on it. Not really fussed as long as I've still got a job at the end of it.'

'I'll pay you some now if you're absolutely desperate,' Dad offered, pretending to reach into his back pocket for his wallet, which he loved to do far more often than he actually opened it.

'Don't be daft. Business comes first. Don't want a penny till you can afford it, you listening?'

And so it was the business in question – Ray's Rapid Repairs and Maintenance – became fully apparent to me that first Monday morning in late May when I pulled on a scraggy pair of jeans and T-shirt and joined them on the drive at half-eight. Pete unnaturally cheerful for a man who'd not been paid in two months. Dad absorbed in inspecting the back of the van, swearing at each other good-naturedly till they noticed me, because I was a girl and obviously not used to it. I didn't tell them I heard far worse at school every day. Pete retreating under his dusty baseball cap, even though he used to give me piggybacks round the garden when I was little and let me beat him up regular.

'Alright, Jess?' he called from a safe distance. 'Ready for work with your old man? Ready for learning all his secrets?'

'Looks like it.'

'It'll be an education,' Dad called from the back of the van. 'A chance to see how the real world operates. Kids get it far too easy these days. Fussed over at school, fussed over at home. Never done a day's work in her life. It's a national disaster if she stubs her toe. A wonder she ever walked to school because most of her mates never could. More than fifty yards and they collapse from exhaustion. Classed as child cruelty if you ask 'em to walk up two flights of stairs.'

Pete agreeing enthusiastically. He loved it when Dad told him what to think. 'Kids aren't what they used to be, like when we were growing up. She'll just have to watch what we do and pick it up best she can.'

Before we set off I inspected the back of the van out of interest, although, being a girl, probably wouldn't understand what I was looking at. It contained three ancient-looking buckets, a garden spade and fork, two ladders, several old paint brushes with stiffened bristles that hadn't been cleaned properly, a knackered-looking grandfather clock Dad had owned years, given to him by a customer who couldn't settle his bill, a set of dusty encyclopaedias also given in part payment, and an electric drill that looked as if it hadn't been used since the day I was born.

'Let's get off then,' he announced, climbing into the driver's seat, grinning broadly. I sat in the middle with Pete nearest the door. In an effort not to touch me, Pete squashed himself against the door at a risk of falling out and ending up on the road. Even coughing into the back of his hand so as not to upset me.

Five minutes later we arrived. The other end of town, a large mock-Tudor detached property in a quiet cul-de-sac, complete with a landscaped back garden and double garage. The last place I expected Dad to be working. They obviously hadn't met him.

The owner was just leaving for work. A small chubby man in a dark pinstripe suit, throwing his briefcase onto the back seat of a 4x4 whilst giving Dad instructions on where to find everything.

'No probs. Be here till five and probably the rest of the week. Plenty to be going on with.'

'My wife should be home at lunch time.' He didn't look at

all worried, as if used to handing over his house to a bunch of strangers.

'What are we doing exactly?' I asked as he drove off.

'Bit of plastering, bit of painting. Fixing a radiator, some wiring. Bit of maintenance.'

The word maintenance cropped up a lot. Dad got Pete using it all the time. Seemed to cover just about everything.

Before they got started the two of them had a good nosey round, upstairs and down, pausing to appreciate some of the tech in the living room. All part of the service.

'Look at this, Pete. Latest bloody iPad! This bugger earns too much!'

'3D telly not cheap either. Want to put your prices up, they can afford it.'

'I'm in the wrong job here.'

I stood around awkwardly, awaiting instructions. Nothing like school. The real world supposedly, though it felt less real than anything I'd ever done in my life. What was the point in passing exams?

After sampling the tech they asked me to put the kettle on, just to check I was up to it. Dad spending twenty minutes on eBay, checking the latest status of whatever he was selling. Shaking his head repeatedly. At one point even diving into the little toilet under the stairs, slamming the door so he could have an angry conversation on the phone. His voice filtering through the keyhole. When he eventually emerged, Pete stood beside him, silently checking his own phone, a mirror image.

'Tea?'

'Yeah.'

'Biscuit?'

Dad nodded, red-faced.

'For a pint later?'

'Probably.'

'See that programme last night? Dodgy builder with that extension? Fell down in a fortnight?'

'There's some scum about.'

I tried to butt in. 'Shall we do something? That's why I'm here, right?'

Blank expressions.

'Hold your horses. Not at school now.'

God knows how the morning went so quick. I didn't seem to do much except get under their feet, repeatedly put the kettle on and ask daft questions. Not that I planned on having a career in the building trade, but it would've been nice to learn a skill.

According to Pete, my tea was crap. He pulled a sour face every time he took a sip. Dad did the same, even though he'd tasted my tea hundreds of times and should've been used to it.

Pete reckoned it was because everyone left school unable to do anything useful. Dad confirmed this to be the case.

'We always did useful stuff at school. Stuff we could use in the real world.'

'They're too busy teaching 'em to pass exams. She's got certificates for scratching her arse.'

'They weren't invented just to rub your nose in it. They do actually serve a purpose,' I butted in, feeling slightly depressed. What if he was right?

One of the jobs they'd been asked to do was paint the bathroom mint green. I felt uncomfortable the second Dad sandwiched his massive frame between the shower cubicle and toilet, knocking a picture off the wall as he spun round. Everything brand new and spotless, straight off the pages of a glossy magazine.

I needn't have worried so soon. He sent Pete to search the van for paint brushes and found they were all set like concrete, a total surprise to them both.

'These have hardly been used. Look. What's happened to 'em?'

'You're supposed to clean 'em, you prat, told you before. You'll have to get a new pack. And a roller. Nip out now. You can sign on at the same time.'

'Sign on?' I chipped in.

I'd just assumed Pete was employed by Dad. No idea he'd been signing on since he left school.

'Bloody inconvenient at times,' Dad admitted after he'd gone. 'They're trying to send him to job club again. What's the point? Been five times already. Sit around all day looking at newspapers scratching your arse, filling out application forms. Might as well be here working.'

'But he's breaking the law. If he got found out you'd both be in deep shit.'

Too busy surfing the net looking for spare parts for his bike.

'Dad?'

'Eh?' Nodding slowly. 'I know what you're saying. Always someone looking to interfere. All I know is he's got a decent job with me and he's a good lad. Not as if he's claiming housing benefit or got half a dozen kids with different women. He's alright, Pete. People need to get off his back. Besides, it's cheaper this way. Imagine the state we'd be in if I had to pay out a proper wage and pension and all that crap. How do you think I manage to pay the bills as it is?'

Nudging me in the ribs till I cracked a smile.

'Come on, least we get to spend a few days together. Make the most of it, eh?'

A lump in my throat from nowhere. Something nagging at the back of my mind. I didn't give a shit about Pete. Pete didn't give a shit about himself. Dad always thinking it was funny. When would he ever stop laughing at stuff that wasn't funny?

I was about to argue further when something unexpected happened to distract me. He used the opportunity while Pete was out to crack on.

'He makes more work by being here. Come on, we'll get

started while he's gone.' Shoving a knackered old paintbrush into my hand. 'Use that till he gets back. You're a million times smarter than he is.'

'So why the sexist remarks?'

'Eh? Since when?'

He prepped the walls by running a hand over them, carefully removing all the nails. He opened the paint and gave it a good stir, until I told him it was the sort that didn't need it. Then straightened up and somehow in one swift movement yanked the shower curtain from its pole, tearing it at the top. Handing it to me without a word. His hands far too big for fiddly jobs, which I actually didn't mind until I heard the front door slam and a breezy female voice calling from the bottom of the stairs.

'Hello! Anyone at home?' The chubby man's wife, keen to check on progress.

Suddenly a strange sensation at my feet. I glanced down. A huge mint green puddle seeping between the immaculate polished slate tiles, inching towards the skirting, already half covering the bathroom scales. He'd knocked over the tin without noticing. Already moving onto the sealing strip above the bath, examining it minutely, even though it wasn't on our list of jobs.

'Dad!'

'This sealing strip's not too handy, could do with replacing. We'll do it as an extra. That's a good tip for you, from your old man, always ensure the customer's happy and he'll come back for more.'

While I clutched the shower curtain, my only decent pair of trainers ruined, listening to approaching footsteps on the stairs.

22   Lisa

Thank God I'd fallen into the habit of calling round at Carol's rather than letting her come to me. I knew how she interpreted it, especially since we moved. I was being stuck up. I didn't want her sipping coffee in our conservatory, running a hand over the soft furnishings and questioning the price. Shaking her head over a scatter cushion, as if I'd turned into the most frivolous person in the world.

Hadn't she loved it when I was stuck in a freezing flat, thin as a whippet? Never imagining I'd meet someone like Jim, who she couldn't understand anyway. What on earth was he thinking?

'Couple of inches?'

'If you don't mind.'

My visits had lessened over the years, a mutual relief no doubt. Two or three times a week at one point, banging on the door, shouting to be let in, neighbours lifting the curtains. Desperate to hear whatever news she was prepared to impart, agonising over her motive. It mattered back then. Convinced she was trying to be Jess's mother and that she'd planned the whole thing from the start. Ray as innocent as myself, Carol encouraging him just so she could have a kid of her own. Taking advantage of us both.

Now down to once a month, showing my face, reporting for duty. Anything more far too risky. Jim believed she was an old friend – when he bothered to consider such things – somebody I met for coffee now and again. Two hours max. Time to chat, not just about Jess but about Jim, Harrison, Jim's job, being rushed off my feet, even the weather, just so we could both say we'd done it.

She draped a towel across my shoulders. The wind howling down the chimney. Same room Ray carried Jess into that fateful day, tearful and confused, blood trailing the carpet. A lifetime ago. I used to feel so jealous of the place, the sanctuary it must've been.

In reality it was both poky and old-fashioned, like the whole neighbourhood. Some streets pulled down to make way for a new shopping precinct, despite protests. Carol's narrowly escaping somehow. They wouldn't dare. A slight musty smell due to the north-facing windows and lack of natural light. Barely enough room for a two-seater sofa and to open both doors. Like travelling back in time. Why hadn't she changed the curtains or re-wallpapered at least? I doubt she'd ever been in the yard except for a fag. This had been Jess's whole world. Some of her old toys still in a plastic tub in the corner, even more upstairs. Stubbornly clinging on, just like Ray.

I wondered whether she'd have the nerve to bring up his recent demands or whether I'd have to. She was a good gossip if nothing else. I could explain my position, knowing she was bound to pass it on.

'We're going to Australia early next year for three weeks.'

'Australia? Goodness!'

She would've said that about anywhere. A weekend in Blackpool too good for me.

'Jim's been twice on business. Says it's fantastic. Harrison's told the whole village. He packed a bag last week.'

'Mmm.' Glancing over her shoulder. 'Where've you parked?'

'Right outside. Plenty of room, don't panic.'

Obsessed with my car being a problem, especially since I'd had the Range Rover. Not my fault there was no regular parking spot.

'Carol?'

'You conditioning? Feels a bit dry again.'

'Can you have a word with Ray when you get chance? Obviously in trouble again.'

'Trouble?' Straightening up and coming round the front. 'You mean, owes money? May come as a surprise but quite a few people do. Not uncommon.'

'Don't be silly. I mean he's desperate. Ringing all the time and leaving messages. He knows the situation; he knows what it's like.'

'Oh. Sponging? Can we call it sponging in this case?'

'If it's every other day, yes.'

Why hadn't I called time on these visits long ago? For both our sakes. I didn't need to know what Jess was up to, I could guess these days or send a text if necessary. She was older and things were different. Of course, Carol wanted Ray to live off me. It saved him having to go to her.

'We're still paying for Harrison's treatment. The drugs seem to work but he's still got to see a specialist every other month. There's no end in sight.'

'How much is he after?'

'More than I've got. The more I give him the more he'll ask for. Not exactly helping, is it? I've got to draw the line somewhere.'

'And I suppose Jim's asking questions? Suppose you're constantly lying?'

'Sometimes,' I answered reluctantly. More titbits for her to store away. The details she thrived on. 'I don't want Ray making demands that affect Jim or Harrison. It's not just about me anymore. It's not fair. If I were on my own it might be different.'

'Fair?'

'You know where I'm coming from. If I thought there was the slightest chance of me and Jess being together I'd never have even looked at Jim.'

'But I suppose if you'd been honest with him from the start. Only made life difficult for yourself, don't you think?' A long pause. Smug silence on her behalf. 'Has Ray told you she's been questioning him?'

'He tells me anything just to get his own way. I've switched off, to be honest.'

Snipping sharply. 'Well, it's true for once. She's put me on the spot quite a few times, wanting to know what happened that day. Always going back to it. She knows something's not right. Living with Ray has sharpened her wits. If you were hoping she'd turn out as clueless as him, think again. I said it from the start.'

My mouth parched. She hadn't even offered a coffee. Always the upper hand. 'I know Ray can be a bit simple but it's not in his best interests to encourage her. He needs to nip it in the bud before it's too late. If you can tell him.'

'Oh right. How exactly? With a teenager? Much experience in that department, have you?'

'He should've thought of that, shouldn't he? It's in nobody's best interests, none of us, for Christ's sake.'

I glanced at my watch. Collecting Harrison at half-three. And tomorrow and the day after. The holiday to Australia. Half the village knew. These things were going to happen; even Carol couldn't stop them.

'Want it layering at the front for a change?'

Why did I always feel the past so strongly in this place? In Carol's presence. Park Field, Ward 2b. How many people had she told? They all thought I was going back and that I belonged there more than anywhere. Life with Jim and Harrison the temporary bit.

'For God's sake, please speak to him. If she's asking questions he needs to treat it seriously, if it slips out...'

'I'm sure he won't want it slipping out, but you can't plan for everything, even you. He knows to ring you on your mobile, he won't ring the landline, don't wet yourself.'

Glancing over her shoulder again. She rushed to the front window and lifted the grubby net.

'Next door's struggling to get in. Best move it or she'll be moaning again.'

'I parked right up to the kerb, I always do.'

'Not used to big trucks down here, I've told you.'

I needed to get away permanently. These streets, this house. Everything that happened, lingering within these walls. Break ties with both Carol and Ray, make a plausible excuse and disappear from their lives. Five or six years ago they would've let me. I belonged to Jim and Harrison; no grey areas. I knew exactly where I was and exactly where I was meant to be.

She came back and grabbed my shoulders. 'See what I can do.' Loving every minute. 'Problem is, he's that desperate. Can't stop himself, then runs off and leaves everyone else to pick up the pieces. I've seen it that many times.'

'If you can give him a message from me. I'll get him his money as soon as I can. You know I don't begrudge him; I just don't want it coming out at the moment, you understand? Jim's supposed to be getting a bonus soon. I'll use some of that.'

'Won't he realise?'

'I'll tell him I've bought a new coat.' Amazing how gullible men could be.

'Must be lovely having so much. Can't keep track of it all.'

She finished off with some kind of spray. Humming lightly, snipping at my fringe a couple more times.

'Like a different person.'

'Thanks.'

'Now. Do you want a coffee or not?'

23   Jess

Half-ten, ready to drift off. Karen nodding on the settee before I came up. Dad on eBay, hands twitching across the keyboard, awaiting the result of a pair of Chinese figurines fished from a skip. Our entire future resting on the result.

Suddenly a loud creak on the stairs. Scraping against the wall, followed by more creaks and a groan. No effort whatsoever. Gently nudging the door, his large shadow creeping across the wall.

'You awake, sweetheart?'

'Go away.'

'Can we talk?'

I rolled over and flicked the light. He was smiling nervously, shoulders hunched.

'You know this big landscaping job I've got on? Bloody pain. Might have to leave early. One or two mornings.'

'So?'

'Need you to do something for me.'

'If it involves lying to someone about you being in the shit, forget it. Where's it going to end?' An image of you flashing through the shadows, knife blade coming towards me, blood seeping through a white cotton dress.

He perched on the bed, his weight rolling me towards him, gripping my hand. 'If you can just get to the post before Karen and save it for me. Don't let her see it if you can help it. Never suspect you, will she?'

I snatched my hand away and sat up, struggling to keep it down. 'For Christ's sake!'

'Been doing it years, what's the problem?'

'Oh great!'

'Keep it down, she's only downstairs!'

'And stop dragging Ellie into it. Karen'll kill you when she finds out.'

His head in his hands, staring at the floor, mumbling about it being the last time. The bank hassling him over a credit card he took out before Christmas. He'd promised Karen he wouldn't get another. Once he got paid for the landscaping job he'd clear the card, cut it up and she'd never know.

My English lit exam ten hours away. Feminism in *Macbeth*, W H Auden; *Wuthering Heights* rattling round my brain.

'Don't be awkward.'

'Awkward?'

'Just stop asking so many questions and trust me for once.'

'I'll tell you what's awkward. Finding Mum. Finding the truth instead of swallowing your bullshit all the time.'

'Shhh!'

'Just because I want to know exactly what happened and don't blindly trust you anymore. Karen and Ellie know more than me. Everybody knows more than me. Stop trying to make out you're confiding in me. Tell me what you're hiding, then I'll shut up.'

'Let it go, will you? If we've hidden stuff it's only because we've had to. For the best, believe me.' He nudged closer, gripping my leg through the duvet. Dark shadows under his eyes, exaggerated in the poor light. 'You know them Chinese figurines? Reckon they're fake. Should've fetched at least a hundred, only went for twenty. It'll cost that much to post 'em.'

'Sod the figurines. You've got to change before it's too late. Please tell me you know how. Please tell me you're not just as clueless as the day we ran away.'

'Remember that box room at Carol's? Condensation dripping down the window every morning? All that mould on the walls? Never thought we'd escape. Just look at us now, look what we've been through.'

I clung to him while he muttered his excuses, hopping from one subject to the next. An image of you lashing out, wild frizzy hair tumbling across your face, throwing your full weight against him, refusing to give up.

What made you so angry? Were you really as evil as everyone remembered? Was that what I remembered? Or something else nobody would allow me to consider? Soft hands running all over me after the knife attack. How could I explain that?

'Trust me, sweetheart. Won't let you down, I promise.'

I drew back to look at him straight. Taking in the deep pits under his eyes, the air of panic hanging over him. Not just money. Something else. Something far more serious.

'Obviously not going to tell me.'

'Eh?'

'Whatever you've done. It's that big. You're just going to let me find out for myself.'

His head in his hands again, muttering to himself.

*

'Don't get too downhearted. There's that many school-leavers they can pick and choose who they please. Once you've had a few rejections you'll soon get used to it.'

'Thanks, Karen. Much point getting out of bed in a morning?'

She reached out for my hand, realising she'd gone too far. 'Just reduce your expectations, that's all I'm saying. Minimum wage, part-time, zero hours. No shame in that.'

Long stifling hot summer, just like the one we ran away. In the jobcentre most mornings when not looking after Ellie, filling out application forms, trying to stretch my CV to two pages. Working out the impenetrable titles on offer, requiring qualifications I'd never heard of. Part-time resource planner. Business development team leader. Admin coordinator. Temporary data entry clerk. Miles from home so I'd have to set off at sunrise, catch five different buses and never set eyes on my family again.

'This is what it's like. Difficult economic times.' She paused to swipe the last slice of toast. 'And I don't see why you're getting up so early either. Makes no sense.'

I glanced over her head towards the front door. Dad already cleared off with a large, exaggerated wink behind her back. How could I get there first? What if I didn't?

'Just habit. Can't stay in bed all day.'

'Crikey. Call yourself a teenager?'

I stared into my cornflakes, savouring every mouthful. Potentially nothing the rest of the day. The end of the week equally uncertain. Karen about to scarper and leave me to it.

A few minutes later – or perhaps half an hour – I glanced up and felt my stomach flip. Karen heading for the door, humming lightly. A single brown envelope on the mat. I stood up, intent on reaching the stairs before she opened it. Too late to help him now.

'Where you going, young lady?'

She thrust the envelope towards me. I took it reluctantly, staring at the name behind the window. Miss Jessica Sharpe. The weird sensation of holding a letter that wasn't Dad's.

'Well?'

I tore it open and slid out the single sheet. The admin assistant job I'd applied for three weeks ago, the only one within walking distance, full-time, two quid above minimum wage.

'They want me to come for an interview next week. I've got to ring.'

'Christ.' She sounded gutted. I wouldn't be joining her at the bakery any time soon. 'Can but try, can't you?'

'You mean I've no chance?'

'Don't be so negative. It's all good experience. Hardly likely to succeed in a first interview, are you?'

I sat on the stairs and messaged Dad. Told him there was no post and even more importantly I'd got an interview. Followed by Chloe, hopefully making her a tiny bit jealous even if she'd never admit it. Finally Carol, asking if she'd do my hair, get it under control at last. I couldn't afford to mess it up over something stupid.

Then felt suddenly deflated as Karen rushed into the kitchen and noisily filled the sink. Didn't she realise what it meant? That it had the potential to finally turn our lives around?

Why had I spent so long in the company of somebody who'd never be my mother, pretending to be her daughter, making out we both cared? Whatever you were like these days, however violent, surely you'd feel something? Surely you were real if nothing else?

I clutched the letter, staring at the words till they blurred into a solid mass. Could this be the moment that somehow made sense of it all? Made sense of our relationship. One of those landmark moments we'd both been waiting for, impossible to ignore. Finally flushing you out of my dim and distant childhood, forcing you to pay attention for the first time. A moment that could finally bring us together.

*

The Quality Storage Box Company. A large anonymous warehouse wedged into the corner of an industrial estate, a discreet black-and-white sign above the doorway. I'd never been in a reception on my own. What if I went to the wrong place or asked the wrong person? We never practised at school, probably because it would've been useful. Concentrating instead on fractions, ratios and the English Civil War, pretending they'd come in handy later in life.

Tumbleweed scuttling across the beige carpet tiles. I'd pictured it a million times. About to be ignored. The first person ever to turn up for an interview yet miss it at the same time.

A half-open door behind the desk, leading into an office, the low rumble of voices above a radio. Talk of statements, invoices and a customer's overdue account. The kind of people who'd sneer at Dad for not understanding.

'Can I help?' A woman in the doorway. Small and dumpy with round glasses, in a dark blue stretchy dress.

'Hello, sorry if I'm early, my name's Jessica Sharpe and I'm here for a job interview for admin assistant at half-ten.' No idea if that was how an adult normally spoke in a reception or if there was something obvious I'd missed. The woman looking at me a fraction too long before consulting a list in front of her, as if I was that strange creature she wouldn't normally have to deal with. A school-leaver.

'Right, have a seat, you're a bit early. He'll call you through when he's ready.'

I sat down and tried to breathe. Roasting hot, not surprising considering I was coated in 99% nylon, courtesy of Karen. She'd treated me to a charity-shop trouser suit and scratchy white blouse.

God knows why I was panicking, as if I'd ever get the job. A water cooler at my elbow. Unsure whether it was appropriate to help myself, especially with the woman watching, unsmiling. Like walking a tightrope, destined to fall one way or the other. On one side, acceptance and entry into the adult world, on the other, utter humiliation and rejection.

We sat in silence for five hours. A million miles from school. Chloe and Hannah, Sara and Lucy. Occasionally studying my nails while the blue stretchy-dress woman flicked noisily through paperwork. At school there was always some kind of commotion. I was either doing something right or doing something wrong. Asking what to do next or being told what to do next. Was this the real horror of the adult world that nobody mentioned? Endless silence. Waiting in receptions. No reassurance you were doing the right thing.

Suddenly a commotion. Rapid footsteps down a corridor at right angles to the desk. A tall dark-haired man appeared with a young blonde woman walking a few steps in front, as if he was hurrying her along, unhappy with her pace. She was dressed like me, in a stiff dark suit, a hint of redness to her cheeks. He had rolled up shirt sleeves and a pen jutting out of his hand that looked as if it was always there. He was born in an office and missed out school altogether. And straight away it was obvious he was busy and important, far too busy and important to be wasting time on me.

'Thank you, we'll be in touch.'

He saw the woman out the door with a firm handshake and turned straight towards me in one swift movement, not wasting a second. I stood up and immediately felt like sinking back down. The first adult I'd ever met in my life.

'Hi. Richard. Pleased to meet you. This way please.'

I shook his hand (actually I allowed him to shake mine without joining in), fighting the urge to make an excuse and run back to school, never coming near the place again. Too late. He'd already looked me straight in the eye, forcing me to break contact first, a hard searching stare as if committing my face to memory.

He led me down the corridor to a large office at one end, overlooking an empty yard surrounded by fencing. Vaguely aware of being spied upon as I walked past open doors. Two or three people at least, craning for a better view.

His desk the size of three normal ones pushed together. Covered in stacks of paper, yellow Post-it notes and brightly coloured plastic storage boxes of different sizes, neat and orderly. Each stack labelled, some beside his keyboard as if he'd been working on them, others pushed to the edge of the desk, concealed in brown files. On one corner, contrasting against the paperwork, a large silver photo frame containing a photo of a blonde woman staring steadily at the camera. A vague impression of intense blue eyes and perfect creamy skin. The eyes following me as I pulled out a chair and dared to sit.

'Now. Let's have a look at your application form.' Flicking through a pile of paperwork, nodding slowly. 'Very impressive. So you've had some accounting experience since leaving school. Used to work at Jenkins, we've dealt with them for many years. Probably spoken on the phone before now.' Running his pen down the paper, rapidly underlining a couple of sentences in red. 'We had someone from Jenkins here before. Alan Shepherd? Quality supervisor before he moved on. Then you worked at Shawbrooke's surgery as receptionist, so obviously a confident telephone manner. Followed by two years at Johnson & Co. Excellent. Probably overqualified if anything. Might find this a bit basic to what you're used to.'

I didn't like to interrupt but couldn't help butting in with the words, 'Sorry?' Clearly mixing me up with somebody who'd done something with their life. Karen would piss herself. 'I think there's been a mistake.'

He flicked a page, tapping his pen repeatedly. 'You're not Sally Cross?'

'No.'

'Course not, far too young.' Leafing through the pile. 'Sarah Wilson? Andrea Jacobs? Jessica Sharpe?'

I nodded,

He pressed a button on his phone. 'Deborah? Thought I told you to call in Sally Cross, who worked for Jenkins and Shawbrooke's? This is Jessica Sharpe.'

'Oh goodness, I thought I'd written it all down. I'm sure I did.' A long pause. 'Want me to give her a ring now?'

'Too late, forget it.' Ending the call, his shoulders tense. 'Sorry about that, had so much on the last few weeks with this big contract in Poland. Only got back in the country last night. Left instructions for the interviews to be set up. Obviously too difficult to contact the right person.'

'Do you want me to go?' I crossed my fingers under the desk. I could rush home, get changed and meet Chloe in McDonalds. Who cared if we starved to death?

He looked up sharply, tapping his pen. 'Certainly not, unless you want to. I assume you want the job, otherwise you wouldn't have applied?' At the same time retrieving my application form from the bottom of the pile, nodding in silence while skimming the page. 'Ah yes, it's coming back to me now.'

I tried to remember what I'd put, while he fixed on a spot somewhere over my shoulder and launched into a speech he'd obviously come out with loads of times. 'What we're looking for is somebody who can fit into the environment we've got here, which is a very busy, dynamic environment. A quick learner, obviously, who can pick up on the necessary skills and fill in where appropriate, assist various departments where there's a shortage.' Glancing down again, rubbing his eyes, the pen still jutting from his hand. 'So I'll shut up and perhaps you'd like to tell me a bit about yourself to start with.'

I started mumbling what I'd prepared. Was it appropriate to talk about younger sisters in a job interview? I'd never met anyone whose stare was so intense, working me out, refusing to blink in case he wasted time. 'I'm eighteen. Live with my dad and stepmum, Karen. Got a younger sister called Ellie. Eight GCSEs. Just taken three A levels but I've not had the results yet. That's about it really.'

'Okay.' He'd rather have Sally Cross but was making the most of it. 'And is there any particular skill you feel you'd be able to bring to the job? For example, we have to work to tight deadlines sometimes. Customers nagging that we've not met a delivery date and they might lose a contract because of it. How do you think you'd cope with that? A stressful situation?'

'I've been brought up by my dad, which I suppose you could say was stressful. Or it's probably more appropriate to say we've grown up together since we left my mum.'

'Right.'

'And I've been working with him over the last few weeks since leaving school. He's got his own maintenance business.'

Leaning forward, sneaking a glance at his watch. 'Okay, doing what exactly? What kind of situations have you been in that might help you in dealing with customers here? Any examples?'

I paused. Plenty of examples but probably not the kind he was used to. What would you do in my place? Speak your mind of course.

'Dad's totally useless at decorating. You can guarantee if there's something that doesn't need covering in paint he'll find it. And everywhere that should be covered in paint he'll usually overlook. We had to paint a customer's bathroom the other day and he managed to knock the tin over this really expensive set of bathroom scales. He hadn't put any sheets down because he couldn't be bothered. He's really clumsy in other people's houses. And the owner was coming back at dinner to check up and I had to somehow stop her from coming into the bathroom while he cleaned up.'

'Right.'

'So I kept her talking while Pete, that's my dad's mate, nipped out to buy some new scales. I wasted all her dinner break asking her about shoes because it was obvious she had this obsession, they were everywhere. By the time I'd finished she'd forgotten about checking the bathroom and went straight back to work.'

'And this kind of thing is quite normal for your dad?'

'It's unusual for anything to go right. Do you want more examples?'

'Why not? Just remember to give me your dad's business name so I can avoid him if I need any work doing.'

'He's not likely to work for someone like you.'

'Someone like me?' Pulling back slightly, eyebrows raised.

I hesitated, choosing my words carefully. Tempted to call him posh, not entirely sure how he'd take it. 'He tends to work for people who want a few corners cutting, so they get what they've paid for. Or people who don't know him. When I was little I used to go to work with him on a Saturday morning because we had no choice. I had to stay in the van with the doors locked. Sometimes if he upset someone, which was most weeks, I used to get out the van and stand between Dad and the customer, just to give him chance to put his point across. The customer couldn't get angry if I was stood there. They'd feel sorry for me. Dad would gradually manoeuvre himself towards the van and we'd escape, so I'm pretty good at talking people round and making excuses. That's how we've survived.'

'You're saying he used to hide behind a small child to avoid the wrath of his customers?'

'If you want to put it like that.'

'Anything else? Anything that might come in handy?'

He was obviously laughing at me, laughing at Dad (I couldn't blame him), laughing at our sad lives. Hard to tell, his expression so tricky to read. No idea how old he was. Talking as if he was twice my age. Thirty perhaps.

'I've got plenty of phone experience. I've always spoken to Dad's suppliers and customers if he doesn't want to speak to them.'

'Because he owes money?'

'How did you guess?'

'Just a hunch. And what sort of things do you have to tell his suppliers and customers?'

'That he's out the country or broke his leg. That he'd once fallen through a conservatory roof and slipped into a coma. Dad said I'd gone too far. He was forced to make a miraculous recovery next time he saw them.'

He threw his pen onto the desk and leaned back. 'Sounds like a character. Not sure I'd want him painting my front room, however.' Glancing at the paperwork. 'GCSE grades aren't too bad, nothing special but not disastrous either. A levels still to come through. I'm not sure. I appreciate your honesty. Tend to hear the same old stuff on these occasions. Anything else?'

Perhaps it was because Dad was uppermost in my thoughts. Perhaps because the mint-green paint had trashed my trainers, and nobody had offered to buy me a new pair. Perhaps it was you above all else. I couldn't go back to working with Dad and Pete, forever bailing him out, especially when he wasn't even aware I was doing it half the time.

So I asked a few grown-up questions, not because I was bothered about the answers but because they were the kind that would hopefully get me the job. With a bit of luck they'd convince him I could be normal if I was pushed to it.

He was about to say something when the phone rang. He pressed a button without picking up the receiver. Looking directly at me.

'Yes?'

'Your eleven o'clock appointment's waiting in reception. He's been waiting fifteen minutes.'

'I'll be through in a minute, Deborah.'

He stood up and reached across to shake my hand. The smile vanished, back to business. Had I stepped out of line and made a fool of myself?

'We'll be in touch, Jessica. Been a pleasure meeting you. I'm afraid the accountant's here.'

I stood up quick, not wanting to piss him off. Hurrying back down the corridor, exactly like the blonde woman before me, Richard two steps behind. In reception a tall, suited man paced up and down. Richard shook his hand warmly, sharing a joke about the weather and last night's England game. Blue stretchy-dress woman still perched behind the desk, Deborah presumably, eyeing me coldly as I passed. I wondered whether to say goodbye or thank her. Just as I'd decided she turned her back and disappeared into the office behind the desk.

Half an hour later I got home, red-faced and exhausted, as if I'd been away a month. Karen followed me upstairs as I unpeeled the nylon jacket and blouse.

'Any good?'

'They said they'll be in touch.' I shrugged. 'I'm not sure I'm what they're looking for. He'd probably spend all day laughing at me and taking the piss.'

'He?'

'The man who interviewed me.'

She patted my arm and met my gaze in the mirror. 'Well I think you looked very professional. What did you tell him?'

'The usual crap; about working with Dad. Had no choice. Had to give examples.'

'Jess! What the hell did you do that for? So you have blown it then?'

She put the suit on a hanger, picking off invisible bits of fluff. I felt like bursting into tears.

'Karen? Think you can help with my scar? Help me cover it up every day so nobody would guess it was there?'

She spun round, eyebrows raised. 'I thought you weren't bothered by it. Never have been before.'

'The man who interviewed me…'

'What?'

I didn't even sound like myself. 'He seemed to see straight through me. I just don't think people should have to look at it all day. Not right, is it?'

24   Lisa

Alex had never managed to find me. He'd never loitered in the
street beneath my mouldy flat window, plotting his way back
into our lives. Whenever the phone rang it was never likely to
be him. Whenever somebody came to the door or brushed past
me in the street.

I would've escaped Park Field sooner if things had been
clearer from the start. People crowding my bed and frowning
over paperwork, determined to find something. That nagging
feeling of using up somebody's precious time, ill for the sake of it.

August lasting eight weeks, followed by three months
disappearing in one go. A whole year barely happening. The
Virginia creeper outside the window like a time-lapse video on
a nature show. One minute struggling for life; twig branches
clinging to pockmarked walls, next minute obscuring the glass;
blackbirds and sparrows jostling near the top. Measuring my
life by it. If the creeper was moving at such a pace, if nobody
could stop it, what about Jess and Ray?

I didn't miss any of it. Only the option of being there. Not
too many questions because it was clear I was sick of them
and couldn't handle them well. Turning down the volume on
life itself. Ignoring whatever was happening in the world and
thinking only of number one. Disappearing for weeks on end,
everybody accepting it as the norm because that was what the
place was for.

Dr Williamson trying to convince me there was no shame in it and that it needn't define my whole life. I could live with it and learn to manage it. Softly spoken, with brown eyes that promised not to judge.

Alex had never been in danger of being one step ahead. Pretty obvious these days. Unlike Jess and her sudden thirst for knowledge. Her growing maturity. Her right to know the truth. Who would've thought that one day I'd have far more to fear from my own daughter than I ever had from him?

*

'What if she gets hold of her birth certificate? You can send off for a copy these days; even Pete's done it, it's that easy.'

I perched on the bottom step and gripped the phone, trying to remain calm. Glancing over my shoulder, Harrison's nightlight spilling onto the landing. He was too young to understand even if he did wake up. A few more years, however, what then?

'You're seriously telling me this is the first time you've ever considered it? Seriously, Ray. You hadn't thought of it before?'

'Not just my responsibility, is it? Can't say it's all down to me.'

'So you can't remember the state I was in? If I'd been capable of thinking straight, do you think you'd have her in the first place? You said you knew what you were doing, you were the cocky one, not me.'

She'd found a job. Some kind of office work. Innocent enough on the surface perhaps, but this was how it started. Next would come the questions and curiosity, the outside interference. I couldn't even text in case it prompted her to rush round.

We had to accept she was far quicker than either of us had imagined. In Ray's mind she was still that little girl he used to scrabble with in the backyard, keeping her occupied, keeping her safe. Loving her all the more for having found someone unexpectedly on his own level. While Jess loved him for being permanently grubby, for letting her do whatever she liked. In that twelve-foot square patch there were no rules and no fear. A chance for normality, chance for Jess to rule. Playing hide-and-seek while he pretended not to see her feet poking out from behind the shed. A perfect match.

'Listening? Might have to go away on business soon, once she starts this job. Why don't you…'

'What?' I snapped.

'Break it to her gently? Just the two of you. She'll accept it then, won't she? You know how mature she is.'

'So when you get back it's all sorted? So I face the worst of it?'

'Don't tell her everything, obviously, just the basics. You've got to at some point. Can't keep sticking your head in the sand. Then you can explain to Jim at the same time, might as well.'

He was totally mad. I tried to steady my voice. 'You're her dad, whether you like it or not. The only dad she's ever known. You took on that role, you can't give it back now just because she's smarter than you and sees through you.'

He went so quiet I thought he'd rung off. God knows what he was thinking or what he was about to do. Perhaps he'd done it already. I glanced upstairs. Harrison still asleep. Or was he? Even at his age, they started doing things without always telling you. Perhaps Jess had done the same. What if he suddenly burst out with it one day and blamed me for everything?

'Listen. It may have escaped your notice, but I've got my own life now. Jess is practically grown up. If she needed me when she was little, she certainly doesn't now. I know you're in trouble, I know you're struggling. I'll send you another two hundred but that's an end of it. Please. Enough.'

Before he had chance for another word I ended the call.

25   Jess

'Just a quick tidy up? Nothing too drastic?'

Carol's gloomy back room, overlooking the poky yard that grew pokier on every visit. Two wall lights switched on even in summer. Spot the difference since Dad first carried me in, bloody and sobbing. Same flowery green carpet, same textured magnolia walls, same cream two-seater Dad snored himself to sleep on, even the same low coffee table where she served all my meals with a sharp slap. Why hadn't I set eyes on any of it before that day?

'Excited?' she asked.

'Would be if Dad and Karen hadn't already spent half my wages.'

'Only half? Slipping, aren't they?'

She snipped in silence, mouthful of grips. She'd already slipped me fifty quid to buy a new suit, confident nobody else would. Meticulously planned as always, a bit weird but thoughtful at the same time. Typical Carol. If I fancied driving lessons there might even be a bit more. She'd pay for the first five if I could sort the rest.

'Why keep all my old stuff? After all this time? There's no need, just chuck it.'

She straightened up and glanced towards the plastic crate blocking the corner near the fireplace. Old books, cuddly toys, board games. I couldn't remember the last time I even glanced at them. She hadn't kept them for Ellie's sake, who had plenty of new stuff and no time for any of mine.

'Habit. Never got round to throwing it out, that's all.'

Her spare bedroom – the one I cowered in when we ran away – had a bed permanently made up, on constant standby. Less confidence in Dad than ever. My old school pictures dotting the walls, scribbled drawings dedicated specially to her. Despite the fact I'd only slept over three or four times the last few years, once when Karen and Ellie went to see *Lion King* in London, the rest when Dad was working away.

Almost as if I lived here, my eight-year-old self skipping happily in the yard, poised to skip back in. Although that sounded sentimental, which she'd hate.

Humming under her breath. In a decent mood for once. Surely the right time to jump in and blurt it out quick, especially now I'd found a job. At least she didn't ignore the past. She didn't pretend you dropped dead the second we walked out the door. She remembered the day we first burst into her house, begging for help. She'd held it against us ever since.

'For God's sake, don't tell them I've given you that money. Hide it somewhere or spend it quick.'

'I've stuck it under my bottom drawer.' A long pause. 'Carol? You know our old house? Where we used to live?'

'Not really.'

'Just thinking the other day of the backyard. Practically lived in it, trying to escape Mum.'

'Another half inch?'

I stood up and glanced in the mirror. 'Go on then.' Sinking back down. 'Ever wanted to go back somewhere you knew when you were little?'

'Not really. Lived on this street most of my life. Two different houses,' she muttered. Something else she'd never mentioned before. 'Where's this leading?'

I took a deep breath. All Chloe's idea, which meant it

sounded simple but, in reality, was near impossible with my family. 'Can you give me the address so I can go back and have a nosey? I know somebody else is probably living there but I'd still like to look, and you know what Dad's like, he'll pretend he's forgotten or that it's for my own good. I'll not tell him you've told me. Just between us. I won't do anything daft, I promise.'

She snipped patiently, concentrating round the back so I couldn't see her face. About to rush to the phone and ring Dad. Seeing his point of view, sticking together after all. Leaving school and finding a job making no difference whatsoever.

'Not asking you to do anything, just give me the address. I'll find my own way there. Dad and Karen won't ever know, what harm is there?'

She finished snipping and eventually laid the scissors and hair grips on the mantel, caught in two minds.

'I think I'd know the house if I saw it again, just the street. Keep thinking Thomas Street or Taylor Avenue. If I hear the name I'll know it.'

'I'll think about it.'

'You mean you'll ask Dad.'

'Didn't say that did I?'

'You ever been?'

'Don't be daft.'

'Not even once?'

'What on earth for? Mouldy old place. Heard enough about it from your dad.'

Also a bit weird but said as if it was obvious. That first part of my life completely divorced from the second, Carol firmly belonging to the second.

She dragged the vacuum cleaner from under the stairs, rapidly sucking frizzy hairs off the carpet. The sound drowning any potential for more conversation, whether I was ready for it or not.

*

I treated myself to a non-nylon trouser suit with Carol's money, as a result feeling slightly more confident walking into *The Quality Storage Box* reception Monday morning, except for the fact I'd skipped breakfast again. A straight choice between me and Ellie. A slice of toast for her versus small sandwich for me. The tears, the accusations, the potential for slammed doors. Far easier to just cave in without a fuss.

What if they thought I was weird? That I'd chosen to be this way? One outfit to last the week, no packed lunch, skint until pay day.

This was my chance to show Dad and Karen it could be done. We didn't have to boomerang between triumph and disaster. It was possible to ensure there was enough credit on the meter to last a full month, not one week of extravagance followed by three weeks of panic. Perfectly possible to pay in notes rather than raid an eight-year-old's piggy bank. If we needed a pint of milk or loaf of bread we didn't need to ring Carol and drop heavy hints, we could go to a shop and buy it like everyone else.

I found the dumpy woman perched behind reception again, flicking through a magazine and sipping coffee, wearing the same stretchy dress. I noted her blue name tag with 'Deborah' on it, beside a tiny picture of a storage box.

'Oh there you are,' she said, peering over her glasses, as if I was ten minutes late instead of ten minutes early. 'Obviously didn't put you off then.'

No idea what to call her. She was older than Karen and Dad. Probably rip my head off for getting it wrong.

She licked her finger and flicked another page. Some kind of home magazine, the type loved by Auntie Maggie. Smug couples in the country, posing in front of vast conservatories.

'I think I've remembered everything.' I delved into my leather bag, borrowed from Karen because I only owned a rucksack. National Insurance number, proof of address, GCSE certificates and another copy of my CV in case they lost the first.

'Oh we won't be needing those just yet. Go and sit in that office, the one next to Richard's. You'll be in there for the time being I should think.' Nodding in a vague direction.

I walked hesitantly down the corridor, the same one I went down for the interview, aware she was watching my back closely, desperate for a mistake. Holding my head high. Determined she wasn't going to take it from me. Nobody was.

I entered the only office with an open door. A large room with one external window overlooking a yard and one internal window looking into Richard's darkened office, which I instantly noticed was empty, his black leather swivel chair still bearing the imprint of his body.

Two people perched quietly, a man and woman at large separate desks. I got the impression they were mumbling quietly before they heard my footsteps, both looking up simultaneously as I stood in the doorway.

The man stood up to introduce himself. 'Ed. Nice to meet you. Welcome to the company.' Somewhere in his thirties, with an instantly forgettable face, round and freckly.

The woman was called Jo. Roughly the same age. Reminded me of a meerkat peering over the top of her screen to see what was going on, afraid somebody might be having a better time. Craning to glance at my shoes, my tatty old school ones I'd had over three years, as I tried to hide them behind my bag.

'Make yourself at home.' Eyes sweeping across my hair. 'We've cleared your desk as best we can. I know it's a bit basic but once you get settled we can change a few things. Should do for now.'

I slid onto the chair and instantly became aware that if Richard was in his office I'd be sat facing him, with nowhere to hide.

'You can shift your computer if you like. We just left it there because that's where Andy used to have it.'

Andrew Doyle scribbled several times across a large notepad beside the phone. Also two or three cartoon sketches of somebody who could be Jo, a woman with a stretchy neck and bulgy eyes. Assuming she wasn't aware of it I plonked my bag on top.

'First job?' Ed checked, raising his eyebrows. 'School-leaver?'

I nodded, trying to make it look natural. I hadn't been crapping myself all night.

Jo shaking her head, rocking back in her chair. 'Wow. I can't remember what it felt like on my first day. Ed started here just after the Norman Conquest.'

'Jo came over with the Romans. Fancy some cake for later?'

He pulled a slab of chocolate cake from his drawer, tightly wrapped in foil, waving it under my nose. As if taking the mickey, ready to snatch it back.

'What's wrong? You allergic? Actually, it might have nuts in it.'

'Thanks.' I took a piece; on the basis it could be the only thing I ate all day. 'Did you make it?'

'Course.'

'Er, no,' Jo butted in, grabbing some herself. 'You'll soon get fat if you stay here. I put on a stone in the first two months thanks to Ed's mum.'

He told me where the toilets were and how to get to the kitchen, back down the corridor and on the opposite side, so I'd have to sneak past reception again. 'I have black coffee. Jo has tea, milk no sugar. If you want milk you've got to bring your own.'

I nibbled at the cake, relishing every mouthful melting on my tongue. Ed's lunch box perched on the corner of his desk. Even through the milky plastic it looked amazing, enough to feed all three of us. Jo smiling as she watched. Could she tell?

Half-eight in the morning, stuffing my face. Had Richard told her about the interview? Chuckling behind my back for the last two weeks.

I glanced towards his office and the empty swivel chair half facing the wall, as if he'd leapt out of it five minutes since.

'In Belgium at a trade fair. He comes and goes, don't worry. He'll be out all week.'

Which made me feel miles better, not realising I'd been slightly holding my breath. By the time he returned I'd have rearranged my desk so I could keep my back to him.

'Do you know what I'm supposed to be doing? Nobody's really explained properly.'

'Don't worry, we'll not let Deborah get her teeth in. I've got some envelope stuffing; Ed's got some filing. But first things first, let's have a drink.' Jo wandered past my desk and paused in front of Ed. 'Isn't she sweet? Can you remember when you were that young and innocent?'

'I was never that young and innocent.' Busy peering into his family-size lunch box. 'Oh great, that's all I need. Two sodding wagon wheels and more cake. Jess? Don't suppose you can manage a bit more?'

26 Lisa

'Just thought you would've mentioned it. Normally do.'

Six hundred. When most of the time it was fifty here or there.

'Another handbag?'

'Sorry?'

'That black jacket you wore the other day?'

'Jim?'

'Don't worry, it's not an interrogation. Just curious, that's all.'

He was too absorbed in his tablet to pay much attention. I couldn't remember the last time he noticed what I had to say. At some point he'd stopped prying. Would I be grateful when the time came?

'Just bits and pieces. Couple of tops, pair of silver earrings, some trousers for Harrison for school, birthday present for... '

'Alright, alright, just surprised when I saw the statement, that's all.'

'Can we go away somewhere?'

'Eh?'

'Anywhere, I don't care.'

'I've told you, far too busy at the moment.'

I settled against his shoulder. He rubbed my arm and pulled me close to shut me up. If I told him about Jess he'd never trust another word.

'Oh that reminds me. Somebody rang while you were in the shower last night. Ray? Something to do with…'

'On the landline?'

'The one with two girls?'

'Carol's brother, I've told you.' My heart bursting to life.

'He wouldn't leave a message, in a right panic. He always like that?'

'I sometimes go for a coffee with his wife, Karen. She keeps asking me about Harrison's ADHD. She's worried about her daughter in case she's got the same thing.' Too much detail perhaps. Was it as bad as too little?

He kissed the top of my head. 'I've told you, it's more common than you think. Give her the specialist's name.'

Ellie. ADHD. One day he'd ask for an update and I'd have no idea what he was talking about. If he thought about it, really thought about it, he'd want to know the exact connection I had with these people. Where we met, why we kept in touch, why they seemed to keep ringing out the blue. Saving it all for later, when the truth emerged, his dreams shattered and his trust misplaced. Saving it all for the right time.

27   Jess

'What's wrong?'

'Obviously a mistake.'

'Mistake?'

'It doesn't add up.'

'Why? You reckon it should be more?'

I stared at the figure in the bottom right-hand corner, struggling to picture it, let alone figure out what to do with it. Jo watching my reddened face. She could tell.

'Don't worry, you'll soon get used to it.' She laughed. 'Couple of months and it won't seem nearly enough.'

Another landmark, staring back at me in black and white, my first payslip. Proof that I couldn't always be ignored. Nudging me closer towards you, whatever the outcome.

I scribbled out a long list of things to buy and things to do. A leather handbag like Jo's, a grown-up bag that told everyone I'd left school and was working. Ditching my scruffy old clothes, no longer looking like my old self. I didn't have to be the old Jess the rest of my life. I could choose to be smart and confident, hardworking and successful. Anything but the grubby child you recalled.

I didn't have to wait for somebody else to make the decision. Or wonder how I got there, how it came about. I could sort it myself and take charge.

I'd even take Chloe for a meal to celebrate our exam results.

I'd pay for everything without even glancing at the prices. Two B's and a C, not as bad as I feared, though Chloe naturally did miles better: three A's and a B, easily enough to study child psychology on any course she liked.

I'd buy both Carol and Maggie a small gift each, my first chance to say thanks for all they'd done over the years. Maggie bursting into tears, overcome with emotion. Carol shaking her head whilst secretly caring ten times more, but only after I'd gone.

And most of all I'd buy some bread, milk, cheese, eggs and teabags, because the everyday stuff was important and should never be left till last. Planning was important. Making lists and sticking to them. I'd buy enough for pack-up to last a full week. Ensure Ellie always had enough. Sanitary towels and food. She'd never have to choose. Dad and Karen gobsmacked and hopefully embarrassed. I'd even tuck something away in a savings account. It didn't have to be much, just a couple of hundred. I wouldn't tell anyone, except perhaps Ellie to put her mind at rest because I knew she worried far more than she let on. Above all else, I'd be prepared.

*

All of this swirling round my head as I walked home from work on a warm Friday evening in August. Rounding the final corner, glancing towards the house. Used to seeing Dad's van on the drive, some kind of commotion connected to the end of the week. Either Pete awaiting his money or Dad trying to distract him with the *Racing Post* and a tip for Newmarket the next day.

The drive empty, no sign of either. Probably working late or nipped into town to place a bet. I quickened up. An unfamiliar large blue van parked smack in front of the house, empty and unmarked. Figures moving rapidly in the front room, flitting across the window. Something to do with you. Somebody come to break the news, to let me down gently. My legs weakening, my heart bursting to life.

I nudged the door and found chaos in front of me. Karen sobbing in the kitchen doorway, her whole body heaving and rolling like a ship on a stormy ocean. From her streaky face she'd been at it hours. Craig from next door standing beside her, his arm snaked round her shoulders, his face pushed into hers, pulling her far closer than Dad had done in years. Trying to press a mug of tea into her hands.

'Take a small sip at least and you'll feel better.'

'Can't, Craig, I can't even think about it.'

Two dark-haired men in uniform wandering round the front room with clipboards, scribbling urgently. Ellie following one about like a terrier – the smaller of the two, obviously confident she could take him on – shouting abuse. Still in her school uniform, Pokémon blaring in the background. Every so often he paused in front of something – the new 3D telly, my Xbox, the dining table, Karen's antique sideboard inherited from her gran – while Ellie did her best to block his view, dancing round his legs.

'That's my sister's Xbox, fat pig. Don't you dare touch my sister's things. When my dad gets home he's going to smash your face in.'

'Just move out the way please, young lady. Not exactly helping the cause. To be honest, Rick, apart from a couple of things there's not much here. Think we might struggle. Can you please move out the way?' He glanced helplessly at his colleague. 'Is anybody in control of this child? Anybody?'

'Told you, these are our things and we've paid for them. Sod off and buy your own like everybody else.'

'Ellie, what the hell's going on?'

She left the Xbox and ran towards me, tears trailing flushed cheeks, jabbing her finger repeatedly at my chest. 'Jess, these men are taking all our stuff; they're after my laptop because it's worth something and they've been looking at your Xbox and all your games. Tell them, they won't listen to me.' Like a miniature Karen, filled with rage, pausing to flash a look of pure hatred over her shoulder. 'I've hidden Angry Birds down my top. If he touches my laptop I'll break his leg.'

'Okay, okay, it's alright. Everything's alright.'

'I will.'

'Calm down.'

'Ring the police. They can't touch our things, they can't just walk in. Ring the police, Jess.'

I pulled her close, pressing her face against my chest. Angry Birds digging in. I'd never seen her so upset, even the day she knocked out her two front teeth at Alton Towers. Sensing some great injustice, her whole body trembling, her little face looking up at me to do something.

'Tossers! Get off my sister's stuff! Not yours, is it?'

'Calm down. Where the hell's Dad?'

'Don't know. Craig's in the kitchen with Mum.'

I dragged her into the kitchen as she cast a final glance over her shoulder at the Xbox. Karen still sobbing, Craig still trying to press a mug of tea into her hands, milking the situation for all it was worth. Rubbing her back in a slow circular motion.

'Jess! Where the hell have you been? Got the bloody bailiffs round now!'

'Bailiffs?'

'Bailiffs! Those two men in the living room are bloody bailiffs! And where's your dad as usual?'

'I don't know. At work, presumably. Anybody rung him?'

'I'm pretty certain,' Craig butted in, keeping his voice low and gentle, 'I saw Ray drive into the close half an hour ago, turn round and drive off again. I'm sure it was his van. Could almost swear to it.'

'Oh wonderful!'

'I can't be absolutely certain because he was going so fast when he spun round but I'm sure it was his logo on the side and

I'm sure I saw Pete in the passenger seat waving at me. Seemed to think it was funny for some reason. In quite a hurry.'

'I bet he bloody was. He'll be in a damn hurry when I catch up with him. Owes the builder's merchants over three grand. Three grand! Owed them months and never said a word. Did you know of it?'

'Course not. Don't blame me and Ellie. Not our fault, is it? Why doesn't somebody ring him and get him back here?' I turned away to the sink, staring through the conservatory, seeing nothing.

Craig laid a gentle hand on my arm, making me shiver. 'To be fair we've all tried. Even Ellie's left a voicemail message. He doesn't seem to want to come home for some reason. Don't think there's any point ringing again, do you?'

I yanked my arm away and tried to collect my thoughts. Karen reeling off a list of all the stuff she'd do to Dad when he returned. Ellie reeling off a list of all the stuff she'd do to the bailiffs if they tried to leave with anything.

All my fault. I'd helped him hide so much over the years, especially the last few months. Turning it into a game. Half the time pretending to be asleep so as not to embarrass him. Why hadn't I questioned him more? I should've known he was out of his depth. Hadn't he always been?

My wage slip languishing in my bag, meaningless after all. Back to being that little girl again, helpless and insignificant, unable to change a thing.

'I'll have a word with them.'

'Who?' Karen snapped.

'Bailiffs, who else? Has anybody actually spoken to them yet? Maybe we can negotiate, just pay something and owe the rest.'

'Jess, are you living in the real world? We've no money at all. Nothing. Had to pay the TV licence this morning, got a fiver in my purse. Don't think that's likely to make much of a dent in three grand, is it?'

Craig suddenly piped up. 'Really love to help but I've got a tax bill to settle at the end of the month and it's a bit tight at the moment. You know how it is.'

Ellie grabbing my arm, trying to drag me back towards the front room. 'We've got to keep an eye on them, I don't trust them.'

'Not a game, we're not playing hide-and-seek. They're just doing their job, it's not their fault. Can't blame them personally.'

'I can.'

'It's Dad's fault; he's the one who owes money.'

'You keep them talking and I'll run upstairs with your Xbox and hide it in my wardrobe. Then come back down and get my laptop if you can distract them.'

I grabbed her hand and pulled her towards the stairs. 'Go up to your room and stay there till I call you. I promise they won't take your laptop.'

'But, Jess…'

'Now! Trust me, Ellie.'

'What about your Xbox?'

'Sod the Xbox.'

She stomped upstairs and paused at the top.

'In your room!'

'Okay, okay.' She disappeared, leaving her door open a crack. Stomped about a bit more, then threw something heavy on the floor. I got the uncomfortable feeling she was hunting for a weapon.

The two bailiffs still examining the front room. One near the window, calmly scribbling notes. The other, Ellie's nemesis, in front of the fireplace scratching his chin, unsure how to deal with us. A name badge on his chest. Sam Lewis.

'Sorry, I don't really understand what this is about. It's my dad you're after. I've got some money on me if you'll accept it, I just don't want you taking the laptop though; it's my sister's and she uses it for school. If you have to take something, take the Xbox or the telly.'

'Shall we sit down?' He perched on the sofa, waiting for me to settle. 'Let's start with the paperwork first.' Glancing at my suit, trying to convince himself I was old enough. 'Might be best if we speak to your mum, perhaps?'

'She's not my mum.' Karen still screeching at Craig, who was trying his best to calm her down. 'It's me or no one. Dad won't be home for ages.'

He showed me paperwork that listed the complete details of the debt, how old it was and how much. Over three grand going back almost a year. I read in silence; the whole thing vaguely familiar.

'We're here to seize goods to the value of the debt unless you can pay us something today. Don't worry about the laptop. We're not going to take anything belonging to you or your sister. Only interested in taking what belongs to your dad.'

Karen's voice floating through, drowning Craig's gentle tones. Threatening to ring her mother. Reveal everything Dad had been up to over the last ten years, not shielding him anymore. He was an arsehole and the whole world needed to know.

I grabbed my bag and took out my new purse. Beautiful soft brown leather, replacing the battered old coin purse I'd had years. I withdrew three hundred on the way home, planning to spend it over the weekend.

'Take it, please. I don't know where my dad is, I'm sorry.'

He counted it out and glanced at his colleague, who nodded reluctantly in approval. Far less than they would've liked. They scribbled a receipt and explained they still needed to speak to Dad urgently. The rest of the debt needed paying – in instalments if necessary – or they'd only have to return. They weren't going to take anything today but only because I'd been reasonable.

'Looks like your dad's a lucky man.'

'Only till he gets home.'

I watched them climb into the unmarked van. A couple of neighbours across the road watching at their front windows, ducking out of sight when they spotted me. Probably not that surprised. They'd have seen it coming all along.

*

I didn't wait up for Dad to get home. I tucked Ellie into bed while Karen was downstairs on the phone to Gran.

'You're too old for this,' I muttered.

'They're not coming back, are they?'

'God knows. Don't know much more than you.'

'But now you're working you can pay them off, can't you?'

'Depends how often they turn up.'

She had a nightlight screwed to the wall above her bed, a large pink flower. She'd stopped using it recently, insisting she didn't mind the dark anymore. I flicked the switch, flooding the room with a sickly pink glow and climbed in beside her fully clothed. She lunged towards me and squeezed tight.

'Will you help me with my dinosaur project tomorrow? I've got to make a T-Rex out of papier mâché. Then take me to the park? We can stay there all day, can't we? Please, Jess.'

Almost half-nine when I heard the front door slam. Wide awake, hypnotized by the concentric pink circles on the curtains. Ellie asleep under my right arm, breathing lightly. For a few seconds I couldn't hear a thing. I wondered if Karen had calmed down – highly unlikely – or Dad somehow managed to turn it round in the few steps from the front door to the living room. Much more likely.

Then I heard it. A sound that took me right back to my earliest childhood. A sharp slap followed by a dull thump as somebody's hand connected with an immoveable object. I slid carefully to the floor and crept towards the landing, crouching at the top of the stairs. They were stood near the front door, Dad with his back to it, facing me, Karen lunging at him in exactly the same way Ellie did at the bailiffs.

'Bloody idiot! Bailiffs in my house, intimidating my daughter.'

'Bloody hell, Karen!'

'As if you didn't know!' Aiming a slap at the side of his head, reminiscent of you in your heyday. 'Craig saw you driving off like a coward, everyone saw you, the whole street.'

'Craig? What the hell's he got to do with it? Poking his nose in.'

Flushed and confused, as if he'd wandered into the wrong house and couldn't quite work out what he was being accused of. Taking the rap for somebody else's mistake. I felt a lump lodge in my throat as he started making excuses, launching into a long rambling explanation. Why couldn't he just accept there was no excuse when it got this far?

'Not easy is it, Karen?'

'Easy? Bloody easy?'

'Got to admit…'

'What?'

'Small businesses don't get any help from this government. When have we ever had any help? Struggling for years.'

She clenched her right fist, ready for round two.

'I called in at the builder's merchants last week. Never said a word about bailiffs or sending people round; what's wrong with these bloody people?'

'You serious?'

'I owe plenty of people money. That's what happens when you're in business. Why should this be any different to all the rest?'

Karen rambling now, pacing up and down, struggling to get through. Every time he thought he could make a run for it when she was at the far end, she rushed back and pushed her face close to his. 'Never have I been so tempted in my life to blow your whole world apart.'

'For Christ's sake!'

'Don't think I wouldn't. What the hell do I owe you after this? Messed up my life, messed up our daughter's life; why should I care about your feelings, give me one good reason.'

He looked shell-shocked and panic-stricken. As if she'd crossed some invisible line they agreed on long ago.

'Why the hell should I care about Jess?'

'Steady on, for God's sake, she's only a kid.'

Whack. Another right hook. I didn't think she had it in her. I stood up and spared him one final glance before creeping back to bed. He'd spotted me. Our eyes locked between the banisters. Nursing his jaw, terror trapped behind his eyes.

Karen banging about in the kitchen, threatening him with something even more terrifying than a smack in the face. Gran. She knew all about it. She intended ringing in the morning.

'Oh for God's sake! All we bloody need.'

He'd always been defenceless in the face of Gran's unwavering logic. Her common sense, her inability to waste money, her inability to see other people waste money, her disgust at anyone enjoying themselves far too much for no good reason. His worst nightmare.

28   Lisa

*Bought you a little pressie to say thanks. Soon as I get chance I'll
pop it round. xxx*

Nudging her way in, a hint of confidence that hadn't been
there before. Perhaps she knew already, and this was her way of
letting me know. In reality, what thanks did I deserve? The odd
word of advice over the years, the odd present in the post, only
for it to lead to here.

Two days later, another text. She had something for
Harrison, some of Ellie's old things she had no use for. Hidden
layers beneath the words. Setting me up for some grand
showdown in front of Jim, his parents, his sister, the whole
village. The growing confidence of a teenager.

Resenting my new life, especially the unconditional love I'd
offered Jim and Harrison. Carol engineering the whole thing.
She'd seen it coming and relished it from the start.

The lies we'd spun, the childishness, our attempt to get
away with it, hitting her like a speeding train. Maggie. A name
that meant nothing. A mother watching from the shadows,
refusing to show her face. I sent a vague reply, the kind she
was used to.

*Sorry, love, been so busy with Harrison. Hospital appointments
all next week. Congrats on the job. Will put something in post.
Perhaps leave present at Carol's, I can pick up from there? Love
lots xxx*

Which silenced her for a few days. Unsure if she was hurt or not. Then she sent a strange one.

Sorry not replied earlier, been busy trying to sort Dad. All hell broke loose other day. Won't be able to pop over for a bit, Ellie needs me I'm afraid.

No idea what she meant. Itching to pry. No choice but to text Carol and question her instead. She replied quick. Something to do with bailiffs and an old debt. Ray had scarpered and left Karen and the kids to sort it, only coming home when the coast was clear. A few grand, that was all, not even a great deal, though I had to pretend it was, to be shocked.

Why couldn't I leave their complicated lives alone? I gripped the phone whilst glancing over my shoulder. Carol taking her time, annoyed straight off.

'What now? Don't know any more, Lisa, so there's no point asking. I'm with a client so can't talk anyway.'

She would, of course. Determined not to be put off. I needed to know all I could.

'So it's come to a head, has it?'

'Looks like it. But then what have I always said? He was an idiot before he had Jess and he's an idiot still. Thinks it's funny. That's his attitude to everything he can't understand. Should think there's plenty more to come as well. I once sat down and worked out what he must owe, based on what he's told me over the years, and it must be at least ten grand, if not twenty. Probably not much to you, but enough for him to scarper, that's for sure.'

Between clients, during quiet moments, forging ahead. Clearing her own name first, leaving me and Ray in the shit. Telling Jess she'd been right all along. She'd insisted on the truth, and we wouldn't listen. Favouring Ray slightly perhaps, some residue of sentiment getting the better of her. Revealing my time in Park Field, how I'd failed to protect her against Alex and allowed a man I barely knew to take her.

'Karen won't do him any favours either, if he carries on at this rate,' she went on.

'Karen?'

'For Christ's sake. Pretty obvious I should think. He's told her everything, so she'll hold it against him and blurt it all out. Wouldn't you? Her mother can't stand him, she'll be chuffed to bits if they split. In her element, rubbing it in. Who'll protect him then?'

I knew what she meant before she even finished. Not so far ahead this time. Everybody looking to their own back and protecting number one. Karen would stick the knife in and get what she could, while Ray would run away till it was all over, leaving Carol free to pounce. The inevitable on its way whether I was ready or not.

If I got in first perhaps I could give Jess my version. I'd made mistakes but what choice did I have? Once the lies started it was impossible to stop. All these years later I could never have imagined Ray so helpless, leaving me as the only adult, the only one capable of deciding where to go next. Could I handle the tears and win her round? Prove I was just as much a victim as anyone else. If I could just keep her away from Jim and Harrison, keep her to myself.

'I'll let you get back, sorry if I've disturbed you.' The room spinning with possibilities. I ended the call before she had chance to butt in with another word.

29   Jess

'I only eat when I'm hungry,' I insisted to Jo, which technically wasn't a lie, just not the whole truth.

'So why don't you bring pack-up every day? No way you need to lose weight, far too skinny as it is. I've got a cousin who's always on a diet and it's ruined her metabolism. Ed? We'll have to keep an eye on her, she's practically wasting away.'

'She's fine, just naturally skinny, that's all. My brother's the same, eats like a horse but doubles as a toothpick.' He flashed a sympathetic look. The last thing he wanted was to embarrass me, thank God.

Hard to say what was worse, Jo's blindness or Ed's pity. I tried to keep my head down and concentrate on the job. Jo did the accounts while Ed specialised in sales and marketing. I picked up whatever the two of them didn't have time for. Filing, stuffing envelopes, photocopying booklets, producing endless spreadsheets of price lists, taking the cheques to the bank and if there was any time left making the odd phone call.

I even spent a few days in the warehouse, trying to grasp the complexities of export shipments or sometimes just sweeping the floor, which I felt at home doing. The constant swearing and gentle banter. So much simpler and calmer. Less exposed. Danny and Tom reminding me of Dad and Pete, except they actually got some work done and didn't break nearly as much.

'You'll have to ask for a transfer,' Danny suggested. 'Could do with some female company.'

'Wish I could. Can't believe somebody's been daft enough to give me an office job.'

Three or four times a day Deborah would wander down the corridor and poke her head into the office to have a chat with Jo. If I was lucky she ignored me. If I was unlucky she'd pause to give me a cold searching stare, managing to take in my clothes, my desk, scary hair and pathetic lunch box (if I had one that day) all in one glance. Regretting her mistake, wishing she was staring into the smart face of Sally Cross instead.

'I only got the job by mistake,' I confessed to Jo when we were alone. 'Deborah meant to call somebody else; Richard was really pissed off.'

'He couldn't have been that pissed off, he gave you the job. Deborah's snotty with everyone. Likes to think Richard's her property just because she's been here longest. Gets really jealous if anybody hits it off with him.'

'I haven't hit it off with him. He thought I was a joke.'

Jo had been in the job since leaving college. She lived with her fiancé Dave, a music therapist, in a three-bed new build on the edge of town. Her mum was an English teacher, her dad a retired bank manager. Dave had a property portfolio and played saxophone in his spare time, dabbling in a jazz band with his old college mates. They went skiing to the French Alps most winters. I got the impression she didn't have to work, that she didn't really need the money, she did it for some other reason I wouldn't understand.

'So you live with your parents?' she questioned.

'With my dad and step-mum and younger sister, Ellie.'

'Right. And your mum?'

I lied naturally. Explained that I saw you whenever I felt like it, that we had a great relationship.

'Must be a bit weird sometimes, not living with your mum. Can be so traumatic when couples split, especially for the kids.' Pretty obvious Jo hadn't been within five hundred miles of anything traumatic. She'd read about it in magazines and believed it happened to other people quite a lot.

Sometimes I thought sod it, just be straight. Who cared what she thought? Her typical reaction was to laugh, followed by a sideways glance to check I wasn't winding her up.

'What do you mean you couldn't finish drying your hair?'

'Because we ran out of electric.'

'Wow! Your dad sounds a right laugh. Is he really accident prone or something?'

'No, just an idiot.'

'And what about your step-mum?'

'She's an idiot too.'

'But doesn't she feel like killing him sometimes?'

'Everybody who meets Dad feels like killing him, he's used to it.'

'You'll have to come out with us for a drink one night, won't she, Ed? Jess needs to escape her crazy parents. Driving her up the wall.'

'If that's what she wants. That's what parents are for, driving you up the wall. Mine do it all the time.'

It only took me a few days to shift my computer to the opposite corner of my desk, no longer facing Richard in his office. Not that he was there much. He spent most of my first month in Belgium, Denmark and France. When he did appear it was often a fleeting visit. Popping his head round the door.

'They looking after you, Jess?'

'Yes, thank you, sir.'

'Call me Richard.'

'Sorry.'

I felt quietly confident he couldn't see what I was doing from where he sat, not that I was doing anything I shouldn't. Just as long as he couldn't work me out. Biting his lip whilst trying not to laugh, as I knew he would.

*

Halfway through my fifth week, perched quietly at my desk stuffing envelopes, a new face suddenly floated down the corridor towards Richard's office. The blonde woman from the photo on his desk, a little older and with a different hairstyle but clearly the same. Wearing a tailored dark grey trouser suit, almost as if she worked in an office herself, although Jo assured me she didn't.

'What's she do?'

'Nothing.'

'Nothing?'

'She doesn't have to. This is Helen Whittaker we're talking about.'

As if I ought to know. Flawless creamy skin, highly polished shoes that looked as if they'd never taken a single step outdoors, perfectly arched eyebrows. Even walking differently, a kind of effortless sweeping motion that suggested she was heading somewhere vitally important and couldn't hang around for anyone, especially time wasters like me and Jo.

'Probably going for a manicure. Or lunch with an old friend. Don't smile, Jess, somebody's got to do it.'

'That's what she does all day? Seriously?'

'This is Richard's wife we're talking about.'

He was out when she appeared, so I didn't get chance to see them together, which was hard to picture. Richard with his rapid movements and his drive to get things done, Helen with her elegant sweeping motions.

I couldn't help thinking of you, wild hair tumbling, ready to launch yourself at anybody crazy enough to get in the way. I imagined you coming into contact with her for some unlikely reason – the idea making me cringe – the two of you exchanging words. Your wild face meeting Helen's immaculate frozen face. Your harsh language assaulting Helen's delicate ears. And I wondered what Helen would say if she knew about some of the things I'd witnessed, how she'd gossip with Deborah behind my back. Deborah suspecting all along. She could see it in my face every time our eyes met.

'Can you ring the credit card company for me, Jo? This morning, please. I need the chequebook. If you can sort my insurance. And where's the petty cash? I need to get my car cleaned, it's a disgrace; I told Richard last night.'

'No problem, Helen.'

'And make sure the same thing doesn't happen with my credit card as last time. I'm not having that again.'

The second time she appeared she seemed in an even greater rush, barely pausing to say hello. I watched her sweep straight towards Deborah in reception and reach out a manicured hand, so at first I thought there was a fire somewhere or somebody's life was in danger.

'Deborah! Can you post this letter please? Extremely urgent. First class. Birthday card for my cousin, I nearly forgot.'

'Yes, of course, I'll ensure it goes today.' Deborah's mission for the rest of the day, to put the envelope personally into the hands of the postwoman and if necessary track its course online till she was confident it had arrived safely.

Helen sweeping out, climbing elegantly into her Mercedes, oblivious to the post box she swept past majestically at the end of the estate.

'I know why you come to work now,' I muttered to Jo.

'Sorry?'

'Even if you don't need to.'

'What're you on about?'

'So you don't end up like that.'

*

On my fourth week Richard finished travelling abroad, intending to stay in the office to handle a large contract recently come in

221

from Poland. I felt more relieved than ever that I'd got my back to him, that he could barely see me when sat at his desk.

Most days glued to his phone, especially in a morning when he rang India or China. His chair creaking as he stood up, going over to the window overlooking the yard, leaning against the frame. Stubbornly arguing his point if he believed he was right, refusing to budge. He seemed to win most of the time. I could also sense when he was on a private call when he turned his radio down low and slammed the door, preventing Deborah from barging in. A huge relief, as it meant he was busy and hadn't got time to wander about.

He had four coffees a day, usually making them himself. The first early in the morning before I arrived, his second about half-ten, the third at lunchtime and the fourth at roughly three. I could sense these times approaching without even glancing at the clock.

Ten-to-three Tuesday afternoon. Richard about to leave his office, stride down the corridor and make his final drink of the day.

'Bit dry round here, Jess. Any chance of a coffee?' Ed perched in his corner; eyes glued to his screen.

'In a sec, just finishing this spreadsheet.'

'Go on, you know you want to.'

I grabbed all three empty mugs and shot down the corridor to the kitchen. Rinsing rapidly under lukewarm water. Ed's mug still coffee stained inside. Five minutes max.

'Jess, there you are. If I didn't know any better I'd say you were avoiding me.'

I spun round, almost smashing Ed's mug against the worktop. Richard leaning against the doorframe, watching closely.

'Not avoiding you.'

'Good. No reason to, is there?' He pushed past to rinse his mug, while I fumbled over the sugar and coffee canisters.

Suddenly the most complex job I'd ever done. 'No reason to move your desk round either?'

'No.'

'No reason to avoid my scrutiny?'

'I've only moved it because it's more comfortable. I asked Jo first, she said it was okay. Ed said so as well. I'm sorry.' Then I realised he was laughing again, taking the piss.

'Don't worry, not in school now. You're allowed to move a desk without being in detention.'

I'd managed to scatter sugar across the worktop and dropped a teabag in Ed's mug. He must've thought I was the biggest idiot he'd ever seen. No idea if he was genuinely laughing at me or expecting me to join in.

He hovered in the doorway. I'd never seen him so still. Normally rushing to take a call or make a call or instructing Ed or Jo on something urgent. As if he'd got all the time in the world.

'Everything alright at home?'

'Why wouldn't it be?' I fished the bag from Ed's mug and dropped it into my own. 'Why's everybody so fascinated with my home life all of a sudden? What's it matter to anybody here? I don't go around asking other people personal questions all the time.'

'You do realise you've just put five sweeteners in Jo's tea?'

'Shit.'

'Trying to poison her?'

'No, I like Jo. Might try it on Deborah though.'

'I was just wondering how your dad was getting on with his maintenance business, that's all. Think I spotted his van the other day. Take it you always assume there's an ulterior motive to an innocent question?'

I tipped the contents from Jo's mug into the bin. I spun round, ready to have a go. Ready to lose my job. Sick of people giving me weird looks. Worse than that, ignoring me altogether.

Maybe it wasn't me who was weird, maybe it was them. Who cared as long as I was good at my job?

He'd gone. His quick step down the far end of the corridor, his door slamming. Replaced by Deborah's disapproving face instead.

'Jessica?'

'Deborah?'

Struggling with herself, desperately searching for a putdown although I wasn't doing anything except threatening to poison her.

'You're not wasting Richard's time again I hope.'

'First time I've spoken to him in weeks. He spoke to me first.'

'Glad to hear it. I've got some photocopying for you to do. And some booklets, if you want to follow me.' Stomping back towards reception.

*

I trudged home slowly, unsure what might be waiting at the other end. Bailiffs wandering round the front room, making notes. Somebody else I'd never heard of, with a right to take our things, which had never actually been ours in the first place. Would I ever own anything again without feeling it could be snatched away at any point?

Ellie's small face hovering at the front window, scanning the street, like she used to do for Dad not so long ago. Running barefoot down the drive to greet me, as if she only felt safe when I was around, slightly unnerving considering I didn't know what the hell was going off any more than she did.

It was a Thursday evening when she ran towards me looking worried. Grabbing my hand and pulling me towards the house.

'Gran's here, helping Mum get to the bottom of it. They're in the kitchen.'

'Get to the bottom of what?'

'They're going to find out what Dad's been up to and confront him. Gran's going to expose him for the arsehole that he is.'

'Oh great. And I suppose Dad disappeared three hours ago.'

'He's not been seen all day. Gran says she wants a word with you as soon as you get in. She's not as bad as a bailiff, is she?'

'Ten times worse. If there's a choice on who to let in, go for the bailiffs every time.'

I lingered in the hallway, slowly removing my jacket and shoes. Always immediately obvious when Gran was in the house. A large dose of disgust hovering in the air. Disgust at what Karen had been daft enough to get herself into. Disgust at what her granddaughter had to endure on a daily basis. Disgust at the house itself and what she saw around her.

I felt the urge to bound upstairs after Ellie and hide in my room until she'd gone but guessed I was beyond all that, especially since I'd been daft enough to find a job. The two of them perched at the kitchen table, waiting impatiently. Karen fresh from crying. Gran stony-faced, arms folded, in her element. Between them, on the table, the biggest pile of paperwork I'd ever seen. Loose paper mostly, some drifting to the floor as I walked in and created a draught. A bank statement landing at my feet. I picked it up and placed it on the table, a sickening feeling I'd seen it somewhere before.

'We're just having a little clear out. Thought to myself I'll finally get to the bottom of what your dad's been up to even if I have to turn this place upside down. Thought to myself somebody's not being honest here, somebody's trying to pull the wool over my eyes.' Karen biting her lip to stop it wobbling out of control.

'Leave this to me. About time somebody tried some straight talking in this house. Sadly lacking for many years from what I can see.' Gran turning to face me, briefly taking in my suit, a flicker of surprise shadowing her face. Last time I saw her I was in ripped jeans and a T-shirt. 'Jessica. Hello. Think it's time you explained exactly what you've been up to, what your dad's been up to. This has become extremely serious; it's gone beyond the point of being a joke.'

'I never thought it was a joke.'

'Well that's good because it isn't. It's not a joke for a family to lose their house and end up on the street, is it? It's not a joke that a young child like Ellie doesn't seem to know where her next meal is coming from. How ridiculous in this day and age. I'm sick and tired of my granddaughter sending me text messages to say you've run out of electric, or she's gone to bed hungry again because there's not a scrap in the house. Look at you all. Hope you're proud of yourselves, borrowing money that was never there in the first place, begging from people you barely know. When we started out in life we had to go without if we couldn't afford something. What do you end up doing? You get a loan. If you fancy something you buy it that very day. Can't possibly wait for anything, can you?'

'Jess, how could you?' Karen butted in, unable to contain herself. 'I thought we were mates. How long have you been helping him? You know what he's like even better than I do.'

'How could I stop him? I tried, Karen, please believe me, I kept telling him. You know what he's like.'

She dug her hands into the paperwork, emphasising the depth, letting it run through her fingers. 'How am I supposed to make head or tail of this? He's taken out loans without telling me. Taken out credit cards, owes money left, right and centre. We're behind with the mortgage, apparently he's been in contact with them for weeks and never said a word, hiding stuff in Ellie's room, the bastard. How can I ever trust him again?'

'You're a fool. An absolute fool. I'd love to say Ray's the biggest idiot on God's earth but I've got to say you're not far behind. Never learn, do you?'

'Thanks, Mum.'

'Taken in from the start. The man's a crook, an absolute conman.'

'No he isn't!' I shouted. 'An arsehole maybe but not a crook. I know him better than any of you, I know him better than he knows himself. He needs help but won't ask for it, he's too proud.'

'What's he got to be proud of? The man can barely blow his nose without causing an earthquake. I think you'll find he's had plenty of help. May I remind you that when he met my daughter she'd recently come into a large inheritance from her grandmother; she was doing very nicely thank you, which your father then proceeded to squander on God knows what. He's had plenty of help as you put it, nobody can claim he hasn't. He's borrowed from almost everybody he knows at one time or another.'

'Not that kind of help! Proper help and advice. Can't you see he's useless and can't cope? Everything we've done for him until now has only made him worse. Karen's made him worse; I've made him worse, we've all contributed, we're all to blame.'

'Sounds like you're trying to worm your way out of responsibility, Jessica.'

'Not trying to worm my way out of anything. We've got to put our heads together and help him, so it doesn't happen again. I'll do my bit. I've already done my bit; I paid the bailiffs the other day. I'll pay a bit more if I can.'

'Guilty conscience, it's a terrible thing.'

I stood in front of her, forcing her to look away from the window. Glad I was still in my suit, that she was seeing me like this for the first time. 'Well at least I'm trying to think of a solution. What's the point in slagging him off when we can help instead? I'm sorry I let him hide stuff in my room. And before you ask, yes, I did know he was hiding stuff in Ellie's room. I tried to get through to him but he wouldn't listen.'

She looked furious. Struggling to hold it in, bony fingers gripping the tabletop. And I knew exactly why at last. I'd found a job, I was earning money, finally doing something right. I'd surprised her, the girl with the psychotic mother. What right did I have to make something of my life?

'I thought you'd be happy for me, you of all people. I'm working now, I can help out with the bills. I can understand what's going on a bit better now I'm older.' Couldn't she see we were on the same side? What more could I do?

'Well, Jessica, I'll believe that when it actually happens. All I can see at the moment is an almighty mess. Your father's a liar; we've all shielded him long enough. When the truth comes out you'll realise what kind of man he is, then you'll not be thinking he's so wonderful when you realise the true extent.' Jutting her chin forward, determined to have the last word.

I turned to Karen, demanding to know what she was on about. Sensing some subtle change in expression. The rules suddenly relaxed with Dad out the house.

'Will you shut it, Mum? For Christ's sake, I've told you to leave it.' Gathering paperwork at lightning speed. 'Go up to your room, Jess. I've heard enough, you're not helping. Very disappointed in you. I'm so upset.'

I ran upstairs and slammed my bedroom door, heart racing. I took out my mobile and texted Dad. Told him to get his arse back home, I was getting the blame for his almighty mess. Gran being a bitch, saying weird things. I didn't believe a word, but would he come back quick and make the old cow shut up?

After a few minutes he replied. He was doing his best to pay me back the three hundred, he'd never forget. I told him it didn't matter right now, I just wanted him home. Didn't want to be on my own with Karen and Gran. Sick of hiding in my room like a five-year-old.

I flopped on the bed and stared at the ceiling. Tired of heavy hints, everyone having fun at my expense. Obviously to do with you. Had something happened recently? Somebody making all the decisions without asking me first. Not for the first time.

It took him ages to come back. I imagined him on his way home, racing towards me, pushing aside every obstacle, bursting through the door, finally confronting Gran with all her lies. Instead, half an hour later, he sent a couple of lines.

Need time to think. Won't be home tonight. So sorry. Love lots xxx

30   Jess

'What more could I expect? He'll be kipping on somebody's sofa no doubt. Probably had it planned years.'

'What're you on about?' I snapped. 'He's never run off before. First time he's ever done anything like this.'

'Open your eyes, for God's sake! Where do you get all these daft ideas? Never been wonderful, even before I met him. Like to think you know him. Love to think you're close, the pair of you. Well it's a shame you didn't predict all this.'

Karen trawling through paperwork, trying to make sense of the mess he'd left behind, booking three days off work for the purpose. Curled up on the sofa when I got in from work, paperwork at her feet, consoling herself in front of an old black-and-white film.

'I can't do it, Jess, I can't. Don't see why I should. Not my bloody mess, is it? When I think back to when I first met him, I must've been brainwashed. Mum saw it coming, why didn't I? Doesn't care whether we go hungry, whether we're worrying to death, doesn't care about anyone but himself when it comes to it. Wasting all my holidays on this crap. Don't know what I'd have done without Craig. If he can support me, why can't your dad?'

I felt cold whenever she mentioned Craig. He'd stopped hovering in the garden, trying to catch a sneaky glimpse. Confidently barging through the back, making himself at home in the kitchen. Karen almost collapsing when she saw him, as if he'd caught her just in time.

'We'll sort it, don't worry,' he comforted her.

'Knackered, I can't take any more.'

'There's always a way. We'll figure it together, I promise.'

'Oh, Craig, what a shitty mess.'

'I won't dessert you, not like Ray. You can trust me.'

While I stood at the top of the stairs, wondering whether to go down or keep well clear. A stranger in my own home. My presence making little difference. Acting as if they'd got the whole place to themselves.

'I always thought you were a million times too good for him,' Craig insisted. 'Not as if you've anything in common anyway, not anymore.'

'Suppose not.'

'He's shit on you, Karen. And the kids. Knew what he was doing all along, he planned all this.'

'You kidding? This is probably as big a surprise to him as it is to me, that's what makes it so terrifying. If only you knew half the stuff he's done.'

'Incompetent. How can you share your life with someone like that?' A long pause. I felt sorely tempted to go down and barge between them, bringing Karen back to earth. 'I've always used an accountant. Everything above board, that's what my father taught me. Always put a bit to one side for a rainy day. The value of saving. No nasty surprises waiting round the corner.'

'Savings?'

'That's what it's all about, being prepared. Not stumbling from one day to the next.'

'Oh, Craig! He's been such an arsehole. I should've escaped while I had chance, Mum was right. Shit's about to hit the fan. What about Ellie? If it was just me I'd pack up and clear off no problem.'

He didn't answer at first. Conveniently forgetting there was somebody else to consider. 'Well she's a sensible kid. All that matters to her is that her mum's happy. Karen? Surely?'

She didn't reply unless she whispered it. I gripped the banister, fighting the urge to rush down and slam his face against the wall. What the hell did it matter to him whether Ellie was sensible or not?

*

'Don't know how the hell you can manage it.'

'It's a tin of beans. I'm opening it. What choice have we got? Somebody going to walk in and do it for us?'

Karen didn't seem to realise it had been happening years, that she had no right to be so angry or surprised. We'd been living on the edge ever since she walked into our lives, ever since I could remember.

Ellie convinced everyone was the same. Two weeks of pigging out followed by two weeks of starvation. It was only when she went to a friend's house she started to wonder.

'Two weeks till pay day,' I told them. 'Fifty quid in my purse. If we go steady we can make it last.'

'You go steady, I don't see why I should.'

Gran had promised to feed Ellie if things got really bad. No way she'd watch her granddaughter starve, but she wasn't going to spend 'silly money' on the rest of us, because we didn't deserve it. We needed to learn a valuable lesson and maybe it'd do us some good.

At least Karen had the appetite of a sparrow. Ellie went through phases, sometimes far more interested in catapulting Barbie downstairs, next minute prowling the house like a wild animal, flinging open cupboards and drawers, desperate for something to chew on.

'Sick of beans, why do we always get beans?' she'd say, sighing.

'Cos they're cheap. Shut up and eat.'

'Cos your dad's an arsehole,' Karen snapped. 'I suppose you've texted him today?'

'He said he might ring later.'

'Pete knows more than he's letting on. He's not as daft as he looks.'

'He is as daft as he looks, I've worked with him.'

'But he knows where your dad's hiding, he's bound to. I could probably follow him if I wanted. Sad thing is, can't be arsed. Don't even care right now.'

'You've got to. We've all got to. We've got to carry on as before until he comes home, we've no choice.'

I grabbed the last two slices of bread for Ellie's pack-up. Half a jam sandwich and two carrots. Two tuna sandwiches and half a sausage roll. One apple, one banana, one pear and a carton of juice. She wouldn't dare complain. If there was any left I grabbed it for myself. One eye on my phone, day and night. Still believing, still hoping. Who else was going to do it?

*

Jo went for lunch about one. Ed didn't always take a break, half an hour max, rushing back early as if the place couldn't cope without him. While I fitted in round the two of them, wandering round town texting Dad, waiting all afternoon for a reply.

Please come home. You're not in trouble, we're not angry, I promise. Please. Love lots.

My phone in my bag, pushed under my desk, conscious of its presence every minute of the day. When it started to vibrate I rushed to grab it.

What do cats eat for breakfast? Mice Crispies! Why shouldn't you write with a broken pencil? Because it's pointless!

Still convinced I was six. I pleaded with him to see sense. Pete no doubt looming over his shoulder, egging him on.

Pissing himself over Christmas-cracker jokes while we worried to death. How could I make him realise it was serious? How could I get him to wake up?

'Jess, have you got a minute?'

I glanced up to find Richard blocking the doorway, studying me closely. Totally forgotten him the last few days. My phone clattering to the keyboard. Glancing towards Ed as I stood up. Absorbed in a call, arguing over the lead time on a job. Jo gone for lunch, not back for at least half an hour.

'In my office, please.'

Apart from a couple of brief occasions it was the first time I'd been in his office since the interview. Even more nerve-wracking this time round.

'I'm sorry,' I mumbled. 'Just waiting for an important text to come through. I know that's no excuse, it only took a few minutes. I've sent that fax you asked me to, I did it earlier, I'm just waiting on a reply.'

'What're you rambling on about? Not interested in your damn phone as long as you get your job done.'

He was about to continue when his phone rang. I glanced at the display and read Deborah's name upside down. 'Not now, Deborah. If it's Andrew again tell him I'll ring back, can't be that urgent.'

He leaned back and folded his arms. So still he made me realise how jumpy I must be. If it wasn't my hands it was my legs.

'Tell me to mind my own business if you like but I can't help noticing something's wrong. I'm not here to trip you up or catch you out believe it or not.'

No point lying. Far too smart to fool.

'Go on.'

'It's my dad.'

'What about him?'

'He's disappeared.' My voice breaking as it came out. Even Karen's screaming and shouting hadn't quite brought it home the same way. He'd disappeared and God knows what I'd do if he didn't come back. He might be an idiot, but he was an idiot I knew, an idiot I was used to. He'd always been there for me. I'd looked after him just as much as he'd looked after me. Now I found he was ready to turn his back without a second glance. It didn't feel real and didn't make sense.

'Why?'

'He had an argument with my step-mum over money. Always over money.'

'No idea where he is?'

'He's been texting, so I know he's alright. None of his friends have seen him. That's what they're saying anyway. He has this habit of getting everybody on his side. I've even checked his emails. He's buying and selling as usual, like nothing's changed.'

He sighed heavily and bent down to swipe a plastic bag off the floor. 'Tuna or cheese?'

'Sorry?'

'Tuna or cheese? Wasn't sure what you liked because I've not seen you eat since you arrived. Want to see if you can.'

He offered two pre-packed sandwiches: one tuna, one cheese. My mouth watering instantly. I hesitated briefly, then went for tuna. He tore open the other pack and leaned back.

'You're still laughing at me.'

'No.'

'Feeling sorry for me.'

'Perhaps. Don't worry, won't be an everyday event. You say you've got a younger sister?'

I nodded. Laughing suddenly. 'She's got beetroot sandwiches and carrot sticks for pack-up today. She'll kill me when she gets home.'

'Tasty. What's the weirdest combination so far?'

'Don't know about the weirdest. I once gave her three packets of cheese and onion crisps and a KitKat. She thought it was great. I've tried turning it into a game, so she doesn't get upset. She's too young to care at the moment.'

He smiled slowly, staring at his desk, as if I'd reawakened some memory. Not quite talking a foreign language.

'I'm obviously not paying you enough.'

'I never said that. I'm really happy with what you're paying me. Sorry, I didn't mean to…'

'Glad to hear it. Just don't like to think any of my staff are starving. That wasn't my intention in setting up my own business.' He finished his last bite and threw the wrapper at the bin. 'So what's the plan with your dad? Can't be far, surely?'

'He keeps promising to ring. Obviously hiding something, don't ask me what. He's always hiding something but this time it's even worse because he's afraid to come home.'

'Anything I can do? Any way I can help?'

I couldn't help smiling. If he wasn't handing out advice or offering money or lending something he seemed to think it wasn't enough. Determined to be one of us, terrified he might not fit into his own company.

'What?'

'Nothing. How can you help? Even if I could find him, I can't knock sense into him. Till he changes, what's the point in finding him? Just so he can give me bad news? He's got to want to come home.'

About to reply when the phone rang again. 'For Christ's sake!' Pressing the button. 'Deborah, I'll call him back. Five minutes.' He tapped the table with his pen, studying me closely. 'What makes you think he's hiding something?'

'Just a hunch. He's never avoided me before, not like this anyway.' I stood up, suddenly full of energy. 'Thanks for the sandwich. I'll do you one of my specials next time, tuna and beetroot.'

Deborah's rapid footsteps suddenly sounding at the far end of the corridor, stopping him short. I was even sharper and managed to duck through the doorway just in time, taking the wrapper with me.

*

The worst thing about having a job was getting home and finding everything flipped on its head in a matter of hours. Nobody bothering to ask, half my life wiped out the second I opened the door.

I walked home the day after eating the sandwich in Richard's office, still smiling to myself when I thought of it. It was only what he'd do for anyone and probably did all the time. Looking for solutions without throwing his hands in the air, without panicking or making it worse. He'd been doing it so long in his job it came naturally. Once it happened he dealt with it, like an adult.

I wondered what he'd say if I told him about you. Screaming in the doorway, catapulting towards us, the flash of steel across my throat. Would he be horrified, like Carol and everyone else? Condemn you for the rest of your life? Or perhaps have a different solution nobody else had thought of.

I searched for Ellie's face at the front window. Making me feel as if I'd done a decent day's work when she raced towards me in front of the whole street. She wasn't there.

Craig's sparkling blue Ford Focus parked in front of his house, pretty unusual in itself. Usually found rotting in his garage. The boot wide open, Craig himself shifting stuff about, trying to make room.

'Hi, Jess. Busy day?'

The front door half open, Karen shooting down the drive, a carrier bag in each hand. She coloured slightly when she saw me but refused to change course. Handing Craig both bags.

'More to come, I'm afraid.'

'Plenty of room. If I have to do two or three trips it's no sweat.' They exchanged smiles, ignoring me, full of warmth and something else that seemed to have grown in the space of a day.

'What's going on?' I demanded, barging between them.

'We're leaving. Going to my mother's. Sorry, Jess, I've made up my mind.'

She rushed back towards the house, head down against the wind. I followed quick, slamming the door behind. Before I had chance to breathe a word she was in the front room swiping ornaments off the mantelpiece, wrapping them in newspaper, wedging them tightly in a plastic box. We'd sat side by side over breakfast. She'd watched me make Ellie's porridge without a word.

'This is ridiculous. You can't just take everything and bugger off. What about Dad? You know he'll come back eventually.'

'I don't care whether he comes back or not; I won't be here to find out. Believe it or not, I feel it could be a waste of a life hanging around another minute waiting for your tosser of a father.' She fumbled over the paper. Hoping to finish before I got home. 'Only reason I'm taking so much is because I don't want to come back. Lived here ten years and all I've got to show for it is half a dozen boxes of crap.'

'You're taking Ellie?' A dragging sound across the landing above, wardrobe doors banging.

'Course I'm taking Ellie! Don't think I'd leave her behind, do you?' Softening slightly at my expression. 'You'd make a right pair left on your own.'

'What if she doesn't want to go?'

'She's eight. Since when has she had an opinion on where she lives?'

'She's my sister, Karen, it's got to count for something.'

'Half-sister.'

One little word. Holding it back all these years. Still upset over the paperwork, still convinced it was my fault. Or perhaps just an excuse. Searching for one for a long time.

She picked up the box and lugged it outside. Craig waiting

patiently. When she put her head in her hands, he gripped her shoulder and said something, their heads almost touching. Whatever it was it gave her strength. She spun round and marched back, ready to face me.

She paused at the bottom of the stairs and yelled at Ellie to get a shift on, they were leaving in five minutes.

'You don't need to do this, you're overreacting. What am I supposed to tell Dad when he gets back?'

'I've no doubt the minute we're out the door your dad'll find his way back once he knows we're gone. I've also no doubt you probably know where he is, and he's told you all sorts of things he'd never tell me.'

She grabbed two or three coats off the hooks behind the door. Selecting a pair of Ellie's shoes, two scarves and a bobble hat. Reminding me of that other escape, thirteen years ago. Standing on the other side. How desperately we needed to start again because we had no choice. Was that how she felt?

'Coming with us, Jess?' Ellie racing downstairs, dumping her laptop at the foot of the stairs.

'Don't think so.'

'Staying here on your own?'

I put my arm round her before her face crumpled completely. 'Got your hamster for company, haven't I?'

'Gran can't stand Harry. If we live in her house we've got to live by her rules. Mum won't let me take my bike either. Craig's worried about his car.'

Karen barging between us to reach the kitchen. 'If you're not ready in two minutes, there'll be trouble. Why do you two have to take so long over everything?'

'What coat do you want to take?' I asked her. 'Pick out your favourite shoes, pick out your best stuff while you've got chance.'

'Mum says I can't, Gran's got enough clutter.'

I grabbed her favourite pink sparkly shoes from the pile behind the door, overlooked by Karen in favour of something black and sensible. Also her purple padded coat, ordering her to put it on.

'Not cold. We're coming back eventually. Doesn't matter if I leave stuff behind, does it?'

'What about a book? What about some games? You know what Gran's place is like. Let's fill your pockets, see how much we can squash in.'

We raced upstairs while Karen screamed from below. I grabbed My Little Pony and squashed it into her coat pocket. She went for two *Harry Potter* books, Buzz Lightyear and a toy dog she'd had since she was born.

'But I am coming back, aren't I? This is my home. Don't live with Gran, do I?'

She backed into a corner as I tried to stuff two *Mr Men* books into her left pocket, giggling uncontrollably. Two Barbies in an inside pocket. Cinderella, Sleeping Beauty, Belle from *Beauty and the Beast*. So much more to choose from than thirteen years ago. By the time we'd finished she resembled a purple padded snowman, arms sticking out at right angles as she waddled downstairs.

'Get in the car please, no more excuses,' Karen snapped. 'Alright, Jess, I'll text tomorrow to let you know we're alright, don't worry about us. I've left a loaf on the worktop. Got some money, haven't you? Probably ought to give Carol a ring, she'll be worried sick about you.'

Craig looking ecstatic as Karen walked towards him for the final time, as if she'd been promising years. She stared straight ahead as he started the car, refusing to glance at the neighbours either side, refusing to acknowledge me.

Ellie's pale face looking out from the back seat, the hint of a smile tugging at her lips. Waving Buzz Lightyear behind Craig's back. At the last minute she opened the window as they pulled onto the road.

'Don't forget Harry!'

31   Lisa

'They eat monkeys and lizards!'

'We're going home if you can't stop shouting in people's faces.'

'Buffalo!'

'Pack it in! How many more times?'

I grabbed Harrison's hand to steer him away from a group of older boys giving him funny looks. Would he ever be able to play with such kids? Jim grabbed his other and we marched towards the giraffes.

'Can I have a tiger from the shop?'

'We'll see.'

'Can I have a monkey from the shop?'

'You can't have anything from the shop unless you behave.'

Three minutes with the giraffes. Less with the meerkats. Slightly longer with the black rhinos, nobody else about.

I'd never taken Jess to a wildlife park. Or a zoo or a farm park or anywhere remotely interesting that Harrison took for granted. Did they exist back then?

I remembered certain things as if it were yesterday. She loved beans on toast with the crusts cut off, three or four times a week because it was cheap and easy. Cola bottles and white-chocolate mice if Ray called in at the shop on his way from work. Fizzy gums grabbed behind her back, half a dozen in one grasping handful. Their memories, not mine.

I wish I'd learnt to speak to her about all the little things in life. Fashion and music. What about her hair? Carol got there first. Why had I been so terrified to get to know my own daughter? I'd assumed I wasn't up to it and left her instead to the most selfish people. Perhaps it wasn't too late for us to learn together. Ignore Carol's interference. We could create memories that only mothers and daughters could understand.

'Baby tiger! Mummy, it's a baby tiger!'

Jim smiling, despite everybody staring, which he normally loathed.

'Mrs Spence says they've all got different markings, they're all different, is that right?'

A son was different to a daughter. Jess needn't interfere, she could even help. I could have both without either being pushed to one side. She didn't need my full attention the same way, she could accept less without making me feel guilty.

But what if she ranted and raved, if she did something unpredictable and displayed a side I didn't know? If she didn't believe a word? Her birth certificate, wedged at the bottom of a shell-encrusted jewellery box. Her first pair of shoes and the tiny cardigan my sister knitted her with the pearly buttons. Half a dozen school pictures, not the ones she did for Carol years later, hoarded like trophies. Just the two of us in front of the house, holding hands. She could turn to Ray and Carol for something fake, then come to me for the real thing.

What about the backlash? Ray and Carol twisting things to make me look even worse. No alternative but to tell her how humiliated I'd been, how low I'd sunk. The abuse I'd tolerated despite the risk to us both, my warped view of Alex until it was too late.

Where I'd been vague with Jim, I'd be specific with Jess. Even if she laughed in my face. Even if she thought it impossible I could ever have suffered, sat in the conservatory at the time, staring down the garden, in the middle of my new life. Forced to admit it was all fake. The clothes, the jewellery, the Cavendish Stripe. Everything in life since I'd started running. I hadn't really moved on, it just looked that way to the outside world. I'd been waiting for her to turn up and make it all feel real again.

'Earth to Lisa, earth to Lisa.' Jim waving his hand in front of my face.

'Sorry.'

'And you moan at me.' Pissed off because I'd made him leave his phone in the car.

I bent down to Harrison's level and pointed out the ringtailed lemurs before he raced past. Surely this was the right time for an older sister. Any longer would be too late.

Then it happened. While I was bending down and whispering in his ear, half my mind on Harrison, half on Jess. Standing the other side of the enclosure, twenty feet away, glowing chestnut hair flapping in the breeze. Clutching a little girl's hand, roughly Harrison's age. Chattering away, perfectly content. Nobody would guess. My heart bursting to life in a way it hadn't done in years.

Rachel Unwin. The shocking pink bob long gone, the studs creeping up both ears, the toothy grin not quite so toothy. We'd huddled together over meals and swapped secrets in corners. She'd got more out of me than anyone else. My darkest secrets in exchange for hers.

Quick! Here's my number. Scribble it down, keep it safe! Tears scouring our faces. We'd never make another friend the rest of our lives in the same way. We'd forged something that could never be broken.

I grabbed Harrison's hand, ready for flight. This moment only ever a heartbeat away.

'What now? Great! Nagged me to leave my phone behind but it's alright for you to be a million miles away.'

She'd spotted me. At least thought she had. Peering through the wire and creeping closer, ignoring her little girl. My hair had changed, the context different, otherwise unmistakeable. What if she rushed over and asked about Jess?

'Come on, we'll get you that tiger before it shuts.'

'Monkey as well?'

'If you want.'

We raced back the way we'd come, past the giraffes and tigers, my vision blurring as the shop loomed. She'd be furious I hadn't stayed in touch. Ignoring her texts when she needed me. Happy to speak to her on the inside, a different matter in the real world.

'What the hell's going off?' Jim shouted.

'I'll explain later.'

'Will you stop a minute? Only been here half an hour, what a bloody waste of money.'

I dived into the shop, glancing over my shoulder. Forcing Harrison to choose, pushing him towards the till, thankfully no queue. Within minutes crunching through the car park, Harrison triumphant, Jim still chipping away.

'Sick to death of running away every five minutes. Was it that woman?'

'Her name's Rachel Unwin. She was in hospital with me, we were good friends. A million and one questions, just can't be doing with it right now.'

'Another day out ruined.' Mumbling under his breath while searching for his keys.

'Sorry?'

I bundled Harrison into the back. We sat in the front arguing. How many more years could we get away with it?

'So I've taken the day off work just so we can spend it running away, on the off chance you've spotted somebody you used to know.'

'Not my fault!'

'Are you ashamed of us? Is that it? How can we carry on like this? At some point, whether you like it or not, you're going to run into somebody you knew years ago. And yes, it's going to be embarrassing for us all, especially if it's a works meal or we're out with my sister.'

'Oh my God! Heaven forbid!'

He pressed the ignition, reversing in a spray of gravel and dust. He'd finally said it. Keeping a lid on it. Being able to contain it. The thing that had always terrified him most.

*

'Any idea where I can go for a decent manicure?'

'Why? What's wrong with coming here? I've done your nails before, was it that bad?'

I perched on the top step and gripped the phone. Familiar territory. Carol back to knowing best.

'I just don't like troubling you. I feel cheeky asking all the time.' A lengthy pause while we both considered how long to leave it. 'So you've heard from Jess?'

'Eh?'

'You've rung her?'

'Of course I've rung her. Never find anything out otherwise, would I?'

'Why? What's happened?' She'd pounced already. They'd told her. All part of the plan.

'Karen's buggered off to her mother's with Ellie. Stuck it out a couple of days, then left. Taken half her stuff with her so obviously doesn't intend coming back. Bloke next door's been sniffing round so whether they've been carrying on behind Ray's back, God knows. Right bloody pair.'

I struggled to process. Karen having an affair? Jess had never mentioned anybody next door. I'd never even thought about the state of their marriage. Would it have helped if I had?

'You mean she's left Jess behind? On her own?'

'Well she's hardly likely to take her with her, is she?'

She was almost nineteen, it was hardly against the law. Old enough to get married and to vote. I'd bought her one of those large plastic silver keys for her eighteenth, yet the true meaning hadn't really registered. She must be terrified. She'd never lived on her own before. Like Park Field, especially at night. Unexplained noises and nobody to ask. Even now, with Jim away on business, the walls closing in.

'So there you go. Saw it coming, didn't we?'

I'd seen nothing. I'd left my daughter to people who didn't give a damn when it came down to it, who only cared about themselves yet still managed to look down their noses at me.

'What about meals? Can she cook? Have you been round?'

'I've tried to get her to come here but she's determined to stay. Pretty stubborn when it suits her. Obviously got her own plans.'

Of course. She was working. Not a child anymore. She wouldn't settle for half-truths. The whole truth or nothing. Who was going to give it to her?

'It's Harrison's parents' evening tonight. We're going for a meal afterwards so I'd best tidy up.'

'Very nice. Won't keep you talking then.'

My hands trembling as I ended the call. What was it with Carol? Had she set a time limit? Would it burst out of her one day? Or just making it up as she went along?

Either way, it all came down to the same thing. The truth or nothing. One side or the other. Impossible to have both.

32   Jess

I started in the front room, trying to plug the gaps Karen had left behind. Not that I felt particularly attached to the ornaments, mostly clutter, just that there was an echo without them. They made the place feel like home. What right did she have not just to clear off but take the heart of the place with her?

She'd left an out-of-date loaf in the kitchen, nicked from work. An empty fridge and nothing in the cupboards except a couple of tins and some softened biscuits. Not even a chocolate flapjack or doughnut.

I messaged Dad to let him know. Perhaps Karen was right, and he'd be back in a jiffy once he knew she'd gone. All the vague stuff I'd been worrying about just in my imagination. It was Karen he was avoiding, not me.

Half an hour later the phone rang. Carol, so loud it felt like she was lurking in the next room.

'So what's going off? Just had a text from Ellie to say she's staying at her Gran's.'

'They've buggered off.'

'Buggered off?' A brief pause. 'Left you on your own?'

'Looks like it.' I told her about Craig, knowing she'd lap it up.

'What did I say? Just a matter of time. Pack what you can, and I'll be over in an hour or so. Just washed my hair, I'm not rushing. And don't bring a lot, I've no room for clutter.'

'I'm staying here.'

'What? Speak up, can't hear you.'

'Staying here. This is my home, even if everyone's pissed off. Even if they take everything and leave me just a mouldy loaf of bread, which, as it happens, they have.'

'Can't keep an eye on you if you're ten miles away, can I?'

'Then don't keep an eye on me, I'm not asking you to. Closer to work if I stay here. No point moving in with you, then struggling to get to work.'

She had it all planned. For years probably.

'I need to stay here for when he returns. I don't want him coming back to an empty house.'

'If he returns. Talking like he's bound to. Wherever he is he's obviously happy. Can't hear him complaining, can you?'

'Don't be daft. Unless you know something I don't, of course.'

'Amazed he's lasted as long as he has. Stuck it out far longer than I thought.'

'And what's that supposed to mean?'

'Bloody ridiculous, Jess. Who's going to cook all your meals? Who's going to do the housework?'

'Me. Who else? May have escaped your notice but I've been doing it for some time. If I was helpless I'd have starved long ago. So would Ellie. They'll be back before long, either together or separately or whatever.' Sounding more confident than I felt. Shadows lengthening outside. 'Switch off for once. Absolutely nothing you can do. Stop flapping.'

God knows how it worked but somehow it did. I put the phone down feeling quietly confident she wouldn't be barging through the door inside the hour. Closed all the curtains, double-checked both doors. Switched on the telly and experienced the weird sensation of being able to watch whatever I liked without a scrap.

I messaged Chloe, explaining everything. She came back

in minutes, though it felt like the next day. Something weird happening to time.

Jammy bitch. Why can't my parents be more like yours? Party!

I told her she could move in if she liked; we didn't need our parents anymore. No longer that six-year-old motherless child, struggling to survive. Almost nineteen, able to do my own hair and pick out my own clothes, check the meter twice a day, unlock the house in a morning, lock it again every night. Nobody had broken the law. This wasn't history repeating itself, however much it looked like it.

I perched on Ellie's bed for a few minutes before going to bed. So much crap strewn across the floor it felt impossible she could leave it all behind. The fuss she'd kick up without it. But then, wasn't I the same? Hadn't I left stuff behind, mostly long forgotten? What difference would it make either way? As if she had any say in the matter whatsoever.

*

I started straight after breakfast next day. No more manipulation, distractions or bullshit. This was my chance to discover the truth.

Karen and Dad's room. Everything exactly as before they left. Presumably she ran out of steam after clearing the rest of the house. As far as I could tell she'd taken about half her clothes and nothing else.

I perched at the dressing table and went through the drawers. Hair slides, tarnished jewellery, old pocket diaries. God knows what I expected to find. God knows what it might look like.

As I flicked through the diaries a text came through from Karen. I imagined Gran looming over her shoulder, asking why she was bothering. Ellie should come first.

Sorry, been so hectic trying to settle in. Not much room to be honest. Hope you're okay. Ellie's fine. Speak soon, take care.

The bottom drawer was slightly more exciting. A pile of Ellie's old school drawings on top, everybody lined up in front of the house, names scrawled above. Dad as big as the house, hands like shovels, Karen all glowing blonde hair and beaming smile, Ellie like a mini version. Perfect little family. Then myself to one side, complicating matters. Flowing dark hair, black eyes, a grim expression.

Hidden under the drawings was a plastic bag full of small soft toys. A pink teddy with 'Love' embroidered across the chest. A small dog with large floppy ears. The kind of stuff Dad might've bought for her years ago before she moved in.

Suddenly a sharp rap on the front door. I peered out the window, pulling the curtain to one side. Craig. Rubbing the back of his neck, glancing round as if reluctant for an answer. Were they preparing me for something about to emerge? Not hard to guess what. They wanted me on their side.

I couldn't help preferring your methods to theirs. If you had something to say you didn't hesitate. Why waste time trying to make it look good? Wouldn't be seen dead knocking politely on somebody's door.

I shoved the soft toys back in the drawer. I ought to be shocked. I ought to care at least. Should probably tell Dad about Craig, if he didn't know already. Somehow it seemed unimportant, even irrelevant.

I finally turned to Dad's stuff. He was much harder to pin down. No organisational skills whatsoever. Karen might've been having an affair, but Dad's secrets were even more embarrassing, in his own mind at least.

I trawled through paperwork at the bottom of his wardrobe, stuffed under the bed, in his bedside drawers, even in the pockets of his jeans hanging in the wardrobe. Scanning every page for my own name, a sneaky suspicion it might be there. Relieved when it wasn't.

He was in a mess that dated back years, some of the

paperwork from round the time he broke his wrist slipping off a roof and couldn't work for six months, when they had nothing to fall back on. No idea if it was still relevant or whether he just hadn't got round to throwing it out yet.

Amongst all the letters and demands from various banks over the years, from the council over his tax, from water, gas and electricity suppliers, I found he was offered a ten-grand loan three months ago.

Also quite a few letters in his own handwriting. Full of spelling and punctuation errors, complete with heavy crossings out. He used to let me proofread everything years ago. I'd double-check his spelling, occasionally putting something into words for him. Repeatedly telling me I was a genius.

I perched on the bed, struggling to decipher them. He was asking for help. In broken English admitting he was in a mess, and he'd like to talk to someone. He knew how urgent it was. In one letter he asked them to contact him on his mobile rather than the landline.

I glanced towards my phone on the dressing table. Another text, this time Maggie.

Hi, love. Just heard from Carol. Really hope you're okay. So busy at the moment. Love lots.

The usual. I peeked out the window. Craig finally buggered off. Next door's ginger tom peeing on the roses.

Why didn't he ask for help? I could've written the letters and done it properly. Why didn't he at least hide them in my room? Embarrassment? Pride? I should've realised he was trying to dig himself out of a hole.

I wondered what the bank must've thought. Laughing over his excuses, his badly phrased English, his childish scribble. Then I realised they probably wouldn't have thought anything. I was holding them in my hands.

*

Carol marched into the kitchen shouldering the same cavernous bag she'd had since I was a kid, only this time it didn't contain make-up, moisturiser and nail varnish. Dusters, bleach, fabric softener, vanilla and peach air freshener, industrial-strength rubber gloves and some kind of powder that removed stubborn stains that she seemed to swear by.

'Just give us a list and I'll get through it as best I can. I've got two pedicures and three bridesmaids this afternoon, so can't hang about. I can give you tomorrow morning and Wednesday after two, but I'm fully booked the rest of the week. You can come for tea Tuesday and Thursday. I'll let you have a key, it's time you had one.'

I let her wander round without interruption, thoroughly enjoying herself, flinging open cupboards and drawers. When had Karen last cleaned the fridge? Dirty cow. Had these pots ever been used? What was the point in splashing out on a new kitchen, then never using it?

'I knew she was idle; had no idea she was this bad.'

'You actually here to help or just having a good nosey?'

'Bit of both. It's only confirmed what I always suspected.'

Moving onto the front room, briefly running a duster over the mantelpiece. Tidying magazines, taking a stray mug into the kitchen. Did I need any washing doing?

'All sorted.'

'What about meals? Don't suppose you've been eating properly. Don't look as if you have.'

'Stop fussing, I'm not helpless. Probably eaten better since they left.'

Within twenty minutes she'd burnt herself out trying to find something potentially serious or dangerous. Finally lingering in the kitchen, clutching a duster.

'Well I have to say you're nothing like your mother, thank God.'

'Cheers. Taken you this long to notice?'

'Can you remember the filth you had to put up with? Suppose you've forgotten. Just as well.'

She put the kettle on and five minutes later we settled at the table to pore over the post that had arrived in the last few days. I'd already opened everything addressed to Dad and dealt with it the best I could. She made two piles: one potentially urgent, the other slightly less so.

'I think he was trying to negotiate. I found some letters he'd been drafting out. Don't know whether he sent them or not.'

'Well he didn't try hard enough, did he? I'll have to ring the bank and see if they'll speak to me about the mortgage. Doubt it but I can try. No wonder Karen wanted out. They've remortgaged at least three times by the look of it.'

'So that means we'll lose the house?'

'Means your dad needs to get his arse back here asap. He's the only one who can sort it. Everything's in his name.' She scribbled down a phone number. 'Don't have to be brains of Britain to do this, just a bit of common sense.'

'Is there any reason he's not coming back? Something I don't know? He's never done anything like this before. Whatever people say about him, it's not him. What if he's ill? Seriously?'

'The only illness your dad's likely to have is the thick ear he'll be getting when I catch up with him.'

'He's always told me about his debts. Never been a massive secret between us. Whatever he's hiding now obviously is. He's frightened of something.'

'Four months behind on council tax. He'll have to owe me. Along with the rest.' Scribbling furiously, refusing to look up. 'What about water? Gas? This big loan he's taken on?'

'I've paid the water and gas, it wasn't much.'

She shook her head and took a gulp of tea, loving every minute. Exactly what she'd been waiting for.

'Carol?' A long pause before rushing in. 'I've been thinking about Mum a lot lately. Don't go off on one, just listen for God's sake. I want to go back to the house where I was born, I want to see it again.'

'Oh for God's sake.'

'It's been a long time. If I'm prepared to move on maybe she is as well. Not saying I want to meet her, calm down. Just want to see the place again. Dad's always told me she moved on years ago so there's no danger of bumping into her.'

She finished scribbling, shuffling the paperwork into neat piles, looking thoroughly pissed off. 'Why the hell do you want to go look at some mouldy old house? A house where you were miserable, that you barely escaped from with your own life. Why go back to all that? Lovely house here, brand-new life. Lucky to escape. The more somebody tells you not to do something the more you've got to do it.'

'Just tell me where it is, and I'll go on my own. I'm not asking you to come with me. Carol! Just give us the address.' Running my hands through my hair. 'Don't laugh when I tell you this, I know it sounds daft. The other day I had a flashback to the attack. After she'd done it she was gentle with me, running her hands all over me, checking I was okay. Doesn't make sense. Why try to stab me, then suddenly come over all gentle and calm as if it never happened?'

'Clutching at straws again.'

'Really? Weren't there, were you? Why not let me find out for myself?'

She threw the rubber gloves and dusters into the bag. Pulled out the vanilla and peach air freshener and smacked it on the table. I grabbed her hand before she could pull away.

'I know you care. I know you've always cared and sometimes you struggle to show it. I'll never forget what you've done for us. You've been as good as a mother, better at times, but please, Carol, I can't wipe out the past, I just want to understand it. Give me the address and let me get it out my system. You can shout at me when I get back, tell me you were right all along but don't stop me, please.'

She snatched her hand away as if I'd scalded her, looking hurt as much as pissed off. Not part of the plan. Standing by the window, staring down the garden, brooding silently. Surely she was about to cave in, knowing how much it meant to me. How could she refuse?

'What the devil? That the bloke Karen's been carrying on with?'

'Probably.'

'Well I've seen it all now. She's actually found someone worse than your dad by the look of him.'

'Don't change subject, please. Carol?'

She spun round slowly and leaned back against the sink; arms folded as if ready for an attack. She'd seen through my praise. It wouldn't work because it wasn't what she wanted. It never had been.

'I'm sorry, I can't remember it. Long time ago.' Grabbing her bag and lighting up, exhaling slowly at the ceiling. 'Pushed it to the back of my mind after all these years. Probably just as well.'

'For God's sake, will you stop interfering for once? Give it a rest. Surely you've got something better to be doing? Can't you concentrate on your own business instead of constantly poking your nose into ours?'

'Oh thank you very much! This is all the thanks I get, is it?'

'If you had more of a life then you wouldn't be so bitter about ours, would you?'

She swung her bag onto her shoulder, slowly and silently, patting me on the arm as she went past. 'I'll come back when you're in a better mood.'

'Don't bother. Only come to rub it in anyway.'

Slamming the door and storming down the path, refusing to glance back, driving off in seconds.

I paced the kitchen, pausing to scowl out the window at Craig clipping his side of the hedge. Wasn't it sad she'd never had a proper boyfriend, no family of her own to pester? Sinking her teeth into us instead, pouncing on all our mistakes. Awaiting this moment for years. Couldn't she see I craved the truth, however bad? The real thing instead of something fake?

I threw the vanilla and peach air freshener at the bin, then quickly grabbed my phone, tapping on Maggie's number. Before Carol had chance to warn her. I stared blindly out the living room window at Craig's painfully neat front garden, fearing the worst. Carol might've told her not to answer. Ordered her never to speak to me again.

'Maggie? Sorry to bother you. Alright?' I could hear the relief in my voice.

'Fine. We're all fine. I say that, Harrison fell off his bike yesterday and cut his cheek on a stone. Jim panicked and wanted to take him to A&E but what's the point when you've got to wait five hours? Still, that's kids for you, Harrison's almost as bad.'

Still making crappy jokes. I liked her just the same. She paused, waiting for me to butt in. Panic rising in my throat. I'd never tested her before, Carol always reaching her first. Would she see my point of view or feel she'd got to be loyal to her sister?

'I want to ask you something. The address of the house where I grew up, so I can go back for a quick look. I don't suppose you know it? Just asked Carol and she won't let me have it, you know what she's like. So protective and stubborn. Bloody annoying. Please, Maggie.'

A long pause that seemed to last forever. 'Well… she's always been like that, hasn't she?'

'I think I'd know the house if I saw it again, it's just the street. Keep thinking Thomas Street or Taylor Avenue or something like that. If I hear the name I'll know it.'

'Hang on a sec.'

She put the phone down and disappeared. Silence in the background. Had she rung off? Maybe Carol's voice would be next, asking what the hell I was playing at.

'Taylor Drive. Forty-two.'

'Thanks. Oh thank you.' She wasn't lying; Maggie wouldn't. I didn't need to scribble it down, I'd never forget.

'Just be careful. You will be careful, won't you?'

'Thanks for ignoring her, she's such a pain sometimes, needs to get a life.'

'Of course.' Sounding uncertain, like she regretted it already, perfectly normal in Maggie's world but too late.

'Don't worry, I'll let you know how I get on. Thank you.' Finishing the call before she had chance for another word. I had what I wanted.

33   Lisa

I grabbed Harrison's T-shirt and yanked him back to his chair. It wasn't always necessary to scream and shout, sometimes just a look was all it took.

'How much longer?' he whined, swinging his legs, staring at the specialist's door as if he could force it open.

'Soon. Sit still and behave.'

I'd made the appointment myself, something I'd been doing two or three years, since we first realised there might be something wrong. If the specialist started brushing us off (he hadn't yet but I was ready for it) I'd make another appointment with somebody else. I'd knock on other doors until I found the right one. It didn't matter anymore if I looked ridiculous.

He stopped swinging his legs and slumped back in his chair, suddenly deflated, the meds kicking in. A sudden stab of guilt. I had to ask strangers to explain my son and reassure me what was normal and what wasn't. Just by doing the best for him I'd hidden him to the point where nobody really knew what he was like.

I dismissed the idea quick. I knew him far better than I'd ever known Jess. I wasn't running away or trying to escape, this was totally different. When I considered some of the incredible things I'd done over the last few years (not to anyone else perhaps, just me). One of Harrison's first teachers, Miss Kelly, had excluded him from every special activity because she'd claimed he couldn't cope with routine and disrupted the rest of the class. He'd had no part in the nativity play. She'd forced him to sit on the side during games, showing blatant favouritism towards those of his classmates she considered easier to teach. When I found out I marched down to the school and challenged her point-blank, my voice loud and clear. It never happened again.

I stared at the specialist's door, trying to make out the exact nature of the low rumble of conversation filtering through the crack underneath. Another boy of Harrison's age visible in the sliver of glass to one side. Perhaps he had exactly the same symptoms and same outlook.

I should've argued more for Jess. I should've found my voice in time for her. Yet if I had I wouldn't be sat here with Harrison. Harrison wouldn't even exist. Jim would've found somebody else to spend his life with. Impossible to imagine being a good mother to Jess if it meant not being here.

I pictured a long line of events, innocently started, leading me to this waiting room. Dr Shipley recommending *Helping Hands*. My friendship with Steve, who pushed me to lie on my CV. The nervy interview at the garage with Sue. Jim walking through the door for the first time for his scratch card and chicken wrap. Some of it so faded it felt as if it had always been in my life.

And if I stepped forward now out of the shadows and spoke up, what did I have to offer Jess? I wouldn't have anything good to tell her, anything that would put a smile on her face.

'Mummy! What's up?' Harrison leaning towards me.

I wiped a stray tear from my cheek and tried to laugh it off. 'Nothing, sweetheart.'

In reality, I'd cried dozens of times over the last few years whenever Harrison did the tiniest things. Second place in the school Easter-egg decorating competition. The day he learnt to swim without armbands. The Mother's Day card he secretly made whilst I laid in bed with flu. I always realised those tears could've been for Jess just as much as him.

Thankfully I regained my composure a matter of seconds before the door swung open and the specialist finally emerged.

34   Jess

I perched on the narrow sloping seat at the bus station, poised
between chewing gum and last night's Chinese, rereading
Carol's last few texts. As if she could tell what I was up to, using
that sixth sense she always seemed to have where me and Dad
were concerned.

*Hope you're not doing anything daft after everything I've
said. You go steady. Regret it if you don't. Not telling you again.*

Four days ago. Followed by total silence, allowing me to mull
it over, before bombarding me with four or five a day, each more
desperate than the last. In the end she sent one that sounded like
a last-ditch attempt, all she could think of to change my mind.

*So damn stubborn. Always doing opposite to what we tell
you. Trying to get in touch with some of your dad's mates. Might
be able to find out where he is. Give us a few days. Get him back
here if I have to drag him.*

Which meant I was on the right track, if she was panicking
that much. I could be stubborn and awkward when I needed to
be, but only because it was my life, not hers. Time she went back
to her own life, if she could remember where she put it before I
came along.

I double-checked my purse. Over a hundred quid. Six
days since pay day. I suddenly realised exactly what it was for.
It gave me options in life, greater choice than I'd ever known
or considered before, stopping me having to ask all the time.

Stopping me having to beg. It allowed me to make as many crazy decisions as I liked.

Except I couldn't drive, and the house was over fifty miles away, three separate bus journeys there and back. God knows what time I'd arrive. Not entirely sure I'd find my way back. Who cared? The place lodged in my head. Always had been, far more than anywhere I'd been since.

Chloe convinced it was because those early years were so traumatic. She loved applying her slim knowledge of psychology to my childhood. The house represented my worst fears, and I dreaded going back above all else. I craved the safety represented by Dad, Karen and Ellie. My life was one of two halves, a short spell of extreme danger to start with, followed by a longer spell of extreme safety. Those first six years looming larger and brighter than anything since. I couldn't get it out of my head, returning to it my worst nightmare.

She was only partly right, of course, otherwise why would I find myself waiting at the bus station, heading towards that grubby old house when I could happily be wandering round town on a sunny Saturday morning, squandering my wages instead? Why head towards fear and confusion when I could comfortably stay away for good?

To do with you, of course. You and the house together. Braced in the doorway before catapulting towards us. Pacing the tiny backyard in an evening, fag in hand, scowling at the neighbours if they dared catch sight of you over the fence. The darkened bedroom where you cowered half the time, drinking presumably, occasionally calling out to me whenever you recalled. Patchwork yellow and purple arms. Ghostly face at the back window as I played in the yard, waiting for Dad to come home so I could have some fun, looking through me at times, in a world of your own, refusing to let me in.

And something else. Something in the house nobody ever talked about, always there, hovering on the periphery.

Essential to our lives, however much we pretended otherwise. Everyone trying to make me forget, desperate that I should. A strong sense of trying to escape it, striving to be in the next room. Slightly faded but still there. I couldn't do what Carol was always telling me, I couldn't do as I was told. I needed to face it.

I imagined finding you exactly where I left you in the filthy kitchen, miraculously wearing the same clothes, same haircut, same rage in your dark eyes. Still pissed off for no reason, looking to take it out on somebody smaller than yourself. Still looking for me.

Except I'd changed, of course. Able to look you in the eye for the first time. I could finally ask what it was all about, just the two of us. Was it purely the alcohol or something else? Something I was too young to grasp at the time. Standing in the doorway looking down at you, preventing you from leaving when you got scared. You would be scared. And shocked. You wouldn't believe I'd remembered so much, that I'd clung to it all these years and become strong enough to hit back. I could tell you how you should've treated me, what I really needed in a mother, what I had a right to. Tell you exactly where you went wrong, not that it mattered, you'd not won in the end. I'd passed my exams. Got a job with prospects. Doing far better than you ever could have imagined.

'Jess? Hi. Jess?'

I looked up from my phone. A black Merc pulled up opposite. Richard, shading his eyes as he called across traffic. I held up my hand and nodded. Barely seen him all week.

I glanced down the road to make sure the bus wasn't coming – ten minutes late already – before wandering across. He was wearing jeans and a faded black T-Shirt, the first time I'd seen him without a shirt and tie. Like bumping into a teacher outside school.

'So where you off to? Into town?'

'No.' Reluctant to lie but also struggling to admit the truth, standing in the street with pedestrians rushing by. 'Just visiting someone. Nothing special.'

I told him where it was and he glanced straight ahead for a sec, then in his rear-view mirror to make sure he wasn't blocking anyone.

'Catching the bus? Hell of a way, surely. The bus go straight there?'

'Not sure. I have to change twice I think.' I sounded vague and indecisive, everything he'd hate.

'Why on earth do you want to go there? Sorry, none of my business, just used to have a customer out that way. A bit rough, you don't want to be hanging about.' He paused as his words settled between us. 'Take ages on the bus.'

'I can't drive, can I? What choice have I got?' I stepped back to let an old woman with a shopping trolley trundle past.

He frowned in his rear-view mirror, turned to me and abruptly came out with it. 'Get in the car, I'll drop you off. Take fifty minutes I should think. Hop in.'

'Don't be daft.'

'Why not?'

God knows why, just that it felt wrong, making him go miles out of his way. Even though he gave Danny in the warehouse a sub on his wages last week. An interest-free loan for Tom to buy his first house. Constantly caught between being friends and being the boss.

'Come on, make up your mind. You can wait for the bus if you like but it's easier if I take you.' Staring straight ahead, focusing on the traffic. 'Before I change my mind.'

*

He didn't talk for five miles. Just stared straight ahead, the silence occasionally interrupted by the soft female voice on his sat nav. I sank into the leather seat, feeling part of it. Twenty-two degrees outside. The road blocked by traffic and pedestrians hurrying to cross, yet inside all was quiet except the low hum of the air con.

'Got an exact address?'

I pulled out a scrap of paper, even though I knew it by heart. 'Number forty-two, Taylor Drive.'

He punched the street into the sat nav. Forty-seven miles. Settling back, one hand on the wheel, the other on his knee, occasionally glancing left and right, muttering at other drivers.

'When we get there, if you can just leave me at the end of the road please. You don't have to take me to the door.'

He glanced across, his expression hard to read. 'Fair enough.'

It was only in the silence that his words sank in. A rough area. I'd never considered what kind of area it might be. I recalled playing in the scruffy yard with Dad, scrabbling in a sandpit, the feeling of living on borrowed time, something unpleasant always poised to interrupt. On constant guard, never quite letting go, never quite being what I wanted. Dad glancing furtively over his shoulder whilst trying to keep an eye on me at the same time. Desperately trying to ensure I enjoyed myself while having limited powers. Only so much he could do.

'I used to have a good customer that way when I first set up. Helped get me started.'

'When was that?'

'Just after I left school.'

He fell silent, concentrating on the road, cutting through traffic. I found myself thinking of Helen, wondering what she was up to. Wondering if he realised that apart from Deborah we all enjoyed taking the piss. Perhaps that was why he rolled his eyes sometimes. Did he dislike what she was as much as the rest of us, even though he'd done his bit to make her that way?

'You set it all up on your own?'

'More or less. Got a business loan to start with. Used to work from home. Helen used to help when she wasn't working, before we married.' He paused, concentrating on a roundabout. 'Believe it or not, she used to be a nursery assistant, used to love it. Then when the business took off she decided to pack it all in.'

I couldn't picture Helen going out to work, doing a normal job for a normal wage. I couldn't picture her doing anything other than what she did now, which she'd turned into a job in itself.

'Must be nice having the luxury. I mean, being able to do what you like,' I added.

'Really? Having nothing to do all day? I'd die of boredom. Can you imagine waking up and having nowhere to go? Then at the end of the day you've done nothing, so there's nothing to talk about or discuss, you've not stretched yourself in any way.'

He fell silent as we neared the town itself, the sat nav giving directions every few seconds. I felt guilty as he weaved through narrow streets and over mini roundabouts, negotiating tight junctions and pausing every few metres at traffic lights. He'd never visit somewhere like this unless he really had to.

'So you're visiting a friend?'

'No. The house where I grew up. Been wanting to for ages.'

'Right.' A brief pause. 'Never go back, Jess, it's never the same. I once went back to my old school to give a talk on setting up a business. Thought I'd walked into the wrong place. You keep trying to find all these connections that are never there.' He spun left down a narrow street of terraced houses that probably should've looked familiar but didn't. 'How old were you when you left?'

'Six.'

'Six? You kidding? You've not been back since? I thought you knew the area.'

I clicked on a road map on my phone. 'Don't panic, I've come prepared. If I get lost I'll just ask someone. Can't be that hard, can it?'

'So this is what you normally do on a Saturday morning? Wander round dodgy areas for the sake of it? What happened to walking round town and spending all your wages at the pictures? Getting plastered with your mates? Don't kids do that anymore?'

'That what you used to do? Not much older than me, are you?'

'Funnily enough, I think I'm beyond all that.'

The sat nav barking instructions to turn down a tight side street, past a row of boarded-up shops.

'You don't drink at all?' he asked.

'Don't like alcohol. Makes people violent and sick.'

'Isn't that the whole point?'

I checked the map. The road we were on seemed to be new or had changed its name recently. 'Think the map's out of date. Shit. Should've checked beforehand.'

'So you intend to wander round a strange town looking for a house you can barely remember, that's probably not there anymore, on a street that doesn't exist, and hopefully find your way home before nightfall. Great.'

I glanced out the window, feeling an overwhelming urge to jump out and run for it. Obviously it was crazy but who cared? Life had always been crazy. Getting home didn't come into it, only reaching the house before somebody stopped me.

'Just leave me at the end of the road please. If I get into trouble I'll give one of my aunties a ring, they're always happy to interfere. Not changing my mind.'

Finally we arrived. The beginning of Taylor Drive. My heart thumping as I took in the ancient, twisted street sign.

'Thanks. Feel really bad dragging you out your way on a Saturday morning.' I paused on the pavement. 'You don't have to keep helping, you know.'

'What?' The sat nav still barking instructions because he hadn't quite turned into the road.

'Just because we all work for you. You don't have to feel guilty or anything. Don't have to buy us. You've earnt it all, haven't you? It's yours.'

I left him at the side of the road and made my way down the street. Nothing like I imagined. The house at the end, waiting for me in the sunshine. A For Sale sign planted in the tiny front yard. An air of neglect settled over the entire street, neither entirely lived in nor entirely abandoned, suspended in between, awaiting a decision. I kept my head down and marched on.

35   Jess

I never imagined the place empty and abandoned. Staring at
a building that might as well be anybody's childhood home,
unable to enter, unable to see through the front window because
of a filthy blind. Even the scrappy front yard suggesting nothing.
I glanced again at Maggie's address, wondering if she'd got it
wrong.

Only the narrow driveway seemed to fit. Dad running
down it that summer's evening, carrying me in his arms before
reaching the safety of his battered old van. Neighbours watching
the drama unfold. Had they been surprised to see a bloody child
emerge from that terrible place? Had they even realised a child
had been living there?

I stared at the houses either side and opposite, wondering if
the neighbours had all moved on, if any remained. Richard was
right, it was crazy to return. What the hell did I expect to find?
You moved on years ago. Even Dad. Only me who hadn't.

I walked up to the driveway, pausing at the rusty metal gates,
yearning to go further and look at the backyard. The little step
I used to perch on, waiting for Dad to come home from work.
Still waiting even now. What good would it do me?

'Everything okay?'

I spun round. Richard scrutinising the house, wondering
what the hell was so special. Stepping back onto the road so he
could look up.

'Up for sale then. Obviously empty for a while.'

I shrugged, close to tears for the first time. I'd let it all out on the bus. I wouldn't tell Maggie or Carol. I wouldn't tell anyone.

'I should've guessed. Every other house is up for sale or rent by the look of it. Wasting my time.' I stared at the side door at the end of the drive, the one we burst through into the sunshine that evening.

Richard watching closely. Had I upset him with my comment when I climbed out the car? Did it hit a nerve? He hadn't expected me to read anything into his offer of help. Normally people snatched at it with both hands, barely pausing to say thanks. I'd never taken anything for granted in my life.

I grasped the metal gates with both hands. I could easily jump over but there was another tall wooden gate barring the way into the backyard so there wouldn't be much point unless I jumped that as well. I glanced round to see if anyone was looking.

What the hell was I doing, revisiting mundane things? Expecting answers. You were a pisshead, out of control, while Dad was hopeless with money. The only reasons life was a mess. Wasn't that enough?

I turned to see Richard jump the tiny brick wall and press his face against the front window, trying to peer through a crack in the blinds. Pulling out his mobile, checking for a signal.

'Really want to see inside?'

'I can't, can I? Stupid idea.' Curtains twitching across the street.

'I can ring the estate agent and ask for a viewing, see if they can fit us in today if you don't mind hanging about for a bit. Well?' The same tone he used at work when trying to win an order, No nonsense, to the point. As if it was his search, not mine.

'I've never viewed a house before. What do I say?'

'Or you can stay here all day staring at a driveway. Those are the options.'

I nodded silently. He turned his back and tapped in the number, pacing up and down. He explained he wanted to view the house and that it must be today, next week no good. Yes, he could wait an hour. Job done.

'They're sending somebody inside the hour. Shall we wait in the car? Nothing to see out here.'

*

I had no choice but to admit what it was about. I felt I owed him and at least it broke the silence. He didn't seem surprised or shocked.

'Never had much choice but to accept whatever they've told me but just lately, especially since Dad buggered off, it feels obvious they've lied all along. My Aunt Carol didn't want me to come here but wouldn't say why. Dad's gone quiet on me, which he's never done before. He obviously thought he could fool me forever. If somebody tells me not to ask questions, of course I'm going to. There's no way I'm keeping quiet the rest of my life.'

'People lie for all kinds of reasons. Could be trivial. Perhaps they're trying to protect you from reliving it all. Sure you're ready to see inside? What if it brings something back?'

'Can't be worse than what I've always known. Ever had your mother lunge towards you with a kitchen knife? Ever lived in fear she'd wake up and find you playing in a sandpit and react like you were burning the house down? Ever wondered why your mother couldn't walk straight and always had to prop herself in a doorway?'

'Can't say I have, not exactly. Here's the plan then. I'll keep the agent talking while you have a nosey round. I'll spin it out as long as I can. Okay?'

She arrived within half an hour. Bustling towards the house, hugging a clipboard to her chest. Richard reaching her first, grabbing her hand and giving her some bullshit about how he'd recently moved to the area and was looking to add to his portfolio. God knows who I was supposed to be.

'Oh excellent,' she gushed, visibly relaxing. She'd seen us climb out the car and looked puzzled at first, struggling to work out why somebody like Richard would be interested in a house round here. 'Well it's not a bad area. The rental market is extremely strong at the moment; we've had a lot of people looking to do the same. Here we go.'

It was stale and fusty, even chilly after being in the sunshine. I trailed behind, stepping through the back door into the kitchen for the first time in thirteen years. The black-and-white lino gone, replaced by something brown and geometric. Clean yet unloved. Perhaps nobody had ever got on with the place. I paused in the doorway leading into the dining room, taking a deep breath.

So tiny. What felt like a football pitch in my head, clear boundaries between safety and danger, reduced to a few steps. How could such a massive drama have played out here? How could this house have possibly contained you and your tempers?

'Make a lovely family home for somebody with one or two kids. These are the sort that always go quick.'

'Exactly what I thought. And the asking price?'

I walked across our old dining room. Featureless, except for a dusty grey brick fireplace along one wall. I spun round and walked back, savouring every detail. Wasting my time. Even worse, wasting Richard's. We shuffled into the back room, three or four steps. It wouldn't take more than five minutes to view the whole place, unless Richard could think of something quick. I felt nothing, only a sensation of being stupid. Picturing you in the doorway, in grubby tracksuit bottoms, stained T-Shirt, lunging towards me. Bruises on my arms where you were always grabbing hold. Bruises on your own arms. Something else? Always something else.

'Have you viewed other houses in the area?'

'This is the first. Been keeping a close eye on the market. It's the only one that's come up we've really liked.'

She turned to the patio doors leading out into the garden – I couldn't remember them, obviously new – gesturing for us to go first. I glanced at Richard as I brushed past, willing him to keep the conversation going. If the garden didn't reawaken something, nothing would.

Astonishingly the tiny sandpit was still there, in the same place I recalled. Battered yellow spade and green bucket half buried. Impossible it could form such a large part of my childhood brain. How many kids had played in it since? Were they interrupted as often as I was? Determined to finish the castle, to decorate it with shells and flood the moat.

'Admittedly it's a bit basic but a lot of people who rent don't want a big outdoor space to maintain.'

'Exactly what I'm looking for. Maximum rental value, simpler the better.'

'I'd just slab it over if it were me. Get rid of that sandpit, not doing much. Get rid of the grass, wouldn't cost a great deal.'

And there was the step. Not so much a step, more a small ridge as the garden changed levels and rose at the back. I felt an urge to sit on it one final time. Richard glancing across as the agent turned towards the rickety old shed. Suddenly going into overdrive, telling her some horror story about a tenant he couldn't get rid of, who owed thousands and trashed the kitchen and bathroom before he left. She leaned towards him, shaking her head.

'What I'm really keen to see is the bedrooms. Are we talking two doubles or just a single and a double? Because that makes all the difference. I've seen quite a few properties this size and it's the second bedroom that often kills it.'

I wondered when he last had to view a two-bed terrace. If he'd ever been inside one.

'Pretty sure it's two good-sized doubles,' she muttered. 'Sure it is. Hang on a sec.'

She'd already decided I was irrelevant, Richard making all the decisions. She led him back through the patio doors and upstairs. I sat on the step, bathed in sunshine, legs stretching halfway across the patio. The coldness of the concrete seeping through my jeans.

I closed my eyes and tried to relive one of those afternoons after school where I always seemed to find myself out here, whatever the weather. Blocking out everything Carol had told me since. What did she know anyway? Blocking out some of Dad's comments over the years. Couldn't trust him either.

I used to keep a close eye on the house, never completely turning my back. A glass-panelled door instead of the patio doors. Sometimes I'd shut it to create an extra barrier, gaining more time. If the neighbours were outside I felt happier, especially if they could see me. The frizzy-haired woman waving excitedly from next door's kitchen sink, suds dripping down her arms. She could tell, of course.

Eyeing the wooden gate to the right of the house that Dad would burst through when he returned from work, usually an hour or two after I got in from school. He'd leave his van parked on the road, open the gate and I'd be in his arms almost as soon as he'd spotted me. Reeking of sweat and cement, white bits dotting his hair, as if he'd battled through a snowstorm to reach me. Boots coated in fine dust, his jeans a patchwork of coloured stains.

'That's a lovely dress, Jessie. I'd like a shirt that colour.'

Pressing my cheek against his chest, desperately trying to melt into him so he could take me with him wherever he went. He'd pretend I was crushing him and couldn't breathe. Then fall suddenly quiet, studying some part of my body, an arm or leg, holding it to the light, comparing it to last time. Brushing my skin as light as a feather, despite calloused hands. Rarely

274

commenting on what he saw, as if he felt powerless to do anything, yet always noticing, storing it up for future, awaiting the right time.

I stood up and wandered towards the gate. I placed my hands flat against the warm bleached wood, trying to visualise Dad poking his head round the side, almost as if he was a visitor in his own house, afraid to enter. Suddenly, a question. Why did he always park his van on the road, as if he wasn't staying long? Why not use the drive? I wandered back to the step and glanced up at the house. Richard standing at the bedroom window, his back towards me, gesturing with his arms, asking some long-winded question as if enjoying himself.

Dad used to question me about school and how I was getting on. He'd perch on the step, groaning as he bent down, dragging me onto his knee. I'd ask what he'd been up to at work and beg him to help me build something in the sandpit, though it wasn't big enough for us both to sit in. He had to kneel on the concrete and lean across. I'd persuade him to lever his feet into the pit while I buried them in sand. So massive I always ran out of sand. However tired he was – he must've been most of the time – he always joined in, like he'd been looking forward to it all day.

'Mummy awake?' he'd ask.

I'd shrug, unwilling to talk about you.

'She been alright today? No problems?'

'In her bedroom. In bed again.'

At some point he must've suggested the idea that we run away. I couldn't remember the exact point. Lodged in my brain since the day I was born. The need to escape; the need for the two of us to be alone and have some fun, not be constantly looking over our shoulders. He told me what kind of house we'd have and most importantly, what the garden would be like. He'd still have to work but mostly when I was at school. At weekends he'd take me to work in his van.

'I think you'd make a grand assistant.'

'Will you take me to school?'

'Course. Just the two of us. We'll manage, won't we?'

'You know the way?'

'Course I do! Sure I can work it out. Might be a different one though. Won't mind that, will you? A new school and new house.'

According to Dad we'd made several attempts to escape before finally managing it. You were good at coming round at the critical point. Which didn't make sense. Why not just pick me up whilst we were alone in the garden and carry me to the van? So much drama. There must have been plenty of opportunities to take me without a fuss.

Sometimes I'd jump out at him when I heard his van pull up. Footsteps crunching on the drive... tension building... unbearable at times... tucking myself behind the gate. Sometimes pouncing too early, other times timing it just right, genuinely making him jump.

'Bloody hell, Jess! Nearly gave me a heart attack.'

'Sorry. Love you, Ray...'

That's what I used to call him back then, at least some of the time. I sat on the step again. Crashed onto the step. The sun disappearing behind a small thick cloud. My heart pounding. Freezing all of a sudden. I used to call him Ray. Not sure if he asked me to or whether I really wanted to. It was his name, so that's what I called him.

He was a visitor to the house. He came to see me mostly and you occasionally, after he finished work. Stayed a few hours, then disappeared back to wherever he came from. He seemed to know everything that was going on in our lives. He knew about the violence and the drinking. He knew you were losing control, that people were getting worried. Getting worried himself. Did I see him every day? Not sure. I came to rely on his visits and would beg him to return. I think he took me out sometimes as a treat, to the park mostly, as if he was genuinely in charge, though he obviously wasn't. Just a visitor, creeping into our lives, gradually taking control.

It couldn't be true. It must be true. It was true. At some point I started calling him Dad. Did he persuade me, or did I do it voluntarily? What about Ellie? Karen? Aunt Carol? Who the hell were they? Just a bunch of strangers. When he took me to Carol's house, bloody and sobbing – I remembered it vividly, it definitely happened – was it the first time I saw Carol? She was furious with Dad because she wanted him to take me back while there was still time. She wasn't being awkward; she was being reasonable and sensible.

Carol and Maggie obviously knew the truth. Karen as well. Could I still call Ellie my sister? I always looked like an outsider. Even Ellie sensed it. All those drawings, inserting me as an afterthought, reluctantly scribbling me in. Who the hell was I?

I covered my eyes and fell back onto the grass. Somehow I'd forgotten what mattered most. Had I done it all on my own, without anybody's help? How could I?

Time passed. Possibly hours, possibly seconds. Richard standing beside me, holding out his arm. I stared blindly. Eventually he grabbed my arm and hauled me up, my legs cold and numb, belonging to someone else. I hung awkwardly by his side, unable to trust myself.

'As I said, I'll be in touch once I've sorted a few things,' he told the agent. 'Definitely a contender. Thanks for your time, much appreciated.'

They shook hands and we parted on the pavement in front of the house. Once again locked and silent, no different to the houses either side.

'Okay?'

He pushed me gently towards his car. I slumped in the passenger seat, no memory of the last few minutes. My childish voice calling Dad by his first name. I could even hear the tone, sometimes long and drawn out, sometimes short and sharp, depending what I wanted. How did he come into our lives? Somehow managing to take over and get away with it. Convincing everyone I was his daughter, even himself. More importantly, convincing me.

'For God's sake, what is it? You look terrible. Told you it was a crazy idea.'

'Thanks for keeping her talking. You were brilliant. I wouldn't have known what the hell to say.'

'So was it helpful? Can you remember anything?'

'Bits. I remember bits. Think I used to call Dad by his first name. I don't think I called him Dad.'

'Right.'

'He's not my dad.'

He stared straight ahead, turning it over. The estate agent climbing into her Renault Clio and driving off. A small barefoot child rushing into the road in front, chasing a ball along the gutter. Grubby white dress, spindly arms, dark untamed hair. Turning to look straight at us, a bold unflinching stare.

'You sure?'

'Yes.'

'You've suddenly remembered?'

'Seeing the gate and the sandpit. The gate he used to come through. That's why he won't come home, he's afraid I've found out.'

'It doesn't make sense.'

'He's frightened somebody's going to tell me.'

'Like who?'

I stared at the child as she ran down a passageway between the houses, white dress fluttering in the breeze.

'Not sure. Somebody who wants revenge, somebody he's wound up. There's plenty out there.'

He started the car and pulled onto the main road. For half a mile we didn't speak. So embarrassing. Dragging him miles out of his way, only to witness something I should've worked out years ago. The sat nav barking instructions till we reached a dual carriageway. How did I forget myself? I must've been terrified when he took me away. Then somehow lost that fear and got used to being with him. I learnt to treat him like a father whilst knowing he wasn't. Who was my father? What happened to him? Did I really want to know?

I might never set eyes on him again, once he realised I knew. If he couldn't face his debts, he'd never face this. Carol and Maggie would deny it out of guilt. Karen uninterested because it didn't affect Ellie. The real reason Gran disliked me; she never understood how I got to be part of the family. I was a nobody. I'd come from nowhere.

Gone three o'clock. In the space of four hours my old life had exploded in front of my eyes. Never real in the first place. Everyone around me acted as if it was, they made me believe it. What alternative did I have?

I stared at my lap. A pristine white handkerchief staring up at me. Nobody used handkerchiefs anymore.

'You shouldn't have taken me. I'm grateful and everything but you shouldn't have.'

'What's that supposed to mean?'

'You should've left me at the bus station, I'd have been alright. I'm used to coping on my own. I wanted to do it on my own. I don't need somebody holding my hand all the time.'

'So you could get lost? So you couldn't find your way home?' He drummed his fingers on the wheel. 'Okay, you're right, I do help people too much and they often take the piss. Sometimes I care too much what people think. Sometimes push it too far. Helen keeps telling me to stop. Today's gone much further than I thought, I didn't realise it would be such a personal thing.'

'Me neither.'

'I can't just drop you at home if you're on your own. Is there somewhere I can take you? What about family? Must be someone.'

'Yeah, just drop me at my auntie's. Not really my auntie but what the hell. Or I'll go see my sister who's not really my sister. She'll be overjoyed. Even she managed to work it out before I did.' I scrunched the hanky into a ball, digging my nails into my palm. 'Just drop me in town please, I'll be fine.'

Raining steadily as we neared town. Large black clouds almost as far as the horizon. He pulled up in the market square, just in time to catch the stallholders packing away in a hurry.

I wondered what he'd tell Helen. She'd demand to know where he'd been. She'd need reminding who I was, then order him to stay away, not to get involved, perhaps even laughing at the whole thing. A deep knot in the pit of my stomach, dragging me down to an unknown place. She could say whatever she liked. Beneath all the confusion and shock, something else. Something unfamiliar. Something I couldn't face right now.

'See you Monday. Thank you.'

Before I had chance to climb out he put a hand on my arm, his face within centimetres, his mouth set in a determined line. Square-cut nails, tiny dark hairs, white knuckles. Surely he'd not treated the others like this? Their problems totally different to mine. I needed to get home so I could burst into tears and crawl into a corner where nobody could find me. Work out who I was and what the hell it meant.

'You told me I help too much. You're right, I do. Now let me give you some advice. You're determined to do it all on your own, but you don't have to. Let somebody help.'

'Like who? I'm not like Ed or Jo, my life isn't like theirs. You can't help me, nobody can.'

'Stop trying to fool people all the time. It doesn't work. You're terrified they'll judge you and think you're not good enough. Terrified you're different to them and they're going to laugh at you for it.'

'Well I obviously am, aren't I? Today's proved it.'

'Stop running and face it, you'll only make it worse.'

'Can't you see? We're all on our own eventually. Everyone.'

Out the car and racing through warm rain towards a corner of the square before he had chance to call me back.

36   Lisa

I scrambled over the half dozen cardboard boxes, the last remnants of Jim's single life pushed under the eaves after moving in and ignored ever since. VHS cassettes, faded photos of his dog, Sky, on windswept beaches. His sister snapped beside a Spanish pool. Curled payslips, CVs, birthday cards, wads of receipts. And randomly, dozens of books and maps on hiking through the Peak District, something he'd never mentioned in all our time together. My husband's former life.

The attic stretched the whole length of the house. Jim constantly threatening to convert it into a games room (he'd never find time), which would mean I'd have to race upstairs and make the decision once and for all. Keep hold of the past or let go for good.

I pulled across a box much newer than the rest, full of Harrison's old toys. Noah's ark, jumbo snakes and ladders, tennis rackets and bowling pins. I dragged them out one by one, checked them over and stuffed them in a large bin bag. The school fete in two weeks' time.

My eyes constantly drawn towards the smallest box of all, once home to a combi-microwave, the most mundane packaging I could get my hands on back then. I packed it one evening in my freezing flat before moving in with Jim, hands trembling as I contemplated hiding it from him. Packing away every last shred of evidence to do with Jess. A couple of items of clothing, her first pair of shoes, birth certificate, pictures she'd scribbled at school. Even Pinky the elephant, abandoned that night. Jim oblivious to its presence throughout eight years, while I retained a perfect image of its position directly opposite the stairs, the lid taped on to prevent the casual observer from dipping inside. 'Old clothes' scribbled in permanent marker down each side.

I slumped to the floor and gazed at the cobwebbed ceiling. Jess drawing closer by the day, I didn't need to ring Carol to have it confirmed. A combination of starting work, her first pay packet and passing her A levels. A long list of milestones to tick off, one by one. Find long lost mother. Discover truth once and for all. Her new friends granting her confidence, exactly the way I'd been granted confidence when I started at the garage and met Jim.

I pulled the microwave box closer. The Sellotape starting to lose its grip, lifting at the edges. Eventually it might give up all together and the box fall open by itself.

I closed my eyes and tried to imagine the look on Jim and Harrison's faces. Surely they'd always sensed it coming? Hadn't they proved I could be a decent mother and had nothing to fear?

37 Jess

Karen's nail varnishes lined up on the sill. Hair slides, straightening irons, tangled scrunchies awaiting her return. Dad's old betting slips on the mantel, pinned down with a Whitby fossil. Loose change in a dish on the shelf behind his chair. Familiar, yet unfamiliar. I'd wandered into a stranger's house and made myself at home.

I nibbled on a cheese sandwich, perched on a chair. Checked the meter out of habit, over a tenner in credit. Opened an urgent letter addressed to Dad, an overdue water bill, less than a hundred. Easy to pay without going short, although not quite sure why I should anymore. Stuck in a house I should never have grown up in, paying a stranger's bills, awaiting their return.

I rang Dad's mobile but got no answer. I sent a text, telling him it would be nice to talk, reluctant to put him on his guard. Sooner or later it was going to burst out of me. Then I'd see for myself how interested he was. Whether he just wanted to play Dad, the hero, or whether he really cared enough to come back and sort it.

That night I curled on the sofa under a duvet, unwilling to make myself at home, questions bouncing off the walls. Why did you let him take me without doing anything? Did I imagine you screaming in the doorway? Was somebody else screaming instead? Had you ever screamed in doorways or had I got it completely wrong? Had you ever been wild and pissed and out of control? Not to mention my real father. Why wasn't he looking for me? Why weren't you looking for me? Why did everybody allow Dad to take me? Carol screaming for it to end sensibly. She knew it was wrong, yet nobody listened. He'd broken the law. He'd taken me. All a joke in his eyes.

I woke on Sunday after a couple of hours sleep. No point keeping it in any longer. At ten o'clock I rang Carol. Almost put the phone down before she answered. Almost chickened out.

'Alright?'

'Fine.'

'Good.' A lengthy pause that told me a lot. She was nervous as hell, after our last meeting. 'So what you up to today? Fancy coming over for tea?'

'Did you manage to get hold of Dad's friends?'

'Oh, no luck I'm afraid. I'm sure that bloody Pete knows something. Good mind to follow him one day, wouldn't take much fooling.'

'So you lied then? Just trying to fob me off?'

'Course not. I've rung round and nobody seems to know. Look, he'll come back when he's ready, when he's run out of money. I still think you should come here, ridiculous being on your own. I can keep an eye on you here, can't I?'

'Control me, more like.'

A long pause.

'I went back to the house.'

'What?'

'Yesterday. Maggie told me. I managed to get inside and have a nosey round, including the garden. I know that doesn't mean much to you, but it brought back quite a few memories.'

'Right.'

I'd never heard her sound breathless before, struggling to keep up. I knew exactly what she was thinking. Redouble her efforts, locate Dad and drag him home by the most sensitive bodily part she could find. Anything but face it all on her own.

'I can now understand why you didn't want me to go. Pretty obvious really.'

'For God's sake, I'll kill Maggie when I see her.'

'I wanted the truth, Carol. I've left Dad a message to give me a ring. Get the feeling he'll ignore me. I don't think he'll be able to face it, do you? Only likes the good times. Loves being the hero.'

Silence. Whatever she imagined, it wasn't calmness.

'So are you coming for tea or what? We can watch a film if you like.'

'I'm busy. I know you've probably discussed it amongst yourselves for years and I'm going to hit a brick wall at first. Don't worry, I'll get there in the end. I'm not giving up.'

I ended the call and waited for her to ring back. Made a drink and cleaned round the sink, glancing at my mobile. It wouldn't take her long to contact him. Surely she'd force him to text so at least I'd stop hassling her. I loaded the washing machine, sorted through some work clothes, ready to break off any second. Silence. Stretching through the morning like I'd never known it before. Clearly, neither of them could face it.

*

I returned to work on Monday after first negotiating my way past Craig on the driveway, busy deadheading a rose bush tumbling over his front wall. Did he know my secret? Karen telling him in one of her tearful moments, swearing him to secrecy.

'If Karen's asked you to keep an eye on me there's no need,' I told him. 'There's no point pretending.'

'You obviously didn't hear me knocking last night. Did you have your music on loud?'

'No, just ignoring you. If I see you through the window I'm hardly likely to answer, am I?'

'Christ, no hard feelings. Not my fault, is it? Just wanted to know you were alright. Bloody mess if you ask me. Your dad ought to be proud of you instead of buggering off. Nothing like him, are you?'

'Sorry?'

'From what Karen's always said, done little to be proud of except get himself into debt and make life difficult for everyone. Whenever it gets tough he runs for the hills and leaves everyone to it. You know what? Never had a credit card in my life. Never been overdrawn. Never lent money, never borrowed either. If I can't afford it I go without. Karen couldn't believe it when I told her.'

If it weren't for the wall between us I'd have happily grabbed hold of his fat smug head and rammed it into the rose bush. I was allowed to think Dad useless. So were Karen and Ellie. But that didn't mean he'd got the right. That anybody had the right.

All night an image haunting me. Dad's huge feet in the sandpit, tired creases circling his eyes at the end of the day. Dusty calloused hands lifting me to the skies. Always trying to make things better. He had made things better, whatever else he'd done since. Craig wouldn't do that for anybody because it wouldn't occur to him. Far too busy trying to maintain a perfect credit score. Dad might be far worse in many different ways, but in a million others he was far superior.

Yes, he was the clumsiest person on earth. His shovel hands could locate a breakable object within half a mile, the more expensive the better. But where I was concerned, hadn't they always been in the right place at the right time? Hadn't I always been able to count on them when I needed?

'Running off like that. What on earth was he thinking? Never forget the look in his eyes the day that bailiff called round. Talk about terrified.'

'Surprised you were close enough to notice.'

'Turned round and sped off, didn't he? What could I do

except try to help Karen as best I could? You saw the state she was in. Good job I was home that day.'

'She's obviously been crying on your shoulder a long time. We had no idea you'd been offering so much support.'

'You know me, I'm always happy to listen.' His smile suddenly halted, a flicker of doubt behind his eyes. 'Actually, Jess, there is something I've been wanting to talk to you about if you've got a few minutes.'

'Too busy to listen to more bullshit.' Brushing past the rose bush, marching down the street.

*

Helen breezed down the corridor just after eleven and spent half an hour chatting to Deborah in reception about her cousin's wedding in the country. Probably the most expensive she'd ever been to, yet tasteful at the same time.

'Sounds absolutely wonderful,' Deborah gushed.

'The flowers on the tables probably cost as much as the average wedding. I asked Caroline and she told me exactly how much they'd spent, and it was astonishing, you wouldn't believe it if I told you.'

'Heavens.'

'The bride wore soft pink. A full tiered skirt and lace appliqué bodice.'

'Absolutely love pink at a wedding. So nice to see a bride go for something non-traditional. If you've got the figure for it, why not?'

'To be perfectly honest I thought it was extremely tacky and a huge mistake.'

'Well... I'm sure you could get away with it, Helen, quite easily...'

'Personally, I thought it made her look like Barbie. Not exactly how I'd choose to come across, Deborah.'

While Jo and I loitered in the kitchen, trying not to piss ourselves. Leaning forward to catch every word.

'I thought they were supposed to be mates?' I whispered to Jo.

'Helen's not mates with anyone these days. Don't go feeling sorry for her, she brings it all on herself.'

After she'd finished tormenting Deborah she marched past the kitchen, towards Richard's office. I rushed back to my desk and buried my head in paperwork, glancing up to find Jo desperately trying to make eye contact, nodding at the window behind me. I couldn't see what was happening, could only hear raised voices, mostly Helen's. Having a go at him for being helpful perhaps. For getting involved. He'd gone too far this time.

After a few minutes Helen stormed out and back down the corridor, ignoring Ed and Jo (I didn't count obviously), not even pausing in reception to practise her superiority on Deborah one final time. That upset.

While I kept my head down and concentrated on my lunch box instead, one of the highlights of the day. Sometimes I left it on the edge of my desk for hours. Jo hadn't noticed but Ed definitely had. He'd stopped offering KitKats. The novelty hadn't quite worn off yet. Opening the box and pulling out the contents, eating the same time as everyone else, snapping it shut and planning tomorrow.

After I'd finished I carried on typing, aware of Jo's sneaky glances towards Richard's office and Ed's determination to look anywhere else. Deborah's hovering presence in the corridor, craning to see what Richard was up to. Barging into his office on some pretext. Richard ordering her out in seconds. A terrible dilemma clouding her face. If Richard and Helen fell out, who would she side with?

Minutes later Richard's shadow falling across my desk.

'Got a minute?' he asked.

I tried not to glance at Jo as I brushed past, hunched over her keyboard, struggling not to smirk. I sank into a chair in Richard's office. Noting the dark circles under his eyes.

'Can you send an email please?'

He pushed a scrap of paper towards me, dictating an email to a customer about a quality issue on their last order.

'Send it this afternoon and copy me in.'

'Okay.'

I was about to stand up when he held out his hand. 'Hang on a sec. Everything okay? I thought you might not come in this week. If you need time off, you've only got to ask, it's no problem.'

I glanced over my shoulder through the window. Ed and Jo both on the phone. Lowering my voice just in case. 'I've made a few enquiries, but nobody seems to want to talk to me. I'm going to ring my step-mum tonight. She might let something slip. Don't think she'll do Dad any favours at the moment.' My shoulders relaxing, suddenly shattered. 'Scared to death what she'll say. I was happier when I knew nothing. I didn't need to know, did I?'

'Course you needed to know. It was bound to come out eventually. Can't be a coward about these things.'

'I thought I knew him better than anyone but obviously not. I've got to prepare myself for the worst. He must've known I'd find out. How could he get away with it? He's broken the law, hasn't he? Do I have to tell someone? Am I obliged to tell someone? Am I just as guilty if I don't? Can he go to prison for it?' My voice faltering. 'He took me away and pretended to be my family, built up this world that he convinced me was real. Convinced me all these people I care about are my family. I've been living with strangers. God knows who I've been living with.'

He leant forward, roughly shoving paperwork aside. Surely he had something better to be doing? His argument with Helen.

Jo's knowing smile flashing in front of me. Deborah's bitterness refusing to fade.

'Something not quite right about this. People don't just take kids and disappear. If they do it appears on the news or people get to hear about it. Sounds like your dad took you without much fuss. Sounds to me like your mum knew about it; she must've approved.'

'Too pissed to care more like. She's not given me a second's thought over the last thirteen years. She let a complete stranger take me. What kind of woman does that?'

'Perhaps…'

'She's dead. Fell down the stairs years ago.'

'Or maybe she has been thinking about you, maybe she keeps in touch with your dad. You'd be surprised how hard it is to make contact again. To make the first move.'

'If she knows where I am, why doesn't she show her face?'

'You've no idea what she's thinking. People sometimes agonise for years about these things.'

'I feel like running away.'

'You're not running away.'

'I feel like hiding.'

'Stop being so dramatic. You're going to face it.'

'Really?' I folded my arms against him. Telling me how to react. I didn't even know myself how to react.

'Perhaps your dad still talks to your mum. Perhaps he's putting her mind at rest.' He started picking at a corner of his desk. 'You probably don't know this, no reason why you should, very few people do… I was adopted as a baby. My mother was fifteen when she had me. Her parents pressured her to give me up. They didn't want her to throw her life away while she was still at school, in the middle of her exams. My father didn't want to know, he'd left her to it. She was too young to put her foot down and make her own decisions.' He took a deep breath. 'So four years ago, after my adoptive mother died, I decided to go looking for her, much like you went looking the other day. Only I was on my own, I didn't even tell Helen. Caused a bit of a stir obviously, but there you go.'

Of course. His real reason for helping, other than the fact he helped everyone. He felt sorry for me.

'It took a few months to find her. Imagine how I felt; no idea what reaction I'd get. She'd been wanting to look for me but didn't have the courage. So she said.' He shrugged and started scribbling on his pad. 'We'd never have made contact if I'd not taken charge. Once the idea's in your head you've got to see it through. It's where you've come from.'

'But Dad's not that bright. We're talking about somebody who can't pay a gas bill without going into meltdown. You're describing somebody cunning and whatever he is, he's not that. He can lie like a trooper but it's always obvious. Everybody sees through him.'

'So he's doing it with somebody's help. It's easy to hide things from a child, not so easy when that child grows up.'

An image of Pete, his puzzled expression when we worked together. Surely not? Struggling to tile a bathroom between them.

'My Aunt Carol's always been dominant in his life since his parents died. She's the organiser in the family. Thinks she is anyway.'

Another image. Laid on the sofa in Carol's back room, bleeding and sore, sobbing quietly to myself. Dad and Carol arguing in a corner. Reluctantly she agreed to help. She didn't approve, adamant he was making a mistake, but somehow came round. In the following days they made numerous phone calls. Perhaps you were involved. Perhaps you actually knew where we were. If so, who were we really hiding from? My real father?

'Carol's been a sort of surrogate mum. A bit hard sometimes. We're always doing it wrong as far as she's concerned. Suppose you could say I'm all she's got. Never even had a proper boyfriend as far as I'm aware. Always paid me far more attention than Ellie, which is weird now I think about it. I guess she thinks she can control me easily.' I paused. 'She's tried to mould me.'

A vague idea. Carol always treating me like a daughter, some kind of project to sink her teeth into. Cutting my hair, doing my nails. Lecturing me on the right creams, how to look after my skin. How would Carol feel if you suddenly reappeared? How would she feel if you wanted to make contact? Would she prevent it if she had to?

I touched the scar on my throat. Harder to find than ever. Carol always making the biggest fuss, insisting it would never go away.

'I think I've been blind as well as stupid. All this time.'

He shuffled some paperwork and tapped a couple of keys, checking his emails. 'Sorry if I've interfered. Got a bit carried away as usual. Hope you don't think I've pushed you too far.'

'You'd do the same for anyone.'

He glanced above my head, into the corridor. 'Can I be honest? You reminded me of myself when you first walked through that door.'

'I thought I'd blown it. I just assumed you were laughing at me.'

'Never.'

I was about to add something but stopped myself. Standing hurriedly, almost forgetting the scrap of paper with the scribbled email.

'Thanks for the advice. I'll let you know how I get on.'

I went back to my desk, ignoring Jo by ducking behind my screen. It worked for about twenty seconds until she lobbed a pencil sharpener at my head.

'Spending a lot of time in there these days.'

'So?'

'You want to watch Deborah, she'll be after you.'

293

I typed quick, barely pausing to correct mistakes. Nowhere to hide in this damn place. A weird sensation tugging my stomach. Along with something else, a sick feeling washing over me. Your wild face wherever I looked, refusing to budge. Bracing yourself in the doorway, ready to catapult. I'd imagined you all wrong.

38

Jess

'Jess!'

'Jesus!'

Feet scampering across the hallway. Ellie launching into my arms, knocking me back against the kitchen worktop. Leaves, damp grass and fruity shampoo. Inhaling slowly, relishing her return. Taller and lankier than a month ago. What else had I missed?

'We had to choose an endangered species and make a model and paint it blue. Supposed to be a whale. For you.' She pressed a hard lump into my palm and glanced round hungrily, taking it all in, on the lookout for change. 'You've moved my elephant picture, it used to be over there!'

Karen shuffling about in the front room, helping herself to more stuff. Couldn't even be bothered to say hello first.

'Staying for tea?'

'I don't think so. Had it at Gran's but it was horrible. Have to finish everything on my plate or I'm not allowed a pudding or anything for the rest of the day. Once she gave me carrots, told her I didn't like them and she gave me exactly the same next day, only more. She said it's not down to me what I eat.'

I unplugged the iron and folded away the board. Thankfully the front room was spotless. Karen would have to admit I was coping much better than she thought.

'She says Mum and Dad have been too soft with me.'

I put my arm round her slim shoulders. Eyes darting about, unsure whether to remove her coat. I let her carry on, half listening to next door.

'I can move back in with you, can't I? Just the two of us? You're old enough to look after me. Then I'll be nearer school. Megan lives with her older sister; she takes her to school every day and picks her up. We can do the same, can't we?'

'If only.'

'Don't really need Mum and Dad, do we?'

'I know that, and you know that, but it doesn't quite work that way I'm afraid.' How could I explain that we couldn't go back to the way we were? Even if Dad returned. How was it possible I could feel so close to her just as I was about to lose her? How come she'd never felt more like my sister than this moment?

'Then you could do my pack-up instead of Gran. She gives me wholemeal bread and celery sticks, searches the shops for the most disgusting stuff she can find. I have to throw it over the wall at break time. I liked it when you let me have crisp sandwiches, that time you gave me three Wagon Wheels and a sausage sandwich, that was my favourite.'

She threw her arms round my waist and squeezed tight, while I stared out the window at gathering black clouds. Would she still remember this when she lived God knows where in years to come? Would she laugh over it, realising I often felt as clueless as she did? Not nearly as grown up as I appeared.

Suddenly a large bang from the front room. I shot down the hallway to find Karen clearing the sideboard. Not even pausing to remove her jacket or shoes. A pile of books strewn across the carpet.

'Don't mind me.'

'Alright?'

'Great.' I glanced over my shoulder. Ellie sneaking upstairs, a finger pressed to her lips. 'Apart from the fact I don't know what the hell's going off. Every time I step outside I'm being watched by that creep next door. Strange how he seems to think he's got a vested interest in this family. Then, of course, I've not heard from Dad for weeks, except daft texts designed to put me off. Carol's tried taking over but even she's given up now she thinks I know the truth. Nobody wants the shitty job, do they?'

'Don't be so melodramatic.'

'You don't think I have a right to be after what I've discovered?'

'Depends what you've discovered.'

Plucking photos off shelves, dropping them in a cardboard box at her feet, selecting only the ones of Ellie as a baby or Ellie and herself together. By the time she'd finished it was obvious what remained. Me and Dad, the way it used to be.

'I know the truth, there's no point lying any more. Dad's not really my dad. That's what Gran's always been hinting at. Talking about it amongst yourselves for years. Did you think it was funny?'

She finally turned from the sideboard, sighing heavily. 'For God's sake, I knew it'd come to this. I had the misfortune to marry your dad. Whatever crazy stuff he did before we met is none of my business. God knows whether I'll be coming back. Might as well take what I need, no point fighting over crap. Half of it's not been paid for anyway.'

'I thought you said there was no room at Gran's. What's the point in taking more junk?' Still reeling from her reaction. I'd discovered the truth and she'd barely blinked.

'We'll see.'

I blocked the doorway so she had to listen. Possibly my last chance to get it off my chest. 'This is ridiculous. You like to make out you're a million times better than Dad but you're not. You know what I've discovered the last few weeks? It's not that hard, Karen. You've made a dog's dinner of it, both of you. Admit you're as bad as each other. Everything that's gone wrong didn't have to go wrong. We didn't have to go hungry half the time. You could've paid some of those bills if you'd bothered to open them.'

She turned to the bookcase near the window. 'Well I think a few weeks living on your own hardly qualifies you as an expert on the subject. Let's see how you cope after six months, shall we?'

'You keep making out you're blameless, but the truth is, you wouldn't take responsibility either.'

'What? I tried to keep it together! How dare you suggest otherwise?'

'Deep down you know you messed up just as much as Dad. The only difference is he takes all the flak while you walk away pretending to be perfect. You were just as reckless when it suited you.'

She pushed past and ran upstairs without a word, shouting at Ellie to leave her stuff alone. Sobbing occasionally. Her last resort. Running back down with an armful of clothes, make-up and toiletries. Stinging red eyes.

'Can't believe what you've just come out with.'

'The truth hurts.'

A brief pause. 'I suppose you'll end up at Carol's?'

'Hopefully not. She said she's going to negotiate with the bank. If Dad comes back we might be able to stay here, especially now I'm working. We'll work it out. It's worth it, isn't it?'

'I thought so a couple of years ago. That's why I used to bang on to your dad. Couldn't care less these days.' Picking up the box with a groan. Standing at the bottom of the stairs to yell to Ellie to hurry up.

Ellie running down with a large tub of Lego, clearly crammed with toys. Something bulging in her left coat pocket.

'I'll leave everything else if I can just take this. Please, Mum. It won't take much room.'

'For God's sake!'

'Karen?'

'What now?'

I inched closer, lowering my voice. 'I know you don't give a shit anymore, which is fine, but please, be straight with me at least. I know Dad's told you everything.'

'Oh no, you're not dragging me into it. Nothing to do with me.'

'Why do him any more favours? Tell me who my real dad is, that's all I'm asking. His name, please.'

She fiddled with the strap on her bag. Shouting at Ellie to get up off the step. Of course she was going to cave in, far too tempting to resist.

'Karen?'

'For God's sake!'

'Please.'

'His name was Alex. I think. Don't quote me on it though.'

'Alex?' Was she bullshitting? Hard to tell. 'Anything else?'

'I can't remember. Just leave it, will you?' Like she was really reluctant, breaking her heart over it. 'Alex Phillips or something. As if it's going to do you any good whatsoever after all these years. Sorry, Jess. Really sorry. Just be careful, for God's sake, will you?'

I stood on the step, watching Ellie skip down the street, swinging the Lego, oblivious already. Karen shouting at her to come back, Ellie reluctantly following as Karen stepped over the small front wall and crossed the grass that took her directly to Craig's front door. Craig opening it before she even had chance to knock, gesturing for her to come in out the wind. Trying to attract Ellie with a beaming smile and an outstretched hand. She looked bewildered, glancing at me for an explanation, pulling a sour face. She'd never been in his house before.

I raised my hands and shrugged. The door slamming, rattling the window frames. Gone in seconds. A feeling of inevitability. Within five minutes I found myself sat in front of the telly listening to Ellie's high-pitched whine through the walls. Having a massive tantrum. Fantastic. Craig wouldn't know what the hell had hit him.

After a few minutes it settled to an ominous hush. My heart still pounding, refusing to calm. Alex. Sickeningly familiar. That dark fuzzy thing finally beginning to clear.

*

I made a drink and switched on my tablet. Alex Phillips. Loads of them, dotted all over the world. Blue eyed, black eyed, brown eyed. Dark haired, ginger, blond. As Karen pointed out, what good would it do me now?

I typed the name of the town, narrowing it down that way. God knows why I hadn't done it before. The house itself jumping out. Tiny, grainy. The familiar cracked driveway, the gate leading into the backyard. I clicked on the picture and scanned the article, fearing my own name.

Alex Phillips, twenty-six, unemployed. No picture, unfortunately. He'd rented at the property with his partner and young daughter for six years. The neighbours knew little. He liked a drink, that was all. His wife even harder to recall. Somebody had spoken to her not long after they moved in, for a matter of seconds. The daughter occasionally spotted playing in the yard.

Something dramatic had unfolded that summer's evening thirteen years ago, even more than I recalled. Two policemen standing across the drive, fluorescent tape between the houses. Neighbours on the periphery, craning for a better view. That particular moment frozen in time, waiting all these years for me to find it again.

One of the neighbours, sixty-four year old Ruth Stevenson, had reported non-stop banging against the shared wall. She'd finally summoned the courage to peer through the front window. Seen him lying on the floor. A knife wound to his lower abdomen. They'd taken him to hospital and tried to resuscitate. A little while later realised they'd failed.

Anybody with information urged to come forward. An old dusty white transit van repeatedly spotted in the area. Police interested in tracing the owner. Meanwhile, Alex Phillip's partner and daughter had both disappeared.

39   Lisa

I deleted Carol's texts as soon as they came through. She was furious I'd given Jess the old house address and hadn't thought things through properly, even though I'd done nothing but think things through for twenty years.

She should've realised years ago it was inevitable, that Jess had grown up and matters were outside our control. Perhaps the only thing I'd ever managed to work out first and probably the real reason she was pissed off. Carol playing catch up. At least I was half ready for what was about to come.

I'd shifted the box full of Jess's things from the attic to a corner of our bedroom. The lid still taped shut but easy to peek inside. At some point Jim would either notice it and comment or trip over it and swear, paperwork strewn across the carpet. Or Harrison would dip inside and pull out the elephant, asking innocent questions. His final innocent questions once I told him the answers. Or I might pull out the pair of pink baby shoes and show Jim just to get it over with. Sooner or later one of these things would happen. The box might as well be in the right place when it did.

And at some point there'd be a long conversation with my daughter, the one I meant to have years ago, only much more complicated. I'd discover exactly how much she'd found out and exactly how much I was prepared to tell her.

In the fullness of time I might even discover some things

about her (the things Carol and Ray loved to hide so much). Her favourite film, favourite singer, places she'd visited I never knew, places she desperately wanted to see one day. Finally something to discuss in detail.

All those little things I should've known.

40   Jess

Harrison jumped out the front door carrying a rifle, ran round
the side and squatted behind the wheelie bins, chuckling at his
dad's bewilderment.

'Stop mucking about or you're staying behind. Listening?
Not got time for this.'

Seconds later jumping out, running low across the front
lawn, peppering him with bullets.

'You're dead! Die!'

'In the car! Now!'

Jim's powerful voice floating across the street to where I
sat on the wall. My hair in a ponytail for once. Unlikely I'd be
recognised unless they ventured near. A couple of years since
Harrison set eyes on me; Jim a permanent stranger. I arrived
so early, catching the first bus of the day, I had chance to
watch the house wake up. Maggie snapping open the kitchen
blind just after eight, rushing about and prepping breakfast,
twenty minutes later joined by Jim. Chance to embrace at the
window, Maggie's arms wrapped round his neck, laughing in
his ear. Until Harrison appeared, sending her into overdrive
while Jim stood at the window checking his phone. Eventually
all three disappearing from view, presumably sitting down to
breakfast in some far-off room. Sleek and modern, yet with a
country feel.

A bright chilly morning. I pulled my hat down to cover my ears. An element of surprise crucial. I deserved nothing less.

Finally Harrison agreed to being confined in the car, after Maggie ran out from the kitchen and grabbed his rifle last minute, swapping it for some kind of action figure. Re-tying his laces, pecking him on the cheek, a quiet word in his ear.

Jim pulled out the drive and turned left, driving straight past. Harrison swivelling in my direction, holding up C-3PO, smacking it against the glass. I spent several minutes trying to make out the car in the distance until it merged into other sounds and a delivery van rounded the corner, stopping in front of one of the cottages.

Three people had already nipped into the post office for a paper and they'd all emerged smiling. Maggie back at the kitchen window, leaning against the sill, waving at an old woman walking past with a cocker spaniel. Like she spent all day there, keeping an eye on the place. The woman nodding and smiling, gesturing at the blue sky and bright sunshine. Could I really have ended up in such a place?

I slid off the wall and crossed the road. It was a bonus that Jim and Harrison had cleared off. In a few seconds she'd spy me from the window and it'd be too late. She'd read in my face what was on my mind and perhaps cave in straight away. Her life in this leafy village never the same again. Would she wave at the old woman tomorrow morning? Would her friends remain friends? Would Jim wonder for the first time who he'd really married? Would she ever have that satisfied feeling again, bordering on smugness, as she lounged in her conservatory over a cup of coffee, congratulating herself things had turned out far better than she ever could have imagined?

Carol's sly comments suddenly taking a different turn. 'Landed on her feet there, didn't she?' As if Maggie had no right to get so much out of life. 'How much has that house set her back? Half a million? Did bloody well out of Jim, that's all I can say.'

Dad always claiming it was jealousy, that Maggie deserved every penny. Ordering Carol to leave it out, the only time he dared.

'They know how to save,' he'd say wistfully. 'Don't waste money on crap, do they?'

'Always trying to be something she's not, that's what gets me. Never used to sound like that. How the hell can money change your voice?'

I knocked sharply, my breath steaming up the polished stained glass. Eventually she answered, pulling the door wide. Taken aback at first, instantly trying to compose her face, which I realise she'd always done. Caught between two worlds, delighted yet panicky.

'Jess? What a lovely surprise. Goodness. Who's brought you?' She glanced round. 'You should've said, you've just missed Harrison, Jim's taken him swimming. He didn't want to go but it's good for him, we're not giving him much choice.'

'That's okay, it's you I've come to see.'

She showed me into a massive conservatory before nipping back into the kitchen to make drinks, presumably to compose herself some more. I took in the polished oak furniture, lofty glass ceiling, leather chairs, silver photo frames. Picturing Carol in the corner, arms folded, shaking her head. Had she visited often, to discuss how things were going?

'Goodness!' She sounded breathless. 'This is nice! So how's work then? Keeping you busy? I keep saying to Jim I'll have to get something part-time. It's not the money, that's not an issue thankfully, just to get out the house. As long as it doesn't interfere with Harrison. He's just started some new medication, hopefully it'll work better than the last lot.'

Normally I would've thrown myself at her by now. Staring far too much. Taking in every line, every imperfection. She'd put on weight since she had Harrison. Hair tamed by Carol, of course, no longer wild or scary. Plump and motherly instead.

We sipped our tea, staring straight ahead into the swaying trees at the bottom of the garden. A small plate of fancy cupcakes between us. Had she ever denied herself, worried over food or just bought whatever she fancied?

I noted the ancient-looking stone wall that formed the boundary of the garden, large terracotta urns dotted about, the kind you might see in a stately home. Small veg patch to one side, with every sign Harrison had played his part. Decorated wooden markers stabbing the earth. No scrabbling about in a mucky sandpit for him.

'Medication?'

'Attention deficit disorder. I thought I'd told you? We're going through everything to see what works best. We're trying to get him to bed at a regular time, apparently it makes a difference. Trying to get him to exercise more, so at least it tires him out. Unfortunately it tires us out even more. Jim's done most of the research, he works with someone who's got a son with the same thing. At least we've got plenty of support.'

Silence. Probably only a few seconds, possibly hours. The wind suddenly picking up, bending the rose bushes that bordered the patio almost double.

'I went back to Taylor Drive. Intended going on my own but a friend came with me last minute.'

Our arms almost touching, my shoulder several inches higher. She concentrated on the veg patch, trying to block all else. Focusing on the little things, hoping the rest would fade away.

'I wanted to see the garden more than anything. That's what I remember most, being dumped in the garden, waiting for Ray to finish work. Suppose it must've been cold sometimes, but I obviously put up with it. I couldn't bear to be in the house.'

Hand up to her mouth, as if to stop the truth from bursting out. She'd heard me comment on my childhood before, heard me make throwaway remarks. She'd even chipped in and shown sympathy, offering friendly advice. She'd never heard me deliver it all in a flat voice, no longer looking for advice or support. She'd never heard me sound so sure.

Hands trembling, arms, legs, her entire body, twitching like mad. Finally gasping as she stumbled towards the kitchen, out of sight. A few seconds later something shattering. Glass meeting a hard surface. Maybe she'd collapsed or done herself an injury. How would I explain to Jim when he got home?

The sun suddenly dipping behind a cloud. The warmth draining from the conservatory in seconds. Harrison's wooden markers trembling, threatening to blow across the garden and disappear for good. Wherever I looked little acts of kindness, on every polished surface, on every wall. Drawings, photos, reward charts, scribbled notes. She'd got her act together when it counted.

I didn't want to join her but knew it was down to me to take the lead. She'd reached the same point as Dad, incapable of facing her own actions. Dreading this moment yet relying on it at the same time. Waiting for me to find a way to deal with it.

I walked slowly, mechanically, into the diner kitchen. And there I found you, standing beside the island, a broken dish at your feet, frozen and terrified, lost in your own world.

'Carol always said you'd done well for yourself, but this is unbelievable. Can you remember the poky kitchen on Taylor Drive? They got rid of the black-and-white floor. That day we ran away… it did happen, didn't it?'

I perched on a stool, waiting for you to catch up. Carol always claimed it was some kind of damage. Hardly wild and unstoppable. Gripping the sink for support, eyes wide, never leaving my face.

'Might as well tell me the truth, Maggie. Is that your real name? I always thought it was Lisa.'

'It is Lisa. Maggie's my middle name. Lisa's my first name.'

'Right.' It was going to take a while. What chance of exacting revenge? 'Don't worry, you won't have to tell me who my real father is. I managed to prise that out of Karen.'

You grabbed a cloth and started scrubbing at the marble worktop. Shining and polishing your immaculate home.

'It's Ray I'm interested in. Who is he? Just some stranger who wandered in off the street I guess.'

'Don't be ridiculous.'

'Well?'

'He's a good friend, I've known him years, long before you were born. We used to go out together when we were teenagers. He's a good man, a decent man.' Lobbing the cloth across the worktop and turning away, caught by a sudden movement outside, something in the village that would normally make you smile. 'He's never changed; he used to take me to the pictures and spend all his wages in twenty-four hours on crap. Used to do things on the spur of the moment, then worry later, he's never been any different.'

'So he didn't kidnap me then?'

'Kidnap?'

'He took me, didn't he? We ran away. You let him.'

'It wasn't like that.' Eyes darting about the room. 'Alex used to drink, and I used to join him. I thought I loved him. I realise now that I knew nothing. I wasn't much older than you are now, just a child with a child.'

'Who cares? I never knew Alex and I'm not likely to now. It's Ray I'm interested in.'

A long pause. Wondering how much to reveal. Choosing your words carefully. 'Ray used to come round and try to get me out the house. I can't remember what he did half the time, I was so far out of it. He fell in love with you, didn't he? You used to drag him round the house when Alex wasn't there. Can you remember him taking you to the park? He used to take you out in his van.'

I stared at my dark reflection in the polished marble. Not exactly how I'd imagined. You thought you'd got away with it, edging closer, slowly bridging the gap one step at a time. In a minute you'd be touching me unless I did something.

'People think I've got this perfect life, that I've got it all sorted. They look at this and think it's wonderful. They haven't a clue. People like Carol always slagging me off and making it worse. She wouldn't let me change, wouldn't let me move on, always trying to hold me back. How cruel is that, Jess?'

'So you're saying it's Carol's fault?' Raising my voice to keep you away. Not as if the manicured lawn and massive conservatory wouldn't save you in the end. 'Explain everything. I need to know. Ray didn't kidnap me, but you let him take me. You allowed it.'

You wandered towards the window, staring at the village. Did it appear different yet? Slowly explaining. 'Ray took the lead, he had to, we were in such a state. He suggested he look after you while I got sorted. I kept promising I'd get help and that I'd go to the police. I kept stringing him along. He threatened to go to the police himself if I didn't. He kept warning me Alex would take it too far one day. I couldn't see it.'

'So you did nothing. Absolutely nothing.'

'I couldn't imagine being without him, I was convinced we'd work it out, that it wasn't as bad as everyone said. I remembered the way he used to be; it was hard letting all that go. He once pushed me down the stairs and couldn't even remember what he'd done. Even his own family thought he was a waste of space, that I was just as bad for being with him. Ray tried to persuade me to leave, he said he'd pay for it all, tried to set up this flat for us. Can you believe it? You've got to understand I was ill and not thinking straight. I look back now and hate the way Alex was, hate the way I was, the way we lived, what we put you through. God knows what I'd have done without Ray to lean on. I didn't even thank him; I took it all for granted.'

'So you let Ray take me and didn't bother to get me back? You were happy for him to bring me up?'

'Happiness didn't come into it. What choice did I have? You seemed to love him and he loved you to bits. I thought I'd get my act together and we'd be together again, I counted on that.' Leaning forward. 'I know you don't want to hear this, but my mum died when I was a teenager and my sister blamed me for everything, I couldn't put a foot right. Alex came along and everything seemed perfect for the first time. He was different before he started drinking. Nobody remembers except me.'

'I don't give a shit about Alex. Can't you understand? You left me with a man who wasn't my father and didn't come back for me.'

'I couldn't come back for you. I was in hospital. You wanted Ray to be your dad. You chose him, Jess. He never encouraged you to call him dad, it just seemed to happen naturally. When you were about four or five Alex spent three months in prison for assault. It was Ray who stepped in. He took you out to all these different places and treated you like his own, long enough for you to get used to him and feel comfortable.'

'Hang on a minute. You were in hospital? What kind of hospital? You couldn't contact me?'

Of course. You hadn't been physically ill; you'd been traumatised by whatever happened that night. There'd been a fight and I was trapped in the middle. An accident, of course. The glinting blade through Ray's legs. Alex had been hurt because he'd got in the way. Ray or you? Who'd taken the blame?

Tears swimming in your eyes. For me or yourself? No idea which way it would go. Ultimately, did it matter? Not as if your entire happiness rested on the result.

'I was seriously ill. I could barely drag myself out of bed in a morning, let alone look after a child. When I finally came out it was more than a year later. You'd settled at school, full of confidence. I told Ray I wanted to get to know you again, slowly if necessary. Carol dead against it, of course. She didn't want you upset, that was the excuse. We decided to let you call me Auntie Maggie. You didn't recognise me; you'd completely blocked me out.'

'Doesn't make sense.'

'Ray told you I was his younger sister. Carol interfering all the time, worried I might hurt you or do something stupid. My own daughter, for Christ's sake. The number of times I used to ring, begging for information, just a few words of comfort. It didn't matter what I said, it made no difference, they were in charge. You've got to believe me, Jess. It's the truth, I swear, whatever they say. They were in control, not me.'

In control. As if Dad knew what he was doing. Like any of them knew.

'When Ray met Karen he told her the truth and she agreed to keep quiet. What more could he ask? He considered you to be his daughter. That simple to him, he didn't think he was lying.'

'Except Karen told her mother everything. Gran's always been dying to let it slip. Always made me feel like an outsider.' I touched my throat. 'Still doesn't make sense though. You're still hiding something.'

How long before Jim and Harrison returned? Your eyes darting towards the window, clearly terrified. You might be forced to tell me everything to get rid of me.

'Ray took charge and carried you out the house.'

'I know that.'

'Blood everywhere.'

'Who killed him?'

'What?'

'Alex. I read it online. He died that night.'

Leaning forward, hands across your face.

'Tell me. Then I'll go.'

'I took the blame.'

'Obviously.' No way you could've done it for real. Not intentionally at least.

'I was forced to tell them everything. All the abuse, all the violence towards us both. I had the bruises to prove it.'

'Right.'

'His family chipped in, everybody who knew him. Nobody had a good word to say. Twenty-four-hour supervision. Extenuating circumstances. It was an accident.'

I took a deep breath. 'So it was Ray who killed him? You took the blame for Ray. Why?'

Still covering your face. Still hiding.

It was hard to imagine. Ray didn't act like a man who'd once held a knife, plunged it into another man's chest and walked out never to return. He laughed far too much. He laughed over everything.

'No.'

'What?'

'So much confusion, so much blood. After you and Ray left I didn't even realise Alex had been stabbed. I didn't take it in properly. He was screaming at me just like normal. Slumped on the sofa. I went to bed half pissed, then crept downstairs in the night and cleared off.'

'And?'

'They found me in the park and took me in. They told me what happened. I couldn't believe it. Practically hysterical. One of the neighbours had found him. He'd punctured his spleen. He bled to death while I was in bed.'

'An accident? That's what you're saying? He'd fallen on the knife or something? It wasn't you? It wasn't Ray? Yet you took the blame?'

I stared out the window, barely recognising a thing. I'd been close to that knife, reached out and touched it. My dress soaked in blood. I'd forgotten my own father for years and blocked him out deliberately.

'Jess? I did it all for you. When he fell on the knife, you were just a child. I couldn't have anyone saying you'd been anywhere near it. He was pissed, he brought it all on himself. Who cares exactly how he died or who held the knife? Does it matter now?'

I spun round and glanced at the clock, my mind racing. Too much to process. The next bus back into town in twenty minutes. Just enough time to collapse on the marble worktop, for you to come to the rescue, to hug and cry for a few minutes before they returned. Nicely contained, minimum fuss.

'I guess they'll be home soon. Don't panic, just tell me the truth, please. I'll only find out anyway. I'll keep digging.'

A long pause. Even though there wasn't time.

'They put you in hospital. Then what? You say you were there over a year?'

More tears, possibly real this time. Worried to death how it would work out. Which part of your life would pull the plug on the other?

'If you can just be patient a bit longer, give me chance to tell Jim; he knows some of the stuff but doesn't know it all, I can't just spring it on him, it's not fair.'

'The truth. Then I'll decide.'

A long pause.

'Ray was given custody.'

'Custody?'

'Of you. He went to court and pleaded his case. They asked you.'

'Asked me?'

'Whether you wanted to be with him.'

'Don't be ridiculous. You mean he did it properly? You're telling me he did something properly?'

Why did that shock me more than anything? Perhaps I had been asked many years ago. Sat in a beige waiting room, toys at my feet, somebody gently prodding an answer out of me. Perhaps they'd observed me and Dad together, believing he was the best person in the absence of anyone else. That I couldn't possibly be happy without him.

I wandered towards the door, leaving you stranded near the island, still awaiting the hugs and tears. Ahead of you, as always. Knowing you'd never be able to handle it, I'd always be on my own.

'Thank you.'

'For what?'

'Taking the rap. It was an accident, whoever held the knife. Like you say, who cares in the end?'

A few minutes later I left the peaceful village behind. The lawns intact. The house still standing.

41   Jess

Chloe turned up at half-six, Lauren in tow, complete with a fifteen-inch pepperoni pizza and nine-inch garlic bread. Lauren glancing round open-mouthed, struggling to believe I'd been left to it, as if she suspected twenty interfering parents about to leap out from under the stairs.

'Want me to move in and keep you company?' Chloe suggested.

'Sure. If you don't mind the house getting repossessed. They've not paid the mortgage in months. Plus Dad owes thousands on credit cards and God knows what else. Actually, I'm almost glad they've buggered off. Least I can eat regular meals now and keep the house warm.'

'Regular meals?'

'I was lucky to get a meal every other day, especially towards the middle of the month. I had to let Ellie eat first.'

She chewed steadily, pulling a face. 'So that's why you didn't always eat at school? Saying you were actually hungry? Couldn't even afford a bag of chips? Or packet of crisps? Not even a 50p sausage roll?'

Lauren bursting out laughing, almost choking on her Pepsi Max. When nobody joined in she glanced at Chloe, swiping her chin on the back of her hand. Chloe nudging the pizza box towards me, away from her sister. 'You've had enough, fat pig! Why didn't you say something? Too proud to tell me, is that it? Even though you're my best mate you were embarrassed?'

'Suppose so. Seems funny now. Just didn't want to make a fuss.'

She munched slowly, brooding silently. Surely there was a chocolate bar or piece of cheese or bag of sweets or something? How could there be nothing?

'You're a bloody good actress, that's all I can say. Lauren, let Jess have the last slice, she needs it more than you.' Pushing the bread towards me, giving me a hard stare till I picked up.

'I've told you, I'm better off without them. I can run this house better than they can, not exactly difficult. I've managed to pay some of the bills. I thought I'd actually try opening the envelopes rather than stuffing them under the sofa, just to see what happens.'

'Cool.' Scrutinising me closely. 'Your hair looks different. Your auntie stopped messing it up? Have you met someone?'

'No.'

'Bloody hell, you have! Who is he? Someone at work? Come on, give us the details.'

'They're all married or ugly. Not likely to look at me, are they?'

She stretched out on the rug, hands above her head, grinning at the ceiling.

'Piss off.'

'I can't believe all this stuff you've been hiding.'

'Piss… off…'

'So secretive it's unbelievable.'

After we'd finished the pizza we put on a film. Lauren falling asleep after messaging her mum, Chloe questioning me further on my childhood.

'Did you ever think you'd reached crisis point?'

A blank look.

'It's all about family systems. They're increasingly complex and diverse in today's society.'

'Is that from your course? Please don't tell me you're

treating me like a case study. Please don't say you're using me as an example.'

'So when you were hungry, couldn't you just get something out the cupboard?'

'If there was something in the cupboard to start with. That's what having no food means. Means having no food.'

Chloe might struggle to understand hunger but clearly not everyone was the same. There'd always be people like Richard who'd grasp it straight away and people like Jo and Helen who'd need it spelling out.

Chloe might believe I was unique but obviously I wasn't. One day there might be someone turn up at work exactly like me, showing the same signs, striving to hide it. In the unlikeliest places. And it might be down to me to understand. I'd never find it funny or put them on the spot. I'd never make them feel out of place.

She nudged the empty pizza box, still kicking herself. Brooding over the rest of the film, struggling to make it fit. The credits rolling, Lauren stretching herself awake.

'So what about a slice of bread? Come on. Not even a mouldy slice of bread? There must've been something for Christ's sake.'

*

Half-three Sunday afternoon, a biting wind rattling the letterbox, blowing a steady stream of litter down the street. Curled up in front of the telly when I heard the key in the front door, an unfamiliar sound of late. Staring at the glowing red coals of the electric fire, daring to believe. He paused in the hallway, checking his surroundings. The sound unmistakable. Heavy breathing held in check, followed by a muttered curse as he smacked into the ceiling light. Unwilling to remove his boots yet. Wondering if he was alone, still chance to do a runner or if I was waiting patiently the other side of the door.

'Jess? Sweetheart?'

His head poking round the side. The breath of winter clinging to his face and hair, rolling towards me across the floor, extinguishing the effects of the fire. Still in his work clothes, dusty ripped jeans and stained checked shirt. Still doing what he'd always done, the only thing he knew well.

'Hi...' I paused on his name, not quite sure what to give him yet.

In a second – if I misjudged it slightly or said the wrong thing – he'd be slumped in his familiar chair, flicking through channels, moaning to himself, legs stretched in front of the fire as if he'd never been away.

'Freezing outside, that bloody wind.'

Rubbing his hands vigorously, his expression frozen, unsure which way it would go. Not the home he expected to return to. Warm and glowing. Tidy and calm. Could he fit into such a place, or had it changed too much? Left him behind in a matter of weeks?

'Sorry, Jess. So sorry, sweetheart.' Leaning forward, his huge bulk balanced on a knife edge. Not quite sure what he'd done right, not quite sure what he'd done wrong. Perhaps I'd shout at him and never forgive. Or fling my arms round him like never before.

I stood slowly, gripping the mantelpiece. 'That all you can say? Where the hell have you been all this time?'

'Where?'

'Yes! Where? Why be so secretive? You really think I'm going to come looking for you again and again? Really think I'll want to know where you are for the rest of my life?'

'Hang on a sec, only just got through the door.'

'Think I'll always wait? That I'll never find anything better to do? You don't need to be afraid I'll come looking for you, you need to be afraid I'll never bother again.'

'Jess...'

'Either sit down and explain yourself or piss off now. Make up your mind either way.'

He shuffled the long way round, eyes glued to my face, back to the wall, skirting the edges till he reached his chair. Sinking slowly, gripping the arms. White powder in his hair, hands dipped in creosote.

'Just been staying with Pete's brother. Bought a new place and wanted someone to share with, to help pay the bills.'

'Pay bills? You helped someone pay bills?'

'Well, I owe him a bit obviously, got a bit behind. Had to do a few jobs to make up. Look, Jess, can't say any more than I'm sorry, can I? For everything. Better for us both if I'm back here, surely. We can muddle on without Karen. Don't need her, do we? Look as if you're coping well without her, look at all this.' Mesmerised by the glowing coals.

'What about Ellie? Conveniently forgotten her? You do realise she's only next door?'

'I'll make it up somehow if Karen gives me chance. Can't stop me seeing her, can she? My own daughter.' He stopped dead at my expression, frowning at the carpet.

'Did you say muddle on? Don't you get it? No way I'm muddling on ever again, either in this house or anywhere. Don't you understand?'

'Just an expression, doesn't mean anything.'

'It's more than an expression, it's you. An excuse to do nothing, an excuse to be stupid and ignorant, to leave it to someone else. Someone like me. Just waiting for me to grow up so you don't have to. I bet you've not given a single thought to this place, to the future, to keeping a roof over our heads. Has it occurred to you to contact the bank?'

'Oh for God's sake. I'm no good at that kind of thing, never have been, you know what I'm like. Only mess it up and make it worse.'

'If you can understand how to spend money, you can

understand where it comes from. If you can understand how to make it on eBay, you can make the effort to read a bank statement.' Pushing my face into his, forcing him back against the chair. 'Not just about the good times. Not just about enjoying yourself and having fun. Not just about playing the hero and looking good, is it?'

'No point when I'm so useless. You seem to understand these things naturally, I don't know how you do it. Seem to have a knack for it.'

'What's the point in sticking around when it matters? What's the point in taking responsibility for your actions? What's the point in keeping promises when you can have an easy life instead?'

'Steady on! Easy life! Spent all morning outside in that wind, laying a patio, painting a bloody fence. Got a massive decorating job on next week, I've barely stopped.'

'What's the point in having the hassle of actually being my father just as long as you can look like him? As long as you can feel like him? What's the point in actually being him?'

'Bloody hell!' He leaned forward, hands braced on the chair, ready for action. 'Bit unfair, considering everything, after all we've been through.'

'What's the point in rescuing me from a shitty home and seeing it through properly? Giving me what I really need when you can get away with less? Understanding me, getting to know me, when you don't have to? When nobody can make you?'

Turning dark red, confused and shocked, as if I'd whacked him across the face without warning. Something he'd been practising while he'd been away. He didn't need to do it for real. Didn't need to do anything for real where I was concerned.

'I bet you're happy now it's all come out; bet you're really glad. Now I know you're not my real father you can stop playing him. You don't owe me anything, free to do as you like. What you've always wanted.'

I fled into the kitchen and leaned across the sink, staring through hot tears into the conservatory. I'd give him chance to leave while my back was turned, make it easy on him. He hadn't even removed his boots yet. Or told me where Pete's brother lived. He could easily return, start a new life, forget me and concentrate on Ellie, the daughter he couldn't escape.

I ran the tap over the dishes, masking the sound of whatever he was up to. Everybody could escape me. Tied to no one. Plunging hands into steaming water, relishing the stinging pain of no gloves. Scrubbing vigorously at the flowery pattern as if my life depended on it. Chipping a glass tumbler, tiny pieces scattered in the bowl. Fingers slipping over jagged edges.

'What's this?'

I spun round. He'd opened one of the envelopes I'd left on the table near the front door. Scrunching his face, lips moving rapidly.

'Bank statement,' he muttered, like it was the first time he'd ever set eyes on one.

'We've opened most of the post. It's in a folder in the front room if you can be arsed. Carol's done her best to pay what she can. You owe her a fortune. She's another one you'll have to avoid.'

'She says I'm dyslexic.'

'She says loads of things. Doesn't get you out of being responsible, does it? Some things only you can do, the rest of us are just covering. We can't go on.'

'Come here.' He pulled me towards him, the statement hanging limply from his other hand. Soapy water in a puddle at our feet. 'Made a right mess of it.'

'Again.'

'Eh?'

'Just tell the truth. Stop running for once.'

The wind howling round the conservatory. Burying into his

chest. I couldn't remember the last time he seemed so calm and still, neither looking forward or back.

'You've been to see your mother. She told me.'

'You really thought I didn't know? That I hadn't guessed you were lying to me?' Breathing in a mix of sweat and cement, damp grass and fresh paint. The smell of childhood. Safety and excitement rolled into one. His grubby hand on the garden gate, head poking round the side, searching me out, determined to find me. The smell of hope and freedom.

'Supposed to be temporary. Just a few months till she sorted herself out.'

'Her husband doesn't even know.'

'Oh well. Got plenty behind 'em.' A small laugh.

'So?'

'She'll be able to shower you with gifts.'

'To keep me quiet? Till she's ready to tell Jim?'

Eventually he released me, throwing the statement on the table. 'I don't even know what it means, bloody dyslexic. Carol's been saying it for years, I've always told her to pack it in. I could understand it if she said it to Pete. If I've got it then I'm bloody sure he's got it ten times worse.'

'Forget Carol. It's just a word, just a phrase.'

'You've obviously not got it, have you? Always understood stuff like that, even when you were little. Whenever I struggled you always seemed to take charge.'

'I'll show you how. It's not a secret, just a discipline, like getting up for work or putting the bins out. Just a habit you've got to get into.'

'Lisa kept saying how grown up you seemed. She said it was like looking at a sister instead of a daughter.'

'I bet she did.'

'The way you talked to her as if you knew all along.'

'You forced me to grow up quick, what choice did I have? I'm not that confident about anything, not really.'

He pulled me roughly towards him, cradling my head against his heaving chest as the wind howled and the lights began to flicker.

'Dad?'

'Mmm?'

'Don't let me be the only adult round here. Please. I need somebody to do it with me.'

Gently stroking my hair with his shovel hands. Back to being that little girl again, forever waiting, forever hoping, daring to believe he'd keep his word.

*

He settled into his old chair opposite the telly but didn't relax completely in case I had a go. Stretching his feet towards the fire, flexing his toes. We didn't talk about Alex. That summer's evening all those years ago. The knife blade glinting between his legs, the inevitable confusion and shouting. The accident. Would there ever be a right time? Would we ever find the right words?

He'd finally sold the ancient set of encyclopaedias on eBay that had been rotting in the back of his van for fifteen years. Perhaps the real reason behind his confident return. Waving fifty quid triumphantly under my nose in case I didn't believe him.

'We'll use that on the electric now it's getting colder.' He nodded at the glowing bars. 'That's the most important thing.'

'Glad you've finally worked it out.'

'Not having you pay it all out your wages. You want to be out enjoying yourself. Have some fun for once, eh?' Counting the fifty from one hand to the other. 'So how much do I owe Carol? If she can get me a final figure I'll draw up a payment plan and start paying a bit each week.'

'Let's not run before we can walk, shall we? She was happy

to pay it and she's not exactly banging the door down. Let's pay the most urgent stuff first.'

I sat on the floor, resting against his knees, his hand perched on my shoulder. Silence settling between us as the fire hummed.

'Not thinking of buying me a present, are you? With that fifty quid? Not thinking of blowing it on something daft?'

'Well funnily enough, I've seen a lovely necklace in town. Silver and mother of pearl.'

'Dad?'

'No? Alright then. We'll go to Tesco instead.' Chuckling to himself. 'Pete's brother's got a new girlfriend; she's moaning at him every two minutes if he's not buying her stuff.'

'You need to speak to Ellie. Don't leave it any longer. She'll probably beat the shit out of you.'

He fell quiet while he contemplated the prospect. 'We'll have a quiet Christmas. No big extravagant presents like last year.'

'We don't need big extravagant presents or big promises. We just need to be together.'

'Karen's stopped texting. Not a dicky bird. Don't reckon she's serious about prat-face, do you?'

'I think you should worry about Ellie for now. Karen can look after herself.' I leaned back so I could see him properly. 'Why did you come back?'

'Eh?'

'Pete's brother threw you out. He did, didn't he?' He was hiding something, incapable of change.

'Gran.'

'Gran?'

'I ran into her in town. Gave me a right earful. Told me I was daft to turn my back on you.'

'You're having me on.'

'Told me to wake up before it was too late.'

'She hates my guts. Why do me any favours?'

'Not about doing favours, is it? She's one of these who has to speak her bloody mind all the time. Can't help it, can she? Just common sense to her.'

I hugged his legs, picturing Gran's face as she tackled him. All that pent-up emotion, the build-up of years of botched DIY jobs and dodgy electrics. The funniest thing ever.

'I had no idea she felt so strong.' I dragged my eyes from the glowing bars, meeting his reddened face.

*

He drew up a payment plan for Carol in a new notebook purchased solely for the purpose. Printing her name on the front with a flourish.

'The most important thing is that you pay her back. A fancy notebook with an eye-catching cover won't pull the wool over her eyes in a million years.'

'Course not. Not daft, is she? I've got thirty quid she can have straight off, next time she pops round. Won't take long, will it?'

In the end, she didn't. She rang instead, two days after his return. Dad launching in straight away.

'Hold your bloody horses, just let me explain. I know exactly what you're going to say. Carol… eh?'

I could hear her on the other end, launching in herself. Dad stopping short.

'Christ.' He glanced towards me, suddenly a different tone. Slumping into the nearest chair. 'Tell Jim he knows where we are if he needs us.'

I knew already what was coming the second he ended the call. His knuckles turning white as he gripped the arm.

'It's your mother, sweetheart.' He didn't want to say it. He could barely get it out. 'She's gone back to that park, the one I used to take you to, probably won't remember. Exactly same place they found her that night.'

42 Lisa

Little things made all the difference, especially to a small boy. Milky chocolate before bedtime, two sugars, lukewarm, in the same faded blue Spiderman mug he'd had since a toddler. Blue or black socks, never brown or grey. Carrots and sweetcorn, even on somebody else's plate. He got funny, whatever the reason. Jim would have to learn.

I'd write it all down and tuck it behind the breadbin. He'd have to complain to the doctors – as I'd done for years – if they didn't do enough. Get Harrison to school on time; speak to his teacher, Mrs Spence, if he had to. Keep his temper and learn to hold his tongue. He'd have to listen to advice, realise that work didn't matter, take a step back and put Harrison first. Would he realise in time?

I packed a small overnight bag. As if it had always been there, nudged under my side of the bed. A spare pair of jeans, two tops, socks and knickers. Two or three days ahead max. Why plan for years when they didn't exist? A couple of photos of Jess and Harrison. My life reduced to a handful of things. Permission to leave the rest behind.

Would Jim really be that shocked? Genuinely claim he hadn't a clue? All the times I could've blurted it out, all the times he could've understood or forgiven. Over a cosy meal, when things were going well. Shortly after we married, when we were most in love. Shortly after Harrison was born. Perhaps.

I had money this time round. Twenty quid compared to thousands. A few more coffees if it turned cold, a sandwich if I grew hungry, the odd luxury I wouldn't have dreamt of all those years ago. Even the luxury to change my mind, the option to turn back. I wouldn't, of course.

No need to sneak out the house either. In the dead of night, stumbling down the street, at the mercy of passing drunks. In broad daylight this time, an absence of drama, ample time to wave at Julie from the post office.

'Don't forget book sale next Tuesday at church!'

'I won't! See you later!'

She'd remember it afterwards, when people asked, astonished how I could've led a double life so successfully. She'd tell Jim and insist there was no need to torture himself, the signs were never there.

*

It wasn't so easy finding the exact spot. Did it matter either way? Surely anywhere would do? Of course not. I hadn't time to grasp something unfamiliar, to grapple with something that both looked and sounded new.

Century Park, a couple of miles from the old house, where Ray used to take Jess at weekends. Long summer evenings after school. A place of refuge away from Alex. Away from me. Rolling home long after he'd promised, Jess always begging for five minutes more. Skinny sunburnt arms wrapped round his neck. Ray breaking his heart over what little he could do, hoisting her onto his shoulders long after she'd grown too heavy for everyone else.

'Pleaseee… don't want to be here, want to be with you.' That tone she saved just for him.

And sometimes he'd agree. Sometimes he'd get sucked in.

'We'll go to the seaside next weekend, sweetheart, once I've finished this job I'm on. We'll go to McDonald's tomorrow after school, once I've been paid.'

'Just the two of us? Pleaseee! Nobody else?'

Where else could it have led? He'd acted like her father long before he carried her screaming down the drive.

Three different buses to get there. By the time I found myself sat on the second I'd already received my first text.

Ray. He knew Jess had worked things out; I'd told him of our meeting. He wondered if it was safe to creep home, if things had fully calmed down. His friend sick of him kipping on his sofa rent-free.

I hesitated at first, wondering if the police could trace my whereabouts from my phone. Should I switch if off if I really didn't want to be found?

Up to you. She was calm when I saw her, very grown up. Probably best to get it over with. Good luck.

I wanted him to work things out for Jess's sake. Even Carol, interfering bitch. She'd made life hell but wasn't ultimately responsible for wherever I ended up. Nothing personal.

I caught the third bus no problem. A group of pensioners parked at the front, screaming toddlers hogging the back. Slotting in between, nothing to give me away. I'd made the decision and felt calmer for it. No more agonising or wondering. God knows how I'd survived so long.

Dusk by the time I arrived. Two horse chestnuts flanking the gates. I'd eaten a tuna sandwich at some point, the wrapper still in my hand. Harrison home from school, straight up to his room, in front of his Xbox. Jim distracted by his tablet, convinced I was shopping and on my way home. Shepherd's pie in the oven. Bread from out the freezer.

I'd even managed a few notes, one each to Jess, Harrison and Jim. Strangers would find them in my bag. An apology to each, a plea to move on and forget, though I knew they wouldn't easily, they'd hate me for years to come.

I'd tried to unite everything and everyone. Those different parts of my life. With Jim's help I'd moved on and ignored the past. He'd swept me along and tried to convince me it could be done. The money always helped, prolonged things without actually changing the end.

It seemed obvious to me now that I could've taken Jess to the park and hoisted her onto my shoulders instead of leaving everything to Ray. I could've been the one to make her laugh, even if it didn't happen naturally, even if I'd faltered she'd have forgiven me, as long as I was still there.

Far more choices than I'd ever realised, far more possibilities and not nearly as much to fear. My teenage daughter had somehow turned out more grown up than I'd ever been, able to understand and forgive, yet still be my daughter at the end of it. She'd learnt everything I'd struggled to understand. She'd learnt the value of those things and would carry it with her the rest of her life.

I didn't deserve to get to know her properly. She hadn't become that person because I'd encouraged her or set a good example. She'd become that person in spite of me and Alex. And just as he'd never deserved her, neither did I.

Fast forward four or five years. An awkward meeting between Jess and Jim, somewhere neutral, Carol's back room perhaps. What could be more fitting? Jess would tell him everything she knew, Jim would reveal his side of the story, the two parts finally slotting together and making sense, perhaps offering some kind of peace. Jim would come to feel relieved I was out the way, though never admit it. Not having to make token visits to some home for years to come, not having to pretend, above all, not having to explain to his sister. Just one shitty thing to deal with rather than a lifetime of pain.

The park was empty, cleared of the last stragglers wandering home. Unlike last time, when I only thought I was alone. The top of the bridge arching against the night sky. A relief to see the swirling black water below. I'd been away far too long. The rail noticeably higher, perhaps because of me. Dozens of complaints to the local rag. Little spikes on top, as if that would be enough.

Louise suddenly floating in front of me, arms folded, slowly shaking her head. Had she ever stopped? 'I'm impressed,' she sneered, beneath the disgust and contempt. 'Look... you're actually finishing something off for once!'

I dumped my bag on the ground. Important not to get it wet. How would it look if there was nothing to find? One leg over the railings, the breeze lifting my hair, a sense of freedom I'd not known in years. So much easier this way. Free to make up whatever they liked. Free to be right, each and every one. Carol, Ray, Jim, Mrs Spence...

Swirling black water desperate to meet me. Nothing to interfere this time.

43   Jess

In the end Ellie didn't launch at Dad when she discovered his return. She waited patiently the other side of the hedge and aimed Buzz Lightyear at his head while he unloaded bricks from the back of his van.

'What the hell's that for?'

'For going away and upsetting Jess. Not answering your phone, leaving us with nothing and being a total shit. Lying to everyone, owing money and refusing to open the post.'

After which she calmed down, mainly because she'd had plenty of opportunity to compare him to Craig. Because he was still good for taking her to the park or swimming, lugging her about whenever she felt like it, and because she hadn't quite reached his level yet. A couple more years to go.

Karen scowling in the background, the hedge in between. Arms folded while Dad waved paperwork in the air.

'You'll have to read it at some point,' he'd shout. 'Got to sit down, discuss it and reach a decision.'

'It's in your name, not mine, therefore your responsibility.'

'Charming! So I'm the only one who's spent it all then? You've not enjoyed any of it?'

'You've enjoyed it far more than me, that's for sure. Craig says you'll never change, just using me as a scapegoat.'

'He would do. What the hell's it got to do with him anyway?'

Karen storming back into Craig's kitchen and slamming

the door. Ignoring his texts, his pleas for common sense, vowing never to speak to him or anyone in his shitty family ever again, apart from occasionally popping round to grab hair straighteners or a pair of sandals.

In some ways, Dad hadn't changed at all. In most ways. Still good at the things he was always good at, still bad at the things he was never going to be any good at. Slightly dazed by it all, as if it might be happening to somebody else. Occasionally revived by a decent bid on eBay, back to his old self.

Ellie hopping over the fence whenever she got bored of keeping it down for Craig, refusing to go back till Karen banged on the door and threatened dire consequences.

'Want to stay here with Jess, this is my home as much as anyone's.'

'Not anymore!' Karen screamed. 'I've explained enough times; what's so hard to understand?'

'But we don't really live with Craig, not properly. He won't let me plug in my laptop downstairs because there's no room, I can't play on my tablet with the sound on, he won't let me do anything that makes a noise. Half my toys are in boxes in the attic.'

'Because he likes it quiet, that's what he's used to, I've told you before.'

Which was perfectly true. Craig didn't mind them moving in just as long as they made no more noise than when he was on his own.

'And he's thrown away some of my games.'

'Don't be daft, they're about somewhere.'

'He's a liar!'

'Well it's the only home we've got for now, can't you understand? Best I can do while your dad's busy acting like a tosser.'

I took the opportunity to pull Ellie to one side to go over a few things. Pretty obvious she needed the help.

'You know all this shit that's going off? Might get worse rather than better. You need to put some money aside if they give you any. Don't spend it all, just keep a bit back for emergencies.'

'I'm eight.'

'So?'

'But I don't know how.' Tiny face beginning to crumple. 'You can do it for me, can't you?'

'If they won't take responsibility, if they won't change, you've got to look after number one. Don't want to end up as stupid as them, do you?'

'No.'

'End up in the same mess?'

'Course not.'

'Then you've got to learn to be smarter.'

I thought she might do a runner at first, tell Karen I was scaring her to death or send Gran a long-winded text.

'That mean you're not going to be here? Because of your psycho mum?'

'Course I'm still going to be here, despite a psycho mum. Just in case you have to cope on your own someday, that's all.'

'I don't want to cope on my own.'

I shrugged.

'Stop being so mean.'

'Just listen to what I tell you.'

'Can we go to the park?'

'If you listen.'

'Okay, okay.' Kicking the wall. Scowling at the floor. 'If it's really so important I'll listen.'

*

The first bus was just like a normal one, the passengers potentially going anywhere. Shopping, sightseeing, out for the day. I could kid myself for a while. Followed by a shuttle bus with bright red upholstered seats, yellow grab rails and a noticeable air of increased comfort. A different language buzzing in the air. Rip-off parking fees, the recent change in visiting hours, the impossibility of getting hold of a doctor. I gazed out the window, avoiding eye contact, focusing on scrappy front yards, washing lines, overflowing wheelie bins.

The place itself an old-fashioned red-brick building, Victorian probably. Park Field Independent Hospital. She'd been there before, while Dad and Carol were busy teaching me how to brush my teeth, arguing over how much sugar to let me have.

I gave my mother's full name at reception, as if I'd been used to it all my life. The woman checked the computer and gave me a ward number coupled with vague directions.

Up two flights of stairs and down miles of corridors punctuated by the odd window, my feet echoing on shiny new laminate flooring partly masking the age of the place. I shouldn't expect too much. She was on medication. I might struggle to recognise her and get upset. What exactly was there to recognise? As if I'd ever known her in the first place.

Second floor, where the smooth shiny walls changed shade from calming blue to calming green. I pressed the red buzzer beside the door and explained to the woman who answered. The door swinging open.

Light and airy. Sprawled out beds and acres of floor space, everyone allocated their own little alcove. She was sat up in a far corner, eyeing the doorway, looking excited and nervous in equal measure. The way she'd always been.

'Jess! Jess! Over here!'

A quick peck on the cheek. No idea what to call her. Fortunately she took care of it by grabbing my arm and pulling me down to her level, squeezing hard. Deep purple bruises covering her neck and one side of her face. Despite that, happier than I'd ever seen her. Almost carefree. Was it for real or down to the drugs?

'Oh, you feel so cold! Haven't walked, have you?'

'It's twenty miles. I caught the bus.'

'Oh, of course.' She blushed furiously; she should've known. 'Thanks for coming, it's lovely to see you again.'

I nodded.

'So how's work? Is it your day off?'

'I don't work Saturdays, only Monday to Friday.'

Chinese whispers. Everything second-hand. A million ways to embarrass her if I wished.

She took a sip of water, the glass trembling. 'So glad it's going well, really am.' She leaned forward and gripped my hand, warming it between both of hers. Criss-cross scratches and bruises up her arms, dark smudges beneath her eyes. God knows what Harrison must think. The transformation before his eyes.

All kinds of inappropriate questions swirling round my head. How she felt, how long she intended staying, whether she had a choice in the matter. Was this a proper hospital or more like a prison? What kind of freedom did she have? Was I missing the point? Perhaps it was freedom she wished to avoid. In the next alcove, to our left, an old woman moaning over and over, a repetitive whine, curled in a tight ball. Impossible not to stare. My mother barely blinked.

'Have you seen Jim and Harrison? Are they okay?' I asked.

'Of course. Jim tries to come most days but with his job and looking after Harrison and everything. Still got the mortgage to pay.' A small laugh. 'What about you? I'm worried they're not looking after you properly, with everything going off. Need to put on some weight, you're so damn skinny. What about Karen? Is it over for good? Where's that leave you? What about the house and everything?'

I gripped her hand and told her what I'd carefully prepared when I first realised she was in here. Life was no different to how it had always been, and I was old enough to look after myself.

There was no need to be so terrified anymore. She might be convinced I'd never fit in anywhere, just as she'd never fitted in, that I'd always stand out, but I wasn't worried any more. I'd met people who recognised me, who didn't see me as strange or out of place.

As I touched the softness of her skin, covered in tiny scratches and bruises, I realised for the first time exactly how much she'd suffered the majority of her life. That hazy old memory of the two of us locked in the loo while my father terrified us by banging on the door. She was still terrified. I'd managed to escape but she never had.

'There's nothing to fear anymore, for either of us.'

She smiled and wiped a stray tear. God knows how much she was able to take in beneath the meds or how many times I might have to say it to get through. I was here for her if she needed me and even if she didn't.

'What about Ellie?'

'She's fine. She's only next door, she can pop round any time.' Ellie wasn't really fine. She was confused and rightly pissed off, but nobody was going to do anything about it.

A visible sigh of relief. Another shaky sip. 'I've been sat here wondering whether to ring Carol or not. Think it might do any good?'

I squeezed her hand and watched her wipe her tears. A sudden premonition. My mother growing older, turning into the woman on our left. In and out of this place. Looking to me for confirmation she'd done something right, always looking till she found it. Looking to me to wipe away all the doubts that might suddenly pop into her mind. Had she made the right decision all those years ago?

'Ray alright?'

'Same as usual.'

'He said he was really struggling for money or something, he rang me up.'

'You know what he's like. Always a pound off being rich, a pound off being poor. Wouldn't want him any different.'

'Here they are!' Suddenly throwing away my hand. Not unkindly, just no further use for it.

Harrison and Jim approaching slowly. Jim with a protective hand on his son's shoulder, stopping him from straying too far. Harrison rolling on the bed to give her a hug, eyeing me shyly over her shoulder.

'Mummy?'

More tears, no longer holding them back, flowing freely. 'What's this you've done?'

A picture of the three of them in a garden.

'I'll get off,' I interrupted. 'No, it's okay, I'll leave you in peace.'

They tried to make me stay, made the right noises but didn't really mean it, especially Jim. Part of his wife's other life, the one he'd never seen and couldn't begin to imagine.

I left them to it. My mother stroking her son's hair. Once I'd rounded the corner I imagined her smiling again, even laughing, taking a steady sip of water, finally calming her nerves.